W9-BWL-840

PRAISE FOR SARA ELLA

"*Unblemished* may have set the stage, but *Unraveling* will forever bind you to this story like a Kiss of Accord. Sara Ella's exquisite writing left me gasping at new revelations and rereading whole chapters just because. *Unraveling* is a sequel that outshines its already brilliant predecessor. Read it. Now. Then come fangirl with me."

—NADINE BRANDES, AWARD-WINNING AUTHOR OF
THE OUT OF TIME TRILOGY AND *FAWKES*

"With plenty of YA crossover appeal, this engaging and suspenseful debut urban fantasy features superb world building and a tightly paced story line. Reading groups will find plenty to discuss concerning self-image, the nature of good vs. evil, and the power of the marginalized to change the world."

—*LIBRARY JOURNAL*, STARRED REVIEW FOR *UNBLEMISHED*

"Sara Ella's debut novel is a stunning journey into a fascinating new world of reflections. Intricately plotted, the story is complex, but not difficult to follow. Eliyana is a strong heroine, yet also has a vulnerable side that readers will definitely identify with. The other characters are also well-developed and have many hidden secrets revealed throughout the course of the tale . . . It will be fascinating to see where the author takes the characters next."

—*RT BOOK REVIEWS*, 4½ STARS, TOP PICK! FOR *UNBLEMISHED*

"Ella has created a captivating, relatable protagonist and never hesitates as she keeps things moving briskly through the many twists and turns."

—*PUBLISHERS WEEKLY* FOR *UNBLEMISHED*

"A breathtaking fantasy set in an extraordinary fairy-tale world, with deceptive twists and an addictively adorable cast who are illusory to the end. Just when I thought I'd figured each out, Sara Ella sent me for another ride. A wholly original story, *Unblemished* begins as a sweet melody and quickly becomes an anthem of the heart. And I'm singing my soul out. Fans of *Once Upon a Time* and Julie Kagawa, brace yourselves."

—MARY WEBER, AWARD-WINNING AUTHOR
OF THE STORM SIREN TRILOGY

"Lyrically written and achingly romantic—*Unblemished* will tug your heartstrings!"

—MELISSA LANDERS, AUTHOR OF *ALIENATED*,
INVADED, AND *STARFLIGHT*

"Self-worth and destiny collide in this twisty-turny fantasy full of surprise and heart. Propelled into a world she knows nothing about, Eliyana learns that the birthmark she despises is not quite the superficial curse she thought it was—it's worse, and the mark comes with a heavy responsibility. Can she face her reflection long enough to be the hero her new friends need? With charm and wit, author Sara Ella delivers *Unblemished*, a magical story with a compelling message and a unique take on the perils of Central Park."

—SHANNON DITTEMORE, AUTHOR OF THE ANGEL EYES TRILOGY

"*Unblemished* is an enchanting, beautifully written adventure with a pitch-perfect blend of fantasy, realism, and romance. Move this one to the top of your TBR pile and clear your schedule—you won't want to put it down!"

—LORIE LANGDON, AUTHOR OF THE AMAZON
BESTSELLING DOON SERIES

"*Unblemished* had me from the first chapter—mystery, romance, and mind-blowing twists and turns that I *so* did not see coming! The worlds Sara Ella builds are complex and seamless; the characters she creates are beautifully flawed. Readers are sure to love this book and finish it, as I did, begging for more!"

—KRISTA MCGEE, AUTHOR OF THE ANOMALY TRILOGY

unbreakable

the unblemished trilogy, book iii

sara ella

THOMAS NELSON

Since 1798

Unbreakable

© 2018 by Sara E. Carrington

All rights reserved. No portion of this book may be reproduced, stored in a retrieval system, or transmitted in any form or by any means—electronic, mechanical, photocopy, recording, scanning, or other—except for brief quotations in critical reviews or articles, without the prior written permission of the publisher.

Published in Nashville, Tennessee, by Thomas Nelson. Thomas Nelson is a registered trademark of HarperCollins Christian Publishing, Inc.

Special thanks to Jim Hart of Hartline Literary

Maps by Matthew Covington

Thomas Nelson titles may be purchased in bulk for educational, business, fund-raising, or sales promotional use. For information, please e-mail SpecialMarkets@ThomasNelson.com.

Two lines quoted from song "Stay with Me," written by Sam Smith, James Napier, William Phillips, with Tom Petty and Jeff Lynne, 2012.

Library of Congress Cataloging-in-Publication Data

Names: Ella, Sara, author.
Title: Unbreakable / Sara Ella.
Description: Nashville, Tennessee : Thomas Nelson, [2018] | Series:
  Unblemished ; book 3 | Summary: Eliyana Ember knows she must annihilate the Void and that only the Verity, the light which birthed the darkness, can put an end to that which seeks to destroy.
Identifiers: LCCN 2017055844 | ISBN 9780718081058 (hardcover)
Subjects: | CYAC: Fantasy. | Love--Fiction. | Kings, queens, rulers,
  etc.--Fiction.
Classification: LCC PZ7.1.E435 Up 2018 | DDC [Fic]--dc23 LC record available at https://lccn.loc.gov/2017055844

Printed in the United States of America

18 19 20 21 22 LSC 5 4 3 2 1

The dedication of this book is sevenfold (one for each Reflection):

For my unfailing readers, who never cease to
cheer me on and beg for the next story.
For my family, because blood or not, you love me for real.
For my dear girlfriends, who are always
there to listen, good days or bad.
For my publishing team—you give me grace when I need it most.
For my daughters, who show me every day
what it means to be truly beautiful.
For my husband, who sees past my blemishes, but
more importantly helps *me* see past them.
And for my Creator, who brought me out of
darkness and covered me with light.

Third Reflection: Venice

Venetian Lagoon and Sandbar →

Adriatic Sea

Grand Canal

The Ghetto
(Bianca Moretti's Flat)

Rialto Bridge
(Council of reflections
secret meeting place)

St Mark's Basillica
(Threshold to the Second)

Bridge of Sighs

The Hidden
Jewels of Venice

The Phoenix

N
NE
E
SE
S
SW
W
NW

Fourth Reflection

Tecre Sea Threshold

Tecre Island

GREATEST
HOWEVER
IS WATER

Therakytain Island

Aniach Bay

Aniach Canton

Mount Nespach

Rosalmy Bay

Mynoreth Canton

Mount Ritisspilor

Sarames Bay

Dosgav Island

Vanlib Sea Threshold

Dai Island

Rahkerlion Canton

Palace of Sonsosk

Thatsou Catacombs

Rahkerlion Canal

Kaide Agi Marketplace

Sithila Canton

Tecre Thruway

Mount Kitdi

Onisi Kouf Island

Rysich Island

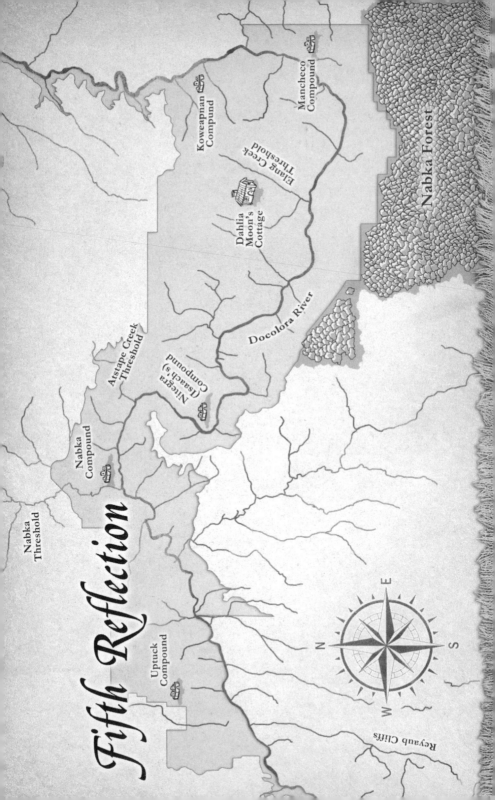

Fifth Reflection

Nabka Forest

Mancheco Compound

Koweapnan Compund

Elang Creek Threshold

Dahlia Moon's Cottage

Docolora River

Aistape Creek Threshold

Niteera (Isaach's) Compound

Nabka Compound

Nabka Threshold

Uptuck Compound

Reyaub Cliffs

unbreakable

Past poses a riddle.
What will come of the morrow?
Future stands untouched.
Who reaches forever?
Day offers a chance.
Will night prevail?
The answers are dreadful indeed,
And so my warning do heed.
Ne'er allow your heart to fall;
Its death remains the most tragic of all.
My only cure for this blight
Remains to find the girl with the light.
My curse will end with her final breath,
For a broken heart is its own kind of death.

—FROM *THE LAMENT OF THE FAIRY QUEEN*, AUTHOR UNKNOWN

prelude

You can't understand the beginning until you reach the end, so here it is . . .

After all this time it comes down to this?

I never wanted this to happen.

Somehow I always knew it would.

"It's okay." His rasp is little more than a final breath. "I'm ready."

I'm not. "You idiot. Why would you do this? There had to be another way."

But even as I speak the words, I know . . .

This is the only way.

My forehead meets his.

His eyes lock on mine. "Time for you to go."

I kiss his knuckles, bating my sobs as I force myself to rise. Now it has to end. Here. For good. So I do the only thing left to do.

I. Die.

ACT I

IN MY OWN
Little corner

meek as a mouse

What is that wretched odor? Am I dead? Because I smell dead or death or something close to it. I can't open my eyes. Not yet. Opening my eyes makes it real. I just need a minute to collect myself. My thoughts. My memories . . .

Memories.

I squeeze my eyelids, rummaging my brain, digging and sorting. Compartmentalizing. *Retrace your steps.* That's what the proverbial *they* say, isn't it? That's how to get back to what you've forgotten?

Or who?

The sound of trickling water plays a part in the symphony of recollections trumpeting through my mind. Except this performance is broken, missing instruments, clusters of notes omitted here and there. A sad rehearsal not quite living up to what the full experience is intended to be.

It's winter. Feb—Second Month. I was in the Fifth Reflection.

Mom is there, and Evan, my new baby bro.

And Kyaphus, the Void's vessel. In fact, he's the *last* thing I remember before falling into the draining Threshold behind the cottage. Did he push me? The idea fits. Darkness and light are at war. But the former won't win.

I simply refuse.

So I open my eyes.

The sky is shrouded in grays. I'm lying on my back, legs and arms sprawled, and what's above dominates my vision. The only color filters in, and I can almost imagine I landed on the set of

Pleasantville or *The Giver*. Worlds bathed in drab hues with only a twinkling of pigment ushered in by the odd man out. Or odd woman in my case. The lack of vibrancy mirrors my mind. The things I do remember are livelier than ever, standing out among the other faded, hazy memories.

Oh, fine. I might as well admit it—I want to cry. And not just cry. I mean a full-on ugly sob. Like snot everywhere, red-rimmed eyes shedding unstoppable tears. Bring on the tissues because the waterworks are about to commence. And why not? No one's here to see me lose it. Not a single recognizable soul to witness the vessel of the purest light identify as a mama's girl.

Yeah. I want Mom.

Sitting up, I swipe at my eyes and nose. Could things get any worse? I'm in the gutter, literally, which explains the smell. Water streams, rushing down the grate beneath me. The sidewalk a step up is paved in unevenly cut gray stones. I scoot onto the curb and ring out my drenched mocha hair, combing through the tangles with my fingers. My bangs are no more, having at last grown long enough to tuck behind my ears. The purple ends have faded to gray. And not the pretty, "hip" gray everyone's wearing nowadays. I'm talking the kind of gray that looks as if it were stripped off a dead sewer rat. Which totally fits right about now.

Straight across the street sits a vintage baby-blue car, its tires flat. Since I know nothing about cars, all I can think is how it reminds me of that scene from *Back to the Future Part II* when Marty is sneaking around the 1950s wearing a fedora.

I could sure use Doc Brown. And not because he's a genius. Truth is, I'm pretty sure I'm in a foreign country with no ID and zero cash, minus a phone. A flying car would be great. I'm sure Harry Potter and Ron Weasley would agree.

Mixing film references? Wow. Lack of sleep plus wormhole suction really makes a person insane.

I rise and shove my hands into my hoodie pockets, playing eeny meeny miny moe in my head before deciding to head upstream from the sewer grate. More tears threaten to expose themselves and I sniff them back, though the effort is halfhearted. I'm not the naive and fragile girl from what seems like a lifetime ago. I mean, I can walk through a flipping mirror, for Verity's sake.

But crying doesn't make me weak either. It makes me human. A human who is—I touch my throbbing face, then lower my hand—bleeding and disoriented without the slightest clue where the nearest US embassy might be. Why didn't I pay better attention in my foreign language class? Not that speaking Latin would help me now anyway—nor anyone in this century, for that matter.

I'm not even sure what language actually *would* help me. Italian? My surroundings feel very Little Italy to me, though much more authentic, and there are no buildings painted in the colors of the Italian flag.

Why does such a trivial detail from my life in the Third Reflection stand out, yet I can't recall major events from the past twenty-four hours?

All the more reason to keep moving.

A café with an outdoor patio waits ahead, naked rosebushes lining the sill of the shop's front window. I pause beside it, straining to make out the chatter between two cappuccino-sipping women. They whisper beneath their breaths, talking too fast and . . . hmm . . . *buongiorno* is definitely Italian. Score one for the queen of the Second.

Hurrying past, I continue up the street. Daylight recedes with each step, twilight pronouncing its grand entrance through tufts of cloud cover. Passersby are few and far between. Each person I cross unsettles my gut further. A heavyset man with shoulders hunched, a cigar hanging from his mustached mouth. An elderly woman speed walking, practically dragging along a little girl who can't be older than five. A couple with heads bent together, tones hushed, the man with one arm around his sweetheart.

No one notices me, and the realization injects an all-too-familiar feeling into my center. I shove it deep and walk faster. Why do I get the feeling these people are *afraid*? And not afraid of me or the mark I bear, because no one has even made eye contact. No, these people carry a tangible anxiety that's impossible to ignore. Even the air feels ominous, like the deadly fog rising after an epic battle scene in *The Patriot* or *Wonder Woman*.

Right arm cradled against my soaked middle, I cut across a main road. Eerie quiet settles in, sets me on edge. What time does the embassy close? Is it like a twenty-four-hour thing? Doubtful. Darkness will blanket the area soon, and then what?

Asking for help it is.

I choose the next person I near and touch a bony, pin-curled young woman on the arm.

Her pointy shoulders peak, then she glances over one with narrowed eyes. It's the exact look I'd expect her to bestow, especially considering the handful of anxious people I've witnessed thus far. She's early twenties, dressed in a suit that would probably cost me a kidney, and the perfume wafting from her person makes me think of what liquid gold must smell like.

And me? I appear as if I just washed up from the sewer. Which is, ugh, accurate. I cringe inwardly, waiting for her to turn her probably plastic nose up at me.

But then her expression softens and her maroon-painted lips curve into a smile. "Oh my! Signorina, what on earth has happened to you?" English! Sigh. Her accent is thick and undeniably Italian. Familiar. In many ways like home.

A cringe dominates my insides again, but this time it's from my own stupid bias. By now I should've learned not to judge people based on appearances. My disheveled mien doesn't seem to faze her, let alone the mirrormark spiraling up the right side of my face like fraying scarlet threads. She sees me as human, equal. A rarity in this Reflection or the next.

I swallow and clear my throat, force myself to hold eye contact. She may not realize who she's speaking to—vessel of the Verity, queen of the Second—but I know who I am. Or I mostly know. "I was in an accident." That's a fairly true statement, right? Unless it . . . wasn't an accident. "Can you tell me where—"

"Certainly, but first you come with me." She wraps an arm

around my soggy shoulders as if it won't ruin her outfit. As if it's nothing.

Maybe there *is* some kindness left in the Third after all. At least, my intuition tells me it's the Third. Then again, this could be the Sixth or Seventh. For all I know I've died and gone to the First.

The woman ushers me down the stone-paved walkway, her lace-up ankle boots *clack, clack, clacking* in contrast to the squeaky shuffle of my Converse. We turn one corner, then another, heading deeper into what seems to be a residential area. Up one hill, then down the next. Level streets and curved streets and streets that end nowhere. How very New York. Not a stand-alone house in sight, but what the city lacks it makes up for in an overflow of historical architecture.

Some of the structures are built from old brick, while others are coated with peeling paint or yellowed stucco, all topped with Spanish tile roofing. Curving iron cages cover white-framed windows. Clotheslines droop between windows across the alley. An old woman with a kerchief swathing her hair beats a rug on a mini balcony. A wisp of gray looses and she tucks it back. Instantly I'm reminded of Reggie and my heart leaps. I've only known the old cook who helped raise Mom a short while. Surely my memory loss can't be as serious as it seems if I've retained even an ounce of my short-term recollections.

Right?

When we round another corner, my rescuer makes a sharp right and enters a building with a green door. My breath catches and something inside cracks. The Void's vessel has one brown eye and one green. The color of envy, jealousy, money, and any other corrupt thing you can think of.

I peek back at the door as it snaps closed. Anger rises with each step up the steep stairwell. Man, I hate that. I hate *him*. That much I remember. My reaction to the green door rings true to this, at least.

The woman withdraws a single key from her handbag. It's an old key, large and brass and artistic looking, a tattered red ribbon looped through its end. Like something you'd find in a souvenir shop but not intended for actual use. Reggie mentioned Mom found a key once, in the Second's castle.

"Never did learn which door it opened." Reggie shook her head and the story was forgotten.

Unimportant. Trivial, but also not. Because with each random detail that triggers a new memory, I'm one piece closer to a renewed mind.

My chaperone inserts the key into the lock. *Jiggle, quarter turn, click.* The door opens inwardly. A quaint one-room loft rests undisturbed across the threshold. It's full and bright and not at all what I'd expect to see on the inside of such a dilapidated old building. Everything is the color of eggshells, not white enough to be actual white, you know? Eggshell rafters, eggshell cabinets, eggshell gossamer curtains, eggshell bedposts. A window on the far end of the space allows a small breeze, the curtains billowing like an elegant gown on royalty.

"Sit, sit!" The woman gestures to a chair, which is of course also eggshell, and I obey. The familiar ping in the back of my mind, a.k.a. Mom's voice, doesn't call a warning, reminding me to proceed with caution, let alone not to go home with a stranger. The Verity settles cozily, grounding my trust. This woman is genuine. There's just something about her that assures me she means no harm.

She bustles about the loft, switching on antique lamps at every corner. Then she moves to the kitchen, pulling an eggshell teacup and saucer from a high cupboard. An eggshell teapot and tea tin from another. The tea tin is silver, standing out as a diamond in a quarry. A closer look informs me it's white tea, the words *White Earl Grey* engraved onto one side in fancy lettering. My cheeks perk. It's a sign, has to be. Earl Grey is Mom's favorite. The Verity warms my core, further infusing me with calm. I may be lost and confused, but I'm safe.

I smile and yawn, relaxing a smidge as the woman, who remains unnamed, prepares tea in silence. A folded newspaper rests on the round eggshell table before me. I pull the paper near and examine the front page. And that's when the first twinge of uncertainty rises. I glimpse my rescuer from beneath my eyelashes, take her in again. Noticing the distinct Agent Carter hairstyle sweeping the wavy strawberry locks off her face. The classic red of her lips. The style of her jacket and skirt. Even the laces of her vintage ankle boots stand out now.

I look down at the paper again. At the date printed there. The timeless voices of Doris Day, Frank Sinatra, Perry Como, and Bing Crosby bombard my brain all at once, their refrains meshing into unsettling noise rather than soothing ballads. This is much more complicated than I first realized. When I was transported through the wormhole, I knew I had no idea where I'd end up, which Reflection it would spit me into. I was not prepared, however, for this. I may not know exactly where I am, but I know when. And when is not then. I've been sent to a completely different decade. A different century, for that matter.

Even if I could find the US embassy or another Threshold and make my way back to the Second or Fourth or Fifth, what good would it do me?

Because it's February 7, 1945. And I have no clue how to get back.

A gain!" I heave. "Don't go soft on me now." My weapon arm supports my middle. Every muscle and bone aches. My head pounds, and if I had a shirt on it'd be drenched with sweat. It's been twenty-four hours since Em disappeared through the wormhole. Since then the pain hasn't stopped. Without her it won't. Without her love it's up to me to keep my mind about me—and my heart. My goals rush through my thoughts, racing to keep up with my raging adrenaline.

Find Em. Take her to the Fountain of Time in the Seventh. Change the past. Fix the present. Restore hope for the future.

It all seems too simple. My blade swipes the air. We're missing something, but what? I wipe my seeping brow with my forearm. Dahlia's been around longer than any of us. I trust her when she says we must go back in time if we're to destroy the Void and set things right in the here and now. My opponent grits his teeth but makes no move to charge again. Still, *I've* been around long enough to know this isn't a game . . .

"I think we've had enough for one night, boy." Saul Preacher lowers his battle-ax and heads for the back door of Dahlia Moon's cottage. Over one shoulder he adds, "You know I enjoy a good sparring match, but I'm beat." He scratches his jaw where gray whiskers grow over claw-shaped scars. "We'll pick up where we left off next chance we get."

I straighten my spent body and narrow my dry eyes. The moon-light is hardly enough to illuminate my target, but I'm no amateur.

"Think again," I call. Then I flick my mirrorglass blade directly at his shadowed back.

He whirls, all two hundred–plus pounds of him. He may be short and stout, but Preacher's not a man to be trifled with. Swift as a clipper ship he blocks my throw with the flat side of his ax. My knife pings the metal and clatters to the dirt.

Preacher snorts, then scratches his trimmed beard. "You'll have to do better than that, Kyaphus."

"One more hour." My skin itches so much it's maddening, the Void-filled veins pulsing against the surface. But I pin my arms to my sides. I will not let it change me. And that includes acknowledging the torture and agitation. "I need to stay strong if I'm going to keep the darkness at bay." He doesn't know there won't be a next time. No one does.

His right eye twitches. Do I detect a smirk fluffing his whiskers? "Fine. But be warned I'll not go easy on you. You may be bleeding before we're done." He snatches my knife and slides it across the sand toward me.

I grab it and wipe off the dust on my pant leg. "No problem." I flip the knife in my hand and crouch into a defensive stance. "I've always said blood is more a luxury than a necessity anyway."

He laughs at that, ax raised once more. Then he charges.

⌒∞⌒

One hour quickly turns into two, then three. I won't relent and Preacher accommodates me nicely. A Guardian without a Calling, he's always had to compensate with the tough-guy act. At least that's what I've sensed. People try to hide from me, but I read them. I see them.

Just like I saw Em. And, eventually, she saw me too.

When I'm so out of breath I can't catch it, I finally agree to call it a night, or morning as the case may be. We head inside and Preacher commences snoring the second his head hits the cot, boots on and ax in hand. I roll my eyes and cross to the bedroom window, holding my blade up to reflect the waning moonlight. I'll never forget the day I obtained my mirrorglass blade. For some, a weapon is a trophy. For me, it's a hefty reminder of who I am and where I come from, of the person I will always aim to be.

But it isn't the light on the blue-silver knife that gains my attention. Instead, it's my own altered image. I haven't looked at myself since she left, couldn't bear to see what she saw that caused her such terror. But there it is. There *I* am. Blackened veins everywhere, clawing at my torso and creeping up my neck. Even my honey-colored hair has darkened, my eyes displaying subdued shades of their original colors. The gold flecks in my green eye have vanished, leaving a scum-like circle of puke in their place.

I smirk and roll my shoulders. What's the outside? The shell I'm stuck in? This doesn't define me. Never has, never will. As long as I serve the Verity, as long as I cling to love, nothing, not even the Void itself, can take me.

"You can't fight forever. Eventually I'll come out. I have before and I will again."

The voice belonging to the darkest part of my soul croaks from deep within. I press him down. I've done this for years, had plenty of practice. I'm not about to give in now. Not when remaining myself is vital to finding Em. She told me once bound souls always find each other. Whatever Josh did to her, I have to believe that, at least, is true.

I sheathe my blade and turn from my reflection. The sun'll be up within the hour. I should rest, but what's the point? I won't be at ease until I've located her. And unfortunately, to do that I need a favor from someone I hoped never to see again. He may be a traitor, but he's also a marauder. A treasure hunter. Attention to detail has served me well in the past, and I'll bet my mirrorglass blade he possesses what I need.

"Jonathan Gage." I grunt his name beneath my breath. Servant to Isabeau Archer, the immortal Fairy Queen. He helped Josh, that Shadowalker downstairs, and he can crowe well help me.

I step around Tide Toshiro, my chief cook from *The Seven Seas,* sprawled out on a floor mat. Streak, who showed up to the party a few hours following the others, sleeps standing up in one corner. Whether he's truly sleeping or just resting is up for question. I don't dare startle him and invite his fury. And by fury I mean his wretched sailor breath.

When I exit the room and tread through the cottage, the loose boards creak and buckle. I pass Elizabeth and Makai's closed door. I almost think I hear baby Evan stir and I pause, bating my breath. When I'm certain I haven't startled him, I continue on, more cautious than before.

The front room is noiseless aside from the girls' breathing. The fire has long since died. Robyn Song lies curled up on the rug in Bengal tiger form, though she resembles a harmless kitten more than the ferocious beast she is. Especially with that purple clump of hair on her cheek.

Dahlia Moon—Regina Reeves—took off late last night for Nitegra Compound, Flint in tow.

"Time waits for no man," the Ever woman had announced, floured hands flailing. "And those Thresholds won't be waitin' either, ya hear. Betcha Breckan and Isaach'll have news. They keep tabs on all the happenings here. Bet yer left boot that pair'll know if there's any Threshold worth its water left. If that's the case, we'll have a plan when we reconvene." She clapped. "Besides, it's never too good to stay in one place for long. That means you too, Miss Elizabeth. Time we found you a new hideout."

"Regina, please." Elizabeth touched her arm, their history made clear with a look. "We can all depart in the morning. Together. Is it wise to split up?"

"Nonsense, child." She pecked Evan, asleep in his mother's arms, on the head. "Y'all get some rest now. I've been around enough years, sleep's become a luxury. If it'll make you feel better, I'll take Flint along with me. I've not been feelin' my best and could use the extra hand." She winked and lowered her voice, spoke behind her hand. "Besides, that boy's a bit of scrum and umptious, if you know what I mean."

I think everyone in the room knew what she meant. Poor Flint went beet red. It was all I could do to keep a straight face. Hopefully he's survived the night, and the two will have news for Makai when they meet up.

I take a head count, then glance out the window. Stormy is nowhere to be seen, probably off on a morning jog or something. She's kept to herself since arriving, and I don't blame her. Her husband, Kuna, is gone and Em is her best friend. The water Magnet must feel so alone.

Guilt weighs heavy on my fighting soul. If I were to take anyone along, it'd be her. But I can't. I have to take this on alone. I will not have Josh or Stormy or anyone else interfering.

In the end my gaze rests on Ebony Archer and my adoptive sister Khloe. For all I know, this could be the last time I see them. I lean over Khloe, brush her frizzy hair off her face, and kiss her forehead. The girls share the couch, spooning, the elder with her arms wrapped around my baby sister. *Our* baby sister, I guess. Both are Tiernan's biological daughters.

And me?

I belong to no one.

Never even met my real parents, whom I now know to be the former King Aidan and Queen Ember. What's more, the man who claims to be my brother is insane. It's really too bad I need him. Joshua David is the only one who knows exactly what's happened to Em. The only one who's been in contact with Gage and Isabeau recently.

To top it off, his Ever blood is useful in these times. Granted, we have Dahlia, but I'd rather not cut into her if it's not necessary. She's been acting ill, a reminder Evers are just as human as the rest of us. The Shadowalker is our blood supply, and even if we have to bleed him dry—

I smack myself hard on the head. The sinister thoughts come before I can stop them. I have to stay on full alert if I'm going to keep the Void from taking over.

Fine. Always liked a good challenge.

My surge of confidence is quickly followed by resentment as I make my way back down the hall. Wren Song rests slouched beside the door to the cellar. I nudge her boot with the toe of my own.

Nothing. Not even a change in breathing.

I comb my fingers through my greasy hair with one hand while turning the knob on the cellar door with the other. For the dread of Dragons, David. Why'd you have to be such a moron?

He's locked away again. It took the lot of us against him and Wren to keep him down there. Even Commander Archer, who's like an older brother to David, saw it as an essential precaution to contain him. But I know all too well the battle he faces now. David allowed the Void to take hold of him. Permitted his darker side to surface. And that's the most dangerous game of all. I've told Makai exactly what's going on with the Ever. He and the others can handle the Shadowalker when I'm gone, no sweat.

With a long exhale, I exit the hallway and head down the stairs into the cellar. Might as well get this over with.

josh

Ah, and so he shows his pathetic face once more. I jerk against my restraints, the ropes binding my wrists chafing the already-raw skin. What's it been? Eight hours since we last had a chat? It's about time he came back down here. Does he believe he holds a semblance of authority over me? When I forced Eliyana to drink the Unbinding Elixir, *I* harnessed the Void within *Kyaphus*. Which means *I* am in control, not the other way around. And now that my brother's bond with Eliyana is broken, I can find a way to lock him away. Let him rot from his dark insides out.

"*You're delusional,*" my weaker half says inside my head. "*Haven't you figured it out? Get it through that sick soul of yours. The mere fact Kyaphus is the only vessel of the Void means he's the one who cares for Eliyana most. By attempting to break their bond, you have only strengthened it further. Have you forgotten what Rafaj said—?*"

"Quiet, fool," I hiss as Kyaphus tromps down the cellar stairs. "Grandfather has nothing to do with this."

"*Are you daft? He has everything to do with this. Or have you forgotten his last words? Kyaphus will figure it out if he hasn't already . . .*"

I ignore him and his voice departs. If I don't acknowledge his presence, he'll be forced to leave me be.

"*Amusing.*" He laughs. "*That's exactly what I assumed about you, and look where my folly landed me.*"

I witness him reclining in my mind's eye. At first Joshua was in agony over his internal prison. Now he acts more like the man standing before me for the second time in a day. Cocky, arrogant, and so sure of himself.

I square my shoulders and glare at my twin.

He looms over me, convinced, just as Joshua is, he'll make it out alive.

I spit to one side.

Not if I have anything to say about it.

THREE

i obey

I've told myself the same thing a million times over. *Don't panic. Do not do it. Panicking helps nobody, least of all me. Think. Use your brain, for Verity's sake. What are my options?*

Mirror walking. I can do that, right? I close my eyes. The Callings were dying, and my voice had vanished. Then it returned. My Mirror Calling *does* work. Because Joshua saved that girl—Khloe, my half sister—from bleeding to death when Kyaphus tried to kill her. His Ever blood was one of the first to cease. He couldn't save Kuna—ouch, my heart grieves the loss as if it's fresh—but he did keep Khloe alive. Which means the Callings are functional. I can mirror walk myself right out of here. I have no limits, I can just—

Double ugh and duh. As if passing through my reflection does me any good. Where would I go? If this were the present, I'd put myself right back where I began. But mirror walking only transfers me from here to a place I've been. I've never used it to travel to an alternate year, let alone an alternate century. Is such a thing even possible? I could try—

"Do you take sugar and cream, *mia cara?*"

My head whips up. I'd almost forgotten someone else was here. "Yeah. I mean, yes, please."

The woman skirts the kitchen island, a saucer-supported teacup in each hand, and joins me at the table. Every move is elegant, grace-ful, classic. From the purse of her lips to the sway of her hips. She's Mom and Ebony rolled into one.

I palm my forehead. Ebony. My other half sister. She taught me how to use my butterfly Mask. We're . . . friends now? Why is everything so jumbled and misplaced? Is this how amnesia works? Fragments of facts falling back into place, bit by bit?

"I am Bianca Moretti." The woman's hand covers her heart. Finally, a name to go with the face. Bianca passes me one of the saucer-and-cup combos. The cloudy tea wavers. Steam rises, warms and dampens my face. "You are a long way from home, no?"

I sip and swallow, thinking of Robyn and her father, Wade. Bedtime tales over tea and soup in the Haven seem far removed. The returning memories allow me time to form an answer for Bianca as the overly sweetened tea runs down my throat. *Long way* doesn't even begin to cover it.

"Yes, a long, long way, I suspect." She sips from her own cup, not a decibel of sound releasing as she does. Her sepia eyes remain locked on me, consideration in her undemanding stare. "You are fortunate our paths crossed, signorina. Had a Shadowalker found you, I am afraid you would have been dead before the sun dipped below the Tyrrhenian Sea."

Though I'm berating myself for not paying better attention in geography class, my ears perk and I choke on my tea midgulp. Hot liquid dribbles down my chin. *Nice. Real regal, El.* "Did you say Shadowalker?" I've heard that term before. In the . . . Fifth Reflection. A woman storyteller. A bonfire. A chill caresses my side, as if something should be there warming me.

Joshua. He was there that night, arm wrapped around me as Breckan relayed her tale. Mmm. Good memory. Better hold on to that one.

"Do not be alarmed, *bambolina*. I will not turn you in. I belong to the Third Alliance. It is my duty to guard and protect the Called of this Reflection." Crossing her right fist over her heart, she closes her eyes and inhales deeply, as if paying homage to a saint.

A weighty sigh escapes. The Verity must be looking out for me. I may be lost in a different century, but I've stumbled across someone who might help. "This *is* the Third, then? And you're

a Shield? What's your niche? Who else is in the Third Alliance?"
Questions flow like the notes of an up-tempo opus.

Bianca giggles, her whiter-than-white teeth gleaming. "Slow
down, *amica*."

Signorina, bambolina, mia cara, amica? I can't keep up with these
terms. I hope they mean good things. The tone of her voice suggests so. I'll take that as a good sign.

"First we must clean you up. Make you presentable for the
meeting *questa sera*. All shall be revealed then." She rises and posi-
tions herself behind my chair, pulls it out, and helps me up. Then
I'm whisked off to the loft's other end where a claw-footed tub
waits. "Most apologies, but the water is *freddo*."

I shiver. I don't have to speak her language to guess what *freddo*
means.

"Still, it will wash away that nasty smell." Her nose wrinkles.

My cheeks flame. If my subjects in the Second could see me now,
would they look on with pity or disgust? Certainly they wouldn't view
me as queen. I hardly got a chance to act as ruler before everything
began to fall apart. Is everyone all right? Did Joshua leave someone
in charge in my absence? Are the people—*my* people—waiting for
my return as they did for King Aidan's? Or will the disapproval of
many compel them to find another, worthier monarch? Does their
loyalty to the Verity trump their disappointment in me?

Only time will tell.

❧

My head pounds. Never in eighteen years has my hair been yanked
this tight. Bianca seemed to enjoy making me up. I didn't notice evi-
dence anyone else lives with her. Maybe she's lonely or bored or a bit
of both.

"You look exquisite, *bambolina*." She pushes one last bobby pin
against my scalp. "Or, what is it you Americans say? You're the cat's
meow, doll." Her sweet titter, unfortunately, doesn't make my head
hurt any less.

I follow her up and down the streets of what I've learned is Venice. I scratch my temples where my locks are pulled up and pinned back, twisted into curls and secured with way too many bobby pins. I press my lips together, the sticky red painting them way too pungent a flavor for my taste. The worst part is the outfit. A knee-length khaki skirt and a poufed cream-colored shirt accented with an even puffier chiffon scarf. And the heels. Oh, the heels. I shouldn't be complaining about the black, character-style shoes. But still, they're *heels*. Ebony would be jumping for joy at my vintage fashion, while all I want is a pair of dry jeans and some worn-in sneakers.

I look to the night sky and moan inwardly. *You couldn't have sent me to the eighties? At least then I'd be comfortable.*

Bianca remains close to building sides. I mimic her moves, keeping an eye out for a reflective surface. As much as I sense no danger with her, I'm still not sure it's such a wise idea to just up and go wherever she tells me. Perhaps mirror walking *is* my only option. I could at least *attempt* to mirror walk through time. Who knows? It could totally be a thing.

Then again, another part of me, miniscule but present, wants to know more about the Third Alliance and the deal with Shadowalkers. In my time they don't really seem to be an issue aside from Void lovers such as Jasyn Crowe and my absent father, Tiernan Archer. What happened? Did the Shadowalkers go into hiding? If so, why?

As Alice would say on her way through Wonderland . . . "curiouser and curiouser."

We approach a shop with a wide front window. Flyers and posters written in Italian deck the glass. One catches my attention and I peer closer. Yep, that's definitely Humphrey Bogart. This must be a film advertisement, though I don't recognize the two actors with him. The other papers blast headlines I can only guess announce failures and victories. Wins and losses. One featuring a photo of Mussolini is hard to miss. I shudder and rip down his picture, only to find grime and filth beneath. Still, it's the perfect target for my hypothetical ticket out of here.

I find my escort in the corner of my vision. Bianca is so focused on her destination, she doesn't notice when I lag behind. I clear my throat. The dust coating the glass is thick, caked on. When's the last time someone washed this window? My reflection isn't a reflection at all. Perhaps if daylight peeked over my shoulder I might be able to make out at least an eyebrow. But night wins this one, leaving me in the dark. Literally.

No bother. I don't need to see where I'm going to know where I've been.

Eyes closed, I open my mouth. Shut it. Open it a second time. But no lyrics form. No song flows easily from my lips. What in the Third? This should be routine for me by now. Why can't I perform?

Bony fingers wrap my wrist.

I jerk back, but her grip stays firm.

Bianca stands before me, brows knit and eyes narrowed. Everything from the way she glances over one shoulder to her white knuckles on her handbag suggests anxiety. Same as the other residents I happened across earlier. Are the Shadowalkers so terrifying? They worship the Void, but that doesn't mean they have any power.

Does it?

Wait. Hold the rotary phone—1945 is wartime. It's February and ha! That's one thing I recall. World War II ended on September 2, 1945. In your face, history class.

A far-off siren blares, reminding me of home. My heart hammers as Bianca pulls me onward and picks up her pace. Her hold doesn't give. I don't fight it either. Does the siren mean a curfew? A bomb raid? I'd rather not find out. I don't recall much regarding the politics of this war, but honestly I'd rather run into a Shadowalker than a Nazi any day. My safest bet is to stay with Bianca and see whom she might lead me to, what other Called I might find.

When we reach the Grand Canal (which I only identify as the Grand Canal thanks to my guide), we wait at the water's edge. Tiny waves lap at the walls containing them, begging to rise and be freed. We stand there for what seems like an eternity. Bianca withdraws a pocket watch from her purse, flicks it open, and checks the time before pocketing it once more.

An internal bell pings my memories. I've . . . seen that watch before. Haven't I? Then again, tons of people own pocket watches. Just because I've seen one doesn't mean it was *this* one. Still . . . there's something about it—

"Look." Bianca gestures toward the water, drawing my focus.

A gondola glides toward us, the water below parting beneath it like melting glass. When it arrives, the man on board assists in lowering us off the ledge where we stand, Bianca first, then me. It feels awkward in a skirt, and I nearly knock the straight-faced Italian over from trying not to expose myself. When my feet meet the boat's bottom, my ankle twists and one of my heels breaks. See? This is precisely why I don't wear these kinds of shoes, which really aren't shoes at all. This sort of thing never happens with Converse. I slip them off and shove them to the side. Barefoot it is.

Our pilot pushes off with his slender oar, sculling on one side and then the other—

Wait. Since when did I become a boat junkie? How do I know the man steering is the pilot or what he's doing with the oar is called sculling?

The Seven Seas. The ship Ebony and I were taken captive on before Joshua came to our aid in the Fourth. My time aboard must explain why I've retained some sailor lingo. Did one of the crew teach me? Tide maybe? Or Streak? Couldn't have been the captain. I never saw him. He stayed in his chambers the entire time, the coward.

But back to the gondola at hand. In movies the Italian guy serenades a cute couple as he rows merrily down the stream. Sort of like on *Lady and the Tramp* when the spaghetti guy and the accordion player sang to the dogs. But there's nothing warm or happy or romantic about this. We endure the ride down the canal in silence. Bianca sitting with knees pressed together and shoulders back. Our guide staring straight ahead, unblinking.

And me? I'm here for answers. Like how do I get back to my

decade? Why do I feel the Verity within, but when it came to mirror walking, my song list was cleared? Could my Calling be used against me here? Bianca must know something about my mirrormark. Has she read Queen Ember's *Mirror Theory*? Is the *Mirror Theory* even written yet? Does she know the power of the curved lines climbing my skin?

An all-too-familiar wrench in my gut materializes. I glance across the boat at the woman who willingly took me in. Was I too quick to trust her? Did my time-traveling disorientation-slash-amnesia play against my better judgment? Could Bianca be another Jasyn Crowe, with an ulterior motive eager to take center stage?

Mom, where are you? You're supposed to be my Jiminy Cricket, for the love of Infinity!

Infinity. As in Kiss of? Another memory brushes my heart, and I respond by lifting my fingers to my right cheek. Joshua gave me this. I allow my eyes to close a moment. Allow my mind to whisk me away to our first kiss beneath the grand staircase in the throne room. The kiss was everything I'd dreamed and more. Brought with it Joshua's first admission of love.

I grasp for my treble clef–heart necklace at my collarbone, as if somehow the familiar token will help the missing memories return in full. But the charm feels different. Double. I dig it from beneath my blouse. My eyes widen when not one but two charms appear. Joshua's treble clef–heart has been joined by a copper button engraved with a rose. I recognize the button as the one from my favorite pair of jeans. Problem is, I have zero clue how it wound up hanging from my neck. And where is Joshua's engagement ring?

Just another complication to add to my growing list.

The boat drifts under an arched bridge, and the pilot steers us toward the edge of its shadows. Bianca offers him a nod, releases my wrist, and exits the boat, stepping out onto a small platform.

Hesitation keeps me glued in place. I may or may not be in danger, but it's not as if I'm helpless. My mirror walking is off-key, but could my Mask be in tune? I can always butterfly my way out of here if escape becomes imperative.

Still, I need my song for every aspect of my Calling. If it won't vocalize, I can still find it within. I've done it before.

I'll do it again.

Bianca rummages through her purse, giving me my window. I draw the music from deep inside, waiting for it to rise to the boundaries of my heart. Longing for it to spill from my soul. To transform me. To give me wings.

But I feel nothing. Nothing at all.

My guide withdraws an object from her bag and *click*. A flashlight illuminates the upward-curving wall ahead. Unlike my venture with Joshua in the subway last November, I know what's coming now. I can't help it. I can't detect it in this light, but I'm able to guess it's not a barrier at all. Bianca examines the concrete, then walks through unhindered.

Metamorphosis apparently out of the question, I follow her.

"Well done, signorina." Bianca slings her handbag over one arm, flashlight brightening the tunnel before us. "Come now, we mustn't be late. His Majesty would be most disenchanted if we delayed our meeting with the Second Alliance."

The *Second* Alliance? As in the Second Reflection? I riffle through names, subtracting years, guessing ages. It's 1945. Could someone I know or recognize wait here? Wade Song, traditional Physic a.k.a. Robyn and Wren's dad, would be too young, maybe not even born yet. Who else? Preacher? He's pretty old. And Reggie, oh Reggie! She's an Ever, more aged than any of us knew. It's totally possible she'd be around. And knowing her, my time travel–slash–wormhole story wouldn't sound crazy at all.

Hope wells as Bianca and I venture deeper into the underground. The way narrows the farther we travel, her heels clacking, my bare feet padding. At the tunnel's end a frosted glass door waits, a circular knocker fashioned from silver at its heart. The art-deco door seems random, nestled inside so much concrete. Then again, nothing is random. Not when it comes to the Called and Reflections.

Swirling silver designs climb up and cascade down the door's front. Mesmerizing. Unique. But also achingly familiar. The Fourth's council meeting was held underground, an out-of-place circular door waiting to admit us. Joshua read the most tragic tale of the first Verity's vessel. How her heart broke into a million pieces.

Horrible. I can't stay stuck in the past. I need to return and help the others set things right.

Bianca takes the knocker between two fingers and her thumb. Two quick taps precede three slow ones. The door swings inward. To a room full of . . .

Teens?

A guy who can't be older than a high school senior waits as we enter, then shuts the door behind us with a rattle. I study his face. Nope. Don't know him. Then again, he could have wrinkles and be bald by the time he gets to my century.

The room before me is arranged like a lounge, wingback chairs set up in a circle bordering a round Venetian rug. Several chairs are occupied, just more almost-twentysomethings I can't identify. Hope falters. Not one friend? Not that they'd know me. Still, a little familiarity on my end would be nice.

Bianca, the oldest of the group, though that's not saying much, takes a seat at the far side of the circle and signals for me to do the same. I choose a floral-patterned chair a few people down from her. Wait. Anticipate. I drum my fingers on the chair arms. I cross my right ankle over my left, then switch. A fire crackles in a hearth to the right of the circle. Where does the smoke release without raising suspicion? Is there a house above us? A factory?

One boy with a cigarette tosses it into the fire, clears his throat, and waves for those standing to take the remaining seats. Everyone tunes their gaze to my channel.

I sink deeper into my chair. What's with the staring?

Oh-kay. Guess I'll introduce myself. "Hello." No ums or likes. Be straight. Queenly. "My name is—"

A throat clears behind me. I crane my neck and look up. Gasp and hole-ee Verity! Not just one, but *two* guys I know stand there. One I've met, the other not so much. But I'd know his face anywhere.

Because it's Joshua's face. Uncanny.

King Aidan Henry steps forward, assuming his place at the circle's core. He's young, maybe Bianca's age, with honey-blond hair and jade eyes. Though Joshua has cerulean eyes and brown hair, these features are familiar as well. I take the smallest second to stow away the thought in the folder of my mind labeled "Save for Later," then blink and focus on the man behind me.

He doesn't look down, just rests an elbow on the high chair back and keeps his eyes trained on the king along with everyone else. But my gaze remains on this man. I can't take my eyes off him. He's so much like Makai it's crazy, with shaggy dark hair and a strong jaw. There's even a bit of rebellion sparking in his gray eyes, though it's more reserved.

Nathaniel Archer notices me then, considers me through thick-rimmed black glasses. He's pushing midtwenties? Probably the most mature of the bunch, which, again, isn't saying much. And now I realize why I recognized Bianca's pocket watch.

Because when my grandfather peers over me and winks at Bianca, I know.

Because when she winks back, a blush taking up residence in her cheeks, I see it.

Bianca Moretti is my grandmother.

f O U R

KY

"We don't have time for Dragon games. Son of a crowe, David. Just tell me what you did! I know you messed with her memories, but I need you to explain how you accomplished it."

Back against the opposite wall and knees bent, my enemy emits a heartless laugh. An alternate tactic is inevitable. Acting as his superior is getting me nowhere. Perhaps it's time for a little sibling bonding.

I remove my sheath and knife from my hip, then set them on the bottom cellar stair. David doesn't glance up as I move toward him across the dusty floor. When we're half a fathom apart, I sit before him, legs crisscrossed and elbows resting on my bowed knees. I clear my throat, which itches as if a cough might be coming on. Though I'd wager it has less to do with the mold and dust and relates more to the blackness attempting to take hold.

And this is when he lifts his head. He glares, unblinking, and we sit that way for quite some time. There was a day he saw me as at least a worthy comrade. Someone who could guard and protect the one thing we both cared for most.

Except now he cares more for himself, for his love of darkness, than he does for her. A Kiss of Infinity is a powerful thing. Whatever David did has interfered with a force I'm not sure even he understands.

I swallow hard, biting back the choice words I ought to sling. I drive patience into my bones, into every muscle and tendon that throbs in anticipation of pummeling him. He wants to wait, we'll wait.

At last he ceases and says, "You and I both know we do not have the time to sit here at your leisure." His eyes are downcast, head hanging between his knees. "I divulged as much as I could the first time you came down here. I've no clue as to Gage's current whereabouts, and as far as Isabeau is concerned, it seems the others are prepared to leave at first light."

He jerks his chin toward the low ceiling. "I shall be left behind to live out my days as a prisoner, just as our grandfather Rafaj before me. Makai Archer will sweep his darling Elizabeth as far away from the Fairy Queen as possible. And you." His glare tightens. There's no mistaking the malice in his gaze. "You will search for *my* true love, only to come up short. Eliyana will never know you as she once did. Sure, she'll recognize you. She will even gain back her memories of you piece by broken piece. But the love she held for you? The bond you two shared?" He shakes his head. "I am afraid that, dear brother, is broken forever."

He's been too helpful. Too much of an open book. He's trying to distract me from something. Doing his best to give me everything so I won't notice I'm missing the only detail I need.

"What's your name, Shadowalker? Josh, was it?"

He grunts.

He must gather I'm on to him. We all are. Even his voice is off, different from before. It lacks warmth, life. When he introduced himself as Josh yesterday, I knew he had more than a mere alter ego going on. "I suspect Joshua David is still in there somewhere. I'll deal with him if and when he chooses to surface." I lean forward. "But you and me?" I gesture between us. "We can't come to any sort of arrangement unless you help me out here."

His shoulders sink like a weight in the water. He cocks his head. Now I've commanded his attention.

"You think you're clever, don't you, *Kyaphus*?" He places the emphasis on my full name, anticipating it will faze me, no doubt.

Though it lights a smoldering fume deep inside, I won't give him the satisfaction of seeing the effect he has. "Kyaphus is the name of the lesser man within." The name my farce of a father, Tiernan Archer, called me when he was beating me black and blue for not living up to his impossible expectations. "It's just Ky." The shortened name my mother bestowed. She said it meant "strait of water."

"*You are destined for greatness, my son,*" she would explain as she tucked me in at night, Khloe propped on her hip. "*One boy intended for a much larger purpose. You may see yourself as small now, but one day the grand picture will come into focus. Then you will see. You are designed to join oceans. You will change the Reflections as we know them.*"

Every mother holds high hopes for her child. But mine wasn't even my *real* mother. I didn't know at first, but she was always aware of it. And she treated me as her own anyway.

"That's real love," I mutter.

"Come again?" David who is not David watches me now. "What are you rambling on about?"

I smile to myself. Another thing Em and I have in common is getting lost in our own heads. Which, I'll admit, was much more fun when I was actually *in* her head, and when she was in mine. All the more reason we're perfect for each other.

"As I was saying, it's Ky." I scratch at the Void snaking around my right bicep. Clench and unclench my left fist. Kyaphus will not surface. I won't allow it. The last time he showed up, he nearly got us both killed. "Now then." My fingers intertwine in my lap. "Explain what you did, and we can go from there."

He shrugs and leans back. His hands are bound and attached to a vertical pipe beside him. If he's uncomfortable he doesn't show it.

This guy really is a piece of work. David kept his own darkness suppressed for so long, when he finally let it loose, an egotistical monster arose. "You haven't fooled anyone, you know. You may think you can pass as a jaded version of yourself, but I smelled Shadowalker the moment your sword ran through my baby sister."

The reminder makes me question my own sanity. *How am I this calm?*

"Are you so weak you can't invoke justice on the man who almost killed Khloe?" Kyaphus chimes in, ever the pest.

Ah yes, that's right. I'm attempting to keep my personal issues with him out of this. Otherwise there's no telling what I, or Kyaphus, might do to him.

I fight the umpteenth urge to rearrange Josh's face. "The others are aware of what you've become. Wren is the only one who isn't convinced, but even she must realize"—I rub my chin—"you're a Shadowalker. You bow to the very darkness trapped inside these bones." I twist my arms, palms up.

His forehead creases. "Believe what you like, but Shadowalkers are a myth. A story created to keep children from hitting their siblings or running away from home." The lie rolls off his tongue.

I shift and bring one knee up, clasping it against my chest. "Josh." My upper lip curls. Man, I wish Em were here. Aside from the fact this guy is basically her ex, we'd make a great interrogation team. Like one of those good cop–bad cop scenarios on the Third's TV shows. "I know your secret. If Shadowalkers are a myth, then I'm looking at a legend."

He scowls.

I lift one eyebrow, a talent of mine. "Anyway." I rise, dusting off my rear, and retrieve my knife and sheath. "Now that your identity is cleared up, tell me what you did to her and we can begin to undo your mistake."

He laughs again. The sound echoes. "It can't be undone, you fool. The break is permanent."

The break. Indeed. "'Nothing is permanent . . .'"

He winces at my words, the start of a phrase my mother used to quote. I wish I could remember the rest of it. I'll have to skim through the book of fables Countess Ambrose gave me at the nearest opportunity. Volume 1 of *Once Upon a Reflection* is teeming with useful information for those who know where to look. Not really a book of fables at all. *The Scrib's Fate* was based upon what happened when the Verity created the Void. What other stories might be events in history rather than mere parables?

"That's where you're wrong, Brother." And this would count as the second time he's acknowledged our relationship. "The Elixir destroyed your soul bond. It's nearly impossible to restore."

"Nearly isn't completely." The hope I already contained continues to grow, grabbing on to my heart, guarding it from the Void.

"It doesn't matter," he spits. He's coming off 99 percent confident. But I see that 1 percent. And it's telling me exactly what I need to know. "The likelihood of you sharing the antidote is one chance in a million. A splinter in a pile of ruins."

It won't be easy, but it *is* possible. And possible is all I need.

"Here's something you haven't considered." This time I'm the one diverging. "And perhaps this will enlighten us as to why the Callings seem to be returning, but why the Thresholds—at least the one behind this cottage—continue to drain. Em—Eliyana—doesn't remember me, or more accurately, she has forgotten *us*. I'm afraid you have the upper hand there. But a connection remains. When I touched her, she knew me, and not just me but the love we shared. Just as the Kiss of Infinity is more than a physical act, our touch raises something deeper. Something much more lasting than even your Elixir could alter. The Void enters the one who cares most for the Verity's vessel. As long as that's me, I will not stop fighting until she and I are together again. Heart and soul."

"You and your feeble hope. Hear me, now. The longer you're apart, the more her memories of you return. But without your soul bond, everything will be tainted. She'll remember you as the Void's vessel, not as her love. I'm elated she's been taken to another Reflection. It only aids me further in keeping you two as far from each other as possible. I don't know why I didn't think of it before."

He closes his eyes and bares his teeth. His gloating is getting to be a little much. "My plan was to control the situation, to keep her by my side so I could keep an eye on her. But this? This is so much better. By the time we find Eliyana, even when you make contact, she'll have made up her mind about you. She will feel nothing but disgust for what you have become."

I fold my arms over my puffed chest. "Explain." His desire to boast about how well things are working out trumps his need to remain mysterious. Good.

"The man who gave me the recipe for the Elixir—Rafaj Niddala, our grandfather—pressed that time is of the essence. Time heals all wounds, correct?"

I nod. Where's he going with this?

He sits a tad straighter. "Your bond with Eliyana was a wound that needed healing. It ruined everything—*everything*." His chest heaves, his dark rage too fiery to control. He exhales and regains composure, though his expression remains hard as a conch shell. "She belongs with me, understand? In time, you will surrender to the Void inside. Darkness and hatred will consume you, and your love for her will turn to resentment. That is when the Elixir will have done its job. That is when I will have conquered."

Staring more intently, I look for the man I can't see. David is in there. In some dark corner where Josh would have him rot away, lost forever. But he's the least of my concerns. What he's done to Em is sick.

And what of the Reflections? Wasn't it our unique link that set us on this course in the first place? If the bond between us is severed completely, will the link between Reflections break for good as well? It's the only thing that explains why the nearest Threshold is nothing more than a muddy pond when it was once a rushing river. We thought it was our soul bond that *caused* the problem, the too-close link between Void and Verity that created the chaos. But what if it's the opposite? The Void came from the Verity, after all.

What if our connection is the force holding everything together?

The realization sets in like a storm at sea. Nowhere to go but directly into the squall.

When we were together the Callings faded, the Thresholds drained, yet *her* Calling grew stronger. We made it into the Fifth by the skin of our teeth because of Em. The Callings are returning now, but at what cost? What if the reunion of the Verity and Void was the beginning of something far greater than we knew? A force to be reckoned with. They'd been separate for so long, the darkness and light removed from each other due to a tragic heart-break. Of *course* things began to fall apart at first when the two were reunited.

But then things started to shift.

What if our love began to mend things, return them to their original intended state? Return them to the way they were in the Garden of Epoch? What if our love set a course of action that Josh-Joshua-whoever has carelessly interrupted?

"One last question."

"What now?" He rolls his eyes.

"Where did you last see Jonathan Gage?"

"I told you yesterday. He was with me in the Fourth. We parted ways this side of the Fifth's Threshold."

"And you have no notion as to where he might've gone?"

His flattened lips are all the answer I require.

"Why protect him? What's he ever done for you? He tried to kidnap Em—Eliyana."

Josh exhales. "I am not protecting him. I am seeing how clue-less you truly are."

My defenses erect, I'm at the ready with my next retort. But then I catch the humor displayed in his calculating eyes. He's stall-ing. This *is* just a game to him.

I turn my back on my brother and tromp up the stairs, open-ing then closing the cellar door. I've half a mind to slam it and rattle the entire cottage. But this is no one else's concern aside from my own. I creep up the hall and grab my pack, which is already bulging with supplies. The books I included only weigh me down more, but I can't leave them behind. The written word has saved us before, and I won't underestimate its power now.

The same loop of thoughts tumbles through my brain as I exit through the front door and ready for my jog. If Em and I remain apart too long, the passages between Reflections will cease to exist. I'm sure of it. The Verity will lose its connection to the Thresholds, the Callings, everything. I must find her and restore the connec-tion, allow the course we set out on to play through.

I'm about to set off, but a sigh keeps me in place. When I peer over one shoulder I find Elizabeth. Why am I not surprised? Should've known I wouldn't make it out of here without her say.

"Good morning." The greeting is meant for me, yet her eyes don't abandon the fleece-bundled baby boy in her arms.

I turn to face her, bowing my head as I do. "Ma'am."

Her smile takes over, the spitting image of Em's. My heart contorts. *Keep it together, man.*

"Oh, Ky." She sighs again, this time shifting her gaze toward me as she rises from the stone bench beside the door. "I believe you and I both know I am no 'ma'am' to you. You love my daughter. I feel, in the very least, we ought to be on a first-name basis."

I swallow hard and offer a nod.

"Makai felt he should be the one to speak with you. He knew you would try to take off. He thought you should know something before you decide to leave everyone who cares for you behind."

The corner of my mouth twitches and my feet itch to run. I respect Em's mom enough to wait and hear her out, but my head's already halfway across the valley.

"You should not be trying to go this alone. Nothing good will come of it."

Each word digs deep as the Void pulses along my veins. I'm reminded of something I once said to Em. A smirk surfaces because, oh man, did she despise me. It was kind of cute. She was bleeding from the inside out yet, stubborn as ever, didn't want my help.

"Either you let me help you, or you die right here. Your choice."

She caved after a minute, and I lifted her onto the horse. There was no way around accepting my help. Is now any different from then? Except I'm the one in need of assistance.

The Void stings again, each time harsher than the last.

Stay with Em. Focus on Em. Love will keep me sane. Keep me from letting the Void take over as it's attempted to do so many times before.

She sighs. "Joshua is a good man."

I realize, deep down, she's correct, but where's she going with the change of subject?

"He loves my Eliyana as well." She moves toward me. Before I can protest, she's offering me baby Evan and placing him in my arms.

It appears the Void doesn't faze her. She doesn't even seem to notice it.

"But you." Her fingers slide into her son's blanket. She tugs it down to reveal his full sleeping face. "There is a difference between true love and *soul* love."

My heart coils tighter, nearly cutting off my air. Em's brother is heavier than I expected, much more solid than Khloe at his age. I find myself swaying in place without prompting. His face stirs a long-forgotten feeling. My throat clears. I need not ask Elizabeth to continue. She will. It's why she's here.

"Do not mistake my meaning. True love is the most powerful emotion. So strong, it can be mistaken for soul love. Joshua's love for my oldest child is true. Yes, it is very true indeed." The baby's mother strokes his full head of dark hair. One wisp curls up above the rest. "But the love you have for her is much more. The kind of love that cannot be denied or broken. No weapon, no potion, no enemy can stand against this love." She eyes me. The look is so Em.

I sense she's waiting for me to catch on to what she's trying to relay. Okay. I'll bite. "Are you referring to the Kiss of Infinity we shared? The Shadowalker—"

Elizabeth eyes me again, this time in warning.

Duly noted. Joshua is no Shadowalker to her. "Joshua . . . gave her something. He claims it—"

A shake of her head. Brown hair that could be Em's, aside from a few silver strands, falls into eyes the color of teakwood. "I spoke with him while you were sparring with Saul. Joshua does not know exactly what he has gotten himself into. His seemingly simple solution is not the remedy he hoped for, but a test of your unbreakable bond. A cord of three strands is not easily broken, just as a love sealed with three Kisses of Infinity is not merely forgotten."

She's exactly as Em described her. All the wisdom of a Scrib, decades older than she, radiates from her every word. Yet . . . "I'm sorry, you're mistaken. We only shared one Kiss of Infinity, the night she saved me from the Void injection. All the others after that were . . . normal." I reposition Evan in my arms, diverting from the awkwardness. Nothing about kissing Em is normal. I'd prefer not to discuss the details with her mother, however.

As she places one hand on my cheek, Elizabeth's eyes glisten. "Yes, you did share one, when she saved you and you exchanged an identical connection. And there is also the Kiss you bestowed when you saved her . . ."

Her words take me back to a day I assumed no one remembered, aside from myself.

"And the first one . . ." One finger extended, she traces Evan's chubby cheek. "The Kiss you offered when she was but a tiny baby in my arms."

I am rarely at a loss for words. Then this happens. I don't argue. I don't explain how it was my twin who kissed her daughter as a baby, giving her the mirrormark. Elizabeth was present. I heard Em replay the memory in her mind on more than one occasion. One part always stood out to me, though.

". . . *his eyes almost green in the firelight's glow, his little-boy hair two shades lighter, all curls . . .*"

For a moment I almost hoped it was me. I could've fit the description easily, but—"Tiernan took me," I remind her. "And the boy who kissed Em." I close my eyes and picture the memory as if it were my own. "He said his name was Joshua."

Elizabeth beams. "No. He did not."

I cock my head. Evan begins to fuss and I bounce him gently, just as I used to do with Khloe. A song my mother used to sing fills my mind. I almost begin humming the tune but refrain. The Void has affected my voice as well. I couldn't care less what I sound like, but I don't want to terrify Evan.

My thoughts redirect to the conversation at hand. "Em's memory. She recalled the boy introducing himself as 'Jos-wuh.'"

"The mind is a funny thing indeed." Two fingers tap her temple. "It has a tendency to play tricks on us. To cause us to see

and hear things that are not there. To fill in the blanks of an inci-
dent we cannot quite recall."

"She's a Mirror. Her Scrib ability is extraordinary."

"No one is perfect, Ky. Not a Mask, nor an Ever. Not even a
Scrib. I am sure even you have flaws within your Shield?" She
winks. "These are our gifts, yes, but they do not make us blame-
less. The only perfection is the Verity itself. Even a vessel carries
its shortcomings."

I return Evan to her arms. I need not ask how she knows all
this. If anyone is aware of what really happened that night, it'd be
her or Makai or Nathaniel.

"Stay, son." Balancing her true son, she squeezes my bicep.

Her soft grip sends a jolt through my body. I can feel the Void
recoil from her loving touch.

"Stay and let us figure this out together."

I've always relied on myself, and in doing so I let everyone
down. Perhaps it's time for a new approach. I nod.

Elizabeth smiles. "See you inside?"

Another nod.

She releases my arm and strolls into the cottage. I don't believe
I've ever witnessed anyone else as graceful as she.

Setting my pack on the ground, I sit on the bench, extending
my legs in front of me and clasping my hands on the top of my head.
If what Elizabeth said holds truth, more than one Kiss of Infinity
is possible. And if I've given Em three? It's going to take something
much stronger than an Elixir concocted by a Shadowalker to break
our souls apart. Still, I need to find her if I have any hope of securing our future.

I withdraw a small black vial from my cargo pocket, lift it
toward the dawning light. Staying doesn't change my course. If
anything, having the others by my side gives me more purpose
than ever.

Time for a refill.

I Know

"**B**loody brilliant! You cannot be serious, man! The notion is absurd!" The younger version of my grandfather paces about, removing his glasses and then wiping the lenses on the tail of his shirt as is his custom.

My cheeks perk. I don't take my eyes off him. This is surreal. He's himself yet so different at once. Dark hair like Makai. Gray eyes young and alive and free of shaded, sagging circles. His glasses are thick-framed, the opposite of his wiry old-man spectacles. His walk is sure and able, his shoulders straight though still narrow. I glance at Bianca from the corner of my vision. She watches Nathaniel too. The admiration in her gaze is impossible to miss.

"Hear me out, Archer." King Aidan Henry folds his arms over his chest in the way I've seen Joshua do more times than I can count. He sounds sort of like Joshua too, but for some reason Aidan's voice is recognizable in a different way. It reminds me of Kyaphus, to be honest, or what I remember of him anyway. The idea makes me scoff inwardly. My grandfather had it right. Absurd indeed.

King Aidan clears his throat. "And for Verity's sake, would you stop your insufferable pacing."

My regard passes between the two men who've taken center stage, and my smirk returns. The familiar phrase rolls off Aidan's tongue and I have to stifle a laugh. Did I really believe *I* invented "for Verity's sake"? Nothing new under the sun, right?

I take in the rest of the scene. The hard expression straining nearly every attendee's face. A young woman with pinched lips and fierce eyes reminiscent of Stormy's. A young man sits to her left, face propped against his fist. He rubs his nose and yawns, making a sort of snorting noise as he does. The girl to his left scrunches her face, scoots over in her chair. The next seat hosts a guy who can't be older than I am. He keeps scratching his baby face, his permanent scowl reminding me of Preacher.

Something tells me the banter between Aidan and Nathaniel isn't foreign to these people. Do they see a heated argument? A disagreement between mates? What I'm witnessing is something that raises a feeling I can't quite put into words. Because I know what perhaps no one else here, aside from Bianca, does.

Aidan and Nathaniel are best friends.

It's Nathaniel who introduced Aidan to Ember. My gaze falls to each person present once more. Ember isn't here. I rack my brain. They met when Aidan was . . . thirty. And . . . they both died when Aidan was . . . seventy-five? If it's 1945, I'd say Aidan has a few more years before he meets his queen, but it can't be too much longer. How I'd love to be present for that event.

I graze my right cheek with my fingertips. Push a stray curl from my forehead. What would it be like to witness the Kiss of Infinity that created Ember's mirrormark? How would it feel to see someone else just like me?

"What is there to hear, Henry? What you are proposing we do is madness!" Nathaniel combs his fingers through his hair and crosses to the fireplace, then reaches out to warm his hands. He exhales. His next words come leisurely, as if sifted through a sieve. "If we use our Callings out in the open, the lot of us will be sent to internment camps. Or worse, we'll be used as weapons by our greatest enemies. Is that what you want, man?"

Leave it to Nathaniel to play it safe.

Aidan shakes his head. "The war is coming to a close." His voice never rises. "I feel it, Archer. We all do." He sweeps his hand over the room.

A wave of nods ensues. Even Bianca gives a curt, purse-lipped gesture, her eyes forever trained on Nathaniel.

My grandfather spreads his fingers, then curls them into fists.

Aidan joins him by the fire and places a hand on his shoulder. Nathaniel is taller but the king stands straighter, making him appear the loftier of the two. His next words are for my grandfather alone, but the small space makes them easy enough to decipher. "Think of what you could accomplish, my friend. You are the greatest Physic of our time. Your hands could save hundreds, thousands even. All I am asking is that you give it a try. We can change history. Together."

Nathaniel closes his eyes and swallows, Adam's apple bobbing. After what seems like an eternal silence he concedes. "Relay the time and place and I shall fulfill my duty. To you. To the Verity. The Reflections. For us all."

I'm new here, but even with my jacked memory I can see what's going on. I'm taken back to something once shared with me. It comes to me like a dream. I can't see the face of the speaker, can't even distinguish his muffled, faraway voice. But the words are there, drawing me back to an unexpected but welcome feeling.

Home.

"We had to keep our Callings hidden," the voice says, "as most people in the Third hold no belief in the Verity, the Void, or the Callings. Some do, but they conceal their abilities well, opting for a quiet life rather than becoming a science experiment in some test facility."

This is the life of a Called in the Third. This is why Nathaniel is afraid to use his gift out in the open.

A throat clears and every head turns toward a man in a chair three away from mine to the right. His head is bowed, black bowler hat tilted low over his forehead. Face hidden beneath the shadow of the brim, he says, "I think we are all forgetting we have a much greater power at our disposal. What better way to fight the Shadowalkers than with the very entity they bow to?"

Chills creep along my neck. Because, unlike the dream voice, I know this voice immediately. I swallow hard and have the urge to disappear into my chair. Has the Void already taken ahold of his soul? Does the Verity live within Aidan? It must. Because, black veins or none, there's no mistaking the coldness in my other grandfather's eyes as he lifts his head and locks his gaze with mine.

SIX

Ebony

"Everyone gather up front!" Preacher's razor-blade bellow carries down the cottage hall. "We're assembling two groups. One led by the Commander and the other by the trait—" He clears his throat. "Kyaphus. You'll be filled in on more details once you get your butts in gear."

Ugh. Basically, I have two choices. A, I can run and hide with Elizabeth's Guardian caravan, wait out this whole revenge rampage my mother is on. Or B, I follow Rhyen on his quest to save my sister and, in turn, the Reflections. Either way, I kind of come out a hero.

Then again, there's always option C, which I'm sorry, but am I the only one here who recognizes we so need a third option? This path would take me on the road never traveled. While Rhyen runs full-steam ahead to save his future, and the others do everything they're able to survive the present, my heart can't help but wander to the place I've dared not trespass until now. I'm putting myself out on a limb here. The old Ebony would keep quiet, let the others sort through this mess on their own.

Old Ebony? Those words don't even belong in the same sentence, do they? Which means all I have is the new and, dare I say, improved version of myself. The choice means a trip down memory lane where I'll be forced to dig up old ghosts. If I'm being honest, the idea scares the living fairy lights out of me. Of course, I didn't gain my reputation as a heartless you-know-what without a little effort. Fear isn't something I cower before.

Option C it is, then.

I secure Khloe's second French braid, then immediately start in on my loose mocha-colored locks. The task is one I could do in the dark with my eyes closed and one hand tied behind my back.

Okay, maybe that's an exaggeration, but you get it, right?

I start on the right side of my head, weaving the strands together around the back and finishing the braid off on the left side. Then I take the tie held between my teeth and fasten the do like a boss. Next I grab the only item I was able to salvage from my purse before we were basically shipwrecked. The antique silver compact is the lone thing I still have from my childhood. I wasn't about to let it go now. Excuse me for being nostalgic and all. Some girls hang on to a teddy bear or baby doll. I have a compact, and I don't think it's unreasonable I would want to keep said compact close at all times.

Sheesh, Ebony. Insecure about your security blanket much?

Muffled voices seep beneath the bathroom door. Preacher's yelling as usual and Commander Archer is ordering him to calm the Void down.

Go, Uncle Makai. Never heard him use less-than-appropriate language before, but it's a start. Makes him much more intimidating in my not-so-humble opinion.

Now, for some face time. And I don't mean the digital breed either. I examine myself in the compact's round mirror, tilting my chin, turning my head this way and that. My rich brown eyes look barren without liner on their lids, and my hair is in desperate need of a conditioning mask. The mirror is ancient and extremely fragile, not the plastic kind CoverGirl sells. The natural light streaming through the window above the sink hits the glass just so. No two mirrors are alike, and this one's portrayal of me is by far my favorite. As if it's saying, "Gorgeous, darling. Simply stunning." Even today, with the bridge of my nose peeling and my lips flaking, this mirror manages to make me feel good about myself. I've never been one to pretend I'm not beautiful. I know I am.

But, as they say, beauty is only skin deep. Thank goodness mirrors can't see into your soul. Not this kind of mirror, anyway.

An uninvited image intrudes upon my mind. I picture my other sister. Her fluid voice and the way she seamlessly steps through a mirror as if it's no big thing. She doesn't see what I see. What *everyone* sees. She carries a beauty that can't be created with makeup or a curling wand. Her beauty can't be ruined by a bad hair day or a few pimples. I never got why she never *got* it. At first I hated her for all her sulking and clueless self-doubt. Yeah, I was jealous, so what? I even preyed upon her cluelessness. Sue me. That's yesterday's news. We're past that. And now it's too late. Now I can't even tell my own sister I love her.

Hold the iPhone. Don't even think of getting sentimental, Ebony. It's not your style.

"Hey, you okay?" There goes Khloe again, noticing things that are none of her business.

"Fine." I sniff back the liquid rimming my eyelids. Not that a few tears matter as I'm seriously lacking in the mascara department right now, but that's beside the point. I get up from my crisscrossed position on the floor and scour the cabinets. There's gotta be some here *somewhere*. "What kind of B&B doesn't have oils for guest use?" I may not have eye makeup, but something must be done about my chapped lips.

Khloe giggles from her new perch on the closed toilet seat.

I catch her in the corner of my vision. Quirk an eyebrow.

As always, she defiantly rolls her eyes.

"Okay, what?" Placing a hand on each hip, I pivot to face her. "Just say whatever it is you're gonna say, Khlo."

She smooths her dark hand over even darker braids. "You know what I'm going to say, Eb."

Now I'm rolling *my* eyes. "Okay, okay. I get it, runt. This isn't exactly the Hilton."

"Ya think?"

We both spent a good amount of time in the Third, so we understand each other in a way no one else in our posse does. I flip my wrist in a whatever-you're-right-again sort of gesture. Then I check my complexion once more before I pocket the compact in the steel-blue, waist-length leather jacket I snagged from Charley's trunk on *The Seven Seas*. The Mask may have been a pirate, but I'm not about to deny she had good taste. Too bad she ditched us to rejoin her tribe or whoever. The few times I encountered her, I sensed we could've run with the same crowd.

Could've. Could have. Back then. Not now. Not when I've begun to care about stuff again for the first time in ages. The acknowledgment is nauseating, to say the least. Things were way less complicated when I was in this deal for me, myself, and I.

Curse you, Eliyana Ember. This is all your fault.

Three rapid knocks sound on the door, but the intruder doesn't wait for a response before peeking his head inside. "You two done in here yet? Everyone's waiting on you. This isn't a fashion show."

My cheeks simmer. I turn toward Khloe, pretending to fuss with a frayed thread on her shirt. Tide *can't* see how his hot-but-not-too-hot-casual-surfer-guy presence affects me. "Almost." Oh my flipping *no*. That is not *my* voice coming out sounding like roadkill. I clear my throat in the subtlest way I can and try again. "Al*most*." Better. Much better. "A little privacy?"

Khloe makes a face and I give her a look that says "shush."

"Your wish is my most honored command." I can hear the smile in Tide's voice before the door creaks closed.

And the simmer turns to a full-on boil.

"You didn't have to be rude to him," Khloe says.

How else am I supposed to be? This is just me, and if Tide can't accept me as I am—"I wasn't rude. He's the one entering unannounced." I snap the thread clean off her shirt. It floats into the wastebasket.

My sister rises. She's almost as tall as I am though we're nearly ten years apart. "He knocked." She plants her hands on her hips. Like big sis like little sis.

"Well . . ." Oh, why does she know just the right things to say to get me ruffled?

"He likes you." Khloe's all business. Trying to play matchmaker yet again when it's the last thing I need. How can I even begin to think of being something for someone else if I have no flipping clue as to who or what I am? Am I Called, empowered by the Verity? Or am I something freakish and other, a by-product of an immortal bully? Is this how El has felt with that mark on her face her entire life? If so, this is total crud, that's what this is. I wish El were here so I could talk to her, gain some perspective.

I clear my throat again. "We're friends." I've always handled things alone. How is this any different?

Khloe opens her mouth to speak, but I lift my hand in front of her face. "We're. Friends." I zip my jacket, letting each word sink in. "Tide's a nice guy. He's like this with everyone, not just me." I shove a hand into each pocket of my jeans, checking to make sure every inch of my outfit is in its perfect, tucked-in place. "I'm telling you, Khlo, you're not old enough to understand these things, so don't even bother trying. You're just a kid—" I bite my tongue, tasting blood. *Daughter of a Troll, Ebony, why do you do this? This is too far and now Khloe is hurt. Khloe. With El gone, she's the only person here who even gets you.*

She's past me and to the door in a heartbeat. I almost can't stand to look her in her big brown eyes, but I do. I don't owe anyone anything. Except Khloe. She deserves at least this much.

But the chipped shoulder I would have if the situation were reversed is nowhere in sight. Instead, my sister just flashes her big white smile and says, "We'll see."

Then she skips out the door.

stand

H e doesn't know who I am. He can't. Yes, he keeps staring at me. Yes, he regards me in that sinister, all-knowing, Amulet way of his. But it's impossible for him to recognize me because he didn't know of my existence until he found Mom last year. Until *Quinn* found us. *Just play it cool. Don't look guilty, because you have nothing to be guilty about.*

"Not this bloody nonsense again," Nathaniel retorts in his distinct British accent. "How many times have we told you, Crowe? The Void is not to be trifled with. It is imprisoned in a place only the Verity's vessel knows for a purpose." He faces Aidan. "And he's never going to tell us where that is, isn't that right, Henry?"

Does he want reassurance for Jasyn or for himself? My grandfather remained in hiding when Jasyn took the throne. Could his fear of the Void's vessel have begun long before he realized just how dark Jasyn was?

Sweat beads across my scrunched forehead. Aidan *is* the Verity's vessel. Here. Now. Which means Jasyn is the prison no one knows about. Oh man, oh man, oh *man*. I've never been in this type of situation. Being so totally in the loop I know even more than my grandfather. Nathaniel. The old Physic I once turned to when I knew nothing at all.

A pang strikes my chest. I wish Joshua were here. I rub my palms against the chair's upholstered arms. Close my eyes to shut out the quarrel continuing among the three men. The Verity warms my soul, expanding and swirling. Which raises another question—how can I possess the Verity while Aidan retains it as well? Why is there another question for every missing answer? Why, why, why? How, how, how?

"Ugh!"

The arguing ceases.

Oh crud, did I vocalize my frustrations? Opening my eyes confirms my fear is reality.

It's the king who lifts an eyebrow. "You are new." He eyes my grandfathers. "Perhaps we should save this discussion, gentlemen. For a more private setting." His tone expresses kindness but finality. "I am interested to learn more about our lovely newcomer."

The old me would've been like, "Lovely? Ha!" But now I smile and say, "Thank you."

Compliment accepted.

Bianca rises and comes to stand beside me. Before I can say more, she begins what is an obviously rehearsed speech. "I found her on the streets. As the Representative of the Third, I felt it was my duty to rescue one of our own."

Representative of the Third. My heart falters, though I don't know why this didn't hit me sooner. Bianca's not around during my time. Nathaniel never mentioned her, save a passing comment on a cold winter night . . .

"By then I was already grown and living in the Second with my wife and two boys."

This is where they met. I'm living my own family history. What are the chances I'd land here, surrounded by my ancestors?

"And how do you know she is one of ours, Moretti?" Accusation does not coat Aidan's voice. No. His tenor is more curious, inquisitive. As if he already knows but wants to know how *she* knows, you know?

He's so much like Joshua I want to stand and hug him.

"Because I saw her appear out of nowhere." Excitement speeds her words. "One moment the gutter was sewer water and then—poof!—she was there." She pats my head as if I'm her lapdog.

I twist in my chair, dipping my head away from her touch.

"Wait. You . . . watched me?" I shake my head. "No. I found you. Tapped you on the shoulder."

Her red lips curl. "That is merely your perception, signorina. I had to be sure, you see, to be sure you are one of us." She blinks so fast it makes me dizzy. "We are all Called. And we have a sense about these things." She taps her temple. "We are drawn to each other because each of us has been touched by the Verity. But you." Her eyes glisten, tears welling. "You are special. Different."

Déjà vu makes me shiver. Oy vey. Is that what they say here? Because it totally fits. It's my first day in the Second all over again. Someone change the channel, because I've seen this rerun and I don't have the patience to watch it again. This is the part where my grandmother tells me how my mirrormark sets me apart. How it's a sign there is hope in whatever darkness they're currently trapped within.

But I can't be their savior. I can't stay and help them fight a war I know has already been won. I have to get back to my time period. But how do I tell them? I'd seem like a major jerkface. I wish Ebony were here. She never really cares how she comes off to people. Perhaps not such a horrible trait to carry after all.

It takes everything in me to rise and say what needs to be said. "I'm sorry, I'm afraid you're mistaken. I know my mark appears to be—"

Bianca's eyebrows pinch. "Mark, *mia cara*? I am sorry. I do not understand."

I laugh. Can't help it. "My mark. The red lines on my face. I know what you're thinking." Actually, I don't, because these people are clearly aware the Verity is alive and well. They don't need my mirrormark to tell them it's so. Still, they must think it means *something*. Otherwise there would be no call for such special attention.

My grandmother shakes her head once more. Then she reaches into her handbag and withdraws a compact. Hands it to me. I examine it. A flash of a memory. I've seen this before. But how can *this* belong to Ebony? It can't actually be the exact same one I hid . . .

something in. What did I hide? Paper . . . oh, never mind. I'll never remember right now. Pause, skip, play.

The compact. It's a replica of my sister's. I imagine the first time I saw it, the first time Ebony—at the time Quinn—invited me to her apartment. I cling to something I recall so clearly, it could be happening in real time.

"You can sit anywhere," Quinn says, waving her hand flippantly over one shoulder. "Just don't put your shoes on the bed."

For someone so perfect from lacy headband to nonscuffed heel, her room is a disaster. Bras slung over the bedposts. Seven different kinds of perfume scattered across her vanity dresser, caps off and discarded on the floor. Trash bin overflowing with lipstick-blotted tissues. Guess she spends so many hours on her appearance, she doesn't have a second for anything else. Like cleaning.

If Mom knew my new BFF was this messy, she might restrict our time together for fear of a bad influence. Clothes trail my floor as in any teenager's room, but this is a little much. Is that gum stuck to her mirror frame? Really?

I opt to sit on a low stool at the foot of her bed. A pile of fashion magazines rests atop the stool and I remove them, set them with care on the hardwood floor. Quinn plops onto the bed and dumps the contents of her Prada handbag onto the rumpled rose-gold duvet. Black bobby pins, peppermints, twenty dollars in cash, and an antique silver compact spill forth. Quinn takes a few of the bobby pins between her teeth, then twists some loose hair around her face and secures it behind her ear. Next, she opens the compact and checks her untainted complexion, showing her teeth, then rubbing beneath her eyes where a bit of excess mascara has gathered. Once she's finished, she hands the compact to me.

I shake my head and look away. No and thank you. I don't need a mirror to remind me of what I am already painfully aware of. My reflection never changes. I'll always be marked. Always.

The memory fizzles with three blinks. This is crazy. How connected everything is. Quinn-slash-Ebony's grandmother is mine. What are the chances not only that I would end up in this room with four people I am very intricately connected with but that Bianca would hand me *this* compact? That I would recognize it?

I glance up at her. Maybe there's no such thing as coincidence. Could it be that I didn't end up here, in this time and place, by accident? What if I was always supposed to come? What if my being here plays a role in future events?

Butterfly effect, anyone? And don't think the double meaning is lost on me.

I open the compact lid with my thumb just as I did the last time I held it. The day Ebony and I found a pirate ship on the beach of Coney Island. Hey! I remember that. It's progress at least. If only we'd known the ship was captained by Kyaphus, the vessel of the Void himself. I wish I could recall more of our time at sea. So much after boarding *The Seven Seas* is hazy at best—

A gasp escapes as I catch a glimpse of my complexion. I'm tempted to look Jasyn's way. To see if he's focusing to create what at first I believe is a façade. But no. This is different. Apparently there's more to this time-travel thing than first meets the eye.

Because my mirrormark is gone.

EIGHT

KY

"Here's the plan. We head west." I spread the rolled map flat over the low coffee table in the cottage's sitting area.

My decision not to go this alone solidifies more with each second, with each nod of reassurance I receive from one of the team. We all have something to lose or gain here. Division only causes more division. Did I truly believe I was stronger on my own? Idiot. I need my crew and they need me. With our strengths combined, we just might succeed in achieving the impossible.

Find the Verity's vessel. Destroy the Void.

I don't wanna brag or nothin', but it'll be awesome to say, "Me? Yeah, I was there when the greatest darkness in all the Reflections was annihilated. No big deal." I can feel Em elbowing me now. The thought melts the ice inside.

But back to business. My throat clears as all eyes train on me. Except for Wren Song's. She stands by the front window. Her black hair falls down her back past her waist, the only light a blue streak by her left ear. Arms folded over her chest, she refuses to face me. I've only witnessed one other person be so stubborn. She and David were made for each other.

I ignore her insolence and point to our current location. "Elang Creek Threshold just behind us is useless." I slide my pointer finger a few inches to the left. "Astape Creek Threshold, where we entered the Fifth, would return us to the Fourth . . . if it hadn't drained." I smirk. "But that's not where we want to go anyway." I tap a line denoting a waterway northwest of that. "Our best hope to find Em—the Verity's vessel—is to travel through a wormhole just as she did. The Threshold beyond Nabka Compound may be a viable option. If we can reach it before it drains, we may be able to time our entry just right."

It's a guessing game, a huge risk, but what else can we do? "Nitegra Compound is on the way. We'll stop there to refresh and replenish supplies. We may be permitted to borrow a few horses as well. Isaach and Breckan made it clear their resources are available for our use. By now Dahlia and Flint should have gathered information regarding the status of the Fifth's other Thresholds."

My gaze finds Em's mom and a silent conversation passes between us. Her approving smile speaks volumes.

"With the illustrious Fairy Queen after Elizabeth and Evan, I feel it's best the group remaining in the Fifth surround themselves with numbers, and the Nitegra tribe certainly has enough man—and woman—power to go around." Sound plan, if I do say so myself.

Now it's the Commander who nods his approval. I wait for his second nod before carrying on.

"We have two main objectives. Let's go over them now to make everyone clear." I ignore my timeline anxiety. I stayed behind for good reason. I need to own it. "Isabeau exists because of the Void. According to Dahlia, the original Verity's vessel wants to put Elizabeth to sleep forever with her Midnight Rose. Objective number one—keep Mrs. Archer out of the Fairy Queen's grasp."

The map snaps into a roll upon my release. I rise and stuff the paper tube into the back pocket of my cargo pants. "We can use her determination for revenge to our advantage. With the Troll–slash–Fairy Queen focused on playing the villain, she'll be out of our hair. The last thing we want is for Isabeau to know objective number two—that we intend to annihilate the Void."

"Why would she care?" Tide casually raises his hand. He looks as if he's ordering a drink rather than asking a serious question.

I wave for him to lower his arm. This isn't a classroom, man.

With a slick-back of his Islander hair, he says, "I mean, she's immortal, right?" He stands, speaking while turning in a slow circle, a leadership tactic he learned from Countess Ambrose no doubt. "But according to the story we acquired from my mother—may she drift upon the tranquil waters—all the Fairy Queen's troubles stemmed from a single event: a broken heart." His fist pounds his chest.

I sense his words hold a double meaning, and Isabeau's broken heart is not the only one he's referring to.

"If we destroy the Void," Tide says, "wouldn't it be in Isabeau's best interest as well?"

And here is the million-dollar question.

"On the surface." Ebony speaks up, emerging from the bathroom at last. Khloe joins her, ever the side to Ebony's kick. "But my mother isn't known for being sensible. The single thing she cares about is her own survival. If the Void doesn't exist, maybe she doesn't either. We can't know for sure."

No, we can't. Her double meaning doesn't elude me either. An extinct Isabeau may also mean a never-born Ebony. If changing the past means erasing things in the present, the sacrifices we make may be greater than we know. Still, this must go deeper than Isabeau simply wanting to survive and exact revenge.

I close my eyes, altering Tide's question into a riddle. He's right. Isabeau, of all people, should desire the darkness extinguished. No Void means no pain, no heartbreak. If it never existed, she might have remained in the Garden, living as day rather than banished by night. Shouldn't she want that night gone forever? In a perfect Reflection we could recruit her as an ally and not view her as our enemy. But all she's concerned with is taking revenge on Elizabeth and taking down whomever she can along the way.

I open my eyes. And this is the unseen thing outside the box.

"The Void is all she has." I scratch my throbbing arm. Without Em's love, the shadows would be my sole companion too. "When the Verity abandoned her, the Void was there." Frantic, I dig through my pack, withdraw the old book, and flip to the dog-eared page marking *The Scrib's Fate*. "'She clung to the darkness, and though she was not the Void's vessel, its blackness left a mark. She never loved again. Until Tiernan.'"

I look to Ebony for confirmation. The way she avoids my gaze is all the proof I need.

"I suspect Tiernan was the first man in centuries Isabeau allowed herself to love," I say.

Ebony swallows and I detect the slightest nod, but it's Elizabeth who voices the truth. "He mentioned her only once, after we were . . . together." Her head hangs. "I did not know he was married. Isabeau was not even his true wife, but his mistress, as I was. I am guessing she was not aware of his marriage to Ky's mother either."

Makai draws her close, rubbing her arm up and down.

I clench my fists around the tome. I always assumed the man who raised me did not act in faithfulness toward my adoptive mother. Learning he was Em's father only confirmed my suspicion. But to hear it spoken of again boils my black blood as if I'm hearing the news for the first time.

"All Tiernan said was he would never return to Isabeau, not after learning what evils she was capable of. I had seen him angry but never afraid. Not until that moment. It was the final time I encountered him before I fled with Eliyana."

Wren makes a repulsed sound in her throat, a sound reminiscent of a dying bird.

I've half a mind to put her out of her misery. But, as we may need her shape-shifting talents, I refrain.

At last she turns to face the group.

It's about time.

"Are you serious?" she squawks. "All of this because of jealousy and revenge? It's a little juvenile, don't you think?"

Ha. She should talk. Wren hated Em from the moment she laid eyes on her. It's the same way she looks at me. "No," I say. "Not really." *Listen and learn, Bird-Girl.* "Isn't this what every great tragedy in history has stemmed from?"

I slam the book onto the table, driving my point home. The

pages bare their own history, after all. "An unkind word?" I glare at Wren. "Sour feelings between leaders?" I glance at Preacher. "Mistrust and prejudice?" I consider Josh beneath us. Can he hear my words through the floorboards? "One man from the Third tried to wipe out an entire race because he didn't 'like' them." Em would snort if she saw me doing air quotes right now. She'd be validated too.

That's enough excitement for one day. After shoving the book into my pack, I pull the drawstring tight, sling the bag over one shoulder. "The Fairy Queen has known the darkness of hatred for so long, she's forgotten how it feels to be in the presence of light. What happened with Tiernan only fueled a fire that had been burning for ages."

I make a beeline for the door, adrenaline fueling me to get going already. "Pain is something you get used to after a certain passage of time. In a way, it becomes its own kind of comfort. Because pain is familiar."

The Void pulses in my chest, my speech my own unfortunate reality. Newfound loathing for Tiernan sparks. Will I ever cease despising him for killing my adoptive mother? The man is dead. The only person my hatred affects is me. Even now, the Void feeds on it, every negative emotion energizing the darkness. Then I imagine Em's smile, sense the change as my animosity recedes. Not much longer. We'll be together again soon. "Sometimes heart-break is easier to bear than healing."

Tide's nostrils flare. "He's not wrong. The desire for revenge can consume you." He works his jaw. "Pain keeps the past alive while healing forces you to move on. And letting go . . . it just isn't that simple."

Ebony shuffles to his side and touches his shoulder. I almost expect him to shrug her off. Instead, he makes eye contact. The growing intensity between them reminds me of my connection with Em.

And then I sense it, the shift in the atmosphere that has me backing away from the door. In all the rush I failed to stop and see the details that needed attending. We can't put this off another minute.

I drop my pack and act as the leader I've somehow become. The room watches in silent wonder as I cross to the chief cook of my wrecked ship and place two fingers to my lips. Tide's deep-blue Fourth Reflection Guardian tattoo stands out against a tan background. "Greatest However Is Water" rides on a strip of waves ringing his bicep. I touch my fingers there. "May your mother drift upon the tranquil waters."

"May she ever ride the waves." His response to my condolence is the tradition of his people. A salute to a life well lived.

Ebony follows suit, then Khloe. One by one we pay tribute, empathizing with his grief. When we discovered Tide yesterday, gagged and bound in a hollowed space beneath the kitchen floor, I could tell something was different about him. Originally, when he didn't join us on our journey to the Fifth, we assumed he decided to remain behind with his people.

If only that were true. It would've made things much less complicated.

"My mother has been murdered." Tide pulled me aside as I headed for my sparring match with Preacher. "That spineless son of a squall down in the cellar choked her in her sleep. He didn't even try to hide it. Bragged about it all the way here." The news raced across his rushed speech.

"I'm not one for revenge," Tide shared. "My mother would not have wanted it. I will honor her memory by being the better man, but I do expect justice to be served here."

"And it will be. Trust me."

Tide has kept his word and hasn't stepped within two fathoms of the Shadowalker. Still, I see it in his eyes. He's watching, waiting, wondering what will be done about the man who killed Countess Ambrose.

What will be done, indeed.

The news that David is a murderer only solidified that he is, in fact, a follower of darkness. Another reason to remain with my crew. Makai is aware of the situation, but he has his own troubles to attend to. Staying keeps me and the Void in check, yes, but if I can prevent Tide from doing something he'd regret too? The decision will be well worth it.

Was this not David's folly, after all? Taking matters into his own hands? Hands he claimed were incapable of such horrific acts?

I shoulder my pack once more. Man, Em's mom is wise. I'll have to remember to thank her for stopping me from following the same path as my brother. David requires a constant eye. At this point, is he even capable of being saved?

It's what Em would desire. She wouldn't want to be rescued. She'd tell me to choose the others over her. Even so, I'm going to pour everything I have into doing both. By choosing them, I *am* choosing her. Who better to find her than a group of those she loves? She saved us all. Time to return the favor.

A length of silence passes before I place my hand on the doorknob for the third time today. I wait for a signal Tide's ready, then say, "I don't need to remind everyone how vital it is we find the Verity's vessel. Let's hope Dahlia and Flint have news when we join them at the compound. Without Em—Eliyana—we have no hope of accomplishing anything. The Garden of Epoch and Fountain of Time can't be approached without her. Only the purest of souls are permitted access. She's our ticket in, our guarantee—"

"There are no guarantees."

Ebony's blurt stops me from exiting. Her determination drives through me. *All right, I'll hear what she has to say.* I make a motion for her to continue.

"It's not just the Verity's vessel we need. If we desire to rid the Reflections of the Void, we must first understand it. And we can't do that with a mere tale." She gestures toward my book bag. "Words will only take us so far. It's how we choose to act upon our knowledge that makes all the difference. We need to find out hands-on what's really going on inside my mother's head. Which is why I'm suggesting we break off into three groups instead of two."

What's she getting at?

"One to find El. Another to hide Elizabeth and Evan. And a third to find the nearest Fairy Fountain and get inside the queen's head." Her unblinking stare is hard to meet. Looks like we have another leader on our hands.

"Does anyone disagree with Miss Archer's plan?" I scan the room.

No one protests. Not even Wren.

Wow. That's new. "Tide and Stormy, you two go with Ebony to the nearest Fountain. Tide, you mentioned David brought you through that route?"

My chief cook nods. "That's right." His smile leads me to believe he and Ebony have already discussed this. They weren't looking for my permission here. If I'd said this was a bad idea, they'd probably still have gone.

"Very well," I say. "I agree it wouldn't hurt—"

"Aren't you forgetting something?" Hands on her hips, Khloe steps from behind Ebony. When did Em's sister start rubbing off on her so much?

This ought to be good. "Such as?" I know where she's going with this, and the answer is no, absolutely not.

Eye roll exaggerated for all to see, Khloe says, "Um, I'm going to the Fairy Fountain too." She shrugs. "They might need me."

Ebony laughs. "She's not wrong. Have you seen what she can do? She can adapt to any climate, and don't even get me started on her projection abilities."

"Come on, Cap." Tide uses his nickname for me from our time at sea. "Let Khlo live up to her potential. You can't protect her forever."

Oh yeah? Watch me. I'm about to protest when Em's voice invades my thoughts. If she were here, she'd touch my arm, think something for me alone to hear.

"Let her go," she'd whisper. *"Look who she has for company. Anyone wishing to harm Khloe will have to go through a Shield, a Mask, and a Magnet first. Would you want to be that person? Because I wouldn't."*

As always, my better half is right. "Fine. But if anything happens to her, I swear to—"

The breath is knocked from my chest when Khloe rams into me. I enfold her, give her the tightest hug she's ever had. When she releases, she gives me one of her I-can-get-whatever-I-want smiles, then rejoins her group on the other side of the room.

I take in each person present in turn, really look at them. The empty vial weighs heavy in my pocket.

"I think we're ready, Lieutenant Commander Rhyen." Makai announces my new title for the first time, making everyone aware I'm his official second. Not David. Me. The position belonged to Gage once. I can see him now, all smug in his human strength. My, how the currents have shifted.

"Hold on."

Great. What else could Song possibly have to interject at this point?

"Garden of Epoch? Fountain of Time? We're chasing Fairy tales, Rhyen. Even if such places did exist, how can you be sure a Threshold will become a wormhole that will spit you out in the exact place your precious vessel ended up?"

The griffin's really asking for it. I dig my hands into my pockets. My right hand wraps around the vial. "I can't be sure. As Ebony said, there are no guarantees. I have a pretty good guess my idea will work, though. And we're wasting time standing here arguing rather than moving into action." Placing one foot out the door, I add, "We have to try. Each second we remain here is another we lose elsewhere." Sunlight filters in through the door's crack, highlighting the dust in the air.

"Elsewhere. Right." Wren's scowl makes her look more like Preacher than her father, the Physic. "End the Void. Save the Reflections. I get it. You want to be the hero." An eye roll from David's girlfriend is the last thing I need. "What I want to know is why are we going off on some Dragon chase with *you*?" She points a finger. Come on, that's just rude. "You are the vessel of the Void, the enemy of the Verity. Everyone knows what happens when the Void's vessel is given too much power."

My jaw clenches and I swallow hard as if that will force the

Void to recede down my throbbing neck. It may live inside me, but the darkness does not define who I am. I say none of this, though. Instead, "Which is why we must destroy the Void, as I have already stated." If she makes me repeat myself one more time, I swear—

"Joshua should be our leader." Her words, more snap than statement, have me thinking she might as well take on her griffin form if she insists on behaving like an animal. "Not you."

Now she's gone too far. I will not continue to be treated like a traitor. To be disrespected on my own mission, in front of my own team. They have faith in me despite what I contain. In fact, they probably trust me *because* I contain it, *because* I can be myself while also imprisoning their greatest threat. I pause before issuing my next words, a rarity for me. But I don't have a chance to get them out before—

"Joshua is not himself." Makai clears his throat. "He is a Shadowalker now and cannot be counted upon. We'll take him with us. His bond to Eliyana will certainly prove useful in locating her whereabouts. Besides, his Ever blood may become useful in a crisis. Better to weaken him than Regina."

I grind my teeth to keep my jaw from dropping. His words could be a quote of my own dark thoughts. Commander Archer is closer to David than anyone, the last person I'd expect to take a stand against him, let alone suggest using his blood. Then again, Makai seems to hold truth and justice above any human. What would happen if Elizabeth became a Shadowalker? Would he treat her the same? Let's hope I never have to find out.

Wren keeps her mouth shut this time, and I have to turn my head to conceal a satisfied grin. She may hold zero respect for me, but the Commander of the Second's Guardians can certainly put the Mask in her place.

"Enough discussion." He draws his wife to his side with one arm, then cradles their newborn baby, Evan, with the other. "If you are not ready in ten, you will not go. We depart with or without you."

His confidence causes me to stand three feet taller. So this is what it feels like to be trusted. To have friends.

I cast my gaze to the floor. Friends, yet no one here, not even Khloe, is close enough to know my secret. All have been made aware of our goals. What they don't know? I've tasted water from the Fountain of Time before.

My mind wanders to that not-too-long-ago day as I exit the cottage and wait outside. Hands in my coat pockets now, I rock back on my heels. The desert is cool, the day cloudy, but the chill inside provides the greatest discomfort. I'd take low temperatures over the dark, depressing bite of the Void anytime, anyplace. As I close my eyes I picture that day.

The day a stranger traded a vial of water for passage to the Fourth.

Joshua

Get up."

I blink awake. Did I fall asleep again? Curse this darkness. The environment is Josh's convenience. Makes it much too easy to keep me complacent.

"I said, *move*."

Makai?

"Do not toy with me, Shadowalker. Either you heed my command or I use a measure of force."

I sit and strain to hear more. Darkness surrounds me, but the man I have looked to as an older brother my entire life breaks through.

The world around me shakes as Josh is lugged to a stand. He doesn't acknowledge Makai and I want to tear him apart for his insolent silence.

Defiant fool.

"I know you are not lost to us," Makai says in a low tone. "Return and make things right. Until then, I have no choice but to treat you as a murderer rather than my friend."

I nod, though it does nothing to move the man upstairs. Makai doesn't see my physical agreement. He has no way of truly knowing that, yes, I am still here.

And, soon enough, I will make my return.

NINE

In My Way

"It is all right, *amica*. There is no cause for panic." Grandma B (has a nice ring to it, don't you agree?) rubs small circles on my curved back the way Mom always did when I was younger. The two have never met, nor are they related. The gesture must be a mom thing or, in this case, a grandma thing.

I'm hunched over in my chair and breathing hard. My palm hasn't abandoned my right cheek. As if this will keep the truth from being seen. Not that anyone here would know the difference. I peek from beneath my eyelashes, just enough so it will appear to those present my eyes remain closed. The attendees are distorted through my lashes, but not enough that I can't tell what they're all thinking. Expressions of shock or awe or curiosity contort each face. All except two. And these are as contrary as night and day.

Literally.

King Aidan inches closer, gazing at me with those green-green eyes of his. I suppose he might appear curious, though his countenance suggests a knowing. An observing. Omniscience? I huff a laugh. He's exactly as I pictured him.

Then there's his polar opposite. Jasyn Crowe. The epitome of no and *Void* no.

The vessel of the Void stares at me in the same way he will decades into the future. He looks about my age, but Verity knows he'd never see me as his equal. Reflections to Jasyn, your superiority gene is showing. Might want to do something about that one if you ever want a soul to like you.

I squeeze my eyelids and turn my head to avoid his scrutiniz-
ing gaze. Technically I don't feel any different. My mirrormark
wasn't raised like a scar. My fingertips shouldn't feel a change. But
they do. Now that I'm aware my face is bare, naked, and dare I
say . . . insert dramatic pause here . . . unblemished, I can almost
detect the alteration beneath the pads of my fingers. What I wished
for nearly eighteen years has come true.

So why do I want to hide? It's a repeat of the same chorus, but
in reverse.

"Perhaps you should take her home, my love."

My eyes are closed, but my other grandfather's accent and
endearing words give him away. And his scent, no different from
what it will be many years from now, stale and kind of musty. Odd
how aging doesn't change everything. Nathaniel is still Nathaniel,
thirty-two or one hundred and two.

"Do we dare move her in this state, *amore mio*? She is ill, no?"
Bianca may use a symphony of terms I don't recognize, but *amore*
is familiar enough to translate.

Love.

The affection between my paternal grandparents should warm
my heart. Instead, it pinches, leaving me with a tangible emptiness.
They're each half of one whole, and I can't help but long for Joshua.
My best friend. The one person, besides Mom, who really gets me.

I squeeze my eyes tighter, pairs of lovers scrolling through my
mind. But not the famous ones like Romeo and Juliet or Beauty
and the Beast. Instead, I think of Mom and Makai. Stormy and
Kuna. Aidan and Ember. These represent true and lasting love.
Something many authors attempt to depict but few manage to live
or achieve. Love isn't a fleeting feeling. It's lasting. Real. Something
you do. And those closest to me have shown it better than any
writer ever could.

The way Makai waited for Mom all those years.

The forgiveness Kuna bestowed upon Stormy without question, followed by a sacrifice, his life for hers.

And the love Aidan had for Ember?

I peer beneath my lashes once more, zooming in on the king. Kindness radiates from his being, from his relaxed smile to his twinkling eyes. He loved his wife so much, the loss of her killed him.

Because he's an Ever. And only a broken heart can kill an Ever.

My own heart convulses. Does Joshua wonder where I am? Is he sick with worry, desperately searching for answers regarding my disappearance?

What kind of question is that? Of course he is. I bite the inside of my cheek. Why am I so insecure? This isn't me anymore. I know Joshua will find me.

"Always," he promised.

Always.

I let Grandma Bianca ease me back into my chair. She presses a damp rag to my forehead and I welcome the relief. All the stress has made me break into a sweat. My blouse comes untucked from my skirt in the back, my bare skin rubbing against the itchy upholstery. Groan. Skin protests. Brain hurts. Could I lie down already?

No. I can't. Because one thing still doesn't make sense and I won't rest until it does. Can't ignore the details.

Fact: The Void enters the one who cares most for the Verity's vessel.

Fact: Kyaphus Rhyen, not Joshua, took on the Void. I house the Verity.

I may hate Kyaphus, but he cares for me. Joshua would have me believe Kyaphus is my mortal enemy, but how can that be? Everything points to Joshua. Joshua, for all intents and purposes, should be the vessel of the Void.

It was Joshua who saved me the night Jonathan Gage tried to kidnap me from Wichgreen Village.

It's Joshua who makes my heart do this weird flip thing when I picture his lopsided grin.

Joshua's the one. His name on my heart feels like a breath of relief. Loving Joshua is natural. Normal.

But it's Kyaphus who appears to love me.

Something reeks. And it's not Nathaniel's old-man cologne.

❦

The apartment is way too cold. Even wrapped in wool I'm shivering to the point I'm sore. Normally this wouldn't be my blanket of choice. Too itchy. But seeing as how it was my *only* choice, I couldn't refuse. So this is what it was like to live during the forties. I'd give my mirrorglass crown for the Fifth's desert right about now.

But is it still my crown? I would assume no mirrormark means no Verity, but test after test on the walk back reassures me the light continues to swirl within. How is it possible to have two vessels at once? Does Aidan remain the vessel with me here? He must, but then that means there are two of us. Could it be the Verity lives outside of time?

"Time is a circle. The beginning is the end, and the end is the beginning . . ."

The words of Dimitri Gérard haunt me as I consider the possibilities. As I recall the story . . .

"Once Upon a Reflection, deep in the Garden of Epoch, there shone a light lovelier than any human eye had ever beheld . . ."

No mention of the Verity being created. It simply . . . existed. It just . . . was.

Still, perhaps I only imagined I felt the light. Maybe I became so used to its presence, I didn't notice when it was removed. Like a phantom limb or something.

No. Enough. I know it warmed my core while I sat in the midst of the Third Alliance. Feel it now as I attempt to make sense of past, present, and future.

The events from the Second haven't happened yet. I never battled Jasyn. My coronation hasn't taken place.

Except it has.

But now I'm in the past.

Yet I'm from the future.

For Verity's sake, when did things become so complicated?

I turn over on the rock-hard sofa. I might as well be sleeping on the floor. But how can I complain? There are worse things than Grandma Bianca's humble accommodations. The couch may be firm, but it's clean. When will Makai and Tiernan grace the scene? Will my grandmother keep her eggshell decor then, or will she opt for more child-friendly colors?

Wiggling, I flip onto my back. Okay, that's 1 percent more comfortable, so at least I'm making progress. My ears perk at each sound, straining to hear something other than the eerie quiet of the deadened night. A siren, a plane, *anything* that might remind me of New York and lull me to sleep. I may be getting used to dozing in other Reflections, but I still prefer the album of my childhood.

A muted creak wafts from the hall through the crack beneath the door. My breath hitches, then releases just as quickly. Probably a cat or someone headed to the neighboring apartment after cutting curfew. That's some risky business, if you ask me. And no, I'm not going to make a Tom Cruise reference. Because this isn't funny. What did Breckan say in her story? Shadowalkers *worship* the Void? My body quakes and my mouth turns down.

Sigh. I need answers. Something bigger and beyond is happening. This isn't just about my stumble into the past. Somehow what's going on now with the Shadowalkers is related to Jasyn Crowe. Which means it's connected to the Void. And the Verity as well. Which brings me back to the main goal. Past, present, and future.

Destroy the Void.

Maybe my being here isn't some freak accident. Maybe I'm supposed to be here, now, for a time like this. No one but Aidan knows Jasyn carries the Void. What if keeping the darkness hidden was the very cause of my grandfather's downfall? I know the king meant—*means*—well, but what if I'm here to influence even the smallest alteration that could effect a difference in the future?

Perhaps I was wrong when I believed the past couldn't be changed. Could Hollywood have it backward? Without my Mask Calling I may not be able to transform into a butterfly, but that doesn't mean *this* butterfly can't cause an effect that will start a hurricane.

Can anyone say *boom?*

I free my arms. Sit. My head has had enough of these stabbing bobby pins. One by one I remove them, placing them in a pile on the cushion beside me. My crunchy hair stays mostly in place, so I comb my fingers through it. The effort does little to relax my locks, but at least my scalp isn't throbbing.

When will my grandparents return? They brought me to the apartment, and I got one quick hug in before they promptly left.

"Get some rest now, *mia cara.*" Grandma B patted my head, then cupped my face. Looked into my eyes as if she really knew me. "I will return, *di mattina.*" Her entire face softened then, her lips forming a sad smile.

I looked from her face to Nathaniel's, attempting to find my father and uncle somewhere in between. Tomorrow isn't guaranteed. Who knows if I'll ever see them again?

They turned to retreat down the stairs.

"Wait." I hovered in the doorway.

My grandparents paused.

The brave girl Mom has always believed in did something totally bold and weird then. I threw my arms around my grandparents, holding particularly tight to Bianca's neck. Nathaniel's still around, though it'll be a wonder if another visit to Lisel Island lies in my future.

It was Nathaniel who had the last word. "There, there, child." He patted my head the way Bianca had, but with much less maternal instinct. His touch was more in line with that of Ebony petting a stray dog. "Things will work out in the end. Wait and see."

Did he realize how much I needed his assurance? They looked at me with wide eyes when I released them, but their expressions remained kind. No doubt my sudden outpouring of affection startled them. Which is fine, because I will live knowing I made the moment count. Every moment matters.

Every. Single. One.

Did my grandparents return to the Alliance meeting? Did my shock really warrant my being treated as if I'm breakable? I could be helping them, finding out more information. Instead, I'm stuck here, Callingless, with no game plan. When did I become so obsolete? No mirrormark? No power? What good is the Verity beneath my skin if I can't do anything with it? What am I without the one thing that makes me, well, me?

"It doesn't define you, brave girl." Mom's long-ago whisper brushes my soul.

She's told me this countless times. On days I felt particularly hideous. Do her words ring true now?

I unwrap myself from the scratchy fabric and plant my socked feet on the wood floor. The boards don't creak as I pad to the radiator beside the nearest window. It's the middle of the night, but why tiptoe? Nobody's here except me. The clanging radiator covers the muted sound anyway.

The sheer eggshell curtains act as a veil between me and my reflection. I push them to one side, peering at the girl I've glimpsed only once before. In a dungeon I believed was a palace. In the time and place I'd give anything to be.

Unremarkable. That's the first word that pings my mind as I turn my head left, then right, examining my even complexion. There really is no other word for me but *average. Plain.* An eggshell face to match the curtains. A face that would never stand out in a crowd. My mocha hair almost swallows me now. I pull it back with one hand to catch a better look.

I used to imagine I'd resemble Mom more without the mark. I shake my head. What an utter disappointment. Her natural beauty captivates. Her bonbon eyes with that forever twinkle in them.

And me? I'm flat. I'm—

Whoa. Where did that come from?

I recoil from the window, and the curtains swish back into place. This . . . negativity. It's not me, not anymore. I blink three times, shaking away the tangible gloom overtaking my heart. I'm alone. Lost. Disoriented. But I will never allow myself to be consumed by self-loathing again.

Never.

I inch closer to the radiator, which rattles again. The noise is loud enough it sounds as if an animal is making an attempt to barge through the wall. I stretch my palms toward it, warming them. *Clang, bang, clatter.*

I curl my fingers into fists. I stiffen my body. That encore noise did *not* come from the old-fashioned heater.

I turn slightly, gaining a good view of the front door. The knob jiggles again. A key holder would not take so long entering.

Which means . . .

My palm meets glass. I close my eyes, try for a song. Whispered words release on nipped breaths. They do not resemble lyrics whatsoever.

> *"Somewhere else . . .*
> *I need to be . . .*
> *Anywhere else . . ."*

Nothing.

Worth a shot, right?

My faith in the Verity's power dwindles as I inch backward, toward the darkest corner of the apartment. Darn it for the lack of mirror walking. Great time to be Callingless. Maybe this is just a dream. The time travel. My unmarked skin. It's too crazy to be real, yeah? I'll wake up, warm in my bed, mark on my face, family and friends by my side.

Ha. Nice one. Tried hoping for that once before. No use doubting the insane. In my experience it's usually, more often than not, true.

The door opens to a soundless overture. The man framed by the threshold peers at me through the shadows. Then he removes his black bowler hat, touches it to his heart, and smiles.

Never mind. Forget what I said. This isn't a dream.

This is a nightmare.

ACT II

on my own

TEN

KY

W hat's a fine ship like this doing at bay? She ought to be out to sea."

Those words have haunted me since the day they were spoken. I'd just gained my bearings in the Third again. Between being banished from the Second by David and hightailing it to the Fourth and back to retrieve my sister, I'd decided one thing.

Nothing would make me move from that spot aside from the queen of the Second herself.

I turned from the port side where I gazed out upon the waves. A cloaked figure, decidedly female from her height, build, and sound, stood a cannon's length away. The wool cloak pooled at her feet, the hood draping her head like a tarp over a barrel. Her midsection protruded slightly, but not enough to say she was heavy.

I furrowed my brow. *The Seven Seas* was hidden by a façade, which meant this was no ordinary passerby. Was she an Amulet or something other? "I'm waiting for the right time to set sail," I replied. Waiting for Em, for the day she turned up on my deck step.

"Any chance you'd give me passage to the nearest Threshold?" The voice was timeless, cooler than a bell. I couldn't make out her face beneath the cloak's hood, but I guessed she was middle age. Her tone emanated wisdom, though it also implied a certain youth. But I doubted she was much older than my ship's most talented Mask, Charley.

I crossed my arms and puffed out my chest. "Depends. You looking to travel to the Second or the Fourth? If it's the former,

you'll have better chances in the subway system or Central Park."
I jutted my chin toward the beach behind her.

"The Fourth is what I seek. I have a delivery for Countess
Ambrose." Her words formed a statement, but the slight lilt at the
end of her sentence made it sound like a question. "I'll pay you a
fine price for voyage there."

I pursed my lips. The excursion would take days. Had the
woman come sooner, I could've taken her. What if Em showed
up while I was away? I'd already risked that once. I wouldn't leave
again if I could help it. Not until she was by my side.

The woman held up the vial then, the glass black as a starless
night at sea.

"What's that?"

"Just a token of my gratitude. Want a sip?" She dangled it in
the air.

The motion sent an invisible dagger through my chest. The
woman's gesture reminded me of a sick game Tiernan used to play.
One in which I was forced to perfect my knife fighting until he was
satisfied, which he never really was. If I won a duel, he'd give me a
drink of water. If he won . . . let's just say I went thirsty more often
than not.

"What *is* it?" The words tasted bitter on my tongue. I loathe
nothing more than having to repeat myself.

"Taste and see. If you find it's worth a journey to the Fourth,
excellent. If not, I'll be on my way and never bother you again."

I lifted an eyebrow. Her very presence sent shivers down my
spine. Her words were practiced and precise, almost as if she had
rehearsed this conversation, but also somehow familiar. Her voice
stirred an unwelcome ache I couldn't place. "You're going to pay
me with no promise of a return? And you want me to drink a foreign substance?" Good one, lady.

"That is correct."

"You're insane."

"Aye."

The one-word answer stopped me. Aye? Where had this woman

come from, and why? And how was I supposed to respond? The hour was well past one in the morning. My crew was asleep. My insomnia problem since separating from Em had me exhausted and a touch desperate. I didn't have time for games. I just wanted the sleep I lacked. The rest that would come from one person and one person alone.

"Listen." She grabbed my right hand and pressed the vial into my palm, folding my fingers over the cool glass as she did so. Her skin was pale and cold as ice. "Drink and imagine the person you care for more than anyone or anything. And then . . . see what happens. You will end up where you are needed most."

My heart swelled at her strange words, at the way they drew me in and embedded an odd sense of . . . what? Trust? Yeah, I thought of Em. Could the substance in the bottle take me to her?

The thought was crazy, idiotic, rash. But I had never been one to think and then act. I went off intuition and instinct, qualities I had always prided myself on. It was on intuition I kept one eye open the night Gage and a reluctant Stormy tried to kidnap Em from Wichgreen Village. I sensed danger before her head ever hit the pillow. And when we battled Jasyn Crowe? I knew David's hesitation would endanger us all. So I acted and did what needed to be done.

Before I could overthink it, I opened my fist, uncorked the vial, and drank. I pictured Em. Even if the next time I saw her was the last, it'd be worth it.

The liquid was flavorless, odorless. And then it wasn't.

That's when I knew what death must taste like.

"Daydreaming again, Rhyen? And you expect us to view you as our fearless leader? Pathetic."

Song's voice jerks me from the recent memory. Does she realize how unattractive her attitude makes her? Good luck with this one, David. She's a real gem.

I study the Shadowalker, looking for any sign the Ever is still in there. My personal experience suggests so, though my better judgment would have him thrown in a pit to rot for his current alter ego.

If Josh could shove me he would. Too bad his hands are tied behind his back.

"Song, relieve Preacher and take over rounds." Give her something to do. Maybe that'll shut her up. "Ensure everyone is accounted for."

"I don't answer to—"

"Wren." One word from the Commander is all it takes. "Do as he says."

She doesn't bite back, but her perma-scowl could draw blood. Man, this chick is something else.

Once she's out of earshot, Makai comes closer. Evan is strapped to his chest with a long piece of cloth torn from a sheet. The Commander holds him in place with one hand beneath his rear and the other behind the baby's head. "Have you considered my request?"

I exhale heavily through my nose. "I have. I'm not sure it's possible. He's so far gone—"

"He's your *brother*, Ky. Your twin brother." The arrows in the quiver on his back rattle, ticking off each step, counting every crunch of desert beneath our boots. "You two are connected in a way he and I will never be. You know his anguish. I beg of you to try."

The vulnerability in the Commander's eyes is something I've witnessed in few men. I don't know him well, but I have a way of seeing people, of knowing who they are at their very core, with little information whatsoever. Most men place pride above all else. But here is something different, which causes my throat to tighten and my eyes to burn. Something my adoptive father knew nothing of.

Makai cares for Joshua like a brother, perhaps even a son. What would it have been like to know my father? My mother even? I cannot regret being raised by the mother I knew, but how different would things be if I had known such affection from a male figure?

I nod. "I will do my best."

Archer claps my shoulder. "That is all I ask."

He returns to his wife's side as we venture on. Wren continues her rounds as our caravan spreads and compresses, slows and quickens.

I lengthen my strides, catching up to the Shadowalker. When we're side by side I eye him. I wait for the right moment and whisper . . .

"Do *not* fall asleep."

joshua

I can't continue much longer. Hour by hour, I slip away. Not that time is tangible here, of course. I am only able to keep track of it when I catch a sound from the outside, during the rare occasions when Josh lowers the wall he has constructed around me.

I envision myself shaking my head as I sense my mind wandering, falling subject to the Void. I long to sleep and be done with this madness, to allow Josh to take over on a permanent basis. Makai is perfectly capable of handling things from his end. He and the Guardians have the situation under control.

"I know you're in there."

Awareness surges through my center. Just as when Makai spoke, another voice pierces through.

Kyaphus?

"Keep your eyes on the light, however trivial. It's the only way. Trust me." His voice lowers. "I know."

A series of rapid blinks awakens me further. The smallest pinprick of light grows visible in the distance. Have my eyes been closed this entire time? How did I fail to recognize this?

"Never stop moving. And whatever you do, do *not* fall asleep."

There he is again. Hard feelings punch my gut and I brace against them. Rhyen has been a thorn in my side since . . .

My chest heaves hypothetically.

Since I put him there.

Such is how my descent began, but this will not be the end. It takes all my mental capacity to rediscover the feeling in the legs of my soul. I rise in the darkness, placing one foot in front of the other like a toddler learning to walk. Keeping my gaze focused on my prize, my life, I commence to move forward.

Leaving my thorn behind.

ELEVEN

Ebony

"How much longer?" Khloe tugs my jacket sleeve, bounces on what I'm convinced are spring-filled toes.

"Not much." It's the same thing I've been saying for the past hour. Doesn't she *know* I want to get there as badly as she does? Pressure builds to the point I want to scream. But I can't be frustrated with Khloe, can I? I'm just projecting my own anxiety onto her. Desire and dread clash, warring for my undivided attention. Dread for obvious reasons, and if you can't figure them out, well, not my problem.

Then there's the growing desire—scratch that . . . *need*.

I need this.

Sure, I made a valid argument for why a third group was necessary. But my motivations are of a selfish nature. I won't even try to deny it. I can't not find out who I truly am, where I actually come from. Am I Called or some sort of Halfling? Is that even a thing? Oh crowe, it is, isn't it? I'm a mixed breed. A mutt. A castoff.

I'm precisely who my mother has always said I am.

"Really, Ebony, what is the matter with you? You are sixteen, yet you behave like an infant."

And . . .

"Is that what you're planning to wear, dear? Honestly, I will never understand why you continue to pretend to be someone you are not."

And . . .

"I've had quite enough, Ebony. You may have fooled yourself into

believing it is me you are angry with, but the truth is you simply loathe yourself."

Though I didn't know she was immortal then, I see it in retrospect. In Isabeau's dismissive hand wave. In the way she owned whatever space she filled. My mother was—is—untouchable. Year after year came jab after pointed jab. But what doesn't kill you only makes you stronger, right? I won't wallow in self-pity. Not my style. I can rock the *X-Men* thing. Watched the movie with El once. Totally worth it, B-T-dubs. Those mutants can kick some serious butt.

I slow my pace and Khloe shadows me. What if I don't take the others? What if I simply get "lost," then venture out on my own? Would anyone notice? Besides Khloe, I mean. If I can get her distracted, it could be quite easy to disappear. My biggest issue is Ky's group checks. He keeps glancing back from his position at the front, lips moving in silence. Oh yeah. And don't forget Preacher. Mr. I'll-Circle-Everyone-Like-a-Hawk-'Cuz-I've-Got-Nothing-Better-to-Do.

Drat you, Rhyen. I don't need to be counted or babysat. You get the whole loner thing better than anyone. We both served Jasyn. Both know what it's like to go rogue.

Tide squeezes between Khloe and me. His arm brushes mine, and I curse my decision to wear long sleeves despite the chill.

My sister makes a face at him, then moves to my left side. When she sticks out her tongue, he does the same back to her.

Verity, help us. This is who I'm expected to take with me? If El were here, she'd at least balance this insanity. Maybe alone is my best option. These two may be immature, but they're the closest thing I have to family. Am I so selfish I would risk hurting them?

"Not so fast." Tide takes my hand, forcing me to keep pace with Khloe and him.

I draw up my eyebrows and jerk my hand away. "What?" Why are my words and actions forever the opposite of how I think and feel? Can I get a do-over, please?

He shoves both hands into his shorts pockets.

Now look what you've gone and done, Ebony. You're never getting that hand back now.

"I know that look," he muses. "You're thinking of running."

Eye roll. "Whatever. You don't know me." Except the more time I spend with him, I see he so does. Why must I go on the defense? Every. Single. Time?

"Don't do it." It's Khloe's shot to share her eleven years' worth of wisdom. "You need us."

My knee-jerk reaction is to say in fact, no, I don't need anybody. But I bite my words so hard they bleed into the back of my throat.

"The kid's right." Now it's Stormy who chimes in. "Kuna would agree if he were here."

The Magnet and I are practically strangers, but can I just say her pixie-cut hair is on point? And the color. Neon suits her well. I think it was purple the last time I saw her. Now it's pink, and is that glitter?

Khloe links her arm through Stormy's. If Tide or I had called her "kid," she would've gotten all bent out of shape. But for some reason that is totally beyond me, she takes Stormy's comment as a compliment.

Fickle, fickle.

Tide elbows me, his grief only perceptible in the slight sadness rimming the corners of his almond eyes. Those beautiful, captivating, almond eyes.

Back up. You can fall in love later. If you're still alive then.

"Listen." He takes my hand once more, this time with more caution. And this time I don't pull away. "We're here for you. We're in this and we aren't going anywhere. If you want to bolt now, I'm with you. But can I give my honest opinion?"

Of course you can. Anything to watch those gorgeous lips move.

Oh, gross. No sir. I will not be that girl.

"Fine." Silence. That's all I have. Dead silence. I can do this on my own, no problem.

But should I?

"I spent a lot of years pretending I didn't need anyone." Tide's hand squeezes mine. His dark skin contrasts against my alabaster tone. Perfection. "But it takes a real man to recognize vulnerability is a strength, not a weakness. And the same goes for you. Let the act go, lower the wall, and let people in."

Khloe links her arm with mine now but says nothing. From the corner of my eye, I catch her ear-to-ear grin. Okay, we get it, you little ham. You agree with Tide and your new girl bestie. Tide is wise and all-knowing. Stormy is cool and styling. Yeah, yeah, yeah.

"I'll think about it," I say.

But then we walk faster to catch up with the group. And I know thinking is long gone.

TWELVE

pretending

"I am aware of your presence. Concealing your whereabouts is futile." Young Jasyn exhales, closes the door, and flips the lock in that ever-meticulous way of his. "Come now, child. Divulge your secret."

My heart pounds wildly, a staccato note ready to burst from my throat. One day away from my family feels like an eternity as I stand helpless before a ghost from my past. I palm my chest, hoping the added pressure will force the beats to slow. "What secret?" I rasp into the darkness. Does he know who I am? Can he sense I contain the Verity the same as Aidan? He can't. No way.

Then again . . .

What if this is precisely what's happening, and Jasyn knows all the things? What if he tries to silence me or worse? Am I any match without my Calling? All this light inside and no way to channel it. Fear creeps in, clawing its way back to where it once lived. As a Mirror I was strong. Brave. But now? Now I'm just a girl who happens to be a vessel for the purest light ever.

Except . . . I'm not *just* a girl. There's no *just* about this. My power may have ceased, but I hold the same heart. Same soul. The Verity wouldn't remain a part of me if there was nothing right inside. Or, at the very least, the desire to do right. Maybe I'm not good, but the Verity—it's the definition of good and right and perfect. It was never about what I could do anyway. The Verity is a force to be reckoned with.

And so am I.

Deep breath. Straighten. One foot in front of the other . . .

I step from the shadows.

"Perhaps you didn't hear me the first time, so I shall say it once more. Divulge your secret." My grandfather removes his bowler hat and hangs it on the doorknob. Strolls to the table where I sat when Grandma Bianca first brought me here. Jasyn sits, crossing his legs and folding his hands over one knee. "You know perfectly well what I am referring to." He leans back. "Do you see past façades? Is that it?"

My insides unclench. The Void. He's talking about the Void. "Yes." I take another step toward him. "I do. I know what you are. The darkness you imprison." Let him think I have some semblance of power over him.

Even from across the dark room, I catch his eyebrows rise. "Remarkable. What Calling do you claim?"

The intrigue in his voice is familiar but different. The edge I'm accustomed to hasn't formed. Bitterness still to come.

I join him beside the table but don't sit. He smells of . . . bergamot?

Without considering the awkwardness, I inhale, lean a smidge closer. Mom's early-morning cup of Earl Grey always smelled this way. Of sour citrus. Bitter fruit. Of airy elegance with a hint of after-shave. An odd combination of flavors when I run them through but perfectly paired when placed in a silk bag. According to Mom, at least.

When I was younger, I'd sip a cup of hot cocoa minus the marshmallows while she drank her tea. And once I was old enough I'd enjoy my coffee with soy and sugar. But her drink never altered. Mom is timeless, but this is the first moment in which I've made a connection between father and daughter. And it hits me . . .

Jasyn was timeless once too.

"Are you an Ever?" He tilts his face toward mine. His smile is impersonal but far from menacing.

I knit my forehead. Weird.

"It is rumored select Evers see past façades. Though I have yet to meet one." He winks at that.

Can Joshua see past an Amulet's ruse? I've never asked. Of course Jasyn's not referring to him but to his father. Aidan couldn't see the Void on Jasyn's skin any more than Joshua could see my mirrormark. He knows it's there but sees past it to the point of invisibility. Only the good, the light, is visible—

"You are indeed the thoughtful one, are you not?" Jasyn's deep, melodic voice draws me from my almost–rabbit trail. "Is there much on your mind? Do you not know the precise Calling you contain? Has no one helped you discover it?"

How do I answer? Is it really so simple to lie about my Calling? I have no seal, no mark to show I'm anything at all. If I claim Ever, will my grandfather test my blood? If I claim Shield, or Mask, or Magnet, will he demand a display?

My throat clears. "I'm not an Ever." I let go of the lampstand. Push my hair back off my face.

"Amulet, then, like myself? I would have guessed it first, but I know my own Calling. And, forgive me, but you do not seem the type." His words come slow and even, calculated but kind. Is it really mere curiosity that has him here at Verity knows what hour? This is not the Jasyn Crowe I know—knew. Will know?

All this time-warp stuff is giving me a migraine. "Not an Amulet." Sigh. Out with it then. "I'm nothing." Why not be honest? Lying never leads anywhere decent.

His expression makes no show of surprise. Now *this* is the man I remember. Knows everything before I say a word, or at least that's the front he portrays.

"You, my dear, are far from nothing." He rises now, chair legs scraping the floor. "Moretti sensed it as do I. You see what lives inside me, but do not cower in fear. You know of the power of the Callings, yet argue to have none." Reaching out, my grandfather places a hand on my shoulder.

In a knee-jerk reaction, I twist away.

That's when his gaze darkens and he recoils, wiping his palm on his trouser leg. "Ah, I was incorrect then." He says "incorrect" as if it's a dirty word. "You put on a noble act, but deep down you do fear me."

And then something happens that would take my jaw to the floor if I didn't have it clamped shut. Jasyn's expression descends and his shoulders slump. His eyelids lower as he turns and retreats for the door.

Who *is* he? Defeated? *Jasyn?*

Never.

Could it be the infamous Jasyn Crowe once had a heart before the Void blackened it to ash?

Bowler hat returned to his head and fingertips on the doorknob, he pauses. "You remind me of Aidan, and I thought perhaps you were similar. I had hoped one more soul might see me for the man rather than the mark."

Ouch. Now it's not just Mom who's related to him.

It's me.

"A fool's dream, I suppose." With a sigh he rotates the knob. It rattles as if loose. "People need not be aware of what I am for me to perceive their fear. My black veins are not evident to them, yet they cross to the other side of the street when I pass by. Hurry on their way when I draw close. Anyone who knows of the Void cowers at its very name." He looks back at me, eyes that match mine narrowed. "You will not let on to my secret, will you?" There's a pleading in his eyes.

My heart softens. I shake my head.

He nods. "Very well. Good evening to you." He taps the brim of his hat. And then he's gone.

It's several minutes before I sink back onto the sofa. Myriad emotions wind through me as I stare unblinking at the spot where my broken grandfather stood.

"People need not be aware of what I am for me to perceive their fear." His words play across my mind.

What I am . . .

What is he?

Who is he?

Does the Void define him?

"No," I whisper to no one. Not any more than my mirrormark, or lack thereof, defines me.

My chest pinches. New understanding takes root. We all have light and darkness in us. And we each play a part in bringing out the worst or best in others. Our choices make the difference . . . our choices make up who we truly are.

"There's always a choice."

My hand returns to the space over my heart at the whispered memory. That voice. *His* voice.

How is this possible?

I see Joshua's face, so clear I'm certain he's the one who spoke those four little words. Yet the tonal quality doesn't quite fit. Joshua's tenor is unique, distinguishable from any chorus.

And this sounds nothing like him.

I stumble backward, grabbing the lampstand to my right for balance.

The voice belongs to *Kyaphus.* I know in my heart of hearts the memory ought to move me, stir something deep inside. His words are profound, overflowing with meaning. If I'd read them, heard them recited in a play or film or song, I'd nod and be like, "Whoa." Because, hello, what a simple but powerful line.

But all I feel is out-of-character hatred. I've never been so disgusted with myself. So repulsed. How can the Verity even stand to live within such an angry soul? How is it I feel so much hatred for a boy I hardly know? A boy who carries the Void?

For me.

And what about Jasyn? What does he feel? Rejection? Abandonment? Who aside from Aidan is close to him? He had to have a wife, a woman he loved—loves. Who is my grandmother? Could she have been in the meeting?

One thing Jasyn said struck me, returns to me now.

"I had hoped one more soul might see me for the man rather than the mark."

What happened when Ember graced the scene? Or, more importantly, when she became a Mirror? When her Calling strengthened and she saw past Jasyn's façade to the evil he contained? Was Ember the first to see his less-than-Verity side? Did she turn the king against Jasyn when she became queen? Did my grandfather lose everything he held dear when the truth of what he hid was exposed?

It wasn't his fault. His choice. Before he gave in and relished the Void's power, he was just like . . .

Kyaphus.

But what does that mean for me? Each little piece I recall in relation to him comes bit by broken bit. But each recollection means nothing. He took on the Void when he saved Ebony from Jasyn. The event speeds toward me like a runaway train through clearing fog. Shouldn't his sacrifice strike me in some way? Move me? Why does thinking of it make me despise him even more?

Gah! I'd like to throw something now. Please and thank you. There was a time I wanted to feel nothing. To never love. Never feel. Never care again. Now, to quote Kodaline (best band ever, right?), it's "all I want."

All I need.

Maybe it's all my grandfather needs too. To care. To love. To *feel* loved.

Resolve takes over. I'm off the sofa and slipping on my nearly dry Converse, because no way can I chase anyone in Grandma Bianca's shoes. Then I'm out the door before I can think better of it. A first-floor window reveals my hair is a sight, rivaling an eighties rock star. My untucked blouse and twisted skirt make me appear as if I'm sneaking away from a night in someone else's bed. Which technically I am, but not in the way people would think. Whatever. At least I'm taking action instead of sitting here stewing over what I've lost. Memory. Calling. Everything, really.

I'm ordinary now. Average. But that doesn't make me nothing. I can still do something. I won't stand idly by and wait to be rescued. Maybe Jasyn and I can help each other out. As he is now, perhaps he would want the Void destroyed as well. Which means, for now, he's on my side. An ally.

A smile lifts my frozen cheeks as I tuck my head down against the night breeze. What would those I left behind say about me seeking help from Jasyn Crowe? Joshua would probably be livid, and Stormy might tell me to be careful, and Mom . . .

I pick up my pace, smiling wider as I imagine her words to me now. Not the words of a parent once afraid her child would break. But the encouragement of a mother who has learned to let go and trust I'd find my own way.

"Go get him, brave girl."

On my way, Mom.

THIRTEEN

KY

"Do *not* fall asleep," I repeat, a touch louder this time. I eye the Shadowalker from the side, but it's not Josh I'm addressing.

He elbows me, but a halfhearted dodge is all I need. My boots kick up dust with each shift in the sand. The overcast day warms as the hour wears. Not at all bad for traveling or, once we find Em and make it to the Fountain, *time* traveling.

I smile, exhale a laugh through my nose. The satisfaction is bittersweet, though. My mirrorglass blade becomes my distraction. I draw it, flip it over in my hand, balancing and rocking it across my knuckles.

"Weapons are not toys," Josh says through clenched teeth. "Didn't your parents ever teach you not to play with knives?" He snickers. "Oh, apologies. I forgot you were raised by a traitor. Like father like son, I suppose." He raises his head a fraction.

He thinks he can get to me through snide comments?

Think again. I don't conceal my light chuckle. This Josh character is something else. Petty and arrogant and an even bigger jerk than Preacher. Saul is just a tough old grump, but Josh? Josh is a horse's—

Well, you know.

I don't respond to his jabs. We all have our dark sides. Who am I to judge? I continue fiddling with my blade, tossing it in the air, then catching it behind my back. I keep my black-veined arm twisted behind me and balance the hilt on the heel of my palm.

Josh rolls his eyes.

My grin widens.

"You're a child," he says.

"Why, thank you." Another flip of my blade. A bow for good measure. "I appreciate the compliment, but really, Josh, we don't know each other well enough for flattery yet." One suggestive wag of my eyebrows and that does it.

He scoffs and backs away. Time to take a breather. I'll give him a break before I commence my second round of annoy-Josh-enough-for-him-to-put-his-guard-down. David's in there somewhere. "Come out, come out, wherever you are," I call.

Josh just shakes his head and distances himself farther.

All right already. Sheesh. I'll stop.

For now.

Now's as good a time as any to survey our assets. I take in each of our company in turn. Streak keeps close to Elizabeth on her right, while the Commander and Evan flank her left. Evan hasn't made a peep since we departed.

"Are you sure he's breathing?" Elizabeth places a full hand on Evan's back.

The baby is still strapped to Makai like a bulletproof vest. "Yes, my love."

"Is he too hot?" she asks. "Maybe I should carry him—"

"He's *fine*." As is his trademark, the Commander's tone is firm but kind. "Put your worries to rest. Enjoy the walk." He pulls her to his side and kisses her hair.

She and Em have been torn apart and reunited more times than she'd probably prefer. Who can blame her for being protective?

And speaking of protective, get a load of Streak. Even more unapproachable than Preacher with his eyebrow piercing, missing front teeth, and sleeve tattoos, the man is a machine. Brown dreadlocks frame his stone-cold expression. His steel gaze could fracture my nearly indestructible blade. His Amulet Calling is hard at work, casting a façade around our entire team. Sweat beads his brow, the muscles in his jaw and neck bulge. He's not the most talented Amulet I've encountered, but he's certainly the most determined.

Then there are the girls, doing what they do best. Talk. For once Khloe isn't the biggest chatterbox in the group. She's too content admiring Stormy—who *is* the biggest chatterbox. The Magnet's continuous dialogue with Ebony, my sister, and Tide takes me back to that night in the Second once again. When Jonathan Gage tied Em's hands while Stormy carried out his bidding. Every muscle in my body tenses at the memory. Funny how things come full circle: some good, some not. Stormy and Em are friends now, the past forgotten. From the fond way Em thinks of her, I'd say Stormy is just as much a sister to her as the other two.

". . . and then Kuna slipped in a massive mud puddle. He smelled like clay for days . . ."

Her giggle is so different from Em's. Stormy is a morning bird, full of energy. Never ceasing to share her song. But when Em laughs? How can I describe it? Her laugh is more a rarity. A nightingale you only hear if you wait long enough to listen.

Sort of like Tide. The guy shadows Ebony's every move. Watching her while she pretends not to notice. Listening for the sake of hearing her voice.

"Hilarious." Em's older sister rolls her eyes. "Hey, did I ever tell you about the time Haman lost his eye patch?"

Tide's grin grows wider the faster her lips move. "Oh man, Jasyn Crowe's lackey? Do tell." The guy's a goner. No doubt about it.

The Song sisters are as different as mirrorglass and steel. Loner Wren soars above in griffin form. Her feathers don't do much in the way of hiding the chip on her shoulder. Bengal tiger Robyn prowls from one person to the next, her still-flat tiger teeth glistening. She lifts her head at Makai's hand.

"You're a long way from home." He ruffles the fur between her ears.

She purrs and rolls her neck.

"How are your parents?" The Commander scratches her neck now.

Robyn emits a purr-growl combo.

"Well." Makai laughs. "Wade never was one to step outside his comfort zone, but your mother? That Lark would give any man a dash for his currency."

The tiger nods, shoulders rising and sinking with each pad of her paws.

"I know they would be proud of you, little cat. Though not so little anymore, are you?"

At that, my favorite Song sister roars. Rearing up on her hind legs, then landing with a *thump*.

Sometimes I forget how young some of us are. Khloe and Robyn haven't yet reached eighteen, the Confines on their immature Callings still in place. And no one would know either. The girls handle their gifts like true Guardians. My overprotective, big-brother side wants to keep seeing my sis as a baby in my mother's arms. But the truth is, she's years beyond her age.

I really hate that.

Preacher takes up the rear, another loner. But unlike Wren, he's earned his standoffish status. Stood up to Isabeau the Troll after Em's coronation, from what I hear. Got a nasty wound from the encounter too. He wears his scars like a badge of honor, never complaining. Except when it comes to people speaking, or moving, or breathing, or pretty much interacting with him at all.

We're a caravan of misfits. Some Called, some not, but we each have a mission. Pride makes me walk tall. We may just have a chance here.

As long as Josh doesn't sabotage my plan.

And that's my cue. Time to reel him in again. I move to stroll beside him. He walks away.

This is how he wants to play it? How far does he believe he'll get with no sword and his wrists tied? David is going to need everything he's got to claim his soul back from this imposter in his place.

And by everything I mean love.

Which, according to Commander Archer, is where I come in.

Oh boy, this oughta be fun.

I heave a breath, suppress a yawn. Sheathe my knife and pocket my hands. Then I pursue my brother again. I have half a mind to drape an arm around his shoulders and relish my victory as he cringes. Not much else to do for entertainment mid-desert. I make eye contact with Makai and he raises his eyebrows, nudging me in my efforts to draw the true version of David from the shadows.

A promise is a promise. "So, tell me, *Josh* . . ." I say his name like it's fake and we both know it. "Fill me in on this whole sibling thing. How'd you find out?"

He grunts beneath his breath. Apparently being Josh causes him to make more animal noises than the typical male. "How can you be certain I speak the truth? How are you able to believe anything I convey? How is it you can even stand to be near me when I almost ended that little runt's existence?" He jerks his head in Khloe's direction.

Fists form deep in my pant pockets, my arms taut and shaking. This guy is asking for it, and the swelling Void within agrees. Its power raises both confidence and terror, and I can't decide whether I feel completely awesome or as if I want to puke. But when I catch my little sister's eye and she flashes me a toothy smile that makes her look more five than almost twelve, my fingers relax and the urge to deck my brother subsides.

I shrug. "Valid point," is all I say.

Khloe must sense the shift in my mood. She abandons her fan club and joins us.

Josh's nostrils flare.

Skipping along to his right, my sister sings one of the tunes from Breckan and Isaach's campfire.

> "Oh, little desert sparrow,
> For all you see and hear,
> Can you hear the wind come whistling,
> Softly in your ear?
> The breeze, it sings a song,
> A language of its own,
> The air moves swiftly through you,
> To guide the sparrow home."

Khloe's voice carries, like the wind from her melody. Some of the notes are off-key, but each lyric is full of heart.

The night we spent at Nitegra Compound returns in full color. The night before Em . . .

Disappeared? Was taken? Left?

"*Admit it to yourself,*" my Void-infested side hisses in my head. "*She let go because you weren't strong enough to hold on. You are weak, pathetic, a sorry excuse for a—*"

"Why are you so mean?" Khloe's innocence squashes my shadowed alter-me.

From the way Josh's face relaxes, then hardens again, it's clear he's caught off guard as well.

"Why are you so annoying?" He gazes down his nose at her, at least a foot shorter than he is.

"Why do you smell like rats?" That's Khloe for you. Try to kill her and she'll bounce right back.

"Why don't you ever shut up?" The words growl out of him.

She giggles. "You're weird."

"Well, you're . . ." His eyes shift. Searching for a comeback? Instead, he just grunts again.

Ha. It would appear our friend Josh has met his match. No need for me to continue agitating him when Khloe can accomplish the task just fine on her own. I leave her to her interrogation, slowing until I'm stride for stride with the Commander.

Makai clears his throat. He does not look at me. "Any progress?"

"I'm working on it."

"You are much more than I first assumed, Rhyen. After what he did to Khloe, I can scarcely believe how at ease you are around him. Her too."

"Shadowalker is his vice." I narrow my eyes. "You're right. It's not who he is. We may never be friends, but even I can't deny that having the true, sword-fighting, stubborn-as-Song David on our side would give us a leg up. I'll do whatever it takes to end the Void. To get Em back."

"Indeed. I owe you an apology."

His comment catches me off balance. What am I supposed to say? We stride in sync without speaking for some time, leaving me to wonder about the Commander's relationship with my brother. I put the pieces together. If David is my twin, then King Aidan and Queen Ember were my birth parents. The rest isn't too difficult to navigate. The Verity split between us. And . . .

"Tiernan took me." The out-loud realization brings Makai's apology to light. "It wasn't your fault."

From the corner of my eye, I notice his expression darken. His jaw works. "If only it were that simple."

"Isn't it?" Makai doesn't realize I lived in Em's Scrib memory, seeing clearly what she saw from then until now. The night she received her mirrormark, Nathaniel had accused Tiernan of stealing from him. Only now do I connect the fact it was me he swiped.

Unless . . . what if Elizabeth's claim is accurate? Could I have the facts out of order?

Makai heaves. "No." He rakes five fingers through his shaggy, graying hair and adjusts Evan in his wrap. "My father was in shambles when we realized one of Ember's sons had vanished. She was like a sister to him, and he couldn't live with himself knowing he'd let her down."

The phrase "one of Ember's sons" does not elude me.

"My father remained with one boy while I went out in search of the other."

Uneasiness punches my gut. Where's he going with this?

Makai doesn't say more for a while, as if he's working out what words to use next. Intuition is a gift of mine. Whatever it is can't be good. Otherwise he'd spit it out.

"It was Joshua Tiernan kidnapped. Not you."

But Tiernan raised *me*.

"My brother was a vicious, malevolent, foul excuse for a human being." Makai sighs. "But he was my younger brother, and so my heart grieved for him. He longed for a son, an heir, and my father and I? We were left with two." His explanation is fluid as if practiced.

Remain calm. Do not allow anger to overtake you. It only feeds the Void's hunger, and I need to make it starve.

"The eve before you were born," Makai continues, "just after King Aidan and the queen arrived at my father's home on Lisel Island, Aidan let us in on a long-kept secret. As his wife slept and the firelight faded, he shared a story he had never divulged before. Years prior to meeting his queen, the king took a drink from the Fountain of Time. One sip was all the Fountain offered. One sip to combine his deepest desire, to have children, with where he was needed most, past, present, or future." The Commander turns his head, locking his gaze on mine. "He ended up in the future. *Your* future. Your brother's future. He witnessed a crossing of paths, if you will."

I swallow hard. I'm not an idiot. I know all too well what one moment in time can bring. Everything or nothing at all. "He saw David would become an Ever. He believed David was a better fit to be raised as king. Not me."

Makai's eyebrows arch. He nods. "Clearly even seeing the future cannot tell us everything, can it?"

"No." My thoughts return to our goal once more. "It can't." Makai's words only solidify the Fountain's legend as truth. One sip per customer. Unless someone sacrifices their drink and offers it to you.

Someone like a hooded figure on the deck of my ship. I've yet to uncover the mystery of that day. Why offer something so precious to a stranger? The only answer I've been able to produce is it wasn't a stranger at all. Who, then? And why?

The stories in my pack beg to be studied. Still, I'm no foreigner to them. *The Traveler's Way* is one my mother read often. The singsong rhymes come back to me now, reminding me how precious even one drink from the Fountain's water is.

"*Don't ye waste a sip, not a drop, not a drip . . .*"

And . . .

"*Ye'll never lose yer way, if ye start from yesterday . . .*"

And . . .

"Say good-bye ta sorrow, if ye just skip past ta marrow . . ."

Every story held a lesson, a message for the reader. The one in *The Traveler's Way* was simple—treasure each moment. Don't dwell on the future. Never regret the past. Learn from your mistakes and move forward, making better choices than you did the day before.

"When we discovered Tiernan, we offered him a trade." Makai returns to his story and I return to the present. "You and a pouch full of currency in exchange for Joshua. We didn't let on your brother would grow to be an Ever. If Tiernan knew, he'd have kept him and used his blood for profit, which would've been trouble for everyone. You both carried the Verity. It split between you when Aidan passed, but we never told anyone. It did, however, offer us some comfort in knowing you'd be protected. Tiernan was wary of our offer at first, and who wouldn't be?" He almost sounds pleased with his brother for that. "But a few choice words convinced him."

He moves to place his hand on my shoulder but stops just shy of the action, curling his fingers into his palm and lowering his arm. Evan fusses and his dad soothes him by whispering something inaudible into his ear. "You were such an easy kid, compliant, which is what Tiernan wanted."

Compliant. Good word. Rage rises unbidden. For the love of Em, will it never cease? I push down the darkness again and again, deeper and lower. Makai couldn't have known Tiernan would beat me.

Or maybe he did. Maybe he knew but refused to admit it to himself. The guilt would've been crippling, I imagine. If Tiernan wanted a son so badly, why mistreat him? Was it power, his Shadowalker side? Perhaps it was his desire to ingrain in me the same darkness.

Or perhaps he was just a sorry old drunk who had nothing better to do.

I'll never know the true reason behind his madness. Does it matter?

After clearing his throat, Makai presses on. "Your brother, on the other hand? He cried night and day. He was stubborn, tenacious.

You were also older, making you much more valuable to Tiernan. In the end he made the deal and, with a Kiss of Accord, we agreed never to bother each other again." His voice carries no regret. Only resolve.

I flatten my lips. Anyone else might hate Makai and Nathaniel for what they did. But how can I resent them? Life with Tiernan was a nightmare, sure. But without him I wouldn't have had my mother or Khloe. I peek back at her, still blabbering on to Josh, whose face burns redder every second. "It all worked out for the good," I say. And I mean it.

Makai shudders a breath, then says beneath it, "I see now you would've made a better king. You're so much like her. My father said as much after you went to visit him last Eleventh Month with Eliyana. He said it was hard not to stare at you for how similar you are. Not in appearance, perhaps, but in character."

I don't have to ask for elaboration to know he means my birth mother. I wish I felt more connected to her. I recall the photo we saw inside Nathaniel's pocket watch. Ember Gabrielle Archer, the mysterious E.G.A. and author of the *Mirror Theory*. Hair like Dragon Fire and eyes like David's. How different would my life have turned out if she and the king had raised me, raised us? Would my brother and I be close? Would I have learned how to wield a knife?

Would I have met Em?

Again, what does it matter? Living in what-ifs is pointless. Queen Ember may have been my mother, but nothing will ever change the fact she wasn't my mom. The one who raised me and read to me and tended my wounds and rocked me to sleep. The one who hardly looked like me with skin two shades darker than Khloe's and hair even darker. But her eyes, so green they rivaled the ocean, were mine. Or so I believed.

I always thought I'd inherited a brown eye from Tiernan and a green eye from Mom. It wasn't until I learned I was adopted that this changed. Still, my green eye makes me feel as if I still have a piece of her with me. The Commander's brother may have been a sorry excuse for a dad, but the woman who loved me like her own more than made up for his shortcomings.

"My sweet boy," she would croon. *"My sweet, sweet Ky. Do not let him harden you. Always remain my tender son. Promise me."*

"I promise, Mama." The memory has me stuffing down the Void again, but with greater force and purpose than before. I made a promise. And I keep my promises, no matter the cost.

And then she's there, her face filling my mind. But not my mother this time.

"Find me." Em didn't beg or plead or cry. She simply made a statement, no question in her voice. Her faith in me shakes my core.

"Always," I say aloud. "Always."

Makai's inquisitive look at the voiced assurance doesn't faze me.

I clear my throat and think of my earlier conversation with his wife. "I gave her—Eliyana—the mark, then? It was me all along?"

His silence confirms Elizabeth's story. Why keep this from us? Why allow Em to believe it was David?

My questions require no answers. The shame they must have felt at trading me. The lie they had to live to cover it. Sometimes, continuing in the lie is easier than revealing the truth and making amends.

We trudge uphill, wiping sweat from our brows. We stop by the river now and again, the water seeming to drain with every step. When the narrow entrance into Nitegra Compound comes into view, we make our way toward it. A hot meal and good company call to me. Just what I need before facing the unknown. I close my eyes, ready to welcome the relief.

My chest meets solid muscle. When I open my eyes I find Makai holding me back.

The Commander takes a knee to the earth and scoops up something small in his cupped palm. It's only when he rises I see it's a dead Fairy. At least twenty of them sprinkle the path ahead.

"She's here." Josh comes up beside me. I look at him, at the change in his eyes. For the briefest instant I see David there, and any doubt he is still alive dissolves.

I don't ask who he means, as the dead Fairy is clue enough.

"Fairies don't die," Josh says. "They live off their queen's power and she is immortal. The only one who can kill a Fairy is the Fairy Queen herself."

"How do you know this?" It's Makai who speaks.

Josh shrugs. "Gage told me. If the Fairies are dying, it can only mean one thing."

Sober minded, we crawl through the narrow pass into the compound. No time to waste.

Isabeau is waiting.

FOURTEEN

HE'S BESIDE ME

Here's a thought. Let's go after a man known for lying, kidnapping, and what else? Oh, right. Murder.

On the surface, this has *bad idea* written on it in double-bold Sharpie.

"*A jagged surface . . .*"

I know, I know. A jagged surface doesn't always allude to what truly lies beneath. Fitting words from the one person who has always seen me as I am now.

Mirrormarkless.

Well, my Mirror may be lost, my Scrib memory failing me on so many levels, but the way back to the Grand Canal isn't difficult. I can't help but feel as if someone is following me, though. This whole Shadowalker thing gives me the heebie-jeebies. It doesn't help that the man I seek becomes a Shadowalker someday too.

"*Legend says the first Shadowalker began as a vessel of the Void.*"

What a burden. To be charged with holding darkness so close to your own soul.

"*Rather than fight against the Void, tha vessel welcomed it . . . For when tha Void's vessel began ta love himself more than the one who held the Verity, that's when things went south.*"

And there it is. The difference between a Shadowalker and a vessel. The turning point. Breckan's story was more akin to watching an off-Broadway play than listening to a retelling of true history. Now that I'm living it, desensitization is long gone. Joshua told me once this is the "real world." I laughed at him then, so certain in my naïveté Joshua's "real world" was little more than a fable.

Look who's laughing now.

When I find Jasyn at the Grand Canal's edge, near the same spot Grandma B and I waited for the gondola only hours ago, I tuck my hair behind my ears and step beside him.

"A girl who lacks pretense." He stares ahead. Purple and indigo brighten the horizon on all sides, bringing my grandfather's features into full view as dawn approaches.

Well, *there* is something to be said for the man who kidnapped Mom and almost killed Joshua—he aged well. The differences in his young self are scarce. Hair thicker and two shades darker. Voice smoother, deeper. Posture several inches straighter. He turns his head and muses, "A rare find in this age, but one to be treasured."

Reflections to El. Your modernisms are showing. Heat floods my cheeks. Swallow. Blink. Breathe. "What if I told you I believe there *is* a way to get rid of the Void for good?"

He chuckles at his shiny brown-on-white oxfords. "I would proffer you are a guileless girl with an impossible dream." He reaches into his blazer pocket and withdraws a small, thin object.

It's only when he touches the rolled paper to his lips and lights the tip that I realize he has a death wish. "That stuff'll kill you." I try not to inhale the cancerous fumes.

"And the Void will not?" A cloud of smoke. Another chuckle.

Point taken.

"Come now, I have yet to learn your name, and here you are berating me for my vice? We do not know each other well enough for such niceties." Sarcasm seeps from the words, but his tone remains airy. Teasing.

Jasyn . . . ahem . . . is having fun.

Who *is* this guy? Mom might have an aneurysm if she saw him now. Where's his goal? His purpose? Doesn't he care about anything? He holds the darkest power in the seven Reflections, and he's standing here smoking and inquiring about my name?

My name.

Didn't Bianca announce it during the Alliance meeting? I rack my brain. Come up short. No one's asked yet, not even B. She's called me every term in Italy but never once asked anything more personal than my shoe size. I open my mouth. Shut it. Open it once more. "Elizabeth." Really? "My name is Elizabeth." Why? Am I so afraid he'll recognize Eliyana? Or perhaps I simply miss Mom.

Let's go with that one.

"Elizabeth." He taps his cigarette with one finger. Ash sprinkles the ground. "How very regal. Any relation to England's princess?"

"No," is my autoreply. Then my gears begin to work. Princess? Princess. Right. Elizabeth II didn't become queen until the fifties, when King George died. At least that's what I recall from the documentary we watched in World History class. I kinda had my headphones in during most of it, much preferring the stylings of Owl City and Of Monsters and Men to the droning old British guy narrating the outdated film. If I'd known I was destined to rule, I might've paid closer attention. At least Elizabeth II spent her life preparing for her role. I still don't know the first thing about being queen.

Or . . . maybe I do.

I stare through Jasyn. I don't need to be a Mirror to see past his show. A number of memories elude me, but I'll never forget his final words when I drove the mirrorglass blade through his heart.

"*Thank you*," he'd croaked. The Void left him then, but his soul was already too far gone.

Then what? Something else. Small. A trivial detail, but one oh so vital.

At first, we believed it was the one the Verity cared for most who took on the Void. But the tale of *The Scrib's Fate* relayed the reverse.

My blank gaze alters, focusing, soaking in the man beneath the bowler hat. He loves King Aidan. Like a brother? Father? Friend? Does Aidan hold the same fondness for Jasyn? Perhaps now, yes. Their closeness is what keeps the darkness in my grandfather from overwhelming him. It's why being away from Joshua made the Void in him spread—

When did the affliction transfer to Kyaphus?

It had to have been recent, right? Did Joshua discover a new way to contain the darkness? Did an event occur in which Ky sacrificed himself so Joshua and I could be together? Free of the Void's weight?

Impossible. Why would he do such a thing? Makes no sense.

Not much does these days.

Again, I feel nothing aside from loathing for the boy with the blackened veins. What's wrong with me? No one is this heartless, so what am I missing? The longer I picture his face, the more I want to punch it.

The more I wish he were dead.

I clutch my stomach. The Verity rages, burning at the mere thought of the Void's vessel ceasing to exist.

"What is troubling you?" Jasyn takes a drag. Releases, forming an O with his lips.

"Nothing." The lie is small. Easy. Settles in my center.

"Oh no, my dear. It is never nothing. I am no stranger to lies." He offers me his cigarette. Still doesn't make eye contact.

I wince. Lean away.

He shrugs. Continues in his vice. "Much is on your mind. Now, whether or not you wish to relay your thoughts, that is up to you."

My thoughts? "You love Aidan." It's not a blurt. No word fumble from awkward old me. It's a statement. But also a question.

"He is"—another drag—"my oldest friend."

I wait . . . *three, four, five . . . twenty-five . . . fifty-seven . . .* Yawn. Blink.

That's it? He's really not going to elaborate? Fine.

"How did you meet?" My sockless toes curl inside my dry sneakers. I dug through Grandma B's closet and came out with something at least wearable. Pressed trousers, a loose blouse, and a hip-length pea-style jacket. Her shoes wouldn't do. Good thing the pant hems are long enough to cover most of my Chucks. Who knows? Maybe I'll start a new trend.

Glancing over one shoulder, Jasyn says, "Why would you want

to hear that old tale?" He faces forward once more, expression stoic as ever.

For so many reasons, none of which I can give. My shoulders rise and fall. "Humor me."

With an adjustment of his tie, he begins, "We met as lads. Aidan is several years older and has always been stronger, faster, and better looking."

The admission makes me choke on my own saliva. Jasyn is admitting someone else is better than him? In more ways than one? I really have entered an alternate reality, haven't I?

"I was an orphan. Abandoned by my parents as an infant. Naturally, I followed Aidan around like a horse with a bridle. If he told me to test for traps in the woods, I dove in headfirst. When he lost the wooden sword he used for sparring, I offered him mine with no expectation of return." Another tap to his cigarette. It's halfway gone now. "He excelled at everything. Everyone loved him. Including me. And what would you expect from the son of a king?"

Loved. Jasyn used past tense. Does he resent the king now? Does Kyaphus resent me? I didn't force the Void into him. What right does he have to hate me?

What right do I have to hate him?

"Aidan's parents were good rulers. Kind. His father kept to himself mostly. Rafaj Niddala was his name."

I raise my eyebrows. Poor kid. I'm sure bullies had a field day with that one.

"But most referred to him as King Raf."

Better. I'd want to go by Raf too.

"Aidan's mother was a strict woman who rarely smiled. When Queen Yasmine grew ill and weak, King Raf started to go somewhat insane."

My ears itch. The story is so familiar. Déjà vu. My prediction? Raf carried the Void. His queen held the Verity. A beast and his beauty.

Tale as old as time.

"Yasmine died," I say to the canal. "Aidan took on the Verity."

"You really are more than you appear." At last he drops his cig-arette, knocks it into the water with the toe of his shoe. He coughs twice into his fist before continuing. "You know much of things well beyond your years."

Wait a minute. "You can't be much older than I am." I may still see him as my senior, but he doesn't know our history. How can he look at me as a child when he's probably not even old enough to drink?

In my century, anyway.

"You are not wrong. I turned sixteen this year."

My jaw loosens. Sixteen? Younger than I expected. His speech is so precise. Tuned. This is a forties teen? We millennials really need to step up our class factor.

"When Aidan became the Verity's vessel, only fourteen at the time, the Void remained with Rafaj for a few years. But eventually Rafaj went mad, going on about reversing Yasmine's death. When he could not accomplish the impossible feat, he settled for figuring a way to forget her altogether."

Forget her? Awful. I'd hate to lose Mom. Joshua. Makai. I miss Kuna every day. But would it be better not to remember him at all?

Never.

"Aidan has housed the Verity coming up on seven years now. I have held the Void for one, to this day, in fact."

One year as the Void's vessel? Whoa. "What happened?" I lick my lips, the dry winter air getting the best of them. "For the Void to make the switch, I mean?"

"Aidan locked his father away. He waited for Rafaj's Ever heart to break. Believed the loss of Yasmine would have done it too."

Only a broken heart can kill an Ever. For the love of irony. It was Jasyn who first revealed this truth. Little did I know how deep its effects ran for him.

"But the old king discovered how to forget Yasmine, as I said." He must see the expectancy in my gaze because he adds, "I do not know how, so do not press me. All I can say is Rafaj feared death.

He desired to keep his heart from breaking. Instead, he caused himself to despise those he once cared for. He hated Aidan. A deep loathing that blackened his core." He pauses. "And that is the day the Void transferred to me." My younger-than-I-am grandfather looks down at his shoulder, dusts something invisible off his jacket.

"Don't *you* hate Aidan?" Wow. I have to say, I like the direct approach. So much easier than beating around the bush.

Jasyn looks at me for the first time since I arrived. "What would bring you to such a conclusion?"

Isn't it obvious? "Darkness wraps your soul. Because of Aidan."

He shakes his head. "Foolish girl." He smiles. "The Void empowers me. It gives me purpose. Tell me, how can I hate my friend for giving me all I ever wanted?"

Power. Ugh. He's further gone than I realized. Is it too late to reverse his course? He needs more than the love of power. He needs true and actual love. The kind that gives you a reason to get up in the morning. The kind that makes you know, no matter what, you'll always have someone to turn to.

I consider the boy beside me. So very lost. So very in need of something even more powerful than the Void.

I must destroy the darkness for so many other reasons than to simply be the heroic queen everyone needs. Ending the Void could mean Jasyn's salvation. It could mean saving Kyaphus from the same fate my grandfather met. I reach into the corners of my heart. Seeking. Searching . . .

Nostrils flare. Fists clench.

I. Hate. Him.

Eyelids squeeze. Teeth grind.

Kyaphus. Is. My. Enemy.

And he must be destroyed.

"No!" I gasp the word, clutch my throat. "No," I say again. Softer this time.

Jasyn takes two steps back. Looks at me as if I'm possessed.

I must tear down this hatred. I will not be the person who

breaks another's heart. Rafaj may have tried to block heartbreak, but I'll welcome it if it means sparing another. I must free Ky of the darkness whether I like him or not. Does he relish it as Jasyn does? Is his "love" for me little more than a hunger for power?

Disgusting.

I close my eyes, calling on the Verity within. *Help me know what to do here. Give me some guidance. Some—*

Immediate compassion replaces my disgust. For any being who has ever experienced the weight of life as the Void's vessel. My soul shatters. "Oh, Grandfather." The whispered endearment marks the first time I've called Jasyn this out loud.

"Pardon?"

"Does it hurt to fight it? Is that why you pretend to love the darkness?"

His face is an emotionless mask. If the question pains him, he gives nothing away. "I do not pretend." His tone could turn the canal to ice. "*You* cannot begin to understand these things." On "you" his gaze intensifies, studying me rather than merely grazing. His soundlessness unnerves me. If I closed my eyes, I might not know he's here.

So I do, if only for a solitary, clarifying second. My eyelids flutter, and I tuck away into myself as only an introvert can. Am I the first concern he's encountered? What must it feel like to share life with the Void?

At the internal question a new memory surfaces. Excruciating pain in my arm. The Void snaking its way up, attempting to take hold. The recollection is isolated, a cigarette burn at the end of an old film reel. Dust and debris surround me. I cough, try to catch my breath. I hear voices, cries. Someone speaks, but their words are loose, inaudible. I look down and there it is, the detail I might've missed but can't ignore.

A hand in mine.

Click. I snap a photo with my mind. Grasp for dear life as if the image is life or death. Then I see Joshua, completely covered with blackened veins, a sudden flashback that has me recoiling to my brain's opposite end. I make a fist around his necklace concealed beneath my blouse, clutching a fistful of fabric with it.

"Swear you'll never remove it." Joshua stared at me as I fastened his gift to my neck last spring.

"I swear." It took every bit of self-control I had not to beam like a giddy idiot. *"Never."*

He nodded and that was that. I've worn the treble clef–heart charm for nearly a year.

My fingertips trace the curves of silver, unable to avoid the added trinket resting so close beside. I've decided to call the rose button "the lost thing." An item washed up on the never-shore of my heart, looking for a place to call home. When all is restored, perhaps this memory will return as well. I'll bet it's a good one. Could this necklace be from Joshua too? Doesn't seem like him. Much more me, actually.

"He knows me better than I know myself," I say.

"Are you ill?" Jasyn asks, abrupt as ever.

I shake my head, returning to the task at hand. Perhaps instead of trying to convince him I can help, which he's already decided no one can, I might appeal to his pride. "Why did you leave the meeting?"

"I am merely an accessory. It is Aidan who leads. I simply provide a listening ear. Who am I if I cannot support my liege?" He's back in Amulet mode again, casting a façade around his insincere words. This man does not for one second believe he's an accessory to Aidan.

"I don't believe that," I say, candor fitting me like a new pair of Chucks. "They spoke of Shadowalkers. Who better to aid their cause than someone who has personal experience with the Void?"

"That is the thing, is it not? I must conceal the truth. How can I help when I am unable to let on to my knowledge?"

Now we're getting somewhere. Perhaps he does not love darkness as much as he claims. "Why not talk to the king—er, Aidan? He already knows you carry the Void. Surely he'll listen. He trusts you. He can take your insight and use it against the Shadowalkers."

He rotates his head and quirks a brow. "Aidan wishes only to focus on the good. The light. He is much too pure of heart to consider what must be done." Jasyn says "pure of heart" as if the phrase tastes foul.

"And what must be done?"

He sighs. "Shadowalkers cannot be reasoned with. Aidan believes with the Verity on our side, we have a fighting chance. A way to turn those blasted Void worshippers from their wicked ways. But no matter how much we fight in the name of the Verity, it does no good unless a Shadowalker desires to turn. And even then, the struggle is far from over. The love of darkness is an addiction, and not one easily broken."

At that he turns away, hands clasped behind his back, and walks along the canal's edge. "The only place for a Shadowalker is at the bottom of the sea. A swift death is the only way to be rid of them for certain."

"No. There's another way. A better way."

"Do tell."

"Shadowalkers can't be Shadowalkers if they have nothing to follow. No Void to worship means no worshippers, yeah?"

"No Void?" He continues his stroll, his expression growing more inquisitive with each step. "No Void, you say? Would that not be something?"

I can't tell if his "something" is good or bad. Resolve moves me forward. If you'd asked me last November if I ever thought I'd follow Jasyn Crowe anywhere willingly, I'd have answered with, "Void no!" But now, as I creep behind him, dawn lighting our way, I latch onto my gut feeling. The feeling telling me Jasyn is my best chance to get home. My best chance at changing things.

And maybe, just maybe, my chance at getting to him before the Void takes him too far. Can I change him? Would doing so cause some kind of chain reaction? If it does, would the choice to help Jasyn be worth it? Do I even have a choice in this?

"There's always a choice," a memory whispers in my head. Joshua again.

I ignore the fact he sounds like Kyaphus.

I repeat the words to myself until the sun blinks over the horizon. When it about blinds me, I shade my eyes.

That's when my sixteen-year-old grandfather shoves me into the canal.

ebony

Typical. Perfectly peachy. She's on to us, that much I can tell you. Either that or my mother just happened to choose this particular compound for a raid. Totally random. Nothing to do with the fact we were headed straight for it. Pure coincidence, wouldn't you agree?

Yeah. Me neither.

Fact—Isabeau loves drama. The grand entrance. The shocker at the end. It all reeks of her scent. This is her thing, and we're falling directly into her outstretched claws. She *wants* us to investigate the Fairy deaths. To stop everything we're doing and start what this particular clan does best. Care. She's depending on the hearts of those better than her.

And what my mother wants, my mother gets. She probably even expects me to come after her for answers. If she knows me like a mother should, she knows I'm not like everyone else.

A few dead Fairies changes nothing. Whatever we find inside the compound, we can't let it stop us.

"FYI." I grab Rhyen's arm. I'm the center of attention in a way I so hate to be. I'm a showstopper, not a scene causer. The gawking expressions on everyone's faces are not my idea of self-gratification. "Isabeau is following us."

"You think we should turn back?" Uncle Makai hands Evan off to Elizabeth. Is the kid my stepbrother? Nephew? Neither quite fits. Doesn't change that he's stinkin' adorable.

"No. We keep going. She expects this to throw us off. We continue as if nothing's changed."

"I trust your judgment." Rhyen nods. "We still have to go in. Ensure Isaach and Breckan—"

"No!" I release his arm, catching myself before wiping my palm on my clothes. *The Void isn't contagious, Ebony. Don't be weird.* "We cannot, under any circumstances, go into that compound. Don't you see?" I fling my arm toward the trail of dead Fairies leading directly into the Nitegra entrance. "She's saying come and get me. Come and investigate with all your goody-goody, we'll-save-the-day attitudes." I'm panting now, gulping breaths like some sweaty Guardian. But for once I don't care.

"Well, 'course she is."

Regina appears as if from nowhere, eyes sparkling. She must have crawled through the entrance while my back was turned. "I've known the woman for longer than you, honey." She wags a finger with so much sass I'd say the move was choreographed. "If I've learned anything, it's that your mama isn't the least bit concerned with anyone aside from herself. She couldn't care less if you come on in and lend a helping hand. She ain't trying to do nothin' except find Miss Elizabeth. I'd wager the best we can do is stay with a large group, not go venturin' off on our own."

I close my gaping mouth. I hate to break it to you, lady, but El's mom isn't the main focus in this story. Not any more than revenge on El was my reason for helping Jasyn Crowe. "This goes deeper than Elizabeth, no offense." Hello, don't you people get it? I can't be the only one who sees the light, pardon the pun. Even if revenge is a driving force for my mother, it's only part of it. "Isabeau was angry and jaded long before my father met you."

El's mom nods. Good. At least I'm getting through to someone.

"You go on and do what you gotta do, Ebony." Regina's dismissive hand isn't lost on me. I invented the dismissive hand. She's stealing my moves. Not cool. "We can handle ourselves just fine from here." She sways past me, bumping me with her hip and winking in simultaneous style. Next she wraps an arm around El's mom and leads her toward the entrance. A.k.a. the black hole of death.

Is she for reals?

"Hold up, Dahlia." With folded arms and a hesitant expression, Ky comes to my aid. "If Ebony says we shouldn't go in, maybe we ought to at least hear her out."

Yes. Hear me out. I may not be an official Guardian or anything, but I know my mother. My manipulative, always-out-for-herself mother.

"Hush now." Regina doesn't stop, and Elizabeth doesn't fight the way she ushers her on. "We're safer in there than y'all are out here." Three coughs and a hack before she continues. "The Fairy Queen is long gone now, don't you worry. The Nitegrans shooed her off before she did too much damage."

My eyes plead with my uncle, with Ky, and Tide, and even Preacher. "I am telling you guys, this is a bad idea. We can't go in there."

"Regina says it is safe. My wife trusts her, which is good enough for me." Makai joins Elizabeth, Evan, and the crazy Ever woman at the mouth of the pass.

This is insane. But majority rules, right? I do realize I'm not the most trustworthy person. I've made my mistakes, and everyone knows it too. But can't a girl catch a break? I'm trying to redeem myself here.

"Commander, I feel we ought to consider Ebony's insight." El's guy plants his feet in a wide stance to my right.

For all his Crowe-following, I never would have guessed he'd so readily stand up to authority. Of course, Khloe's life is not at stake this time. Ten bucks says Ky would've ended up in Jasyn's dungeon had our sister not kept him motivated to submit.

Tide joins our small rebellion but takes his place at my left. "I have to agree. At least proceed with caution."

New emotions stir. Is this what it's like to be supported? To have someone on my side? Two someones?

"Caution?" Regina waves her arms, the cellulite underneath

jiggling. She removes her apron, wipes her soiled face. "The Nitegrans need our help. Are you lot just goin' to stand there while people are dyin'?"

Dying? My stomach turns to sour grapes. Crud, this is worse than I'd hoped. I unzip my jacket pocket, fiddle with the compact inside with a nervous hand. Because otherwise I'll want to bite my nails, and I won't stoop to that level. A girl's gotta have principles.

"No. We help them. No matter the cost." Oh no, not Preacher too. He tromps past, adding to Regina's numbers. Of course, it's no secret he fancies her. The brute can try to hide it all he wants, but even a blind person could see his smile appears a little more with each inch he nears our oldest Ever.

The man who calls himself Josh chuckles, but no joy fills his laugh. "Well, well, well. It appears we have a standoff. But which side will win? To go, or not to go?"

"You stay out of this, Brother."

Not now, guys. This isn't the time.

"Oh, I am in this whether you like it or not, Kyaphus. You brought me along, and you've got me."

"We only brought you," Rhyen says, "in case we needed your blood supply."

"Hold on now, Ky." My uncle pats his wife on the back and marches back over. "That is not the sole reason."

For the first time since he joined the dark side, Josh doesn't appear to have it all together. His eyes narrow, then widen, clarity taking over. He shakes his head at my uncle, then glares at Rhyen. "You once told Eliyana everyone has an agenda. Or did you think I couldn't overhear your conversation that day at the creek?"

Ky doesn't respond.

Everyone watches the train wreck as it unfolds. My time in New York told me one thing, and that's that people are fascinated with destruction. Brace yourselves.

"It appears *your* agenda is clear. You desired to turn her against me from the beginning," Josh continues. "And now you wish to pit Makai—more my brother than you will ever be—against me as well?" He jerks his chin in the Commander's direction, making it clear whom he considers family.

Rhyen shrugs out of his leather jacket, then stuffs it inside his already-bulging backpack. "And that's your problem, Shadowalker. You think everything is about *you*. It was never about *you*. It was about helping her see the truth. Showing her who she could trust." He takes a step toward Josh. "And who she most clearly could not."

No, no, no, *no*. Not now. How is it every time I attempt to help, I only make things worse? That's what I get for speaking up. Maybe my mother has it right. Maybe the best option for getting by is to go through life keeping your mouth shut and letting anyone else make the decisions. That way you can't be blamed when things go wrong.

And things, I'm afraid, are definitely going wrong.

Josh and Ky launch toward each other.

Uncle Makai pitches forward, yanks Rhyen away, and pins his arms behind his back. The Shields battle it out, both strong and stubborn. Ky does some kind of ninja maneuver, freeing himself in a one-two-duck-twist move.

My uncle goes into stealth mode, invisibility cloaking him in timely fashion.

Ky falls forward through nothing, lands palms first in the dirt, before he jumps up and shakes it off.

Makai reappears, reaches for Rhyen, but misses him as he lurches for Josh.

Oh, brothers. Can't you work out your problems without resorting to caveman techniques?

Wren caw-growls and swoops in from the sky. Thank goodness she doesn't transform into a human as she places her griffin self in front of Josh. Sorry, girl. You may look good, but no one wants to see your naked behind. That's one thing I'm grateful for. Maybe I don't want to be a Mask after all. I kind of like that I can keep my clothes on with each form shift.

"Stop!" Khloe's voice echoes across the canyon. "This is exactly what that stupid Troll wants." She glances at me. Looking for my offense?

I give her a wink that says, "Nah, runt, you're good." Because Verity knows I've said a lot worse than that about my own mother.

And she's said worse about me. I'm the constant reminder of Tiernan. *"You're just like your father,"* she would say. When I messed up. When I achieved but still didn't quite live up to her impossibly perfect standards.

"We can't fight each other," Khloe says, arms outstretched. One palm faces Josh and Wren, the other Makai and Rhyen. "We have to fight *for* each other. For the Verity. For Eliyana. The Thresholds are draining, and we're wasting time quarreling about nothing."

Josh snorts.

Bad idea, pal. You've awakened the beast.

Khloe stomps to Wren, ducks beneath her wing, and points a finger in Josh's smug face. "You knock it off. You're lucky we brought you. Blood or not, you're here, aren't you? What does the reason matter? You killed Tide's mom and you tried to kill me. A child! For that we should have put you in a fire pit full of venomous snakes. But instead, my brother brought you along. You might be a jerk, but we all know even your jerk side wants to find El. You should be thanking Ky, not yelling at him."

Gotta hand it to her. Fire-slash–snake pit is a pretty creative sentence. Now it's Rhyen's turn for a snicker.

Oh, sheesh, not you too. Better watch out, Khloe's on the loose.

She rounds on him. "Don't you even get me started on you, big brother. You're not even trying. You pretend like you are, but you aren't. I know you miss her." She takes his hand. My heart squeezes. "We all do. We love her too. Don't let the Shadowwalker win. You know how to be a brother. So be one."

The clapping begins with Tide. It tips a domino effect that has everyone, even Miss Griffin, cheering in some way. Robyn roars; Wren flaps her wings and swishes her tail; Stormy hugs my little sis as if she's her own.

"Enough is enough," Khloe says, the momentum of encouragement egging her on. "We're *all* going in there. We're *all* going to see who needs our help. Then we'll go our separate ways. Life is too short not to help people. Isn't that why we want to get rid of the Void anyway?"

Wow. Eleven going on forty. Well said, Khlo. Well said.

She speed-walks to the entrance, turns before giving her final words. "Now let's go, we don't have all day." Then she disappears into the dark.

Makai laughs. The sound is so happy I can't help but smile.

"Well," he says. "Looks like we have a Guardian Commander in the making."

How can I argue? Khloe's not wrong. And now I look like a major jerk. It's not that I didn't want to help the Nitegrans. I just know nothing is ever as it seems with my mother. Dead Fairies? It's too much, a trail of crumbs my mother is counting on us to track.

Even so . . . I make the first move. But I can't ignore the sinking feeling that takes over when I bypass Regina and the others and follow my sister into the hole.

all alone

Shoved. Dragged. Pulled. Lugged. You name it. I've been forced into water enough times against my will it no longer disorients me.

Much.

I jerk my head up, down, left, right. The surface is at a diagonal. Body shifts. Legs kick. Arms propel. Not so difficult. Doesn't hurt that I have expert swimmer's experience now—

Khloe . . .

"Bet you've never seen a Shield do that before."

She had gills. Could adapt to any climate. It's how I made it into the Fourth Reflection without drowning. Another memory pinged by a current event. Maybe Jasyn should shove me into the canal more often. I'll live with raisin skin and mildew clothes if they help me gain full use of my brain again.

Speaking of my brain, I probably ought to . . .

My face meets air and I gulp precious oxygen. I wasn't under too long, but that doesn't make a breath any less refreshing. My first vision of the Fourth flashes like a camera in my mind. The Lost City of Atlantis come to life. A legend proven true. Glittering green and gold glass—mirrorglass—stones embedded in the ground. A Siren for a countess. Guardians with tattoos featuring rolling waves. Joshua on the Fourth's shore, at my rescue once again.

And Kyaphus.

He was the reason we were led to a dungeon. Why Joshua suffered the poisonous coral's sting.

And Joshua?

Tears well and spill, splash into the canal and drift down-stream, lost and forgotten like so many things. This . . . ache. This . . . pain. I miss him so much. How long since he's held me? Since we last kissed? The more I think on it, the more the pain shifts. Because this longing I have inside? This love?

He'll never feel as much for me as I do for him. Even attempted once to convince me he felt nothing at all. I know he cares. He cares so much he bestowed a Kiss of Infinity on me—twice. Yet even this is not enough. Whatever Kyaphus said or did to end up in his position, it apparently mattered more than any kiss from Joshua. Why else would the Void choose Kyaphus?

Maybe a Kiss of Infinity is nothing more than a story in some dreamer's fantasy journal. A plot device created to add a twist. We all want to believe in something more. In a kiss powerful enough to heal or save or bind. What if I never became a Mirror? Who's to say the Verity I think I feel isn't just stomach acid? All the things I believed were real could be a bad case of once upon a dream.

Except I don't know you, I don't know me. Maybe I don't know anyone anymore.

Water droplets stick to my lashes. I blink them away. My blouse is soaked through, which means it's probably also *see*-through. Self-consciousness takes over for a split second and I drown in it, losing my last bit of fight.

"What more do you want?" I scream at no one. "I give up, okay?" Let someone else try to fix Jasyn. The man's a lost cause. Nothing I can do will *ever* change his charbroiled heart.

An old woman passes by on the walkway above. She glares, then turns up her nose, moving along quickly to avoid the most likely homeless girl bathing in the canal.

Go me. Doesn't get much more humiliating than this.

Chin raised barely above the frigid surface, I bob along in the water. The current carries me farther away from where I began, but I don't bother to swim against it. Why should I? I've spent months fighting, and what has it accomplished? Nothing. Nada.

Zilch. How foolish I was to believe I arrived in the past for a purpose. There's no gold at the end of the rainbow. No one ever lived happily ever after. Maybe I never had any power, and I'm just a girl gone crazy from the trauma of the war. I don't even have my mark to prove my identity.

What if I've already messed up something on the timeline? Is it possible to erase my own existence simply by speaking to my grandfather? Better to leave things alone from now on rather than try to correct anything.

"Row, row, row your boat gently down the stream . . ."

It's been too long since melody and I had a one-on-one. I'm off-key and my throat's dry. The children's tune seems to come from nowhere but fits at the same time. I close my eyes, water sloshing around my ears.

". . . merrily, merrily, merrily, merrily, life is but a dream."

The song dies after one round as the cold turns my blood from liquid to solid, numbing my bones. The morning breeze transforms my face into an ice sculpture. I think of all that's been lost and what little's been found. How I once had a goal, a purpose. It all seems so trivial now. Void versus Verity. Light against darkness.

Some wars never end.

"Nice day for a swim."

I open my eyelids with a flutter.

"Are you inclined to float along the Grand like a carcass all day, or were you planning to assist me as you claimed you could?"

I make a point not to give him the satisfaction of eye contact, but my peripheral vision betrays me. "Oh, pardon me. Did you want my help? And here I was thinking you were trying to drown me." My tone is more Ebony's than my own. What can I say? Her snarkiness comes in handy when dealing with arrogant jerks.

"Nonsense. I merely desired to ensure you are not a Shadowalker."

I stare up at the Void's vessel himself. A Shadowalker? Really? He holds the darkest entity in existence and he's checking to make sure *I'm* not the dangerous one? Ha! I turn myself upright and face him fully. "And how would pushing me into a river ensure that?"

"For someone who professes to know a great deal, you appear to know very little indeed." He walks along the street at the speed of the current, hands clasped gracefully behind his back. "There is a rumor circulating that claims water reveals a Shadowalker's true self, its purity too potent for one in love with darkness to bear. I am simply testing the theory." He brushes his lapel with four fingers.

I begin my swim toward the edge. Toward Jasyn. "And?" I huff and heave. "Did you learn anything?"

He stops. Smirks. Then my grandfather crouches and offers me a hand up. Jasyn Crowe stoops to help me.

Unbelievable.

Suppressing the urge to pull him in, I take his outstretched hand, not even bothering to cover my soggy chest. When I'm sitting at street level, I wring out my hair, now a limp mop hanging past my shoulders. I cough and swallow. Draw in another long breath through my nose.

"No," Jasyn finally says, still crouching. "Either the rumor is false, or you are not a Shadowalker. No way of knowing."

My nose scrunches. "And what about the Void's vessel? Hmm? Water doesn't bother you. What in the Third would give you the absurd idea that water would reveal a Shadowalker and not the Void itself?"

"I believe you already hold the answer to that question."

He sounds more like Nathaniel now than the ruthless tyrant I recall. Speaking in vague riddles. I want to tell him to just answer the darn question. Instead, the lightbulb goes on. "Shadowalkers *choose* darkness. The Void's vessel doesn't have a choice." Aside from the choice to love the vessel of the Verity. But I guess, in a way, that *is* choosing light rather than darkness.

And there it is. A firm reminder of what I'm fighting for. I rise and Jasyn does the same. He hasn't chosen darkness, not yet. He's still fighting whether he admits it or not. Until he decides otherwise, I have to help him.

"... I wager we all hold a piece of the Verity ..."

Joshua's face. Kyaphus's voice.

"... a piece of the goodness that stems from the light empowering our Callings ..."

I try to imagine him, the one who actually spoke those words. But all I see is skin drenched in night, a pair of eyes that are hollow. Empty. A lost cause of a man who detests me as I detest him. Fine line between love and hate, right? Maybe it's hate that keeps the Void clinging to his soul. Maybe we had it wrong.

What if the Void's vessel is the one who despises the Verity? Did as much not happen between Aidan and the man standing before me now? He claims he doesn't hate the king. No way I believe that one.

Liar, liar. Pants on fire.

I consider my grandfather, search his eyes. I can almost imagine I'm staring at Mom. Does he see my resemblance to him? I wouldn't put it past him to somehow know everything. Nothing's ever been impossible for Jasyn Crowe. He doesn't need anyone.

Except maybe he does. Maybe he needs me. His eyes speak volumes, two windows overlooking a tortured soul. But his soul can't be gone if there's still life in his muddied gaze. And where there is life there is always hope.

Ding-dang-dong. Dong-dang-ding. A bell rings in the distance, summoning a slew of people to spill from their homes. Jasyn turns his focus to the canal while mine wanders in the opposite direction. It's as if the city is suddenly alive again, the residents emerging once the night no longer poses a threat. Do Shadowalkers prowl about under cover of the moon? What better time for one who bows to darkness to lurk within the very shadows they're named after?

When the echo of the bells dies in the distance, Jasyn faces me again. "Shall we?" His arms sweep inward toward the city. Both his eyebrows arch in question, wrinkling his forehead.

Rolling my shoulders, I purse my lips and nod. What have I got to lose?

As I follow my grandfather and future enemy through the streets of Venice, a small voice whispers in my ear.

"Everything," it says.

Everything.

And nothing at all.

❦

Jasyn hasn't spoken a word since we abandoned the Grand Canal. Venice teems with life, so different from the evening atmosphere when curfew goes into effect and people rush to the safety of their homes. Soldiers patrol the streets, faces straight as statues, eyes always ahead. Uniformed schoolchildren file into what appears to be a schoolhouse or church of some sort. All are girls and all wear solemn expressions with gazes downcast. They're led by a thin woman with a gray streak in her pinned hair, who could only be Miss Minchin from *A Little Princess*, bit-a-lemon expression and all.

The roads are narrow, the turns sharp and angular. The Grand Canal isn't the only body of water in this city, though it's the most famous. Rivers network this way and that, forming streets of their own. We cross several bridges on our way, each one arcing over another passage of water. The houses are crammed together and stacked high, offering a looming sensation of claustrophobia. Just when I think the walls will close in, we turn another corner and spill into an open square.

Jasyn doesn't stop, though my feet are glued into place. This takes the cake. Would definitely be on my Top Ten Things to See list (if I had one). I don't need an A in history and geography to recognize the landmark that is St. Mark's Basilica. YouTube doesn't do it justice. The cathedral is more magnificent than anything I've come across in New York, with domed roofs and steeples stretching for the clouds. Don't get me wrong, St. Patrick's is something else, but this is a sight to behold. Robbing my oxygen. Reminding me just how small I am.

Why would Jasyn bring me here? Are we even allowed inside?

The square isn't exactly bustling with tourists. In fact, the place is probably a target for enemy bombers. I'd bet a hundred lira we're not authorized to step within ten feet of the entrance.

Of course, rules have never hindered Jasyn.

I hurry to catch up, holding the fabric of my blouse out and away from my chest. A group of soldiers stand huddled by a military jeep-type vehicle. A few of the guys glance my way. Their eyes taper, but they must assume I don't pose a threat because after a few seconds, they turn their attention elsewhere.

"Is it not glorious?" Jasyn asks when we're side by side again. His neck is craned, face brighter than I've ever witnessed.

My breath catches. Because seeing him like this, an innocent joy blanketing his entire being, lights a small spark in me. Jasyn laughs then, full and deep. I can't recall ever hearing the sound come from his lips. It reminds me of . . .

Kuna.

Heart lurching at the memory of his death, I have a sudden ache to hug my best friend. The last time I saw Stormy was just after Kuna's Reminiscence. I didn't even say good-bye.

But maybe if I can help Jasyn and find my way back, someday I'll see her again.

My toes squish in my waterlogged sneakers as I take in the wonder before us, attempting to see it through my grandfather's eyes. Darkness plagues him but here he stands, reveling in architectural perfection. Joshua would love this.

Quiet sadness consumes me the longer we're apart. He said he would find me, so where is he?

"Come." Jasyn moves forward but veers right, heading for one side of the cathedral rather than the main entrance.

Nostalgia takes over, transporting me back to a night in New York. Joshua sneaking me into a famous theater. Me more nervous than I've ever been. Us. Singing. Laughing. Us as we were. Us as we should be.

As we may never be again.

No one hollers as we enter St. Mark's through a side entrance.

The guard standing *right there* doesn't even peek in our direction. My gut clenches, nausea threatening my last meal. But then I remember who I'm with and suddenly our ease of passage no longer racks my nervous system. Jasyn has cast a façade over us. We won't have any trouble because we're walking unseen. Is this how Makai feels when he's using his invisible Shield?

Invincible.

Inside waits a palace. My humble castle in the Second feels second rate in comparison. High ceilings and mosaics that remind me of Mom. And gold. So much gold. Everywhere. Adorning the atmosphere with warmth and light. I rub my arms, still damp from my soaked clothing. But, somehow, in here . . . I no longer notice the cold.

"This way." My grandfather seems to know his way around. He makes no move to pause as he works through the interior.

Our game of Follow the Leader continues. I glance over my shoulder now and then. Façade or none, it doesn't hurt to be extra cautious. Deeper into St. Mark's we wind, traveling up stairs, across a hall, then down a few more steps. At the end of one passage, a dull black door waits, out of place amongst so much brilliance. A lion's head the size of my fist guards the door's heart, and in its mouth a knocker begs to be used.

Jasyn stands aside. "Ladies first."

Without hesitation I take the knocker in my hand and rap it once. It's heavier than it appears. The solitary *clang* bounces off the walls around us.

Clank, shuffle, rattle. "Enter," a female voice calls from the other side. Have I heard that voice before?

"After you." Jasyn holds eye contact, unblinking.

After drawing in a deep breath, I shove the door open with my entire body. A chill passes over me as we exchange gold decor for emerald green. Green lamps, green chairs, green ashtrays on green tables. A hint of gold pops up every now and then, in the damask pattern on the sofa or the tassels on the Persian rug. The color combo keeps appearing. In the mirrorglass stones of the Fourth.

In the decor for my coronation in the Second. Now here? What gives?

When the door slams behind us, we venture deeper into the odd room. It's circular, with small nooks branching off to form half circles. One nook contains bookshelves and a cushioned bench, while another houses a round table and two chairs. Plants fill a third alcove, an indoor waterfall over a window playing backdrop, allowing natural light in from the outside.

"This is . . ."

"Amazing," Jasyn finishes for me. "Really quite something."

Adjectives elude me. I lick my lips and nod. The soothing sound of the waterfall tickles my ears. I move toward the miniature garden. Is that a Venus flytrap? I've never seen one up close before. The nearest I've ever come to one was in the old prop room at school. Of course the *Little Shop of Horrors* costume was huge. This little guy is tiny, like a flower bud.

"Don't get too close. She's been known to bite."

Jump. Whirl. A dwarf woman stands directly behind me. I recognize her in an instant.

"Greetings, Odessa." Jasyn gives her a small bow.

Odessa, the governor of the Sixth if I remember correctly, nods in turn. "Mr. Crowe. To what do I owe this pleasure?"

Jasyn meets us where we stand and places an arm around me. I almost shrug it off but think better of it. He hasn't done anything to hurt me. Yet.

"This is Elizabeth. It appears we all share a common goal."

Odessa eyes me. She's half my size. Why do I feel like Thumbelina in her presence? "Is that so?" She taps her toe and pushes her oversized round glasses up the bridge of her nose. How is it she looks just the same as she will years from now? When I saw her in the Fourth, she appeared to be middle-aged. Shouldn't she be younger?

"Her speech is unlike any I have ever heard." Though excitement hoists his words, they are far from rushed, each one spoken with precision. "I cannot place her accent or her odd choice of vocabulary. I have been all over, and yet she has confounded me, Dessa."

My cheeks flush. He speaks of me with awe. Dare I say reverence? What in the Reflections is going on?

Expression unchanging, he gazes down at me, arm still firm around my shoulders. "You are not from here, my dear. You are not from now."

Pulse patters. Breaths shorten. *Keep your mouth shut and your eyes open.* He knows. He knows, he knows. But he can't know everything. Otherwise we wouldn't still be here. Because if he understood I eventually become his demise, it'd be game over.

"And you are here because you want to know if she has passed through one of my cyclones?" Odessa—Dessa?—eyes me.

Cyclones?

"Nothing gets past you, Madam Governor." Jasyn laughs again. I'm getting used to the sound.

One long hushed moment turns into many. At last Odessa says, "I'm afraid I don't have your answer for where she came from, but I might have a way to get her back there. That is, if she is willing to aid us in our quest."

My throat tightens. Tears attempt to well but I shut them down. The smallest ray of hope lingers just below the surface of my heart. How very ironic. That Jasyn might be the one who gets me home.

"What quest?" I ask.

"I have a proposition for you, Elizabeth," Jasyn says. "You tell me what you know of the Void. Aid us in our goal, and we will assist you in returning to your time."

"And what is your goal?" What if all along the answers to being rid of the darkness waited in the past? "To destroy the Void?" What else could it be?

He shakes his head. "Patience, now. A gentleman never reveals his plans until the proper moment."

If only he knew just how ungentle he might become. But he wants to know more of the Void, and that's something. Maybe the good in him can be saved before it's too late. "Deal." I offer my hand and he shakes it. What can it hurt? It's not as if we're exchanging a Kiss of Accord. This isn't a binding contract, just a simple agreement between grandfather and granddaughter. "Now, how are we going to get me home?"

"How else?" His lips curl just enough his teeth almost show. "We walk." His head tilts toward Odessa.

Curiosity must manifest in my features, because the dwarf woman answers before I utter a word. "Time is a façade of its own . . ."

"And I am a master at seeing past façades," Jasyn finishes for her. "As an Amulet I create them, after all."

He doesn't explain his Calling or elaborate on what a façade is. He suspects I already know, and my lack of questioning only confirms it. Bianca said the Called have a way of recognizing each other. Is there something in me even without my Mirror? Something deeper I can't see?

"I know some of what you are," Jasyn continues, "though I do not fully grasp what it is you are capable of at the present time. I am familiar with light as much as I am with darkness. I recognize the Verity inside you."

Eyes close. Breaths deepen. Eyes open. Relief surges. No surprise here. The darkness was created from heartbroken light. Who better to recognize a Verity's vessel than a vessel of the Void?

"This era has a vessel in Aidan." He smiles, full and genuine. "Another time and place needs the vessel in *you.*" His hand on my shoulder makes the Verity dance within. His words are very Mufasa. Wise. Moving. Words I will never forget. "We must return you to those who rely on your light, just as we rely on Aidan. Dessa can help you. We can all help each other."

This side of him is a man I'm starting to like, which just goes to show none of us are born inherently evil. He wasn't born as what he became. He chose it.

What if I can help him choose the light? "And how do you suggest I return?"

"That is where I come in." Odessa turns. And walks into the waterfall.

The only thing on the opposite side is a window. How did she . . . ? Is she a Mirror? Can't be. She doesn't have a mark . . .

Jasyn elbows me. I turn my attention to him, then follow his gaze to the floor.

Holy Verity. Son of a crowe. How did I fail to miss this very important detail? Of all people I should've noticed it right away.

I leave Jasyn's side, follow the path of golden bricks winding throughout the room. They lead back to the door where we entered, then all the way up to the waterfall. Where they stop.

"Follow the yellow brick road."

Would it sound crazy if I said Jasyn sounded like the Tin Man just now? Probably. But he does need a heart. Or he will. What if . . . ? Nah. I shake my head. Don't go there. Because the yellow bricks are enough to contemplate already. I almost can't fathom it.

This is better than finding a reflection of New York.

Better than experiencing Atlantis firsthand.

Because I know where we're going, and I can't help but whisper a tune from my favorite musical of all time. "One short day . . . ," I breathe, the lyrics for my ears alone.

I'm going to the Emerald City.

I'm flying to Oz.

SEVENTEEN

KY

I saach is dead.

Breckan is fuming.

For a woman who's just lost her husband, I'd expect her to act more like a Soulless and less like the fierce warrior before us. The Nitegra tribe's new leader is anything but lifeless.

I fold my arms over my bare chest. The weight of the situation sinks in, a tangible heaviness turning the Void to lead. I wish I could discuss this with Em. Get her invaluable insight. Man, this sucks. I should feel compassion, empathy, anger. But without her I grow more numb, colder and harder. Without her I am the man I do not want to be.

Without her, I am Void.

"I'll kill 'em all. Ev'ry last one of 'em." Breckan stands on a boulder surrounded by her tribe. "I'll not rest 'til me husband's death be avenged and tha' wicked Troll's head lies on a platter." Breckan raises a spear to the gray sky. Strange symbols adorn her face in red paint that matches her hair. The effect causes her sapphire-colored eyes to appear as if they glow.

The tribe cries out, lifting their spears and shaking them, knuckles white against the wooden weapons.

"He will be avenged!" calls a bald man with war paint covering every inch of his skin.

"We're behind ya!" comes from a jeering woman with baseball mitts for hands.

"Lead tha way!" another shouts, though I can't distinguish who through the throng.

Despite my lack of emotion, I can't help but admire their sense of unity and purpose, a family banded together amidst tragedy. I've witnessed people fall apart over lesser things. But Breckan's tribe won't abandon her.

Isaach isn't the only fatality either. While those preparing to fight get riled, others transfer limp bodies covered with white canvas on handmade stretchers. My chest tightens when a stretcher passes me that can only be carrying a child. The stench of death is everywhere, injecting the air with iron and rust.

Relief comes as an exhale. I'm not all gone, not yet.

I glance at Khloe. She has uncharacteristically abandoned Ebony and Stormy to join a group of young women near her age. All have fiery hair similar to most of the tribe. All wear the colored strips of cloth attached to their clothes. My former second mate, Charley Hallen, isn't among the ladies. She remained behind when we left the compound the first time, but I haven't seen her since we arrived.

Another stretcher approaches and the muscle in my jaw pulses. Could Charley be among the lost? The Mask was essential to my crew on *The Seven Seas*, and she even helped push Em to the next level of her Mirror Calling. Without Charley, Em may not have discovered she could transform into a butterfly. I'll have to ask Breckan when she's finished motivating her recruits.

"This isn't jus' a crime against we Nitegrans," the woman goes on. "Oh nay. The Fifth as a unit is under attack, ain't it? Will ye stand by me in tha fight fer our freedom from the Troll's tyranny?"

Another series of shouts echoes across the crowd, a unanimous "aye" from the attendees.

What happened here is a message. A note written in blood. The Fairy Queen wants Elizabeth, and she'll keep wasting lives until she exacts her revenge. I shudder to think what would've happened had Isabeau known about my adoptive mother, Tiernan's true wife. I've only met Isabeau as a woman, never witnessed the

Troll firsthand. However, Makai relayed the details of Em's corona-tion attack. If the Fairy Queen appeared here in her most hideous state, I'd wager rage has overtaken her soul. Anger fuels the Void. Why would this be any different?

I tug my shirt from where it's tucked into my belt and wipe the sweat from the back of my neck. My nose runs and my eyes itch. I use my shirt to wipe my face as well. When yet another stretcher goes by, a lock of red hair snaking over the edge, a sense of dread runs through me.

"Wait." With an outstretched hand I appeal to the men carrying the deceased. "May I?" I have to know.

The carriers exchange a glance, then the one at the stretcher's head nods.

I hold my breath as I lift the top corner of the canvas. Bile rises into my throat. Of course she'd be one of the lost. If the Troll showed up, Charley would've been one of the first to take a stand.

"Thank you." I back away. Every muscle grows taut. The Void swirls in satisfaction at the close-to-home loss.

"See? Death is inevitable. Why fight what you know wins in the end?"

That's what you think. Charley was loyal to the Verity. In her case, death was merely a Threshold leading to the First Reflection.

"Another Fairy tale?" Kyaphus hisses. *"When will you cease listening to stories and learn to grow up?"*

I sling my sullied shirt over one shoulder. "Never."

"Rhyen."

I pivot on my heel to find the Commander.

He removes his bow and quiver, then proceeds to shrug out of his trench coat. "Just the man I have been looking for." He rolls his coat and ties it around his quiver like an oversized bandana, then returns his weapon and ammo to their perch on his back. "Twelve pronounced dead and over thirty injured. Isabeau is nowhere to be found, but she left the mark of her Troll behind. We have counted a dozen deceased Fairies already, but according to the tribe's Physic there is no sign of injury. It is as if they simply . . . died."

"Don't you see what's happening?" Josh, tone mocking, joins

us on Makai's other side. Until now he's been sulking by the compound's entrance with his hands tied behind his back and his tail between his legs. "The woman is desperate. Otherwise she would not leave the safety of her hiding places within the Fairy Fountains. This is not about revenge on El's mother alone. Her Majesty seeks something beyond what the satisfaction of vengeance can provide."

I raise a brow. Her Majesty, is it? "Care to let us in on what that something might be, Brother?"

His teeth clench at the term, but he doesn't growl this time. Way to go, Josh. Wasn't sure you had it in you to be a decent Homo sapien.

"How should I know? I retrieved her blasted Midnight Rose from the Fourth's countess, gave her a drop of my blood—"

Makai places a firm hand on his shoulder. "You gave her your blood? Why did you fail to mention this?"

Josh shrugs. "What does it matter? She's immortal and has no need for the commodity. However, she also fancies a barter. I assumed she wanted it for leverage in trade. I'm sure I am not the first to seek an item of rarity from her."

"And what item of *rarity* would that be?" I ask.

Josh pauses, then glances between us. My brother's eyes narrow, but I can tell he's finally going to give. We share a glare that feels longer than the second it lasts. Despite our differences. Despite the darkness clouding his soul. Despite his stubborn pigheadedness, we still share a common goal.

Find Em.

"A mirrorglass bottle," Josh says.

I grip the blade fastened to my side. Mirrorglass has a reverse effect. My tear on Em's lips . . .

"Son of a Soulless, David. Is that how you did it? By reversing her love and turning it into hatred?"

He smiles.

I will not punch him. He's not worth it.

"Well." Makai sighs, never fazed it seems. "That settles that.

We can come back to how to restore Eliyana's memory—ehm, feelings—at a later date—"

Josh laughs and a huddle of women frown. The heartless Ever doesn't give a Dragon's tail, though. "Restore? Do you presume I would be so careless? Do you believe I would go to such lengths for something that could simply be undone?" His eyes look crazed, wild, with pupils so dilated his dark irises appear almost completely black.

More Nitegrans swivel to gawk at Josh and his boasting. Apparently my brother's dark side has no gauge for propriety. Not that I've ever been one to care what others think, but this is different. People have *died*. People we know. Show some respect, man.

Makai's mouth turns down. "I would like to speak to Joshua for a moment, if you don't mind."

Josh guffaws at the request. "He's gone." His eyes darken more, if possible. "And he's never coming back."

"Nonsense." Makai pulls his gray hair into a short ponytail and secures it at his neck. "Nothing is permanent. Not even death."

My breathing sharpens at his words. I can't hear the line without my mother's voice taking over. How could I forget? The phrase is from *The Lament of the Fairy Queen*. The ending had been lost to me.

Until now.

I step away from the pair.

"Be reasonable." Makai appeals to the man behind the shadows. "Let's talk this out like men . . ." His voice fades the farther I retreat. No doubt his pleadings are met with more sarcasm and disrespect.

I roll my eyes. Will Mr. Invisibility Shield never learn? Not everything can be dealt with by talking it through. Sometimes action is more effective than conversation. I've no desire to be insubordinate, but every bone, every muscle in my body is telling me to step in and take charge. And no, that's not the Void in me. It's simple common sense. We've tried talking to him. What Josh needs is to put his sword to my knife. No interferences. No referees. A little blood and sweat never hurt anyone.

Suppressing a sneeze instead of the Void for once, I creep farther away from the crowd. Shouts of agreement remain audible in the distance, but not so loud I can't think. When I reach the cliff where Em and I sat beneath the stars our night here, I sit with one leg bent and the other dangling over the cliff's edge. Then I withdraw *Once Upon a Reflection* from my pack.

My mother's copy was newer, the words typeset rather than handwritten. This edition could be the original or simply a copy penned by a Scrib. Hers may have been more generic, but she still treated it as if it was sacred text, turning each page carefully and smoothing it out before reading.

I do the same as I peruse. Countess Ambrose was gracious enough to lend this to me, knowing we might need the allegories on our journey to the Garden of Epoch. Interesting that both *The Scrib's Fate* and *The Lament of the Fairy Queen* (or *The Fairy Queen's Lament*, depending on the version and who you ask) appear to be about Isabeau, the original Verity's vessel herself. How many other stories in this book reference her? Could all be related?

At *The Lament of the Fairy Queen* I don't even pause, scanning each page for the line Makai uttered. Where is it? My sister wept every time she heard the tragic tale. Even though Isabeau's immortality seemed a fate worse than death, the phrase gave Khloe hope that death was not the end. Not for my mother. Or Kuna. Or Isaach. Or Charley.

On the tale's final page, I'm at a loss. The quote is absent. My gaze wanders to the next story over. Only a page in length, the title is scribbled as if written in haste. *The Fountain.*

As in Fountain of Time? Why don't I remember this? I read it through, my mind taking me back to a night at the Haven when Em discovered my birth mother's *Mirror Theory*. When she took down those Soulless, her voice carrying across the sand to the south and the waves to the north, I knew I'd never be able to look at her the same.

Hair falls into my eyes as I shake my head and center my focus.

There once was a girl who could not die . . .

Isabeau? Perhaps this really is all connected.

She would prick her finger but never bleed. She climbed to the top of a mountain, but when she jumped, she landed in a patch of the softest grass, not a scratch to be seen. The girl tried everything. Try as she may, she could not harm her physical being . . .

This has immortality written all over it.

The girl searched far and wide for death, but it was nowhere to be found. Life was her curse. And the longer she lived, the more her heart broke into a thousand unbreakable pieces . . .

I don't question why my mother censored most of this. Khloe hates sad stories, and this one takes the cake.

Her only hope for relief rested in the dew of a single rose. For any soul who drank from its petals would be given the chance to save one life. If she could find someone to save hers, she would be free, proving that nothing is permanent, not even life . . .

Wait, isn't that backward? Why would my mother change the line?

To give you stupid, feeble, good-for-nothing hope, that's why.

Let Kyaphus have his fun. Soon I'll be the one laughing.

I slam the book shut, jump to my feet, and sprint back to the camp. Makai and Josh are exactly as I left them.

"Do not defy me, Shadowalker," Makai says, voice escalating. "I told you—"

I grab Makai's shoulder and gasp for a true breath. Their argument can wait.

His eyes widen and he lifts my pack from my shoulders, then sets it on the ground at our feet. "What is it? What's happened?"

Clutching the book, I shove it toward him. "The Midnight Rose," I pant. "It's not exactly what Dahlia claimed. Not even close."

Relief softens the Commander's face. "You mean the flower is not a weapon? Drinking its dew will not cause one to slumber forever?"

I straighten and open the tome, show him my findings.

"The Midnight Rose is the Fountain of Time," he says. "The dew from the Rose is the Fountain water. They're one and the same."

"We've been right on one thing." I gulp another breath. "Saving Isabeau from the heartbreak she experienced is key. We stop the Void from being created, we save her."

"Yes," Makai says. "Except Regina claimed it would put my wife to sleep. Why?"

I shrug. "A rumor. A legend. Who knows? We've all had our turn at being wrong. But the answer's been here." I punch the book with one finger. "Right under our noses."

"But according to the end of the story, the dew must either come from the Garden of Epoch"—the Commander rubs his chin, then stoops to knot his bootlaces—"or be replicated with another life-giving entity."

"Ever blood." Josh stares off into space. "So that's what the hag was up to." He scratches the back of his head, and I almost see David. "I put what she needed right in the palm of her hand."

"What of the Fountain?" Makai straightens. "The ending explains . . ."

"'Where the soul's deepest desire meets another's deepest need,'" I finish for him. I know the rule well. Only now am I beginning to fully grasp what my own drink of Fountain water—Rose water—really meant. Was it Isabeau that day on my ship? Couldn't have been. The hooded stranger seemed to know my desire along with Em's need. Who . . . ?

Elizabeth? The timeline fits. She was on her way to the Fourth, maybe the Fifth afterward? This is crazy.

Or maybe it isn't. Maybe . . . this makes perfect sense.

"We stick to the plan then." Makai is business as usual, failing to sense the internal. "We still remain unaware exactly what the Troll seeks. If she is not after my wife, what does she want?"

Someone to break her curse. I hate to admit it, but as much as I want the Void gone, I want Em more. We need her now more than ever.

"She's looking for Eliyana," I say, my tone flat. "Her deepest desire will match up with Isabeau's greatest need. Em wants the Void gone more than anyone, and as she's the Verity's vessel, her intentions are the purest."

"I still don't want Isabeau anywhere near Elizabeth," the Commander notes. "In case we are wrong on this once again. We are trusting a story. A story that could have been penned by the Fairy Queen herself. At this point I do not want to take any more chances than we must."

Fair enough. "Keep Streak, Flint, and Robyn here with you." I'd make Wren stay too, but she may be useful in getting Josh to work with us. And we need Josh. David's soul is linked to Em's too. We've a better chance at finding her with him than without him. "I'll take the elder Song, Preacher, David, and Dahlia."

"Streak is casting a façade over the compound now." Makai surveys the area, in full Commander mode now. "Though I doubt a mere illusion will keep the immortal out. I will converse with Breckan and make her aware of our new findings." He takes his leave without another word.

Josh sneers as if he's won some sort of victory. I ignore my brother and find my "real" sibling. Khloe and Ebony, along with Tide and Stormy, prepare to go their own way. I share the new information, watching Ebony's eyes grow with every word.

"Then this can't wait until morning. I need to find her now." Ebony shoulders a pack filled with new supplies. It almost topples her and Tide yanks it away, taking the burden with ease.

"Everything can always wait until morning." I don't say what we're both thinking. Her existence relies on Isabeau's. If the Void was never created, what becomes of Ebony? "We've all had a trying couple of days." Has it really been forty-eight hours since Em vanished? "One more night's sleep won't kill us."

Besides, I've yet to talk to Dahlia. She'll probably opt to remain with Elizabeth, and I need to convince her she'll be of more use heading out with us. Her knowledge of the Thresholds is vital to our journey. I'll need her full report. Breckan's got scouts combing the Reflection. One of them must have returned with news of the water levels. If I'm correct, the Thresholds are draining in a pattern, from each Reflection to the next, and all within a day of the other. I need to run it by Tide—the resident genius of the group, though he'd hardly admit to it—but I'm almost certain the Threshold in Nabka Compound will become a wormhole around sunrise. It's a three-hour journey from here. If we set out early, we should arrive just in time to make the jump as it drains.

"Miss Elizabeth'll be jus' fine now, don't y'all worry." Dahlia comes up behind me, wagging a finger at no one in particular. She sniffs and swipes at her nose, red-rimmed eyes a clue she's definitely coming down with something.

I open my mouth to ask about the Thresholds, but the woman talks over me.

"And you four." She nods toward Tide, Khloe, Ebony, and Stormy. "Y'all get some shut-eye before makin' yer way to the Fountain. Fastest way is to travel southeast through Nabka Forest. There's a shortcut through this here compound."

"Dahlia, I—"

"And as for us"—she slings an arm around my shoulder, standing on her toes so she doesn't drag me down—"we best be gettin' on with bed. Now that we know more about the Rose, we'll want to be getting to Nabka Threshold in top condition. Me and Flint think it's the finest option for what we're trying to accomplish with wormhole jumping and all."

Well, I guess that answers that question. No wonder she was wrong about the Rose. She's all talk and no listen.

"But like I said, sleep first. Verity knows, we need it. If I was lied to about the Rose, who knows what else my old-woman brain has missed. Just goes to show even Evers ain't perfect." She chuckles and walks away, taking cover in a nearby tent.

Everyone else disperses, the Nitegra tribe welcoming us with all the hospitality they can give. I choose a spot beneath a scarce tree. I'll wait until things die down. Then I'll find Gage. I know he's here. It's just a matter of weeding him out.

I settle in and my brain runs rampant through the day's events. I shudder to think of what will happen if Isabeau finds Em first. Will she use her, then kill her? She'd win on all counts in that case. End her immortal curse and slice Elizabeth with the deepest cut imaginable. Our mission is more important now than ever. The Fountain of Time is our answer to everything.

"Don't fool yourself," my unmentionable side taunts. *"If a drink of the Rose's water was a magic fix, why wouldn't Isabeau use it for herself? Her deepest desire is to save herself. Why not drink the dew and reverse the curse on her own?"*

"That's the catch, isn't it?" I utter beneath my breath. According to *The Scrib's Fate*, only one pure of heart can enter the Garden. If the Rose came from the Garden, perhaps the drinker's heart must be pure as well.

My veins throb, the pain in my Void-infested body becoming harder to ignore. I withdraw my mirrorglass blade and make a small incision on each forearm. Black blood oozes from the cuts, relieving some of the pressure in my shaking arms. The blood's deathly scent is pungent, making my stomach churn. If anyone else notices, they make no mention. Good. We have more important things to tend to than the bleeding Void's vessel.

I remove the vial from my pocket and roll it between my fingers. Watch as Wren and David argue twenty feet away. She's guarded him like a hawk—griffin—since we left the cottage. Maybe she can reach into his dark soul and withdraw whatever measure of David is left. Makai thinks it's up to me. But if I'm being honest? I'm pretty sure only one person can bring David back from the dark place he's journeyed.

We need you, Em.

A familiar sense of warmth and acceptance wraps me. I almost feel the Void disappear. My wounds have closed, the black blood dried on my skin. I sense her beside me as I stand and set out through the camp.

Pure intentions, huh? Guess we'll just see about that.

EIGHTEEN

ebony

I can't believe he actually left his junk and walked away. How perfectly convenient Ky Rhyen has more important things on his mind than his smelly old backpack. He takes this thing everywhere? Has he ever washed it?

I pinch the straps. Hold it out and away from my body. From the odor wafting off of it, I'd say that's a big fat *no*. Too bad he keeps his mirrorglass knife strapped to his side. It'd be cool just to see how it works.

"If you bothered to ask, my brother would probably let you see it. No problem."

The words Khloe would say, if she were awake, ping the conscience I've been hearing more often as of late. Oddly enough, it's always Khloe's voice I hear when I'm doing something less than noteworthy. When did I let that kid get under my skin?

"First day we met, duh."

And there she is again, speaking truth. She may be slightly correct. Rhyen probably *would* allow me to look at his books, his knife, if I simply bothered to submit the request. But he's gone off somewhere, and his pack full of reading material is just sitting here for anyone to look through. I'm doing him a favor by keeping it safe, taking it back to my tent with me.

That's what I'm telling myself anyway.

My return stroll through the compound is unpresuming. Tiptoeing isn't my thing. Besides, I'm not some criminal. Don't want to draw attention to myself as if I am either. Nah. I'm simply a girl who's about to do a little late-night reading, if you don't mind.

When I'm ten feet away from the tent's entrance, Tide's shoulders start to shake. One thing I love—*like*, I mean *like*—about him is the way he can see the light in things. His mother was murdered recently, and here he is, poking fun at me.

"Did a little shopping, did you?" He stands and blocks the entrance, folding his arms over his chest and casting one of his loose grins. "What is it you girls call it these days? Vintage?"

A kick in the ribs would do him some good. Instead, I hug the bag tighter, attempt to squeeze by. "Rhyen asked me to hold on to it for him."

"Is that right?" One of his eyebrows arches higher than the other, disappearing beneath a tangle of black hair. "Then by all means." Stepping to the side, he sweeps a hand and lifts a canvas flap. "Be my guest."

I roll my eyes, make an annoyed sound at him in my throat that comes out something like "Ugkh," lower my head, and stoop inside.

"Don't let the door hit you on your way to Liarville," he says behind me, lets the flap fall.

It doesn't hit me. Ha. Who's laughing now?

"Liar, liar, pants on fire." His singsong chanting sends heat up my neck and over my ears.

"Shut up," I hiss through my teeth. *Nice. Real smooth, Ebony. Where'd you come up with that one?*

Tide peeks his head through the sliver at the center. "Your wish is my command." He winks. Then he's gone again.

I stick out my tongue the moment his head disappears, then suck it back in. Impossible, stubborn boy. Look how you're making me act. I've said it before and I'll say it again—this crushing teenage girl is so not me. Why can't he leave me alone? I'm perfectly fine by myself, thanks. No room for a couple here. It's just me, myself, and I.

Ugh, except it's not anymore, is it? I set the book bag down and cover a sleeping Khloe with the wool blanket she managed to kick off in the five minutes I was absent. Brushing her spring curls off her round, baby-doll face, I kiss her forehead. She smells like dirt and more dirt, but beneath that lies her true scent. The little-girl one that goes away when you reach the age of fifteen or so. I can't deny I love her. How much longer can I keep lying about what I feel for Tide?

Long enough to get some things done at least. Back to business, I sit cross-legged on a woven rug. My fingers run over the threads in lilac and azure, indigo and sky. Same colors the Nitegrans wear on the corners of their garments. Colors representing the Verity.

My perfect-shade-of-semisweet-chocolate hair falls into my eyes. The braids have loosed throughout the day, leaving me with what can only be described as travel hair. I remove the ties from my ends, comb my fingers through the new waves. My hair has always done exactly what I wanted. Photo ready at any and every moment. Never needing much product or teasing. My hair just is. The envy of other girls, but still never good enough for my mother.

"Why did you have to look like him?" she'd scream on one of her rampages through our trome at the time. *"You know I wanted to name you Star? Then you were born and I took one look at you and realized you aren't a star at all, but a black hole sucking the life out of everything."*

Five. I was five the first time she said that to me. A five-year-old black hole of a girl whose name matched the color of her mother's heart. And, soon, my own.

Now the colors are returning. Scarlet lifts my cheeks with each blush. And yes, I've got stars in my eyes every time Tide looks my way, though I can always hope he's got Oblivious Guy Syndrome and fails to notice. Maybe it's time I add a new shade to the mix.

I tear off a fraying strip of fabric from the rug's edge, then fashion a braid from my chin-length bangs, using the fabric as the third strand. When it's secure I tuck it behind one ear. What would my mother say if she saw me now?

Correction—what *will* she say? Because I *am* going to find her.

And she *will* give me answers about who or what I am, on top of answers about everything else we've failed to discover about the Void and the Verity. If it's the last thing I do. Which it just may be.

Now that everything's in its place, I snatch *Once Upon a Reflection* from Rhyen's pack. I've been dying to get my hands on this book since I learned the story Rhyen read to us in the Fourth was actually about my mom. Then there's the new info about the Rose, a.k.a. Fountain of Time. I need to read more. To see if there are other passages that can give me some clue as to who she is and was—

The open tome slides forward over my calves and the spine hits the floor. I already know who she is, don't I? Why do I need some storybook to tell me? Do I really believe I'll find something hopeful among children's tales?

Yes and no.

I mean, for the love of lace, this very tent reeks of her blood-stained fingertips. We were offered the humble accommodation by one of the Nitegran men. He lost his wife today. His *pregnant* wife. With twins. The man couldn't bring himself to sleep here without her. I reluctantly accepted his kindness, though the pain covering his face cut me deep.

My witch of a mother did this. How much hate must consume her soul?

A flipping truckload, that's how much.

My own soul softens. That's the thing, isn't it? She hates because she was hated. She tortures because she is tortured. She must really believe if she'd given Tiernan a son, he wouldn't have left her. But El's mom said it was finding out what my mother is capable of that scared my father away. Isabeau probably doesn't want to admit as much to herself, though. I sure wouldn't. Much easier to believe a son would've solved all her problems than to accept she was merely one of Tiernan's playthings.

I feel sorry for her and I don't, all in the same emotion. Do I have any chance of breaking through her wall? I'm either the most likely person to reach her or the last person in the Reflections she'll listen to.

Guess I'll find out which one I am soon enough.

Khloe stirs, rolling onto her stomach and cocooning herself in the wool blanket against the far side of the tent.

Tide sneezes just outside.

I stare down at the tilted open book. To read or not to read. Does it make a difference?

"You girls okay?" His head looks like it's floating apart from his body. Does he ever stop hovering?

"We're *fine.*" My eyes widen. Get the point already.

"I'll guard my girls with my life. Don't forget it." Then he vanishes once more.

I give him five minutes before he pops his head back in. The guy is like a puppy.

A cute puppy.

So what if I flushed when he said *"my* girls"? I won't admit I wish he'd left the *s* off.

My girl. His girl. Tide's girl. Mmm.

Yuck. Eye roll. Gag me. We're not happening. Do I even want us to happen? Tide is so unkempt and laid back. Definitely much too careless for my taste. He laughs way too much and his hair needs a trim. He's . . . he's . . . perfect.

Sigh. *Just admit you're falling for him and get over yourself.*

No and way.

I draw the book into my lap once more, thumb through the thick pages. I'm not a reader. I mean, I can read, but mostly I prefer to stay away from things that make me look too smart. People take advantage of that sort of thing, you know? Besides, I'm no Scrib, and too many little words on one page make my eyes cross. I'd much rather watch a play or listen to a story. Let someone else do the work while I sit back and enjoy.

Except for tonight. Tonight, just this once, under cover of this tent, I will let my inner nerd come out.

I start with *The Lament of the Fairy Queen.* Or *The Fairy Queen's Lament.* Both titles are listed on the page, each in different handwriting. Apparently someone has gone through after the original author and scribbled a bunch of notes. Isn't that a mortal book sin or something? The story is penned in black ink, but the notes are made in bright blue. What a mess. The notes are so detailed, the story almost gets lost. I flip through the other chapters. The blue scribbles are everywhere. How did Ky even read this to us with so much scrawl in the margins and between the lines?

I flip another page, then another. Every few stories, the handwriting and ink color change slightly. Different authors with different pens, but none as vibrant as the blue ink continuing to scrawl the pages until the end. There waits a . . . what? A poem? A riddle? A letter? A bit of all three, it seems, and penned entirely in the same hand and ink as the notes throughout.

Heartsong. Author deceased.

Author *deceased*? Then how in the Fifth did this story get written?

Oh . . .

This is a death note. I shouldn't read this. But whoever wrote it wanted it read. Otherwise they wouldn't have put it in this book in the first place.

Dear reader . . .

Tide clears his throat outside.

I stare at the tent opening. Cue the watchdog . . .

Three, two, one. When he doesn't appear, I release the breath I was holding and continue my read.

If you've discovered this page,
You've sensed my appeal,
For the tale I pen here is horrid yet real.
What breaks with a touch but is stronger than steel?
The heart, don't you know, oh how lovely to feel . . .

What is this? Satire? A joke? The style reminds me of some silly children's book. Did whoever wrote this expect to be taken seriously? I mean, seriously, for all the profoundness of *The Scrib's Fate*, you'd think you could expect a little more literary and a little less nursery rhyme.

> *Yes, how lovely to feel,*
> *But how tragic to know*
> *The death of one's heart,*
> *When broken like so.*
> *A thousand and one pieces,*
> *Or a million at most,*
> *Transform Her Excellency*
> *Into a rotting old ghost . . .*

A rotting old ghost? I'm trying really hard not to LOL. This is ridiculous.

> *Yes, Her Grace's heartsong is tragic but true,*
> *But worse than her fate*
> *Is the one coming for you.*
> *Don't miss the signs,*
> *They've been there all along,*
> *For as mere glass will shatter,*
> *Her heart remains strong.*

"Need anything?"

I'm impressed. He waited a whole ten minutes. I'm about to say, "No and puh-lease just go to bed." But then, "Actually, yeah. Come here."

He cocks his head.

Eye roll. "Fine. *Please*, come here."

Does he have to smile at me like that? Why does he insist on sitting so close? I try to ignore his way-too-nearness. Pretend his very presence annoys me. Which it does, but not in the way I would have him believe. "What do you make of these?" I show him the book.

He gives me a look. "The stories?"

Must I explain everything? "No, genius." He really is a genius, but I'm not about to boost his ego. It would only make things worse. "I mean the blue writing. I can't make sense of it."

"You really need to get some sleep, Eb. You're starting to hallucinate."

"You can't see it?"

"All I see is a beautiful girl in need of some rest. No blue writing. Just a blue girl who needs a mom."

Ouch. Compliment turned soul seeing. Can I take a rain check? I'd rather not get all feely right now. Or ever. Thanks.

He takes the book, closes it, returns it to Ky's pack, and shoves it outside the tent. "I'll watch for Cap's return."

How adorable is it he still refers to my sister's boyfriend as Cap? Not at all. No.

"You go to bed. Stormy's going to take over watch in an hour or so. I'll get a bit of shut-eye, then wake you both when it's time to head out."

"I can wake myself." I narrow my eyes, crawl over to Khloe. I don't utter another word to the boy who's constantly on my mind, because hello, who has time for that?

"Good night," he says in the sweetest way ever.

Good night, I think but can't bring myself to say. I lie wide awake, staring at the plain canvas above. I think of the blue ink Tide can't see and of coming face-to-face with my mother for the first time in years.

It's enough to drive a girl insane.

NINETEEN

I walk with Him

I 'm home.

I blink and blink and blink some more. Still the scene before me remains. I'm standing in the Second again. It appears the waterfall we passed through wasn't a waterfall at all but a Threshold. I suspected, of course, but couldn't know for sure until it brought me from there to here.

And here is home.

I know it's the Second Reflection with my first inhale. If the Second's winter was captured in a candle, this would be the number one Etsy bestseller. My lungs absorb the scents of basil and pine with a hint of chestnut wood. The unfamiliar stream before us babbles, snow melting the closer we come to spring. The trees are thicker here, the earth softer than that of the castle grounds or the constantly trodden paths of the Haven. I don't have to visit where I've been in the past to know where I am at present. The tromes spaced throughout the forest around us are just one clue to our whereabouts. This place has a feel to it unlike any other. This Reflection takes the Tony over New York any day. The difference between a great performance and one that leaves you breathless, drawing you to your feet with tears in your eyes because, oh my word, I've never been so moved.

I. Am. Home.

My heart turns over in my chest. Is this the first time I've referred to the Second as home? Maybe it takes being away to realize how much I've missed something. When I return to my time,

I think I'll finally be ready to accept what I have perhaps known all along.

I was meant for the Second. I want to deny it, but my heart isn't in Manhattan any longer. It's with those I love. There's nothing left for me in the Third. And I'm okay with that.

We exit the stream, follow Odessa to the center of a grassy field. Mud and sod camouflage our shoes. Water drips from our clothes, quenching the ground's thirst.

Odessa says nothing.

I watch Jasyn for some signal as to what's coming. Some warning as to what exactly Odessa meant by one of her "cyclones." Ahem. "Is cyclone a metaphor or an actual—?"

Whip. Swirl. Jerk. Well, that answers that question. Good-bye, oxygen. It was nice knowing you.

"So this is what dying feels like!" My shout is gone with the wind. As is Jasyn. And Odessa. I could say anything and no one would hear. No one would care. My deepest secrets could be divulged and the cyclone would keep them forever.

"Sometimes I wish none of this had ever happened!" I cough, choke, gag. Keep screaming. "A part of me doesn't want to remember! Doesn't want to love the Second! Doesn't want any of it!" Normally the projected confessions would rumble through me. But the wind screams louder, numbing me, putting me to sleep. "Sometimes I wish I could forget everything and go back to the way things were!"

On the final cry the breath is ripped from my body. Sort of like drowning, but way more brutal. A punch to my throat. I'm choking while still fully conscious.

Jasyn *had* to have known what would happen, the Cretan. Thanks for the warning, Gramps. Don't mind me. I'm just the girl swept up in a whirlwind of dust without warning, carried into the sky by a cyclone straight out of Kansas. I suppose I expected something a little more original. Silly me.

Oh, it doesn't take a Scrib to figure out that Odessa is a wind Magnet. Still, nice to learn there's another option for traveling between Reflections. Except I won't ever use it again if I can help it. Thresholds I can handle. Mirrors are a cinch. But twisters? Now that's a horse of a different color.

Slam. Oof. Choke. Cough. Gasp. Ugh.

Ground? We're on the ground! The dust clears and oh, I could kiss these dirty bricks beneath me. I rise and stick my finger in one ear. I twist hard, attempting to get rid of the resounding ring. The howling wind turned my eardrums into ear cymbals. But worse than my newly contracted tinnitus is the constant cough. Give me drowning over wind suffocation any day.

Odessa said I didn't end up in the former Third due to one of her cyclones. Well, thank the Verity for that. Once is enough. With the cough and ear ringing, I might as well have aged thirty years.

I dust off my clothes, scrape the crusted dirt from my shoes. My hair has a lovely dusting of, you guessed it, more dust. I flip it over then back, shake out as much as I can. Once I'm as dirt free as possible, I take in my new surroundings.

They're nothing like I pictured.

Don't get me wrong—the city is unlike anything I've witnessed.

"Everything is green." I can't help but speak the thought. Forest and lime and turquoise and mint. Seaweed and chartreuse and hunter and pear. And, of course, emerald. Because, yeah. Duh. Except . . .

Every hue is tainted, dingy. Worn. Old. Faded. As if the entire city has been run through the wash and hung out to dry more than a few times.

"What do you think?" Jasyn withdraws a handkerchief from his blazer pocket and releases a quiet cough. Evil or slightly less, he's forever the gentleman. "Is it not extraordinary?"

Blink. Wheeze. Sniff. "Are we in the Sixth?"

"We are indeed." He folds the handkerchief into a triangle. Pockets it once more. "How can you tell?"

"Lucky guess." No need to add I came to the conclusion by process of elimination. Still unsure how much I should and shouldn't tell him.

Soft music plays through speakers attached to lampposts. Not the happy, joyous, Oz-ish overture I'd expect, though. This soundtrack is more akin to elevator or grocery store music. Dull and quiet and not at all happy. A hypnotic and creepy lullaby.

My spine crawls. This isn't the Oz I've imagined so many nights in my sleep. Definitely not the inspiration to the times I broke out in a chorus of "Defying Gravity" within the safety of my shower. The dark sky and numerous artificial lights give this place the feeling of being underground. Reminds me of a book I read for school in fifth grade. *City of Ember*, I think it was called.

Ember. How fitting.

"*I think I will call you Ember,*" Joshua said once. "*I've decided it suits you better than your first name . . .*"

I search for the rest of the conversation. What was it he said next?

"*An ember is neither fire nor ash. Smoldering but not truly alive.*"

Ouch. The truth hurts, doesn't it? I've changed since, learned what it truly means to live. But now, inside the walls of this dying city, I feel more Ember than ever.

"This way." Odessa *click-clacks* forward, guiding us up and down bustling streets of dull yellow brick. The people here seem to live in the same era we left behind. Bowler hats and pin curls, A-line skirts and saddle shoes. It's like stepping into the 1940s but in Technicolor. Except something is wrong with the screen and the only shade coming through is green.

Did I mention everything is *green*?

Odessa squints over her shoulder. "Keep up, please. We don't have all day."

I'm starting to think her nose is permanently turned up. Though, to be fair, most of the residents seem a bit snobbish. Not a wave or kind greeting to be found. Now I really know I don't miss New York as much as I used to. The thought of eye-contact avoidance used to be endearing. Now I long for Robyn's warm smile. Stormy's melodic laughter. Even Ebony's eye roll would satisfy my need for human contact.

As if on cue, Jasyn and I exchange a glance. He smiles, and I find it easy to return the wordless salutation. Am I growing fond of him? Are my teenage grandfather and I becoming . . . friends? I stare down at my soggy shoes. Better not get too attached, just in case.

The buildings aren't clusters of thin domed towers like so many artists have depicted. Instead, they're like any other, made of bricks and windows and peeling paint. I understand the need for green-tinted eyeglasses now. In the book the wizard ordered everyone to wear them, his ploy to make the city out to be more than it appeared. Now I sort of wish I had those glasses. Maybe they'd help Oz seem like less of a disappointment.

"Left up here," Odessa instructs before making a sharp turn around the nearest corner.

I try to keep up, stepping on a cat's tail in my attempt. The feline screeches, then scrams. This road smells of used mop water. Mop water that was used to clean some other city, then drained here.

My gaze travels up, up, up. Stained-green windows might look like glimmering emeralds if they were polished. Instead, they're cracked and faded, appearing more as if they're made of mold than gems. And don't get me started on the road. Aside from the odor, the yellow bricks are closer to broken teeth than the golden pathway to a city of dreams. No one smiles, proud to be a member of this society.

"Nice try, wise guy. Now, skedaddle." A police officer in a winter-green uniform drags a Munchkin in handcuffs from an old-fashioned car. "We ain't got all day." His accent is very New Jersey with a Brooklyn undertone.

"Penny for a poppy, miss?" A woman in jade rags sells wilting poppies at the mouth of an alley.

I offer a kind smile. "No, thank you."

Instead of returning my gesture, she glowers. Her stare could kill the flowers in her basket.

This is Oz? Where's the sparkle? The wonder? The wizard?

A sudden sinking feeling in my gut tells me exactly where

Odessa leads us. I'm Dorothy minus the braids and terrier. Except I know how the story ends. I know the wizard isn't the man he claims to be. Besides, in my experience, men with that much power at their fingertips aren't to be trusted.

I glimpse my young grandfather from the corner of my eye. Even King Aidan is up for question now that I've met Jasyn prior to the Era of Shadows. No one is innocent. I'll never believe anything is black and white now that I've seen so much gray.

A car horn blares and I jump, nearly knocking Jasyn into a rusty statue of a . . . monkey? With wings. Not a good sign. Winged monkeys are the bad guys. There should not be statues of them stationed at every street corner. I gulp.

Jasyn steadies me. "You have to keep your wits about you in this place." He keeps his hand on my back, forcing me to match his pace. I can't tell if he's being protective or assuring I don't run away.

We turn one corner, then another. An evergreen stoplight (golight?) marks our next turn onto a street dubbed Pastoria Lane. This avenue is busier than the others, decked mostly with shops and other businesses. A tattoo parlor with flashing green lights in the windows. A diner with a neon-green arrow sign that says "Eat at Moe's." Two plump women exit a salon, hair set in perfect curls with green pins stuck in. We pass them just in time to hear one titter.

"Did you see Winnie's new beau?" Hand to her cleavage, she produces an air of pure shock. "I never! Imagine, a human breeding with a Munchkin."

Her friend nods, lips pinched, hanging on every word the other says.

Is Odessa bothered by their small-minded gossip? I can't see her face, so it's difficult to decipher if she heard.

"Pay them no mind," Jasyn says, pressing his palm into my back. "Just a couple of old crows on about the latest gossip. Odessa has heard it all before."

At the street's end lies a circular square, and at its crest looms a building that could only be governmental with its iconic columns and domed roof. It could almost be mistaken for a cathedral in

Tuscany, but much less grand and not at all pretty. Cold. Structured. Not a place I'd visit by choice.

And we're headed straight for it.

Odessa has to take two mini steps on every stair up to the main double doors. What did Jasyn call her before? Governor? Perhaps she's in charge here. The thought should make me feel more secure. Too bad it doesn't.

A security guard sporting a pea-colored jacket with brass buttons eyes her through a pair of comical square glasses. "What's your business here, Munchkin?"

Rude. She has a name, guy.

Odessa pushes her own petite glasses up her nose, apparently not at all bothered by the guard's degradation attempt. "I'm here to speak with Her Grace."

"Do you have an appointment?" The man is tall, but his nasally voice makes him less intimidating.

"Now is not the time for prejudice, Reginold. Think what you want of my people, but I assure you we were not responsible for the most recent Shadowalker attack."

Shadowalkers lurk here too? Is it the same throughout the Reflections?

"Of course they weren't." Reginold's assurance does not match his cynical manner. "Just like you Munchkins had nothing to do with the southern drought. You think because you have a longer life span than the rest of us, you own the place. Slower to age doesn't equal a higher intelligence, shrimp."

Now he's gone too far. I don't know Odessa well, but no one deserves to be treated with such disdain.

Ouch. *Hypocrite.* I treated Ky that way, didn't I? But wasn't my disdain somewhat justified? I mean, he did make me black out and shove me into the back of his car. I'd say I have more than a little right to hold something against him.

The fists I'm just realizing my hands have formed loosen. What is wrong with me? If I can argue justification in hatred, what's to keep anyone and everyone else from doing the same?

Nothing. And this, oh my chronicles, *this* is where the birth of a Shadowalker begins.

Even I, the vessel of the Verity, am not immune. No more than the original vessel was able to stop the darkness once she chose to release it. Well, hate to break it to you, dark side, but I won't be giving in to my Vader anytime soon. The change starts now. Whatever Kyaphus did, I choose not to hate him. I choose to let it go.

"Blaming the Sixth's problems on us won't change anything." Odessa holds her own as she continues to argue. "We must work together if we desire to return Oz to its former grandeur."

He gives no response. I wasn't too sure about Odessa before, but I kind of like her now. She's got spunk. And she certainly doesn't care what anyone thinks of her, least of all this intolerant sentinel.

"Proceed," he finally says, moving aside.

Once we're within the building's walls, Odessa leads us to a small alcove beneath a curving double staircase. It's so similar to the one in the Second's castle I can't help but reminisce. My first kiss with Joshua lit a fire inside. Thinking of it now gives me butterflies I very much wish I could turn myself into. They fly away quickly, leaving me with an empty, gaping hole.

Odessa digs into her handbag, withdraws a compact, and checks her appearance. "Do not say a word until you are addressed, is that clear?" Is her command meant for me or Jasyn or both? "Her Grace is fierce and will devour you without cause."

Her Grace? Who could it be? "If that's the case, why are we even here?" When I was a kid, *Return to Oz* played on HBO or Showtime or some other film channel we had a free trial for. Gave me nightmares for weeks. There was this lady with a bunch of different heads she kept in glass cases. Mombi. Chills, and not the good kind, raise every hair on my skin. I'll cross my fingers she's not who's waiting to greet us.

After closing her compact and storing it once more, Odessa cleans her glasses with the edge of *my* blouse. Oh yeah, don't mind me. Go right ahead, lady.

"Her Grace does not tolerate shows of bravery or independence. You will get nowhere with her should you choose to act as if you don't need what she has to offer. Humility is the only way to get on her good side. I suggest you begin pondering how best to show her you truly seek her help without malicious intent."

Malicious intent? Is she serious? "If Her Grace is so fearsome, what's the point of even trying? Surely there's another way to accomplish getting me home."

"This is the only way, my dear." Jasyn straightens his tie with one hand, his hat with the other.

I wish he'd stop calling me "dear." The term bothered me when he was three times my age. Hearing it come from someone younger than I am is a little much.

"Time travel is a rare and tricky business. There may be other avenues, but none so close nor direct as what we have before us here."

I clear my throat. Tuck in my blouse. Finger comb my hair. It'll have to do. If Her Grace has a problem with my appearance, oh well. What does she expect from someone who just traveled by tornado? "What about the Wizard? Or Glinda? Or the Wicked Witch of the West?" I'd rather face her than some human-devouring monster woman. Then again, maybe Her Grace is simply another name for the most feared woman in all of Oz.

Odessa scoffs. "The Wizard? Witch of the West? What in Oz are you talking about?"

All right, maybe not. I look to Jasyn for help, but he offers none. MGM's *The Wizard of Oz* released in 1939. They have to know I expect something at least remotely similar.

Understanding softens Odessa's eyes. "I see. You think this is like the motion picture? The one with the girl in the blue dress and the dancing scarecrow?"

I shrug. I don't know what I'm supposed to think, to be honest. In all the movies and plays, the Wizard of Oz is never who you expect him to be. He never has the power to change anything at all, not really. I guess I'd hoped the real-life version would be different. That there really would be a wizard who could help me get home.

The Munchkin woman shakes her head with a *tsk*. "This is not L. Frank Baum's Oz, girl. You will not find a pair of ruby slippers, and there is no Good Witch of the North. If there were, don't you think we'd have petitioned her for help by now?" She dusts off one high-heeled shoe with a handkerchief, then another. "L. Frank Baum was a child who became an author who dreamed of something more for the Reflection from whence he hailed. He had outlandish ideas he wished to become reality." She peers up at me.

I return her mocking gaze with a leveled glare.

"This is the real Oz. Poppies don't make you fall asleep simply by smelling them. Munchkins don't speak as if they have inhaled helium. There is only the Lioness, who is far from cowardly, and she has a continued thirst for hunters to join her army. This story has no hero, and the villain is the last person you'd expect. So, once again, I suggest you figure out a way to humble yourself. It is very rare the Lioness grants a need to a stranger. She can get you to your time, there's no question about that, but it will cost you."

Do I dare ask? "Cost me what?"

"What else?" Odessa asks. "Your heart."

I cover my chest with my hand. Odessa can't actually mean the Lioness wants to take my physical heart from my body. But if she doesn't, that means she requires something far costlier than the beating muscle pumping blood through my veins. And it's then I realize . . . Jasyn wasn't the first ever to create a Soulless.

What the Void have I gotten myself into?

TWENTY

KY

Why am I not surprised? He really should've made himself more difficult to find. But here he is, plain as the Void in my veins.

"Hello, Gage," I say low under my breath. "We meet again."

I pick my way across the outdoor tavern. Large red rocks with flat tops fill in as tables. Men and women gather around them, some placing bets, others hunched and quiet. To my right a potbellied man plays a light song on a harmonica. To my left a woman sings and picks at her ukulele as if she's forgotten how to play. Her lyrics make no sense. Even so, they're the saddest I've ever heard.

> *"What? Oh what? Oh why?*
> *Me, oh my, oh . . . my . . ."*

She sobs and rubs her nose.

These are the men and women who can't get themselves together. I think of Tide and how present he's been, not allowing grief to take him away from the task at hand. I guess we all handle pain and grief in our own way. Who knows what shambles I'd be in if I learned Em was gone for good.

A circular stone bar stands at the center of it all, engulfed by laughter and tears. At its heart lives a fire. And I can't face a fire without thinking of her. When I decided to call her Ember, I had no idea just how well it would fit, or the fires we both would survive.

She doesn't need me to save her. I shrug. Going to do it anyway.

On my way, Princess, I mouth to the rising smoke. Then I take a seat on the stool beside him.

Words are unnecessary. From the irritated expression tightening his face, I'd say he knew the moment I set foot inside the compound.

Gage gulps a swig of whatever amber drink he fancies. A bandage to cover deeper wounds nothing but time will ever heal. He stares at the fire too. His glower could burn a hole of its own.

Like the seats around the tables, the majority of stools are occupied, only a few openings here and there.

Stein empty, Gage raises two fingers.

A boy not much taller than Khloe hurries up, retrieves his empty glass, and replaces it with another. Foam billows at the lip, but not for long. In one swig the drink is half gone. Gage wipes his mouth with the back of his arm. His face is unshaved, hair too long. Healed eyes stare through a sunken and lifeless glaze. Last time I saw him he had hardly any sight left. Did the Fairy Queen fix him? Or perhaps a Physic did the work? Or David's blood?

"What is it you want, traitor?"

Ah. So he speaks. "Good one, Gage."

The boy returns with yet another full drink, but Gage waves him away. He offers it to me instead. I decline, tossing him a few coins and sending him on to the next man in need of a refill. I've never tasted a drop, and I've no plans to change my mind anytime soon.

Being a Soulless and Shadowalker changed Tiernan, sure, but the drink made him a monster. He lost control with the bottle. Fists went flying and they always landed on me. He aimed for my mother. For Khloe. But I took every blow. Because of this he began swinging in my direction, knowing full well he couldn't touch them. Not if I had anything to say. What a disappointment of a son I turned out to be.

"You're weak." He'd kick my ribs and spit.

I never stayed on the ground long, though. I'd rise and he'd spit on me again.

"Hit them," he'd jeer. "Be a man. Show the women who's in charge."

Never. I never hit them and I never fought back. I think that's what bothered him most.

So much for being the son he always wanted. The son Makai believed his brother would value. I was of no more worth to my adoptive father than an empty bottle of ale. Did my real father love me? He wanted my brother raised as king. Did he hold high hopes for me as well? Even if he didn't, it doesn't matter. I choose who I am and what I will become.

With that, I slap Gage hard on the back. Weak? Ha. We'll see. "I'm here to make a trade."

He laughs. The sound couldn't get much darker if he took on the Void. "I am not into trading anymore. Try your luck the next compound over. Maybe someone there will have what you seek."

He moves to leave, but my hand on his shoulder stays firm. I push him back down.

Because I'm not backing down. "I know you helped David."

Another chuckle.

My mistake. The sound just got darker.

"You and David are not of equal breed, traitor. As Guardians, Joshua and I once fought on the same team. We were friends. But you and I?" He shakes his head. "You were never anything more than a bug to be squashed."

"Really, Jonathan? Is that the best you can come up with?"

He fists the bar, hands clean despite his stench. "Do not address me so casually. I am still your superior—"

I'm on my feet and drawing my knife. "Like the Void you are." What's a little scrape going to hurt? He'll heal. I'm about to make my first cut, swift and easy. And then I see them.

My father in a rage, trying to drown Khloe. Forcing me to ingest Void-riddled water.

Em shaking her head, telling me I'm better. I'm stronger.

And my mother. The woman who died to protect me. Tiernan came looking for his sorry excuse for a son that day. Instead, he found the girls in my place. My mother took his wrath full on, the wrath he'd been waiting to unleash all those years. If I'd been there, she might still be alive.

My knife meets its sheath. This man isn't worth my anger. But I do require him. And that is very much worth the most precious possession I own.

"What if you were to trade again, for a fair price, of course?"

Shoulders quaking, Gage hangs his head. "And what of profit do you have to offer?"

I wield my weapon once more, but this time I set it on the bar between us.

He lifts his head, glances between me and the mirrorglass blade. The day I received it still holds firm in my mind. I push the memory away. If I dwell on all this item has meant, I might change my mind.

And I cannot change my mind. I've come too far.

Gage is practically foaming at the mouth over the loot between us. Good. I've got his attention.

"Make your request, traitor. Let's see if we can strike a deal."

His coy response can't fool me. The man's already sold.

Still, I'll play. "I thought you might say that." Smirk in place, I remove the vial from my pocket. "How's about a refill?"

"You just proved what I knew all along. You are, in fact, a fool."

"I know you have it. No use denying it."

"Oh yeah?" His fingers tap stone mere inches from my knife.

I watch him. If he thinks he can swipe my offer without an exchange, he's got another thing coming. "Your snakeskin dagger." I lean into the bar. "It's not wrapped in snakeskin, is it?"

Now it's his turn. He withdraws his knife, lengthier than mine, the blade steel. He sets it on the bar. "Good eye, traitor. I will give you that."

"Dragon skin is hard to come by." I stroke my chin.

He grunts. "Not when the Dragon is already dead."

"What?"

"Never mind."

"Are you saying the Fervor Dragon guarding the Garden of Epoch in the Seventh is dead?" If so we may not need to solve a riddle. Fine by me. We still need Em to get in, Dragon or none.

"I'm not saying she is; I'm not saying she isn't."

He can lie all he wants, but . . . "I've heard Fervor Dragon skin is as difficult to cut as mirrorglass. In fact, rumor has it mirrorglass *alone* can cut a Dragon's hide."

"Don't believe everything you hear." Licking his lips, he eyes my knife once more. He's practically drooling. Got 'im. "There are other ways to attain such commodities. My dagger, for example, was already wrapped in Dragon skin when it came into my possession."

The hope I'd placed on a guess fails. "So you haven't been to the Garden or the Fountain?" Crowe, I was counting on this.

"No." His tone falls flat.

I grab the hilt of my knife. Our business is done here.

Gage grabs my wrist. "Tell me this. How did you recognize the Dragon skin? I am merely curious."

I shrug. "As a boy I loved Dragon stories. Learned everything I could about the beasts. Fervor Dragons are said to be myth, unlike the common Dragons of the air and sea. A Fervor Dragon cannot fly, and all are female. Her breath is so hot it turns her skin black as ash, welding it into armor with every exhale."

"You know your mythology." He releases my wrist and sheathes his weapon. "I am not giving you my knife, though."

I incline my head. "Are you saying you do have something to trade?"

He considers me for a good while. Then he unscrews the handle from his blade and out spills a vial identical to the one I carry. "The Fountain gives one drink to each. I have never ventured to the Seventh myself, but Mistress Isabeau is generous when she so desires."

I'll bet she is. I shake my head. The man has no clue we've discovered the Rose and the Fountain are one and the same.

"This knife and its drink belonged to none other than the infamous Dimitri Gérard," Gage goes on. "I am sure you have heard
of him?"

Is my mouth hanging open? Because I'm pretty sure my mouth
is hanging open.

"If I sacrifice my drink for you, I may never have the chance to
change a moment in time again. Who knows if I will ever make it
to the Fountain myself."

Typical. Gage thinks a sip from the Rose Fountain works for
his personal use. Do I break the bad news? Explain what the dew
actually does?

Nah. I'd rather humor him. "What moment would you
change?"

"Honestly?" He gives me the sort of look only a defeated man
can offer.

I nod.

"The day I was born."

If you'd told me I'd one day feel compassion for this scoun-
drel, I'd have laughed in your face. Now empathy raises the hair
on the back of my neck. Gage carries no Calling. No true friends.
No family that I'm aware. He's a loner. He has no one. What must
that be like?

With a flick against the dark glass, he says, "Here. It is probably
expired by now anyway."

Did the son of a Soulless just make a joke? "Thanks."

"Use it wisely." He grabs my weapon.

I stop his hand before it retreats with the blade I will never see
again. The weapon that's been with me since boyhood. An unwelcome lump forms in my throat. She'd be proud this is what I traded
her gift for. I know it.

"Use it wisely," I tell him, repeating his warning. One can only
hope he'll heed it the way I have. Doubtful, but I'll hope so just
the same.

He says nothing, stumbles off the stool, and staggers away.

I'd like to say this is the end, but I know better. With the full vial in my possession, I can't deny the truth.

This is only the beginning.

ASIDE

Joshua

Eliyana!" I call to her from my pit, invisible hands cupped around a nonexistent mouth. This dematerialization experience has become second nature, a comfort I welcome and dread in the same instant. She's Reflections away, but saying her name acts as its own weapon, driving a nail into the heart of my greatest enemy.

Myself.

Reaching to all sides, I hope for a wall, or a stairwell, or any path that might lead me to the light. In my mind I have walked for hours, forcing my soul to remain alert. I hear those who surround me conversing, yet they do not acknowledge my desperate attempts to be heard. Have I made headway? No way of knowing when my entire world is ink. The darkness is an exhaustion of its own, one I don't know if I can endure much longer.

"She can't hear you," my dominant self jeers. *"Face it, Joshua. Your time is running out."*

Running out, eh? His goading only fuels my determination. I mistook love for hatred as I pursued the Unbinding Elixir, believing it was my love for El that truly drove me. How could I have allowed myself to become so blind? My desperation to have her forget Kyaphus and return to me became my undoing. Was it worth being trapped within my own soul?

"Yessss," Josh hisses.

"No." I break into an envisioned jog to keep my hypothetical heart pumping and legs moving. I cannot feel my body, but the action isn't difficult to imagine. Does my fight have any effect on

Josh whatsoever? Am I simply doomed to be an insect in his ear until I'm lost to nothing? I almost stop to take a mental break when a voice breaks through. But not Josh's voice this time.

"*I need to hear you say it, Joshua.*"

El?

"*Say it.*"

Her voice is clear as the daylight I can almost see.

"*Don't even think about it,*" Josh responds in his typical tone of condescension. "*It won't work anyway.*"

My soul picks up its pace. Could my efforts be taking form?

"*Stop,*" Josh orders. "*Your attempt is futile.*"

I move faster still. I can almost hear my breaths become life. The darkness seems to dull, the blackness not as sharp as it once was.

"*Say it,*" I hear El say again. She was so angry that day in Wichgreen Village. Angry and hurt and jaded. The lie I let loose was a sword across my sternum. I could not bear her heartbreak, yet at the time, what option did I have?

"*Say it.*"

I draw a deep breath, feeling my actual physical lungs expand in my chest.

"*What are you doing?*" Josh says. I feel his body—my body—jar.

I'm going to say it. But this time I'm not going to lie. This time I will break free from the chains I've locked myself in.

"I love you," I say aloud. My own voice rumbles my throat. "I love you with all my heart."

"*I love you too,*" I hear her say.

I blink, picturing her standing beside me. She's smiling with lips that cannot exist without being kissed. The image is hazy but it's there, outlined in the shadows before me, a cool drink of water in this wasteland, not of the Fifth, but of my soul.

"*No!*" Josh's voice comes out distant and far off. Muted as if he's calling from beneath a pile of rubble.

"I love you," I say again, hoping to the Verity my words carry through. That it's my voice and not Josh's telling her how truly, deeply I adore her.

"Well, it's about time."

I open my eyes to a desert landscape blanketed in night.

I've broken through. It is not Eliyana beside me, however.

Wren laughs. "Welcome back."

I flex my hands, roll my neck, and feel the stubble on my chin and cheeks. I swallow hard. I hate to hurt Wren, to tell her my words weren't meant for her. "Wren, listen—"

She stops me with a palm in my face. "Don't bother. I know."

Lips pressed, I nod my silent apology.

"This won't last," Josh jeers. *"You don't have the strength."*

We'll see about that. I'm alert to my shortcomings this time around, not about to give up so easily again.

I have, indeed, returned.

But for how long?

TWENTY-ONE

'Til Morning

Can't see the forest for the trees, huh? Well, I've got news for you. Because I can't see *anything* for the trees. No ceiling, no walls. No way to decipher if we've stepped outside the Emerald City and into an actual forest, or if this is some sort of indoor arboretum. I inhale, long and deep. The aromas of earth and cedar infuse my senses. I welcome the homey fragrances. One reminding me of Joshua and the other pinging my memory, taking me to . . .

My. Dark. Place.

The Verity pulses alongside my heart. A warning to stop. *Don't. Cease. Desist.*

Is this what a Shadowalker fights each moment? Constant anger and bitterness? Depression? I feel like I have PTSD. How could the scent of earth trigger me into this spiral of resentment?

Poke. Blood on his shirt, Kyaphus tosses an unconscious Joshua into the Threshold.

Prod. A dark gaze. A seemingly innocent plea. Then I'm fooled again. Kyaphus brings a rope over my head, pulls it back against my neck.

Ping. Kyaphus supports Gage. Watches as my wrists are bound behind my back.

The Verity plays tug-o-war for my heart and mind. But the Void?

"It's okay." The darkness billows across my soul. *"You have a right to feel this way. He deserves for you to hate—"*

No. I'm not hurting him. I'm hurting myself.

"Yes. Let the anger build. Stop fighting what feels oh so natural."

No. Think of Joshua. Of good and right and real.

Running full force into him after Gage's adaptation of *Invasion of the Body Snatchers*.

Cold and weary, sinking into Joshua's arms inside the cabin of a ship.

Holding each other on the beach in the Fourth.

And the kissing. Oh, the kissing. Joshua's a good kisser, an amazing kisser. The hatred subsides, my mind slips into ease. He's autumn. Cedar. Cinnamon. Cloves. He's color-changing leaves, Thanksgiving dinner, pumpkin pie, cider, hayrides. He's cranberry and plum and auburn.

I expect the Verity to thump brighter. Hotter. To jump at the pleasant memories. Instead, my anger seems to billow and grow, overshadowing the light with a blanket of thick darkness.

So, for the smallest moment, I let the darkness come.

What is this new surge of rejuvenation? This sudden burst of desire to scale the trees surrounding me? I feel strong, I feel . . . alive.

"This way." Odessa's whisper jars me. She wags two fingers in a beckoning motion above one shoulder.

Shoving away my tangled emotions, the new longing to stay close to the shadows, I follow. The ground is so soft my feet sink into the dirt with each step.

"Stay close," Jasyn says. "I have never met Her Grace, but I have heard rumors. I fear she is all that is relayed about her and more."

Rumors. Right. I doubt he'd share even if he had time. Gotta keep the mystery going and all. Because in no story ever does anything just get revealed.

I lick my lips and swallow, feeling the weight of my Mirrorlessness. It's been too long since I've sung, I mean really belted a tune. Without my Mirror, is there even any point?

Yes, a voice whispers within. *Always.*

A roar resounds.

The trees quake.

The earth trembles. And the still, small voice retreats.

Odessa hesitates, then moves forward with caution, her steps not quite as sure as before. The trees space out more until they form a circular clearing. Golden poppies surround an emerald throne, an unbroken road of yellow brick paving a path through the poppies into the clearing's center. And there, atop the throne, is none other than Her Grace the Lioness. She's cloaked in a robe of ruby red, and her tail swishes back and forth.

She's a lion. Like, a real one. Move over, Nala. Behold the true queen of the jungle.

When she opens her fearsome mouth, I almost turn and book it. Then I remember who I am and stand a little straighter. Because I too am a ruler, though no one here is aware of the fact. Still, I refuse to cower.

"Come forth, Matron of Munchkins."

Matron of Munchkins?

Odessa dips her head and slips off her shoes. When she follows the brick path leading to Her Grace's throne, she keeps her head bowed. Reverence radiates from the tip of her black bob cut down to her stubby bare toes. When she arrives at the foot of the throne, she lowers herself to both knees. "Your Grace."

The Lioness nods. "State your purpose." Her voice carries the feminine tone of Countess Ambrose's but the command of Makai's.

"I have found her, Your Grace. The girl we have been waiting for."

Wait, what? I take a step back.

Her Grace focuses on me and then on Odessa once more. "And what makes you so certain?"

Odessa turns her head and nods toward Jasyn. Without a glance in my direction, my grandfather removes his shoes and steps forward, following in the Munchkin woman's footsteps all the way to the opposite-of-cowardly lioness. He takes a knee beside Odessa, but does it in a way that makes him seem more above than below.

"Your Grace," Jasyn says in an even deeper voice than normal. "Allow me to elaborate."

"As you will." She licks her lips.

Please don't let her be hungry.

To Her Grace's feet Jasyn says, "The girl bears no Calling, yet there are traces of the Verity on her. No one is closer to the Verity's vessel than I, Your Grace. The Second's king is my oldest comrade. I am well accustomed to detecting the light. And this girl carries it."

Would someone please fill me in? I thought I was going to help them on some mission in exchange for a ticket home.

My breath hitches. Oh . . .

"Allow the girl to speak for herself then." The Lioness rises. Prowls around her throne. When she comes full circle, I know what's next. I brace myself.

Gulp. Maybe trusting Jasyn Crowe was a serious case of poor judgment.

At her approach, I stand my ground. I will not bow before someone, man or beast, who has yet to earn my respect.

As if reading my mind she asks, "You do not bow?"

I force myself to make eye contact with her glassy brown orbs. My heart ceases its rhythm.

"You will not answer me, child?" Her kind words carry a menacing aftertone.

I peer past her to find Jasyn and Odessa watching me with anxious expressions. I do my best to ignore their scrutiny. Focus on the queen of this jungle.

"What girl are you looking for?" Does she detect the earthquake rocking my insides? As brave as I may appear, I'm cowering within. A little Dorothy Gale who's a long way from home. What did Odessa say? Her Grace would devour me without cause?

"It is hard to say." She answers me without a hitch, speaking as if I am her equal and not an insubordinate foreigner. "We have been plagued by Shadowalkers for far too long. They are careless, selfish. Some believe they should be . . . reconditioned." A pause. "Saved, as it were. These so-called heroes have made it their mission to help the creatures find the correct path. The one that leads to light."

Because Shadowwalkers *choose* darkness. She must be speaking of Aidan and the Council of Reflections. His conversation with Nathaniel makes perfect sense now. "What does this have to do with me?"

"As the Void's vessel mentioned, you carry traces of the Verity. Now that I see you up close, I sense it myself." She sniffs. "There is goodness in you that radiates from your very being."

Goodness? I hug my stomach. Guilt festers. How good can I be if animosity tastes so sweet? There was a point when I believed something twisted inside caused the Thresholds to drain and the Callings to dwindle. Maybe I was right all along. How can the Verity stand me?

"However." She tilts her head.

Ah, and there it is. I plant my hands on my hips. Ebony would be so proud. Okay, let's have it, lion lady.

"While there is goodness in you, there are also hints of the Void."

Hearing my greatest fear vocalized is acid on my skin. I wrap my right bicep with the fingers of my left hand. The blackened veins of the Void covered this arm once. Now it appears normal, but is it? Really? Maybe nothing ever leaves us. Perhaps deep down something so powerful and soul altering can't ever really be gone. The idea crushes me, but . . .

If this is true, then I'm still a Mirror. I just have to find a way to make it manifest. To make my mark return. Perhaps then I can squash the Void in me once and for all.

"Do you care to explain how you can possibly carry both Verity and Void?" Her head tilts the other way. She never blinks. "Up until now I had assumed to carry both was almost impossible."

My theory is confirmed. I voice what I am now certain of. "We all have light and darkness in us. We all have the choice to take either path."

The Lioness dips her head, a wide grin spreading across her golden fur. "No, child. Sometimes there is no choice at all. Some-times there is only one path."

"Which is?"

Her eyes twinkle.

I've never been more terrified.

"Why, the path that leads to death, of course."

Oh. Crud.

TWENTY-TWO

KY

Good riddance, Gage. Good-bye, mirrorglass blade.
Hello, Princess.

I make my way back through the dark compound. The tents sleep now, most every lantern extinguished. How many hours remain for rest? Do I care? I have my prize. Snoozing isn't my favorite pastime anyway. At night my guard lowers, and then it all comes back to me. Every punch and blow feels fresh.

But worse than any bruise Tiernan could have given is the gash that never healed.

"Mom?" I forced steadiness into my voice as I pushed the already-ajar door inward. "Mom?"

My gaze landed on a shoe. Her shoe. In the middle of the entry. If the open door didn't ignite fear, the abandoned piece of footwear did. My mother wasn't one to be careless. She always locked the door and never left anything lying around.

The floorboards creaked as I rounded the corner from the foyer into the main hall. Our modest home near the docks in the Third was nothing to boast about, yet it was more home than the Second ever was. A safe place for my mother and Khloe, where they could live in peace far away from Tiernan and his drunken dissatisfactions.

Until then. Until I saw her lying at the bottom of the stairs in a rag-doll heap.

I fell to my knees. "Mama." I hadn't called her that in years, but in the moment the word was everything. Her hand lay lifeless. I took it in mine and held it to my lips.

I'd never felt skin so cold.

It was minutes before I rose. When I finally gained the strength, I punched a hole through the nearest wall. Then another, then another. I swung until my hands were a bloodied mess, but I couldn't help it. The loose board on the middle step was something I'd been meaning to repair. But the faulty stair structure didn't end her life.

He did.

"Yessss," Kyaphus eggs. "Remember. Remember how good it felt to let me out. To release all your anger and frustrations and become the man you truly are. Me."

"Get out of my head, monster."

"No can do. When you tried to kill Tiernan after what he did to our mother, that was when you finally behaved like a man. You sought justice for the wrong done to us."

"Don't be a fool," I say beneath my breath. "I've learned my lesson. When I let you out that night, you almost killed us both. I won't be so negligent again."

"Details, details."

The pain I've kept below the surface threatens to rear its evil head. I harness it before it causes a shipwreck in my soul and gaze up at the stars, a clouded half-moon hanging in their midst. My mother loved stars and chose her own names for the constellations, just as she did for most everything else. Flowers were "color wheels" and trees were "shade makers." The Callings were "gifts" and the Void was "death" itself. The Verity had many names, but my mother's favorite was simply "morning."

"Because morning always comes," she said. "Just like the Verity."

Her unshakable faith in something better kept me going then in the same way it inspires me now. I think of her eyes and see through them, keeping my own eyes on the stars and returning to the most memorable night of stargazing.

"Legend says mirrorglass is nothing more than fragments of shooting stars." My mother kissed my twelve-year-old mop of hair as she drew me into her side. We shared a blanket atop our flat cottage roof, peering through the treetops. Tiernan was gone a lot back then. "Guardian business," he called it.

Guardian business, my rear.

I was a little old for forehead kisses and bedtime stories, but I couldn't deny her affection.

Accepting her tenderness, even as I grew, made me feel more like a man. The man my father would never become. He thought she babied me, of course. Always had a problem with something.

"Someday. . ." She shivered and I moved off the blanket, wrapped it around her bare feet. "I'm going to be a real Guardian." I stood on the roof, pointed to the sky. "I'll travel the Reflections and find you one of those shooting stars. You and Khloe."

"Oh, my sweet boy." She looked up at me, clasped my hand, and squeezed. "You've been a Guardian since you came to us." Her voice shook. She hung her head.

The guilt in her stature undid me. I wanted to tell her it was all right. That I was proud to protect her and my sister. I crouched beside her, squeezing her hand back.

"I have something for you," she said. "Come."

I followed her down the ladder and into our home. We stepped lightly, careful not to wake a sleeping baby Khloe. Once we were in the kitchen, she opened the knife drawer, reached to the very back, and withdrew a blade I'd never seen.

"Your father never cooks." She laughed, wiped her teary eyes with the heel of her palm. "Never needed a better hiding spot for this than the one right under his nose." Then she took the knife and cut a gash straight across her cheek.

The blood in my head drained. I scrambled for a towel, something to stop the bleeding. Tiernan had finally broken her. My mother had gone insane.

That's when she grabbed my arm. Her very touch forced a calm I couldn't explain.

"Watch," she said. "Wait."

I did as she asked, paying close attention as the cut healed right before my eyes. The blood remained, but it was as if the wound never was.

"I want to try!"

My reaction nearly put her into hysterics as she wiped the blood off her cheek with a damp towel. I ran the knife across my palm, hissing through my teeth at the pain. But as quickly as it came it vanished, leaving only a trickle of blood behind. I bent over to try it on my leg, but my mother stopped me.

"That is quite enough, son." She took the knife and cleaned it. "You've had a demonstration. No need to put yourself through more pain, even if it is short-lived."

The questions spilled out after that. "Where did you get this? Is it magic? It's mirrorglass, isn't it?"

"It's yours. A way for you to defend against your enemies and save them at the same time." She handed it over. I haven't let it out of my sight since.

Until now.

My eye twitches, thinking about my younger, naive self. Tiernan tried for years to break me, to turn me into a son he could use as a weapon at will. I know it's only because of my mother that the good in me survived, though I can't deny I've considered alternatives to her plan. That a knife that cuts and heals could also be used as a torture device.

"Come near her again and you'll wish this blade was made of steel."

I imagined cutting Gage again and again. Allowing him to heal and then injuring him until every inch of his skin had been broken. A fire awoke in me the night he tried to take Em. It burns now fiercer than ever.

My gaze finds the stars once more. Out of habit I grope for my knife. I feel bare without it, but I'll get used to it. What I'll never get used to is life without the ones I love. My mother is gone, but I still have my sister. And soon I'll have Em back too.

"Hey." Tide walks toward me, my pack in his grasp. "Ebony borrowed this. She wanted to look at your books."

"She could've asked." I take it. "They're more your books than mine anyway."

My chief cook shrugs. "Yeah. True. But you know Ebony. She's never asked for a favor in her life, and she's not about to start now." He elbows me.

I comb my fingers through my hair. Scratch my arm. Goose bumps make my hair stand on edge. Anyone who claims the desert doesn't get cold has never experienced the climate after sundown.

Ebony emerges from the tent behind Tide. "Oh." She shakes her head. "It's just you. I thought I heard my name." She looks away. Is she embarrassed?

Tide leans back and folds his arms. "You heard right. Ebony, Ebony, Ebony."

She narrows her eyes. "Oh, shut up. I'm going back to bed."

"Hey, wait," I say. "I may not see you before we all split up in the morning. I wanted to say—"

"I'll take care of Khloe. She's as much my sister as she is yours. Stormy feels the same."

"Thanks." I can't bring myself to say good-bye. Who knows where we'll be at the end of everything. As much as I'd rather Khloe go into hiding with Makai's group, I know she'd never have it. "There's one more thing too."

"Spill." Ebony flips her hair over one shoulder. She keeps glancing at Tide as if he might run away.

"What do you know of the Midnight Rose? Any additional information you could give would be useful moving forward."

Ebony shrugs. "She's searched for the Rose as long as I can remember, only I didn't piece it together until David told his story, and then Dahlia flipped out. On top of everything, finding out my mother is the immortal Fairy Queen . . ." Her voice trails.

If she's about to cry, she contains it. "Why does she want the blasted Rose anyway? Another's need has nothing to do with her deepest desire. Isabeau has always been, and will forever be, out for her, herself, and her." This time I know I catch her sob, though it's more angry than sad. "I guess that's where I get it from, right? Like mother like daughter."

"Wrong." Tide goes to Ebony, tugs on her hair playfully. "You changed. You chose good. You put others first. You're on our side." My shipmate turns to me then. "The original Council of Reflections was formed because of that flower. My mother always told me they were guarding something important, but I never knew what."

Gaze darkened, Tide raises his voice. "When the Shadowalker stole the Rose, he put a great power back in the Troll's hands. My great-grandfather passed guardianship down to my grandmother and then Mom. I was to be next in line. I'll do whatever it takes to rectify the mistake Josh made."

As if on cue Josh and Wren join us.

Stormy emerges from a nearby tent, yawning and scratching her neon-pink boy-cut hair. "What's all the fuss? I thought we all agreed. Sleep, then save the Reflections. It's not too difficult a concept."

"What are you lessers doing up, anyway?" Ah, Wren. Always condescending. Can't even last an hour without putting someone down.

"We could ask you the same question," Ebony retorts. Looks like Wren's met her match. Nice.

But I'm not paying much attention to the girls. It's Josh who catches my eye. I peer at my brother through the shadows. He stands there in silence, staring into the night. Something about his expression has altered and I step closer.

Tide follows my gaze and says, "I'd keep moving, Shadowalker. I've kept my cool near you, but I wouldn't expect it to last."

Josh clears his throat.

"Let's go. He's not your judge." Wren touches his arm. Who knew she was capable of such tenderness?

"No." He clears his throat again, this time louder than before. "He is."

I recognize the change in his tone immediately. David?

He makes eye contact with Tide. "I will never ask you to forgive me for what I have done, Tide. I was foolish and took things

too far. The Fairy Queen claimed she and your mother shared a
Kiss of Accord over the Rose. Countess Ambrose promised to keep
a matter quiet in exchange for the blossom. I do not know all the
details related to the exchange. I do know nothing is so important
it was worth sacrificing your mother's life. I am truly sorry."

Tide's fists clench at his sides. The anger I've been expecting
to surface seeps through his tight knuckles. Crowe, this isn't good.

"Leave," Tide says. "Leave and you'll go your way and I'll go
mine. It's what my mother would want."

Ebony touches Tide's arm, no doubt trying to calm him before
he needs it.

"I deserve to die." David, or I am almost certain it's David,
scratches the back of his head. "I will not blame you should you
agree."

I step forward, positioning myself between my brother and
my friend. My gut tells me what's coming. Here we go.

"Don't come near me. I mean it." Tide's voice elevates a hair
more, making the quiet desert around us seem smaller. He's not a
big guy, but his voice carries.

A few surrounding tents illuminate, the residents within lighting their lamps, awakened by the commotion.

David's face contorts with pain. And that's when I know
more than ever this isn't Josh. Because Josh would be proud of his
despicable actions. Someone who worshipped the Void wouldn't
own up to what he's done with remorse the way his better side is
doing now.

"I ended her life in an attempt to better mine." David hangs his
head. "My regret runs deep."

Tide launches himself forward.

Ebony half gasps, half squeals, "No!"

Khloe's eyes go wide, fully awake from her sleepwalk.

Wren steps in front of David, but he dodges her, making no
move to defend himself.

Oh man, I hate that I have to take this measure. But I can't let
Tide exact his revenge now, not like this. He'll regret it later.

"Tide!" My voice is a step down from Makai's commanding boom. Still, it gets Tide's attention.

His gaze meets mine long enough to matter. I've caught him off guard, and he'd never expect me to use my Shield Calling against him anyway.

He freezes in place, eyes narrowed because now he can't move. "Let me go, Cap."

I raise my palms. "This isn't the way. You know that. You've said as much yourself."

Eyes like slits now, he gives a jerk of a nod.

Taking a broad step back, I release my power over him. He staggers but doesn't fall. Without a word he marches away in the opposite direction, Ebony trailing after him.

Khloe shoves her finger toward Ky's chest. "What did you do, big brother?"

"Me?" I'm all mock innocence and charm.

She rolls her eyes and shakes her head. "Do I have to take care of everything around here?" Her arms rise and fall in a quick toss. Then she marches after Ebony and Tide.

When they're out of earshot and eyesight, I say, "Give us a minute, Song." I don't look at Wren. Neither does David.

She hesitates but obeys, taking off after no one. Once a loner, always a loner.

When we're without an audience, I say, "So you're back."

David nods. "I cannot tell you for how long. It's all I can do to focus on speaking. I've been screaming to be heard for days."

I understand. More than he knows.

"How did you break through?" Khloe was my motivation back then. Now Em's been added to the mix, only making my wall against the darkness stronger.

My brother looks away.

So. He thought of her. The battle with Josh may be ending, but the war for Em has just begun.

"What do you propose?" David shifts topics. "I am here, and I can help. How do we reach Eliyana?"

I hate the way he says her name. As if they share a secret she and I will never have. I don't dare waste my time by questioning his motive to work with me. Em is the obvious reason. We'll worry about the logistics of our complicated connections to each other later.

"Well, now we know the Fountain of Time isn't actually in the Garden," I say. "We don't necessarily need to venture there." Maybe. Maybe not. "I suspect the place everything began is still where we'll end up. But, for now, we continue on the same path toward the nearest wormhole. That's the only way to get to Em."

The way he cringes at my nickname for her is oddly satisfying. David nods, though I've studied him well enough to know—he doesn't fully trust my risk-and-chances plan. Of course, he also isn't aware I hold a secret weapon. He'll find out soon enough.

And if the Garden does play a role in the end? Our entrance still depends on the Verity's vessel. I'd wager Dimitri didn't enter of his own accord. He penned *The Scrib's Fate*. Of course he'd want to paint himself in the purest light possible. Still, I believe the Verity saw him before he entered. I could be wrong, but is it so unfathomable that the Verity was also the Dragon? With as many forms as Isabeau seems able to take, I wouldn't doubt it's only with permission from the Verity's vessel that one is allowed within the Garden's hedges. With her by our side, nothing will be impossible.

"If Josh returns," he says, cutting through my musings, "swear to me you will take necessary measures to ensure he never nears her."

I exhale. I'm hesitant to fill him in, but Khloe's right. I do know how to be a brother. I promised Makai I'd try. Here goes. "*If* Josh rears his ugly head again, we'll wait until you find your way back. There's no you or him. It's just a matter of which side you will choose. Even Eliyana, the pure heart chosen by the Verity, has a little darkness in her. The Verity chose you before. It's chosen me as well. Pure of heart doesn't mean without darkness, Brother. It means a desire for the light."

"Now you sound like Nathaniel."

If I didn't know better, I'd believe that was a compliment.

I don't acknowledge it. Stuff like that is better left unspoken between men.

We begin walking in the direction Tide and the two girls ran. No need to find Song. She'll show up in the morning, chipper as ever.

David exhales. "The Void? What will become of it when all is said and done?"

I shrug. "The Void was created by a broken heart. I can only imagine Isabeau wishes to save herself from that very fate. But, unlike us, her intentions are selfish. There's no knowing what she's planning at this point. We're kind of shooting in the dark here."

"The Fairy Queen *is* the dark. Her heart is permanently black."

"Not even death is permanent." Any heart can be redeemed. I glance at David, then think of Ebony, who once held as much hatred toward Em as Isabeau harbors for Em's mom. If we ever discover what really happened that day in the Garden, not from Dimitri's perspective but from the Verity's, we may be able to reach Isabeau's heart beyond the walls she's constructed around it.

Then, perhaps, she not only can forgive but will finally learn to love.

ACT III

DO I LOVE YOU BECAUSE YOU'RE BEAUTIFUL?

ebony

Well, isn't this a lovely little pickle we've gotten ourselves into? Alone at night in Nabka Forest with a Mask who can't transform outside water, a Shield whose Calling can only go so far as to protect us from the climate, and a Magnet who could only make things worse with rain pour.

Perfect. Just peachy. *Great plan, Ebony. Lead your group into certain death, why don't you?*

What form do I take? I'm not much help either, am I? A Shield who's not really a Shield. How pathetic. Oh sure, I could make myself look like Jasyn Crowe himself, but where would that get us?

Yeah. That's what I thought. No and where.

"Maybe we ought to ask for directions." Oh, Stormy, our chipper sunshine and rainbows girl. Want me to get you some pom-poms, honey? You can shimmy and shake us out of here in no time.

Okay, that was mean, even for you, Ebony.

I'm sorry, but a lot of stress comes with taking the lead. Usually I just boss people around, tell them what to do without having to suffer any consequences. But this? Even if nothing happens to me, these three get the sour end of the deal, don't they? Soooo supportive now, but what will they say when we're still lost in a few hours? I know people, and one thing you can count on? They turn on you the minute things go wrong.

Money back guaranteed.

"Too bad you can only change into different humans." Leave it to Khloe to remind me of my limits. "Otherwise you could become a bird and scope out the land from above."

"Maybe we should stop. Take a breather. None of this is familiar. We might've taken a wrong turn somewhere." Tide attempts to take my hand.

I fidget with my bang-braid, pretending not to notice another one of his way-too-sweet-to-be-happening-to-me moves. Don't misunderstand, plenty of guys have tried to make a move, but my hand was not their body part of choice. No way does this super nice and sweet and somewhat normal guy truly like me. Maybe I'm intriguing now. Oh yeah, I'm all mysterious and whatever. But eventually he'll come across a girl without a tainted past and zero attitude. The kind of girl he can take home. A girl who doesn't come with baggage.

I'm so not that girl.

He jogs past, then flips around to face us. "We've been walking since sunup."

Has it really been a day since we left Nitegra Compound? How far have the others gotten? Did they find Nabka Threshold? Was Ky's plan to travel through a wormhole successful?

"This looks like as good a place as any to settle down and gain our bearings. Start fresh in the morning." Hands on his hips and chest puffed, Tide appears as if he could start crowing at any moment. "We can eat and get a fire going. What do you girls say?" He crouches, patting a soft-looking patch of grass with the hand that tried to hold mine. Guess Stormy isn't the only one whose outlook is sunny-side up.

"We don't even know where we are. You said you knew the way, when clearly you're just as lost as we are." Now my hands are on my hips. I'm a replica of how he stood moments ago. Except I'm being realistic and he's off in Neverland. "Are we even in Nabka Forest still?"

I look around. Are these the same types of trees we encountered when we left the desert behind and entered this jungle? I thought we were in pine territory, but these seem more tropical.

Bizarre. "This trip was a waste. We should just head back, see what we can do to help the Commander and the others."

Khloe marches to where Tide crouches and stands beside him. "You're just going to give up? After how far we've come? Never thought of you as a quitter, Eb. Fine. Go." Hand shaking, she shoos me off. "But we're staying. I trust Tide when he says he can find his way back to the Fountain. We'll find that mean old Fairy Queen with or without you."

I clench my teeth. I'm not one to be caught with my mouth hanging open. But seriously? My own flesh and blood is going to take his side? Not cool.

"I agree with Tide and Khloe."

Stormy too? What is this, a mutiny? Who's in charge here?

"If I've learned anything, it's that you can't see where you're going until you know where you've been." The oldest of our group takes a natural place between us. Stormy makes eye contact with me, then the others, then with me once again. "Tide's been through the Fountain with Joshua before." She turns her attention to him. "Are there any landmarks you can remember? Anything specific that might help us retrace your steps?"

He rises and holds his chin between his thumb and finger. Gazes up at the wide-palmed trees as if he's contemplating the meaning of life. "We crossed a creek at one point. It was shallow, but the stones in its bed were black. We're talking they might as well have been charcoal."

"That's good. See?" She rounds on me again. "I say we sit and strategize. Make a list of everything Tide remembers when he came through the first time. Then we go from there. Sound good?"

I nod, but I'm not on board. I don't see how we're supposed to form a plan when we're already lost. *Some leadership skills you have, Ebony.* Like, oh, I know, we'll just figure it out as we go along. Surely Tide can remember how to get to a place he's been to all of once. When he was under a great deal of stress and grieving the loss of his mother. Makes perfect sense.

Not.

"Sounds great to me." With a wide grin Tide heads off through the bushes to his rear.

"Where are you going now?" I call.

Not that I care, but we should stay together. Another film I watched in the Third once became the ultimate warning for stuff like this. El couldn't make it to movie night so I watched it myself. So what if it was a horror flick? I could handle it. Anyway, these stupid teens were running from some ax murderer or something. They were fine when they remained in a group, but the moment one of them went running off? Let's just say the amount of fake blood that production went through was enough to fill Dawn Lake.

"Don't worry." Stormy places a consoling hand on my shoulder. No wonder El likes her so much. Her positivity really does start to get to you after a while. "He'll be fine."

Her words send a bad vibe into the air. Like an omen or a jinx. Only seconds after they leave her mouth, a shout resounds from beyond the spot where Tide vanished. *Crash, snap, thud.* What follows is deadly silence. The wail that echoes afterward is enough to rip through me.

Well, this is just fabulous. I try not to show my terror as I speed in his direction. It's okay. He's not dead. He's *not*.

Oh my word, what if he is? If he is, I hate him.

And if not?

If not I'll kill him myself. How dare he scare me like this. How dare he leave without saying good-bye.

∞

I'd slap him but he's already in enough pain. No need to scold the poor guy. He's doing that well enough on his own.

"Gah!" Tide's agony pierces the night. "You'll have to pop it back in, Eb."

"No, no, no." *Don't freak out. It's just a dislocated shoulder, nothing serious.* "I'm not a Physic. We'll find a Physic. Someone lives here. They have to live here."

"We haven't seen anyone else for miles." Stormy sits with Khloe. Both remain calm. Why are they so flipping calm?!

"You're the oldest," I tell Stormy. "You do it."

"No." Tide's voice is steady as a rock despite his injury. "It has to be you. You can do this."

Why does he insist on being so darn stubborn? If he wants me to do it, he's got another thing coming. Hope you like a useless arm there, bud. "I'm not a Physic."

"But you can become one." Khloe's eagerness has her bouncing on her knees.

"Transforming into a Physic doesn't give me the Calling."

"Have you ever tried?" Stormy really needs to stop agreeing with these two. I'm totally outnumbered and it's super unfair.

I'm ready with my answer but stop myself midbreath. Have I ever tried to exude another's Calling? My mind scans every previous alias. Lincoln Cooper. Quinn Kelley. Tide. I've even attempted to become my mother behind closed doors, just to see what it'd be like. In all those transformations, did I once stop and think, *Hey, I know—maybe I can make myself a dolphin or Troll it up just for the Void of it?*

I'm such an airhead sometimes. "No," I say, dumbfounded. "I haven't."

Tide's smile would fool anyone into thinking he's just fine. "So give it a try. Change into a Physic and see what happens."

Hesitation fills me. Partly because I don't want him to prove me wrong and partly because I'm terrified he will be wrong and I won't be able to help him.

He places his good hand on mine, which is pressed into the soil beneath us.

I can feel the dirt digging deeper and deeper into my nails, and I don't even care.

"You can do this," he says again.

Lips pursed in uncertainty, I nod. Then I close my eyes and think of all the Physics I've encountered. One stands out. Dennielle. Skin the color of midnight and eyes like winter mints. I met her right after I ran away from home. In Dewesti Province just west of Jasyn's castle at the time. I was trying to figure out where I'd go. What I'd do to survive. Then Dennielle found me and offered me a place to sleep.

"My son is away," she said. "So I have a free bed. We live in the Haven but left a few things behind in our home here. I was hoping to retrieve them, but it appears we've been looted. Have you heard of the Haven?"

I shook my head, not sure what to say. I'd never met someone so genuine and kind.

"Times are getting darker. The Era of Shadows continues on with no end in sight. But there's a safe place for those wishing to stand against Jasyn Crowe and his growing army of Soulless. It lies south of Lynbrook Province, beyond the sea. A place untouched by darkness as long as it remains undiscovered by those who seek to douse the light."

Sounded like a fantasy. A place free of darkness and night? I was only twelve at the time but already far past jaded.

"You should come back with me," she said. "There's always a place for someone else loyal to the Verity. I know the others would be glad to have you."

I just stared at her. She could think what she wanted, but I wasn't loyal to anyone or anything. When had the Verity ever helped me? If the Verity was so real and light and good, where was it?

I thanked her for the meal and bed, let her touch up the few scrapes I had attained since escaping my mother. Dennielle talked and I listened. She spoke of her Physicness and how proud she was of her son and daughter, waiting for her return to the Haven. She talked about how she grew up in the Third by the docks and how she longed for her childhood home.

If I had gone with her instead of fleeing while she slept, would things have been different? Haman never would have found me, and I never would've gone to work for Jasyn Crowe.

Sigh. If only.

"Eb, I'm serious." Tide's urging pulls me from the memory. "At least try."

I nod. Then I rise and step back. I haven't shifted since the Callings returned. The broken boy before me has placed all his hope in what I may not even be capable of. Still, I can't say no to a challenge. I picture Dennielle, her kind face and green eyes. Then I take on her form, hoping to the Verity I now believe in that I'll have her healing touch too.

Khloe gasps once the transformation is complete. Mouth gaping, she scrambles to her feet.

I look myself over, notice the way my clothes are way too tight for my more filled-out frame now. Doesn't look too bad, though. I glance at her. "What is it, Khlo?"

"You're, you're . . ."

My eyebrows lower. "I'm what?" I kneel beside Tide.

He helps guide my hands to take hold of his injured arm. "It's okay. I believe in you."

Deep breath. Focus. I look over my shoulder at my sister who's still staring at me wide-eyed, at Stormy who's trying to get her to snap out of it. Stormy mouths something inaudible, then ushers Khloe away, probably to see if she can get her talking, or at the very least blinking, again.

Tide and I are alone now. So not good.

"Please, Eb." He brushes the hair off my face with his working hand. It's the lightest touch, but I can feel it resonate through my entire body. "I need you."

Oh, for the love of Prada. I can't deny him. "This may not work."

He smiles. That stupid, tingle-inducing smile.

I hate how much I like him.

"You're a Physic now." He winks. "Just pop it back in."

"Oh, is that all?" This guy is something else. "Well, why didn't you just say so?" Oh pardon, is my sarcasm showing?

"Mmm-hmm."

Would he stop smiling already? I'm not even Ebony right now, but he sees right through my Shield, doesn't he? His sweetness is going to make me kiss him. And I am definitely not going to be the one to make that move. No sir. A girl's got to draw the line somewhere. If anyone is kissing anyone, he is kissing me. And he'd better not kiss me when I'm not me. Because that would be weird.

"Okay, this is going to hurt." My hands shake. I steady them. These are Dennielle's hands, not mine. She could fix this and I am her.

At least that's what I'm going to tell myself.

He winks again. "Thanks for the warning." He's trying to hide it, but I detect his wince as I move one hand to his forearm and the other to support his elbow. I rotate his arm into position. How in the Reflections do I know what I'm doing?

He braces himself on his knees, leaning into me.

Three, two, one . . .

His scream sends sleeping birds into flight.

or are you beautiful?

The path that leads to death? Lion lady must be tripping if she thinks I'm following any path but the one that leads me home.

This is all backward. I thought she was going to help me. Odessa claimed my heart was involved in the price.

I shoot a glare saved for Jasyn alone. How could I believe he stood a chance at being anything but exactly who he's always been? I'm done with the good Samaritan bit. My only goal now is to get out. Now.

I clear my throat. "I respectfully decline your offer." Right, as if she'd let me. "I'll find another way home."

The Lioness prowls around me. A low purr emits from her throat, rumbles my core.

So yeah, I'd rather not be treated like dinner, thanks. It's really not helping.

"You are a smart girl." Her Grace pauses before me once more. "I think we both know a declination is not an option here."

Swallow. One step backward. Two.

"You will not cooperate?"

Another step. Wait for the perfect moment. Don't run yet.

"I see." She turns and saunters along the brick path. Once she reaches my grandfather and the Munchkin woman, she converses in a hushed tone.

Really? She's going to make it so easy to up and walk away?

Guess so.

I pivot. This is too eas—

My heart sinks. Never mind.

Two guards step from behind trees, each dressed in some sort of governmental garb similar to what the man at the door modeled. They carry green staffs. Their faces are as straight as the poles they grasp. How very imperial. Their weapons cross, making an X. Path officially blocked.

Here I am again. Trapped and clearly out of the loop. Whatever. It's not as if this is new territory, existing amidst secrets and lies.

"Everyone has an agenda. Everyone."

Joshua's warning stills my heart. Always protecting me. Never letting me down.

And there it is again. Why is it every time I think of Joshua, the Verity grows hot within? Not the warm, comforting sensation of a blanket and a cup of cider in the fall. Closer to sitting on hot pavement beneath a blistering sun with nowhere to go. What do you want, Verity?

"Trust me."

Joshua's words. And Mom's. But their voices don't quite fit. This voice sounds more like—

No. Couldn't be. A monster and a coward isn't capable of such tenderness. Hatred boils and the Verity cools it. Calms it to a simmer. I know I shouldn't hate the Void. The Verity's vessel is supposed to guard it, keep it from harming anyone else. Which is why I have to get back. Without me, what's become of the others? If Kyaphus has so much as looked at anyone wrong, so help me I will lock him away and throw the key into the Fourth's ocean.

Sigh. My soul falters. The harbored anger is almost easier to unleash. Why fight it?

The trio continues to discuss me without, well, me. I have to wonder how the Lioness is able to speak. She seems to be an ordinary creature, nothing fantastical about her aside from her fluent use of human language. I doubt she's a Mask. Robyn and Wren can't speak as a tiger or a griffin, so why would a lion be any different? Any relation to Aslan?

Okay. Bad joke.

If they're planning to take all day, fine. I have better things to do. Like rediscovering my Amulet and telling these guards where to put their fancy walking sticks.

"Hey." Chin jutted toward them, I prepare for target practice. "Want to move?"

They glance at each other and laugh. The one on the right says, "Have you lost your marbles, girl?"

"Probably." Controlled breath. Swallow. You can do this. "Should we find out?"

Eyebrows raised, they ease their stances. "Looky what we have here, Oscar," Lefty says. "The widdle goil wants to pway."

Perfect. He's a jerk. I won't feel so bad messing with him.

They set their sticks aside and begin to circle me.

I yawn and enter the forest the way we came, though I've no clue which way to turn for the front door. I'd nearly forgotten we aren't really outside. Within the trees, I can almost imagine I'm in some unexplored corner of the Second.

"You boys coming?" My exhale comes as a blow through pursed lips as I sway deeper into the woods. *You got this. As long as you act the part, you're in control.*

Behind me, the guards share a sick laugh. The kind that makes me want to be anywhere but alone with the pair. A quick peek through the branches gives me a visual of the clearing. Jasyn and the others continue their exclusive club meeting. I'm not so naive I think they're oblivious to me. It's just they don't care.

A stick snaps. My stomach churns, but I'm able to force my body to remain steady enough so my internal quivering goes unnoticed. I let my eyes search left and right, scouting the area. Trees with branches too high to reach tower over me. Climbing's out then. What about—?

"Not so fast, doll." A meaty hand claps my shoulder, spins me around. "Wait for us."

"Yeah," the one called Oscar says. "Stay awhile."

I inhale and shut them out, tuning to the light within. Despite my brush with my less-than-Verity side, I know my Mirror's in here somewhere. It's crunch time.

A breeze sweeps through the forest, rustles the leaves so they titter above me. One of the guards begins to whistle. The sound is eerily calming. I listen and wait, seek the rhythm of the atmosphere. If I didn't know any better, I'd say the trees had a song of their own.

> *"The breeze does blow,*
> *Sweet and low,*
> *Through my branches.*
> *The wind does sweep,*
> *Soft and deep,*
> *Through my branches . . ."*

The melody soothes me, making me feel less alone.

Then Oscar moves behind me.

And everything tilts.

His hands find my waist. He sways me. "Wanna dance?"

Don't they sell deodorant in Oz? One whiff of this bottom-feeder and I'm gagging on week-old BO.

I attempt to regain my lungs—and my personal space—but his hold remains firm. "No, thank you." My voice is not near as commanding as I'd like it to be. Not even close. I can't lose my resolve now. Not when I need it most.

"There is another way . . ."

The new voice moves in a wave through my head. Mine, but darker. Confidence bordering on arrogance. Who are you?

"I am you."

The nameless guard takes his place in front of me, joining in Oscar's poorly executed tango.

I gulp. Crud. This isn't going as planned. Granted, my only plan included practicing my song, seeing if one of my Mirror abilities might manifest. But now things have gone too far.

"Don't panic," the other me says. *"Panicking is for weaklings. You still have a song, just not the one you're familiar with."*

My gut grows cold. Ice. Snow. No light. No warmth. I can almost imagine the Verity isn't here at all.

"*That's it,*" she whispers. "*Harden. If you're hard, no one can break you.*"

My jacket comes off. Oscar tosses it to his friend, who chucks it into a nearby tree. They snigger.

Enough.

Front dude gets my knee to his groin.

The move they clearly didn't expect catches Oscar off guard, but he's quick. Yanking my arms behind my back.

I scream, then twist and bite his hand, using my weight and the split second his yelp of pain gives to escape his grasp. I could run now. Didn't I do as much when Kyaphus tried to attack me on Eighty-First back in New York? If I join Jasyn and the others, I'd be choosing the lesser of two evils, right? Maybe not, but I've dealt with my grandfather. This is a nightmare turned sick reality TV show.

"*No. Defend yourself. They deserve it. They were going to—*"

I am fully aware of their unchivalrous intentions. Just let me think for a second.

"You've asked for it now, girly." Oscar has returned, licking his lips as he creeps forward.

Mom would say go.

"*Stay,*" a voice shouts inside. "*Sing.*"

For the first time in far too long, I find my voice. Emotions rise, anger and hatred at their helm. The melody is my medicine, the cure for the pain that ails. But instead of releasing a song filled with love, I find something new and different. Other. The black notes coil around my heart, squeeze. The only way to breathe is to let them loose. So I grab a fallen branch and sing.

> "*You are the reason for my rage,*
> *Locked me in a cage,*
> *Tried to tear me like a page,*
> *I said no to your yes,*

> But you persisted anyway.
> Enough."

My muscles move as if they belong to someone else. Oscar catches the branch on my first swing, heaves, but I hold strong. He tugs and I pull. When he's close enough, I claw his face, then grab his shirt, digging my nails into the skin on his neck. I make a noise that is neither scream nor cry. "Get the crowe away from me!"

He stumbles backward into a tree, eyes bulging. "You're insane."

"You've surprised him now. Good. Keep going. Don't stop until he's learned—"

I should go. He's not going to hurt me. His buddy's already run off . . .

"No . . ."

Yes.

I drop the branch, hold my head. Breathe, breathe, breathe. Gasp, gasp, gasp. This is crazy. *I* am crazy.

Oscar scrams and I do the same, but in the opposite direction. When I reach the edge of the clearing, I pause. Catch my breath. Glance up to find Jasyn, Odessa, and the Lioness exactly where I left them, none the wiser to my dilemma.

What was that? My mind . . . it's like it had a mind of its own. I need some water, or at the very least something to counteract the shadows I let get too close. A memory. Focus on something from before.

One from my childhood surfaces. Here, in this land that's broken the borders of my imagination, defied every hope and dream I ever held for the City of Emeralds, how can I sing anything else?

"Somewhere over the Rainbow" pours out, not from my throat, but from my heart. My Mirror song may be lost forever. This new version of me seems to keep clawing her way to the surface, a relentless disease of the soul inspired by the Void itself. I dare not try to find my Mirror for fear I'll be let down once more. But this song isn't for anyone but me. It's not meant to get me anywhere or accomplish anything. To save anyone or help everyone. This is just mine.

Because I love to sing. Joshua understood. So much he even wrote me my own melody, played it on the piano while we were trapped together beneath the deck of a ship. But my need for melodic oxygen goes back much further. Even when I was alone, song was my companion. During my darkest moments, music never left my side.

My soul swirls this way and that, one of Odessa's twisters, cycloning within. My thoughts wander to a day I conquered one of my many fears. As much as I still hated my complexion, hid from my reflection, the day my elementary school caught fire was when I stopped hiding my song from the world. I'll never forget the older boy who helped me. A stranger who showed me that true kindness wasn't a Fairy tale. I never saw his face, but I didn't have to. His touch warmed me the way the Verity does now, melting—no, *crushing*—the ice that formed beneath the trees.

"You know what I like to do when I'm scared?" he asked from the other side of the bathroom stall. His voice induced a foreign ease that almost scared me more than the bullies who'd taken my shoes and shoved me into the toilet.

I shook my head. I never got the name of my rescuer. I used to think he was some kind of angel or ghost sent to save me but not actually real. A hero in a dream like the ones in the stories I refused to believe. Peter Pan to my Wendy. Prince Charming to my Cinderella. And because I thought I'd dreamed him, he never really crossed my mind again.

Not until Mom's gallery burned down. When the police told me there'd been a fire, *karma* was the first word that popped into my mind. Had death been after me all along? The first person I ran to was Joshua. When I found out later he was my Guardian, I couldn't help but think of my own fire escape. Could the boy who saved me have been him? He said we always had a connection. It's possible, isn't it? His voice soothed me then as it has since the first day we sang a duet. He used music to rescue me, as it has so many times.

"*. . . once in a lullaby . . .*"

The boy's adagio hum made the song its own lullaby. As he hummed I closed my eyes just as they're closed now. For a moment I forgot the smoke. Forgot the bullies and the names and my absence of shoes. The large wet spot on the back of my school uniform that smelled like urine. His song made me come alive. And it was in that moment I sang aloud without thinking. I knew the lyrics but had never sung in front of anyone other than Mom.

"*. . . where you'll find me . . .*"

I'm there with him now, singing as he hums along. I've tried so many times to picture what his face might have looked like. Now I see a hazy version of Joshua, younger, cerulean eyes not so wise, brown hair not so tame. His voice has stayed with me.

A voice I continue to hear in my dreams.

Anger wells. Rises and falls.

Kyaphus invades my thoughts once more. Will I ever be rid of the Void's vessel? He taints every good memory, nearly every perfect moment that belongs to Joshua. Why? Leave me alone, Kyaphus. Just leave me the Void alone. It's your fault a semblance of a Shadowalker even exists in my soul. If not for you, I wouldn't be in this mess.

"Odessa, take the girl to her new chambers." Her Grace's voice is like a lather, washing away the fog and drawing me back to the present—or in this case the past.

I step into the light, within the clearing's borders once more. The ominous trio stares at me, each of them looking at me as if I'm property rather than a human being.

"My maids will prepare her for a celebration held in her honor."

Celebration? Honor? Ha. Figures. Jasyn has to have his show, doesn't he? He must hold a bigger influence here than I understood. Or perhaps it's the Lioness who gave him the idea. Put on a party, force everyone to attend, then show who's in control. Scare everyone into submission. Who's in charge here? Odessa? My grandfather? This whole betrayal thing reeks of Crowe. He figures I'm something he can trade, does he? What does the Lioness have that he wants?

I cross my arms. Didn't work so well for you last time, did it, Jasyn? My eighteenth birthday may be years in the future for him, but it's in my past. Joshua and I defeated him once. I'll do it again. I'm not truly alone, not really. I may not be a Mirror, but music will always give me courage.

And I will fight like the Mirror I will someday become.

Odessa scurries up the path toward me, grabs my hand. She doesn't mention the absence of guards or my scream in the woods. Either the woman failed to notice or she simply doesn't care. "You shall not be disappointed, Your Grace," she calls over her shoulder. "I assure you—"

For the first time since our arrival, the Lioness roars. The trees seem to bow their branches in respect behind me, while the poppy petals tremble.

"You assure me of nothing," the Lioness says. "This is your final chance, Matron of Munchkins. I sincerely hope I am not disenchanted again. The last girl you brought only made things worse, becoming one of the most infamous Shadowalkers in this Reflection. We don't need another one like her, stalking the countryside on her wild, flying broom."

My breath hitches. Wild, flying broom? As in the Wicked Witch of the West? This is too much to take in all at once.

"Of course, Lioness." Still gripping my hand, Odessa bows as she backs away. "I will not fail a third time. I am quite sure this girl is the one. She has a strength inside I have never witnessed in all my extended Munchkin years."

"That is what you said the last time and the time before that . . ." Her Grace yawns.

Her voice becomes more familiar with each word that crosses her lips. Why do I get the inkling I have heard that voice before?

"But I'll confess this girl does seem different. Let us hope she will be the answer I have long awaited. With the Verity in my grasp again, I may finally be allowed to reenter my Garden."

The Verity in her grasp *again*? What the—?

Without warning or prelude, the Lioness transforms. Her head shrinks from feline to female, her muzzle shrinking inward, molding itself into a petite nose with a perfect point. Her golden fur lengthens into waist-length sunshine hair, and her eyes fade from brown to a lovely ice blue. Her clothes remain intact, revealing she's not a true Mask at all but something much more powerful.

Is this where Ebony's unique Shield Calling stems from? Not from water infused by light but from her mother?

I want to run and hide in the same instant I want to end her life. She started all of this. I'd like nothing less than to destroy her, the woman who'd love nothing more than to see Mom dead. But I can't. Because if she's here, and just as young as always, then she's either an Ever or, more likely, the character from a tale I heard not too long ago.

The pieces fall into place like rainfall. This is the immortal woman from *The Scrib's Fate*. The original vessel of the Verity herself. My theory comes back to me, the one I formed after hearing the story from *Once Upon a Reflection*. The woman needs to love and, more importantly, to be loved if we're ever going to destroy the darkness her broken heart created.

There's just one problem. As she stares me down, winter in her icicle eyes, one question keeps any hope I might have had from blooming.

Who could ever love this monster?

TWENTY-FIVE

Ebony

It's fine." Tide scoots back against the nearest tree, supporting his bruised arm with the other. "A little ice and I'll be good as new."

"Right. I'll just head on over to the nearest freezer. Oh, wait. There are none. Because we're in a forest."

His light laugh unnerves me. Does he have to look at me in *that* way?

I bite my lip. Suck in my cheek. Twist my hair around my finger. I'm Ebony again and I think a silent thanks to Dennielle, wherever she is now.

"I've had worse." Tide laughs again. "Besides, that was amazing. I knew you could do it."

So this is what a racing pulse feels like. And not the kind that starts from doing something I totally know I shouldn't be. This is much more levitation worthy.

Oh man, oh man. Is he going to kiss me?

He better.

Tide brushes my hair off my face for the second time tonight. "You're always so afraid. Why?"

His question is a shove and I lean out of reach. Seriously? He's going to insult me? Now?

"I'm not afraid." The retort comes out accusatory. He just had to ruin this, didn't he? I turn away and rise. "I should go find Khloe and Stormy."

"See what I mean?" He stands and moves behind me, never allowing more than a few inches of space between us. His mouth finds the space above my shoulder and next to my ear. "You can't even look at me without chickening out."

I want to slap him in his perfect copper face. How dare he see through me. How dare he go around smelling like sea salt and sand.

"Ebony. Look at me."

No. It's too late. I've let him get too close. We aren't happening like this. Not when he thinks he has something to hold over my head. I won't let him use vulnerability against me. I'm better than that. Than him.

Ennnt. Wrong. But don't tell.

"Just get some rest?" I move out of reach again. "I'll be back. Stormy and Khloe can't have gone too far."

"They're fine. Talk to me."

I can't let him see me cry. I won't.

"Tell me something true." His hand covers mine. "Something real."

Sigh. El told me once how Rhyen broke through every wall she constructed. How he was so different from Joshua in that regard. Because instead of pushing her away, Ky drew her in. He made her open up and see who she really is.

Is that what Tide's doing now? I sense the need for release, how good it will feel if I just let it go. Every bitter memory I've held in, used to become an emotionless robot. Nothing and no one will hurt me. I can say what I want, do what I want. Mean words? Ha. They don't faze me. Betray me? So the bleep what? I can get you back twice as hard.

"Talk to me," he urges again.

Something about those three words seeps through a crack in my armor. And I spill it. I let the words flow because why keep trying to hide? "My mother never came to look for me. When I left to work for Jasyn."

My past can't be news to him. Tide was close with Rhyen, so he must know we both worked for Crowe. Does Tide even understand the concept of an unhappy childhood? What was it like for him to live with the Countess in a palace by the sea? I've never

known how it feels to truly love and have someone love me uncon-
ditionally in return. Countess Ambrose loved him. Even Rhyen
had one loving parent. But me?

I had no one.

"You haven't told me much about her," Tide says. "Your mother."

"What's there to tell?" Bitterness coats my question. Who cares?
"She's a monster. Maybe I am too. Am I even a Shield? I've always
taken pride in my unique ability to assume another's appearance.
Now I wonder if I'm some sort of mutant offspring." I kick a nearby
stone with my toe. It doesn't go far.

His lips press, then part. "You're not a monster." As he adjusts
his stance, his face contorts in pain from the miniscule movement.
Tide's the type of guy who's good at reading people. I wish he
wasn't. I wish I could hide from him. That I didn't have the impulse
to tell him everything that's on my heart.

"Who knows why your Shield ability manifests the way it
does." His chin comes to rest on my shoulder, his nearness warming me.

I want to shove him and lean back into him at the same time.
Fall asleep right there in the crook of his shoulder. Correction—his
good shoulder.

"I don't think you hate your mother as much as you'd like me
or anyone else to believe. You're not a monster. Your mother is, I
won't argue that. But was Jasyn Crowe much better? When you
worked for him, I mean?"

Loaded question much? Still, it causes me to really think.
Something I don't prefer to spend too much time doing. I don't
respond right away. Can he expect me to? Serving Jasyn had its
downsides, but we were cared for. Sad, right? Loved more by darkness than by a parent, a person meant to protect me. It's nauseating.

Welcome to life as we know it.

I glance toward the stars. Tide's breathing slows. We stay
that way for a while. He doesn't try to hold me and I'm grateful.
Knowing me, I'd leap away from such affection. And I don't want
to push him away. Not now.

After a spell of silence has passed, I say, "In some ways, Jasyn was the lesser of two evils. He never spoke cruelly to me, always treated me with the highest respect. As long as I did what he asked, I received praise. And I never didn't do what he asked."

The last part releases beneath my breath. Dark memories surface as I recall my time in the castle. Guardians older than I was who would've liked to take advantage. Experiences that made me harder than ever. The way Haman watched me, as if he was waiting for the right moment to pounce. I shudder. He never got his way, thank the stars. But knowing what he wanted was enough to make a girl crazy. Every time I walked down the hall I'd be looking over my shoulder, never fully trusting anyone aside from myself.

"Ebony."

Why does my name on his lips make my soul dance? When did I become so sentimental? I'm starting to sound like El. Perhaps that's not such a bad thing.

This is becoming too close for comfort. I force myself to step away, knowing the boy who keeps weeding his way in won't give up so easily. Still, I need some air.

"I'll be back."

I don't wait for him to answer, just walk and walk and walk some more until I'm far enough I can pull my head back down from the stupid clouds it's floated into. Doesn't matter. Because the look on his face when I glanced back at him said it all.

I'll be waiting, he mouthed.

I squeeze my eyes shut. That's exactly what I'm afraid of.

TWENTY-SIX

KY

D awn blinks as we move into the third day without Em going on a lifetime. How do people keep living apart from loved ones who end up missing for years? We're approaching seventy-two hours apart come nightfall, and the hole in my chest only continues to gape.

Nabka Compound is a ghost town. The dome-like octagonal homes appear as boulders in the desert. Weeds thrive, running over the paths, making it unclear if there are any at all. Not a soul peers out a window or exits a home to investigate the newcomers. It's different from Wichgreen Village or even the Fourth, where residents were curious but remained at a distance until they knew we meant no harm. Nabka is just forgotten and looks to have been for some time. Which tells me something about the Threshold we seek. That I may have been wrong. Perhaps it's been gone awhile and the people here simply moved on.

"Well, that's just great," I grunt, low enough so no one can hear me. No need to worry them. Yet.

What next? The nearest compound over is Uptuck, at least a two-day journey. Do they even have a Threshold? The map Dahlia provided at the cottage didn't record one. Then again, that's not saying much. We might have hope if there's nothing left for us here. We can't give up. If it takes me forever, I will find the Second's queen. Good things come to those who, what is it, wait? Nah. I say good things come to those who go and get them. The end.

We travel in pairs. Me and Preacher. Josh and Wren. Dahlia's the lone wolf. I'm still trying to figure her out.

"Get a move on, people!" She's taken the lead, huffing and puffing and picking up her muddied skirt. She's probably used to being the loner by now. What a secluded existence it must be. To have Ever blood and live for so long. She must have a strong heart for it never to have been broken. Or maybe it has and she just doesn't talk about it. In fact, I don't know much about her at all aside from what everyone else does. She's an Ever. Elizabeth has known her since childhood. And that's . . . it.

"You got a plan in case this one goes sour, Rhyen?"

I look up at Preacher, my traveling buddy. His gaze never stops, always darting. You'd think the guy had a nervous tic or a lazy eye. Really he's the most aware of us all. Why I brought him, actually. That and he doesn't talk much.

"Not yet." I withdraw the rolled map from my back pocket. "But I will by the time we need one." Which, let's hope, is never.

The abandoned homes thin, giving way to rock formations different from what we've encountered. These are gray and towering and remind me of my time on Lisel Island with Em and Nathaniel.

"Only way through is over," Dahlia says. And believe it or not she begins to climb. You wouldn't think it from the looks of her, and the fact she's had some sort of flu, but the woman is strong. If I were an Ever and could live and live and never worry too much about physical injury, I'd take more risks.

What am I saying? I'm the riskiest guy I know. Ever or not, I know how to live. Unlike my brother, who moseys just behind us with human Wren by his side. They don't look at each other, don't converse. In fact, it appears they're purposely avoiding eye contact, *any* contact, for that matter. Could something be there? Are they suppressing feelings and just need a matchmaker to work his magic?

David catches me staring. His eyes narrow. The slightest shake of his head says, "Don't even think about it."

Fine, fine. But it was worth a try. Live a little, man. Venture into the unknown.

When this is all over, if we ever find our way back, I'm doing what I promised Em months ago. I am taking her to climb Pireem Mountain. Shoot, I'll take her to climb every mountain ever if we make it through this. The look on her face the night we scaled the rocks on Lisel was worth my shortened breaths.

"I can't believe I've lived my whole life without experiencing that," she said through quick heaves.

I faced forward and uttered, "You ain't seen nothing yet, Princess."

My anxiety over falling has slowly dropped off since I met her, lessening with each adventure. I'll do all the falling when it comes to her. Would David do as much? Elizabeth said it was I who kissed Em, gave her the mirrormark. After the story Makai relayed, I have to wonder.

Has it been me all along?

I grab a protruding section of stone and gain a foothold. I grunt and heft and flex and hoist. The way up? Painstaking. I can't help but think of Frodo on his quest. I'd go to the ends of Mordor for Em. Would David?

"Stop comparing yourself to him," Kyaphus hisses. *"Your own birth father didn't have enough faith in you to become king. And a queen deserves a king, not some lowly, unwanted pirate."*

I ignore him. He won't get the better of me. Not this time. We're so close, I can almost taste her kiss. Not much longer now.

On the other side of the rock wall, I exhale my relief. We pick our way down, down, down to what might as well be a large puddle for what's left of it. The bright-green light at the water's center still glows, indicating a way in remains. Green marks our point of passage, and green means go. I'm counting on it.

When we all have our feet on the ground, I don't even stop. I approach the water's edge. Halt just short of getting my feet wet.

"Are you certain this is a Threshold?" Song can't get two words out without contradicting me, can she? "I thought you said the wormhole that took your girl was like a swirling whirlpool of death. This"—she clears her throat—"is a puddle."

Aren't we the observant one? Also, Em has a name. Why is it so difficult for the Mask to say it?

"Maybe not all the draining Thresholds become wormholes," David says. "Didn't you say it was Tide's *theory*, not a fact?"

His jab at my best man does not elude me, though I'll choose to ignore it for the time being. I rack my brain, think back to what my chief cook relayed to Em on *The Seven Seas*.

"He said it would create a wormhole *if* the Threshold was part of a larger body of water. Like the creek behind Dahlia's cottage." I incline my head in her direction.

She sits on a nearby stump, shaking out her boots and wiggling her free toes.

"But," I continue, "he also shared that a hole would remain within that water, which would've been much more convenient. We simply could have followed Em through then. Instead, the Threshold disappeared completely."

"So it would appear," Wren says, "your guy doesn't know everything. And neither do you."

"Never claimed we did." I lift my hands in defense. "If you thought any of this was a sure thing, you joined the wrong crew. I'm a pirate, not a prophet. I follow clues that, more often than not, lead to a treasure of nothing. Still doesn't stop me from hunting for the next chest of gold." A fine metaphor, if I do say so myself, and one that shouldn't be too difficult for Miss Thing's brain to comprehend.

"What now then?" She folds her arms across her chest and leans back in her signature stance. "We just hop in the puddle and hope it takes us wherever the Verity's vessel has gone?"

I shrug. Sounds good to me. I can't put it off any longer. I have to tell the others my plan. Well, this ought to be as much fun as a barrel of rum and then some.

"I say we regroup." Arms folded over his chest, David addresses me like his equal as opposed to his enemy. I kind of like having him around again, though I keep waiting for Josh to rear his ugly head. "We can't just jump into this and hope for a favorable outcome. We need to think this through. If this Threshold isn't a wormhole, it will only take us exactly where it's connected."

"The Sixth," Dahlia chimes in. Her boots have returned to her feet, but the laces remain loose. "And why not? We travel through and hop on over to the next one on the other side. We'll be that much closer to the Seventh, and maybe the Sixth is exactly where Eliyana ended up. Ever considered that?"

I hadn't, but she has a point. Still, could my drink be of use here? Worth a shot.

"What do you say, Brother?" Brow arched in question, David eyes me.

I don't generally stare at another dude, let me make that clear. But it's kind of hard to look away when I'm beginning to notice distinct similarities between us that I missed before. A first glance says we're nothing alike. A closer inspection, however, says there's more than meets the eye. I find myself staring at an altered version of myself. Different color eyes and hair. Distinctive height and skin tone. Opposite in the most noticeable features, yet it's obvious we've descended from the same gene pool. Square jaws, thick waves of hair, and the ability to quirk a brow only graze the surface of our matching traits.

How much of our parents did we inherit? How much of our behavior was learned from those who raised us? David is strong and silent, usually slow to speak when Josh isn't hanging around. Me, I say what's on my mind. Most of the time.

"We do as Dahlia says." Out of habit, I check the blade at my hip, only to remember it's gone. I exhale. I need to come by another weapon, though nothing will ever compare to the one I possessed. "What other options do we have?" I'm starting to feel it. The anxiety pressing in. The absence of the Verity since Em left. The loss of everything good. The Void inside fights me. "I feel as if this is our best choice right now. We jump in headfirst and go from there."

"Not long now," the voice says. *"I'll be taking over soon."*

We'll just see about that, Kyaphus. With Em by my side again, nothing will stop us.

The worst part of me laughs in my head. His voice is growing louder. We don't have much time.

"Always going off your feelings, Rhyen," David interrupts with a shake of his head. "Feelings are what landed me in my mess with Josh. I suggest you use your brain and leave your heart out of the equation."

I relate to the bitterness he houses, I really do, but . . . "Without the heart, there is no life." I clap him hard on the back. "Sure, you got into trouble, but that's not your heart's fault." I poke him square in the chest. The shocked expression on his face is worth it. "It's *your* fault for not guarding it better. I suggest *you* remember *that*." I move away from my brother, leaving him to ponder my wise advice.

"Let's get this show on the road." Dahlia dips one bare toe in the water. "The Sixth waits for no man."

I hesitate. Withdraw the vial.

"Drinking again, Rhyen?" Wren rolls her eyes.

My brother and I exchange glances. "Got an Elixir of your own, I see."

"Close, but no cigar. This"—I hold it up for all to see—"is a drink from the Fountain of Time."

If ever a hush fell over the crowd, this is it.

"Where did you get that?" David doesn't remove his gaze from the vial. He wants it, that much is clear. His right eye twitches, and I see the shadow the moment it crosses his face. Josh is fighting his way out.

Stay strong, I think toward him. Though he can't hear me, he also can't mistake the meaning behind my gaze. "A traveler once told me this water would take me where I was required most. To think on my deepest desire, drink, and see what happens. I've seen the tale become truth, and I believe when combined with the power of a Threshold, one sip will take us where we need to be."

"You're mad," Song says. "Joshua, we can't follow him. He's leading us nowhere. We've accomplished nothing. We're walking in circles and everyone is just fine with it."

"Stay behind then." I stomp into the puddle. I can feel it suck me in like quicksand, the green light dying every moment. Whatever we find on the other side doesn't matter, as long as it leads us to Em. "If you wish to come with me, you'll have to hold on. The drink is for one, but I'm betting, just like Em's mirror walking, if you're touching me we'll stay together."

David joins me, places a hand on my shoulder.

I wish I could say his support is encouraging.

"Why don't you let me take that?" He reaches for the vial.

I hold it away from his grasp. "Don't." My voice shakes. "We have one shot at this, and I'm not letting you ruin it like you've done with everything else."

"Just give me the bottle, Brother."

"Stop your grousing." Dahlia puts her hand on my other shoulder. "We're all in this. I love Elizabeth's oldest more than you two combined and then some. I want to find her as much as anyone. We can't do it with your constant bickering, though. I say the one who knows her best takes the drink. Seems to me Joshua has known her longer—"

"See?" he says. "What did I tell you? Now give me the drink."

"Don't interrupt me, son," Dahlia says, wheezing. "I was sayin' you have known her longer, but I believe Kyaphus here knows her better. The Void he's taken on is proof. He loves her more. The drink belongs to him."

David says nothing as Wren joins us. Attempting to touch me as little as possible, she pinches the sleeve of my shirt between her fingers. Preacher's the last. His firm hand on my arm feels almost fatherly.

Here we go.

The process is slower than ever as we sink deeper and deeper into the puddle. Just before our heads go under, I think of Em. The water took me to her before. I have to believe it will do so again.

Just as the vial reaches my lips, David grabs it, downs its contents.

Then the puddle swallows us whole.

∞

I can count on one hand the times in my life I've felt so much pain I wanted to die. Surprisingly, the Void is at the bottom of the food chain on that one. Pain can be physical, but not always. Sometimes heartbreak bruises deeper than any cut or jab.

The day I found my mother unmoving on the stairs.

The moment Josh ran his sword through Khloe. The thought still makes me want to pummel the guy.

The second Em's fingers slipped from mine as she was sucked through the wormhole. I promised I'd find her, though is that a promise I had the power to make? Am I the only one she's forgotten? What if messing with her memories caused her to contract full-on amnesia? She could be anywhere without the slightest clue she's supposed to be searching for us. For me.

The Threshold to the Sixth sucks us in, twisting and squeezing, as I recall one other time I've experienced this amount of pain. I've hesitated to let the memory fully resurface. Guilt rolls like a tidal wave about to crash into me. A not-too-long-ago conversation pulls me back, reminding me just how connected we are.

"Who did this?" Em thought while within the private walls of my ship's cabin.

"Some came from Jasyn's Soulless." The mix of terror and hurt on her face about destroyed me. Even so I knew it was only a matter of moments before she asked about the—

"And the burn?"

How could I answer her in truth? Would she have believed me if I'd told her? The last thing I wanted was for her to think any of our relationship was somehow orchestrated. So I answered, "Next question."

Much to my relief, Em didn't bring it up again. And I worked hard to make sure that part of my mind was closed off. Couldn't have her knowing I'd kept this to myself, not when she'd just started to trust me again.

I thought of her as I tipped the vial to my lips, as the cloaked stranger disappeared from view. Yet what came to be afterward was not what I anticipated. Standing before a brick school, the scent of smoke filling my nostrils? Where had I ventured and why? I longed for Em, someone so familiar to me. Thinking of her is equivalent to breathing. But a school in a city on a street I've never seen? What a waste of whatever it was I drank. Surely the stranger couldn't have meant for it to bring me here. She said to think of the person I cared for most, that I would be where I was needed. How could I be needed anywhere other than where Em or Khloe were? And this place was neither.

Then again, I've never been one to write off anything until the full picture grew clear. So rather than walk away, I waited. For what? You got me.

That's when the alarms went off.

The school doors burst open. Uniformed students piled out through a cloud of smoke. Girls screamed and boys shouted. The younger ones cried while the older ones hugged them. Sirens blared as fire trucks came to the rescue. Smoke seeped from windows, from vents. Law enforcement arrived just behind the firemen, and soon enough medics piled out of ambulances.

"You will end up where you are needed most."

Okay. I got that part. But what good would my Shield do in such a crisis? This was a job for a Magnet, someone who could either control or douse a fire. Come on, lady. There must be some mistake. All I carried was a mirrorglass blade plus one paralyzing Calling. A lot of good that would do me in the case of a fire.

Hands shoved into my pockets, I turned on my heel.

And saw her.

The details still stand out to me now. Funny the things you remember, huh? Her light-gray sweater hung to her knees, and her brown hair was wrapped in one of those twisted mom-type styles at the back of her head. She approached the school steps, both hands covering her mouth.

I froze and stared. Squinted. Was it really her?

Closer, closer. Identity confirmed. A younger Elizabeth Ember. There was no mistaking it.

I looked left and right. She must have sensed me staring because she glanced over her shoulder and made brief eye contact. But her gaze didn't remain. She didn't know me. Had never seen me before in her life. Was this some sort of nightmare? Did the vial contain a hallucinogen?

A man who I assumed was a teacher or staff member passed Em's mom. She touched his shoulder.

Everyone knows I have excellent hearing. Still, I moved closer to catch the full conversation.

"Please," she begged. "Eliyana Ember. My daughter. I can't find her."

The man's mouth turned down.

I hated him already.

With apologetic eyes he pointed her toward the gathering of firemen and paramedics, then moved on.

I nearly intervened at that point. The coward should've, at the very least, escorted her to someone who could have given her information. Where have all the men gone? For the love of sea salt, show some decency.

Elizabeth stopped another teacher, a woman this time, and then a fireman. I listened intently, desperate to know what had happened to Em but unsure what to do. It wasn't real. I was watching a scene that had already taken place. Like a movie. Some memory of Em's I was supposed to know for whatever reason.

But no one Elizabeth stopped helped her. No one. Was that it? Was that the end of the vision? No way. I couldn't help it. Every fiber of me itched to talk to her. So, naturally, I did. I kept it casual, trying not to disturb the order of things. As much as it seemed like a dream, it felt completely real. I could walk, talk, jump, flex.

I found my place next to Elizabeth, keeping my head down and face turned away. She didn't notice me at first, too distraught to see past her worry. "Your daughter is in there?" I asked.

Tears streaked her younger face. "She isn't with her class." She gestured toward a group of students in the park across the way. "No one has seen her. I don't know what to do."

"I'll find her." What else could I say? Dream or reality, I wouldn't let Em die. I would always save her.

Always.

I started to walk away, but she grabbed my jacket sleeve. "Don't you want to know what she looks like?"

I smiled but didn't lift my head to face her. "I'll find her." Then I jogged up the school steps two at a time and entered the building. No one stopped me, too busy tending to the chaos. Smoke filled my lungs in a snap. I sprinted down the hall, my boot soles squeaking against the floor. My eyes watered. Sweat seeped from anywhere it could.

"Em?" I coughed and hacked, drew the collar of my shirt up over my mouth and nose. Inhaled again. "Eliyana." Her given name sounded awkward, but for all I knew, she wouldn't answer to Em yet.

I can't pinpoint the moment it occurred to me. But sometime between finding myself standing before the school and calling her name, my intuition kicked in. My venture into the smoky halls wasn't a dream. My encounter with Elizabeth happened in real time. Somehow I'd journeyed to the past, to New York. Two things occurred to me at once. One a question, the other a realization.

One, what was in the vial?

Two, I had to save Em. Again.

I jerked each classroom door open. Searched in supply closets and beneath desks. In the cafeteria. The auditorium. The gym. The heat and smoke pushed me back toward the exit. I continued on. I'd not crossed a single flame. The danger wasn't too bad. I'd certainly faced worse.

Where would the future queen of the Second be? The place was abandoned, for crowe's sake. I tugged on each locker. Shouted until my throat dried out. Maybe it was my inherent need to save her that drew me into the girls' bathroom. Whatever it was, when I pushed the door inward and heard her crying, I knew Em's sobs before I ever laid eyes on her.

"Hello?" I called through my shirt mask.

The crying ceased.

One corner of my mouth curved. I peeked beneath each stall. And there, in the one at the far end, waited two bare feet. I knocked.

She sniffed and sobbed again.

My heart twisted. "You okay in there?"

No answer.

"Hey, look, I mean no harm." I winced at my empty words. As if she'd believe me. I knew what she'd gone through as a child. The bullying left a deeper scar than Gage's bullet to her knee. What else could I say? "Your mom is looking for you." *C'mon, man, you can do better than that.* "I can't leave here without you." Oh, very chivalrous. I sounded like a moron.

She opened the door but wouldn't look up at me. At least a foot shorter than me, the girl couldn't have been older than seven. But it was Em without question. Dark hair to her shoulders. Mirrormark covering the right half of her face. Her eyes looked different from those of the girl I'd fallen for. Same spirit, but way more fear. *Too much fear.*

"They took my shoes." She swiped hard at her eyes, making them redder than they were before. "Then they shoved me in here and I fell in the toilet." She speaks to the ground, bites her lower lip, and tucks a lock of hair behind her left ear.

Man, she was adorable. I wanted to comfort her, to tell her I would always save her and she'd never be alone. Instead, I reined in my heart and held out my hand.

She didn't take it. Of course she didn't. This was Em before. Em scared. Em afraid of everything.

"I can carry you."

She shook her head. Hair fell into her eyes and she blew it away. "Can you just go get my mom? I really want my mom."

"I promise I'll take you to her. We can go right now."

Another head shake. She backed away into the stall. "I just want my mom. Please, I need my mom."

Her desperation made me want to punch whatever barnacle

had made her so afraid. I had half a mind to pick her up and carry her over my shoulder like I did the night I saved her from the castle dungeons. I wouldn't terrify her, though. But I couldn't leave her there either. How to get through to her? The smoke grew thick, leached through the vents. She gagged and I choked. I blinked away the burn in my eyes.

To say I was at a loss can't do the feeling justice. I was torn between acting and empathizing. I don't believe in accidents. A random stranger gave me a vial of something that tasted like death. I didn't end up next to a terrified mini Em. I was sent to her. What was it she said to me once? Something the younger Song sister had shared with her.

"Bound souls always find one another."

Maybe our soul bond ran deeper than either of us knew. Could it be once bound always bound?

Only one way to find out.

The opposite side of the Threshold into the Sixth is nothing to call home about. I gasp for air as my hand searches for the hilt of my weapon. Gah, I won't get used to its absence anytime soon. I whirl, examining my new surroundings.

I'm standing in a shallow well. The wall isn't high and water isn't deep. In fact, it's almost completely gone. The Threshold became a wormhole, I'm certain, but did the drink from the Fountain control where we traveled?

The drink. Crowe, David. Why did you have to go and mess everything up?

I climb out of the well just as Josh shows up behind me. I knew he was Josh before he snatched the vial. The look in his eyes, the way he talked about "feelings" as if they were a disease. Team David lost another point while Team Josh took the lead.

Dahlia and Wren soon follow. Then Preacher. The well dries up with a loud sucking sound only moments after the last of us exits.

"Well, this is lovely. Nice going, Rhyen. You've taken us to the middle of nowhere."

Wren's snarky comment makes me wish she'd stayed behind. If this is how she's going to be the entire journey, maybe she needs an Unbinding Elixir. The kind that makes her forget how to talk.

"This ain't the middle of nowhere, Miss Song." Dahlia wrings out her wet dress. "No, ma'am. This, doll, is the Sixth Reflection, otherwise known as Oz."

Oz, huh? The ache inside me grows. The burns beneath my shirt feel fresh. But not because I regret saving Em from the fire that day. "Did you hear that, David? Or should I say Josh now? We're in the Sixth. The wormhole took us exactly where the Threshold led. We were supposed to find Em and now we're not any closer to getting to her or destroying the Void. Are you happy? We can't do this without her, and time is slipping through our fingers. Who knows if the next Threshold will even have a drop of water left!"

"Cool your head, Brother. Maybe *Eliyana* is here, did that cross your mind? The Threshold behind the cottage in the Fifth led into the Sixth as well. Perhaps she went through before it became an actual wormhole. Perhaps she has been here in the Sixth all along."

I grind my teeth. I can't argue, though my dark side is begging to rip him a new one. Fine. If he's wrong, I'll deal with him then. There's still an ounce of hope. If Em is here, we'll find her.

"Where to?" I turn toward Dahlia and take a look around. The shallow well is at the center of a cornfield. I sense no immediate threats. At least none aside from Josh and Wren.

Dahlia licks her finger and sticks it in the air. "We follow the south wind."

"And where will that lead?"

Ha. As if Josh cares. I believe David, at least, loves Em enough to know she and I are connected—were connected—in a way they'll never be. The real David would have let me take the drink.

Hitching up her skirt, the Ever woman begins to cut through the dried cornstalks. "The Emerald City won't wait all day. Hurry up."

"You heard the woman," Preacher says. "Move out."

We take our places behind her. I don't know enough about this

Reflection to even guess what awaits us at the end of our trek. But if it takes us one step closer to Em, I'll run if I have to.

I just hope someone in the city can help us. If I remember correctly, Oz has a Wizard. Maybe he can at least tell us where Em has gone. Give us someplace to start.

Picking up my pace, I abandon Preacher and pass Dahlia. Navigation isn't foreign to me. I follow the wind to the road, then I sprint down its unearthed yellow bricks until I'm too tired to breathe.

I'll find you, Em. I'll find you.

ASIDE

josh

He's quick, I'll give him that. Figured I was back before I even had a chance to catch my breath.

"Things will change when they find El," Joshua says. *"She'll see right through you. I know the way out now. And I will find it once more."*

I may have let my guard down with you before. I will not be so careless again.

"Is all of this really worth it?" Wren asks.

She's cute, I won't deny it. But El is something else. Joshua and I at least agree on that.

"What do you love about her?" Joshua asks.

What do you mean?

"I mean, El is good and kind and vulnerable and insecure. But she's also confident when she so desires. And she is smart. Everything about her is beautiful. If you hold the Void in such high esteem, what could you possibly love about El? She's opposite of the Void. In every way."

Oh wow, has my too-good-for-anyone conscience been so clueless this entire time? Does he truly believe I love his girlfriend for her heart?

"I can hear you," he says.

Can you? Can you really? You have been so focused on getting rid of me, on escaping and redeeming yourself, you have failed to see into the farthest corner of my thoughts.

I feel him searching, digging through the mind we share. I

sit back and wait. Wren's yapping about something or other on the outside. My fellow Ever doesn't trust me, so I steer clear of her. Preacher? The brute won't be a problem. As with Makai, his loyalties lie with me first.

"That is where you are wrong," Joshua says. *"Or did you forget Makai named Rhyen his second in command?"*

Unimportant. A minor hiccup.

My brother leads us, and I let him believe he's really in charge. The Void will take him over soon, and then what? He'll be nothing. Because he fights it. If only he would give in, he could see what I already see.

The Void is beautiful.

"You can't. She'll never fall for it. Never." How thrilling.

Ah, and so Joshua has figured out my secret. My lips curl into a smile. Because as beautiful as the Void is, nothing is lovelier than turning something from light to darkness.

Eliyana, get ready. The shadows are coming for you.

TWENTY-SEVEN

Ebony

Let's see, where do I begin? You want the moment I decided I hated my mother? Sorry to break it to you, honey, but there wasn't any specific turning point or anything. I mean, sure, she probably loved me as a baby, didn't shake me or knock me upside the head. But as long as I can remember, we never got along. I was never good enough and never would be.

What will she say when she sees me now?

Stormy and Khloe didn't go far, just as I expected. When I approach them where they lie amidst a bed of fern and clover, Stormy looks up and places a finger to her lips. "Shhh."

My gaze follows her to Khloe, fast asleep in Stormy's arms. The kid is wiped and I can't blame her. This is a lot for anyone to take, especially her. I can't help but be proud of her, though. She hasn't complained or asked to slow down. A real trooper.

"Did she say what shocked her?"

Stormy shakes her head. Whispers, "She fell asleep without saying a word. I think she's just exhausted. She'll be better tomorrow."

Tomorrow. Right. Another day lost. I can't keep wasting my time on sleeping or stopping or waiting for the next thing to fall into our laps. "I'll go get Tide. We should all stay together."

With a nod she closes her eyes and cuddles next to my sister. Jealousy rises unbidden. *You are not being replaced, Ebony. Stormy is a fill-in. She'll never have the relationship with Khloe you have.*

You sure about that?

No. Not at all.

I begin the short trek back toward Tide. It was this way, right? Then why is that bush new? It was on the left and now it's on the right. And these flowers weren't here. They start off tiny, no larger than a quarter. Then they grow the farther I walk. I know this is the wrong way, so not the way I came, but I can't help it. The blossoms intrigue me, creating their own little path that seems to beg to be followed.

The ground softens and sinks the farther I venture. Mud covers my shoes, but what do I care? This isn't a runway. And those flowers, they smell like honey and cherries. The scent is so familiar I want to eat the petals. Is this what nostalgia feels like? Because if so, I say bring on the memories. I can recall nothing pleasant from my childhood. But this? This could be the sweet memory I've been waiting for.

I keep walking.

Is that water? The noise trickles and bubbles. *Curse you, Ebony. Why don't you pay better attention?* It's going to take a miracle for me to find my way back to the others. But who cares? My only concern is how much stronger the scent grows, how much closer the water sounds. Tide mentioned a creek. Could I be closer to the nearest Fairy Fountain than I realized?

The creek comes into view. The water seems to be lit from underneath. Black stones, just as Tide described, lie in its bed.

No. Not black stones. A closer observation shows what lies beneath the water are sunken pieces of wood. Wood carved into various shapes and sizes. Hearts and roses and crescent moons and stars. Polished wood, too dense to float.

Ebony. The wood is ebony.

I tread into the water. It rushes around my ankles, guiding me along its path. I pick up one of the carvings. This one is a heart, small enough to fit into my pocket. I store it next to the compact, still inside my jacket. Then I'm running through the creek, throwing caution to the wind.

You go, girl. Let your inner five-year-old out.

The moment I step foot within the Fountain's perimeters, I know I've been here before. The scent of honey and cherries is stronger than ever. I didn't know it was a fountain back then, obviously. But I remember being five or so and playing where the colors were brighter than anything I'd ever seen. Where the water tasted sweet and the trees seemed to sing.

This is that place.

But she isn't here.

Why would she be? Did I expect it would be so easy? That I could just waltz up to the Fairy Fountain and she'd be waiting on some sort of Fairy throne? Nope. I'm not an idiot. I get that things don't just fall into one's lap and all.

And why am I so sure she's absent? You know that sinking feeling you get in your abdomen when you're about to be chastised? Yeah, I don't have that. I should turn around. What was I thinking? Who follows a smell? What kind of freak takes a swim in a river at midnight?

Sure as crowe not me. Good thing no one saw. I'd never live this down. Tide would get a kick out of it, and I can hear Stormy and Khloe's titters already. Blush.

Yep. I'm going insane. This is happening, people.

On the shore I pick my way back to the place I entered the water. Branches slap my face and arms, scratching my skin and nearly taking an eye out. When I hear a bell-like giggle through the darkness, I exhale a fuming breath through my nose.

"Okay, Khloe, you can come out now. Go ahead and make fun. It won't bother me one bit."

But my sister doesn't answer.

Pelted by another bendy branch, I grow more furious with every step, cheeks growing hotter. "I know you're there, Stormy. This is so hilarious. I get it." I'd throw a clod of dirt at them if I wasn't worried about it containing rocks. "Be serious, for once. Oh right, I forgot. I'm the only serious one here."

"Way too serious, if you ask me," a voice I don't recognize calls from above.

I crane my neck and gaze upward. The glow of a live Fairy makes a leaf look like a lantern. The light dances, and I know in an instant this is the one who's been laughing. My young memory fills in the blanks. This was a lightning bug to me back then. Or that's how I recall it. Have I really known of Fairies all along?

Do I talk to her? What if I scare her away?

Wait, is that me caring about another being's feelings before my own needs? Weird. Cool, but weird.

"Hey," I whisper. "Er . . . Fairy. Hey."

I expect her to flit away, far away. Her fellow Fae are dying—being murdered? We haven't quite solved the mystery of that case yet. Still, she must be terrified out of her tiny mind.

But she's stronger than she appears. She flits down, hovering in the air before my face. She's sort of plain but still pretty, with pale lips and bronze skin. Her eyes are brilliant turquoise, and her hair is flat white. She places her hands on her hips and lifts a brow in a "what do you want?" sort of gesture.

Now she's speaking my language. "Where is your queen, Fairy?" The question comes off sort of rude and much more me. Back on track, thank goodness.

"I have a name, human."

Smirk. I like her. "So do I. It's Ebony."

She gasps and covers her mouth. "Ebony? *The* Ebony?" She curtsies midair. "Forgive me, Princess. I did not recognize you. I did not realize you had returned."

Princess? Returned? Say what now?

"You have arrived just in time. Come with me. Your mother is not well." She grabs the corner of my jacket collar.

"Wait, you want to help her? Isn't she killing you all?" Come on, it was the easiest thing to assume. Don't deny it.

Another tiny gasp. "What? Oh no, Her Majesty would never harm us. We are her humble servants. She saved us from our horrible fate. And now it is our duty to protect her. But we must hurry. Our lives are connected to the beat of her heart. As she gets worse we fade, one by one."

"Wait, what fate?" I'm so confused here. I follow the Fairy toward the Fountain, in the opposite direction of the creek's flow.
"You want me to walk through a waterfall?"

"What are you, scared of a little liquid?"

Ugh. "No." Yes. I can't see my mother looking like a wet mop.
What will she say?

What *will* she say? And what do I care? Defiance brewing, I follow the Fairy through the waterfall to find the most glorious pool,
lit from within like the river. The shore is lined with more ebony
wood carvings. The walls are what draw my attention, though.
Markings and drawings in blue ink cover every inch of stone.

"The blue ink." I part my wet hair, which falls like curtains
around my face. "I've seen it before."

"Of course you have." She sounds annoyed, as if this is her own
way of saying "duh." "Some of these drawings are yours."

My eyes widen. I take in the drawings. My gaze flashes from
a sketch of a daisy to one of a doll. "I drew these? What's the blue
ink from?"

The Fairy sighs.

Sheesh, it's just a question. Excuse me for having no idea who
I am or where I come from.

"The blue ink, as you should well know, is something only
Fairies and their kind can see."

"Yeah, I got that part. But where does it come from?"

Another sigh.

Is this how other people feel when I act annoyed? As if their
existence alone is a burden?

"To answer your question." She tugs harder, forcing me toward
the center of the pool behind the falls. "The ink is not ink, it's sap
from trees watered by the Fairy Fountains. And to answer your
earlier question . . ." Her yank on my collar chokes me.

Ease up, will ya?

"Our fate was one worse than death. Some called us menaces,
while others knew us as the dark ones."

I think of Josh and how opposite he was from David. She can't mean—

"But most everybody called us Shadowalkers." One last tug has me swimming. I take a deep breath just as she says, "Now come. I have something you'll want to see."

TWENTY-EIGHT

KY

"This way now." Dahlia's steps grow slower. Odd ones, these Evers. They can survive most anything. Still they grow weary, feel pain like everyone else.

Song's on the ground too, though she's making sure we all know she's not happy about it. She keeps looking at the sky, braiding and unbraiding her blue-streaked hair.

"Stop your fussin', Wren. You'll get yer chance to take on griffin form soon enough. For now, we want to draw as little attention to ourselves as possible."

Song's shoulders slump.

Aw, what's this? Poor baby can't fly? Is she ever not mad about something? For all her brooding, I'd think she'd win most likely to become a Shadowalker. Yet she's as loyal to the Verity as any. Just goes to show you can't judge a book, or a Mask, by its cover.

The muggy, almost-polluted air casts a gloom over everything. Cornfields wilt and roofs sink. Weeds crawl and grass appears as a patchwork quilt. Not like the clean desert of the Fifth where every breath brought relief. This place carries a thickness, a gravity that pulls you down. The sooner we find Em and get out of here, the sooner I can inhale without protest.

Despite the foul air, walking brings me solace, provides time to return to the past once more. I tune out Song's complaints and relive the memory of the fire. As the stranger said, the drink would take me where I was needed most. Much like the Void and Verity are connected, one forever relying on the other, the Rose's dew seems to bond with your soul.

"I can't breathe!" Em rasped. "We're going to die!"

I seized her hand. She still wouldn't make eye contact, but it didn't matter. "No, we won't. I promise."

I removed my jacket and wrapped it around her slender shoulders. "Put your arms in. It will protect you."

She did as I asked. My Guardian jacket looked like an oversized sail on her mast-thin frame. The double doors at the hall's opposite end were hardly visible due to the thick smoke. We were ready to make a run for it, both of our faces half covered with our shirts, but then—

Boom!

"What was that?" she cried, whipping her head this way and that.

"Gas leak." I didn't mean for her to hear the mutter, but my mouth ran ahead of my mind. Flames crackled and licked. My pulse raced, and I could feel Em's heartbeat through the underside of her wrist. This was no high jump, but the fear was just as tangible as if I were a thousand feet aboveground. I couldn't let her see I was scared too. Couldn't defeat the whole hero persona and all.

I looked left and right. Closed my eyes so hard my head ached. What good was Guardian training plus all the torture Tiernan put me through if I couldn't escape something as miniscule as a fire?

My eyes opened. There, just a few feet behind us in the wall to our right, was a vent. I dragged Em to it. Crouched. Listened. The faintest echo of sirens and shouts pierced the walls. The vent led outside. I was 99 percent positive.

"I'm going to remove the grate and then you crawl through. Follow it until you're outside. It will be smoky, it will be dark, but you should be safe from the fire."

Her lower lip quivered as she stared at the vent in horror. "But what about you?"

"I'm too big. I'll find another way." I forced my tone to make it sound easier than it was.

"Promise?"

"Always," I said. *Always.*

I pecked the top of her head. It was innocent, the same kind of kiss I've given Khloe since the day she was born. I never imagined something so small and quick could strengthen our bond even more.

Em never looked at me. Not before she crawled into that rectangular hole in the wall or even when I called after her to keep going. I remained on my knees, waited until I heard the signal.

"I'm out!" Her voice came as an echoed murmur. But it was all I needed.

She was safe. I'd done my job. I rose and dusted off my pants.

Another explosion blasted the hall.

"Crowe! Void! Gage!" Knocked on my rear, I groaned every curse-worthy word in my vocabulary. I cradled my arm. The fracture was undeniable. I'd have to see a Physic and soon. But first I had to get out. And fast.

I didn't see little Em again. Not when I exited the building, clothing singed and smelling of burnt flesh. I looked everywhere, but she and her mother were already gone. In the time it took to blink, I was returned to *The Seven Seas.* The stranger was gone, along with one of the ship's lifeboats. It was just as well. Em was alive. What else mattered?

Did Em tell Elizabeth I kissed her that day? She must have. Now more than ever I believe her mother was the hooded stranger. Her talk of soul love, the three Kisses of Infinity. Who else would know for certain Em's greatest need matched up with the desires of my heart? The Scrib didn't have a delivery for Countess Ambrose—Elizabeth simply needed an excuse to board my ship as an anonymous passenger.

I may never know the answer for certain, but whatever happened always would. In Em's life, I always went back to save her. She never knew any differently. I've not once questioned what would have taken place if I hadn't chosen to drink the strange substance. Because I will always choose her. No questions asked.

I can only hope this time isn't different. Josh stole my drink today. Let's hope he loves her enough. That her location is where he's needed most. And if not?

Let's just say I might allow Kyaphus out of his cage long enough to do a little damage.

∽∞∾

"Trust me, you don't want to eat those."

Dahlia's warning is useless. Wren reaches for an apple hanging from a tree loaded with an assortment of fruits.

Dahlia bats her hand, blocks her path. "Take a bite from one of them and you'll get your fingers gnawed clean off."

"Is there anything we *can* eat? Or perhaps you'd have us all starve."

"Not my fault you didn't pack supplies," Dahlia says.

"I'm a hunter. If I could take on my Mask I'd be just fine."

For pity's sake, we ate a few hours ago. I remove a container of jerky from my pack and toss it to her. "Don't eat it all."

She glares. Gives no thanks, surprise, surprise. But she devours it. The sight is enough to make me laugh, though I don't know how she can think about food right now. My stomach rumbles, filled with an endless ache that won't subside until she's found. Em is the constant on my mind. Is it the same for Josh? For David maybe, but Josh?

We'll see.

"This place stinks." Preacher swipes at his snout. "I can't wait to be home in my own bed again."

Home. What is that? I've moved around so much. The sea felt like home for a time. I can tell you one thing, I won't be settling in the Sixth.

Rural countryside melts into suburbia. Uprooted sidewalks zigzag down graffiti-infested streets. Trash cans overflow. A woman in some sort of Onesie getup smokes on her porch while her baby's cries carry through the window.

"Now that's just sad." Josh finds his place beside me. What a change. From avoidance to pestering. Now I'm the one who wants to be left alone. Does he notice how the Void wears on me?

I snort. "As if you care."

"I do care. I care enough to say she ought to shut up her kid so others can have some peace and quiet."

Wow. "Well, that settles that question." I look down at my boots. My clothes are starting to carry a stench. I need a shave, a shower, and probably a follow-up shower just to be on the safe side.

"What question?"

Cue the smirk. "Oh, nothing. Just that Shadowalkers aren't human."

From the corner of my eye I catch his arm tense, his hand fist in his pants pocket. "Go ahead and try to punch me," I say. "See what happens."

He stops. Turns. "Maybe I will."

I face him. Finally.

The others cease their trek. Dahlia speaks up, the mother hen always *cluck, cluck, clucking*. "Now—*cough*—boys . . ."

"Back off, Regina. This is not your concern." Josh slides one foot forward.

I match his action. "Indeed it is."

"*Oh yes,*" Kyaphus whispers. "*This is what I've been waiting for.*"

Suppressing my inner villain is the least of my worries. David needs to hurry up and get his behind back here. Him I can at least stand. Maybe the only way to put Josh in his place is to put him in his place. "Tell me, Shadowalker. Does it kill you how connected I am to her? That I'm the one who stepped in and took the blow of Crowe's sword?"

The veins in his forehead have joined the party. His pupils seem to antidilate.

"When Em saved me from the Void injection," I go on, "our soul connection was made complete."

"*Finish him. Do it. You have it in you.*" The jeers sounding from Kyaphus grow louder and louder.

"We believed that kiss linked the three of us. From you to her and her to me and back again. Because you kissed her as a baby? Right?"

"Rhyen, maybe this isn't the best—"

"Shut up, Saul!" Josh says. "I want to hear whatever pathetic thing he has to say. Then there will be no questioning why I broke him."

Preacher rolls his eyes, tosses his hands up, then retreats to a bench on the curb five feet away. "If the Commander were here, he'd have none of this." He grunts.

The man may be correct. But Makai isn't here, is he?

"We created a triangle, all connected by the Verity, the mirrormark, the kisses." My throat burns, the walls stinging. Reminds me of the poisonous coral from the Fourth, only my insides possess the poison. "We wondered if your Ever blood somehow saved me as it had saved her."

"It did." He grinds out the words. His fingers curl and flex. Neither of us carry weapons. It's his strength against mine.

"That's where you're wrong," I say. "The truth is, love is powerful. And the choice to love despite pain or darkness or sorrow even more so. Love kept me alive, gave me strength to overcome the Void. And yet, I'm connected to you as well. We shared the same womb, split the responsibility of the Verity. It is our connection, Brother, that connected you to her." There it is. The hit that will hurt him most. "I am the one who gave her the mark. Not you."

"Revenge. Isn't it sweet? You've held your tongue, but now. This? Doesn't it feel amazing?"

No. I feel sick. This was not the way to tell him. Makai and Elizabeth would be ashamed.

Love. Heartbreak. Revenge. The ultimate combination for once upon a time.

"You're a liar and a traitor." Josh grabs a fistful of my shirt. "I can't see her mirrormark, idiot. You don't need more proof than that to know what she and I share is special. Something you can never duplicate, no matter how often you lock lips."

Valid point, though I'd never tell him and boost his alter ego.

I clear my throat. "Are you certain the creation of her mirrormark is why you can't see it?" My birth mother's *Mirror Theory* comes to mind.

"*When bestowed by the Verity's vessel, a Kiss of Infinity imposes an unusual outcome upon the subject's soul . . .*"

"A Kiss of Infinity given by the Verity's vessel creates a mirror-mark, yes?"

Josh steps back. I've caught his attention. Good.

"Since we shared the Verity, it's safe to argue either one of us could've made her a Mirror."

He nods, though he's far from happy about it.

"Here's a new theory for you. Listen in." I lick my lips and swallow. "Perhaps the reason you can't see her mark is not because you gave it, but because you didn't."

"Reality check, moron." Oh, so Wren's decided to defend him? This ought to be entertaining. "We all can see her mark, and none of us kissed her, thank Havens. Get your facts right. David's the only one who can't see it." She stares into the distance as she speaks, her tone flatter than I've ever heard.

"Are you sure about that, honey?"

Dahlia? Does she have some wisdom to impart?

Song glares at the Ever. No respect, I tell you.

"You callin' me a liar, Miss Wren?"

"Maybe I am."

Our matron does something I've never seen her do. She removes her apron, balls it up, and tosses it to the wayside. Then she stomps over to Wren and gets in her face.

Whoa. If any of us guys did that, it'd be borderline harassment. But an older woman getting too close? Song can't say anything. Not a word. Not when she's been inviting a reprimand her entire existence.

"I'll let you in on a li'l secret. Are ya ready?" Grabbing her ear, Dahlia yanks Song down to her level. "I can't see the mirrormark either, no more than I or King Aidan could see Queen Ember's. Never have, never will. It's not in our blood."

Wait, what? Oh man, this is some solid stuff. I fold my arms. The fight between my brother and me has subsided, our attention pulled elsewhere.

"Evers live outside of time." Releasing Wren, Dahlia wipes her hands on her skirt, then reattaches her apron. She makes eye contact with each of us. Me, Wren, Josh. "Why are you three so darn shocked? I thought this was common knowledge. Saul?" Her eyebrows arch, eyes bulging in Preacher's direction. "A little help here?"

He lifts his hands in mock innocence. "Leave me out of this. This is the first I've heard of it."

"Bah." Another wipe of her hands. "If we Evers would stop worryin' about people usin' us, maybe we'd be more understood. I thought everyone knew we lived outside time." She spins her finger in the air. "Someone once told me time is a loop. A circle. Well, it's that way with Evers, ya see. Our beginning is our end and our end is our beginning."

Whoa. The answer I couldn't give was here all along. Though I feel like I've heard the line before.

If David were here, the news would crush him. But Josh is a statue. Unmoved. "It doesn't matter." He resumes walking, the first to break our stagnant state. "I'm the only one of us still linked to her. Whether I gave her the mark is irrelevant. But the Kiss of Infinity I bestowed on her birthday? That's what will lead us to her." He speaks of their kiss as if it's a weapon. One he'd like to use to take me down a few pegs.

Try again, Josh.

"Bound souls always find one another." I don't elaborate. Don't say he's full of hot air, that she and I are more deeply linked than he can imagine, and it's my soul that will find her, not his. We've had enough banter. We know where we stand. Maybe it'll never be together, but we can at least try to *work* together until we reach our goal.

"Now we've had our Ever lesson for the day. I say we get ourselves a guide." Dahlia laughs. "Whaddya say? Y'all up for a drink?"

Preacher rises and follows her. "You know I am, Reg."

"Good. My knowledge of the Sixth is vast and all, but if we really want someone who knows the ins and outs, our best bet is one of my oldest and dearest friends. She knows this place and all the gossip that comes with it." A slap to her knee and then Preacher's back puts a little more spring in his step. "If anyone's heard of Eliyana comin' here, it'd be her. Good thing for us I know just where ta find her." She taps her temple.

"And where would that be?" Song voices the question we're all thinking.

"The Lazy Lime." The Ever woman gives another wink, twists, and sashays down the road, humming a little tune.

Anyone else would annoy me with their redundant patronization and constant cheery disposition. But Dahlia is one of a kind, and I can't help but love her like a relative with each bat of her eyes.

"The Lazy Lime, eh?" I call after her. "Sounds like some sort of pub."

"That's because it is," she says. "The finest pub in Emerald City."

Pubs always smell like one thing and one thing alone to me—Tiernan. The man couldn't stop drinking to save his life. It started when Khloe was born, his final attempt to sire a son of his own. That's when he started beating my mother, which means he started beating me. The more I disappointed him, the more he drank to console himself. If, on a rare occasion, I pleased him, he'd celebrate with a bottle in his hand and a lazy smile plastered across his lips. But no matter the reason, slap happy or depressed, Tiernan always ended his binges with a round of beat on Kyaphus, the little twerp who would never be good enough because I didn't share his blood.

Classic.

"*Stop, Tier!*" my mother would cry. "*Please.*"

He never listened, never cared for anyone but himself. Now that I know Em, I can't be anything but grateful it was me and not her he unleashed his pain upon. Perhaps, in a way, I've been protecting her all along without even knowing it.

Dahlia saunters up to the bar of the Lazy Lime, hefts herself up onto one of the stools. The four of us join her on either side, Song and Josh remaining a pair, Preacher and me taking stools to the Ever woman's left.

The bartender, a lanky man with beady eyes and a nose too big for his thin face, braces himself against the bar. He fires each of us the stink eye until his gaze lands on Dahlia. Then he grins, a golden tooth shining like buried treasure.

"Ma'am." Spittle drips from one corner of his mouth. He swipes it with the back of his arm. "What can I do you for? You're lookin' like you need a strong drink to knock out that cold you're fighting."

I shudder to think what bodily fluids end up in the drinks he serves.

Dahlia's mouth turns down. "I ain't sick, just tired. I'm looking for the bartender, Wart Langley."

He shakes his head. "Only barkeep here is me. Has been for at least a decade now."

If Dahlia is shaken by his answer, she doesn't let it show. "All right then, well, how about a Munchkin woman goes by Odessa? You happen to have seen her?" Her talk is smooth, as if this is a normal visit and we aren't foreigners in a new Reflection. "Last I saw her was right here on this very stool. 'Course, Wart was the barkeep then."

He begins cleaning glasses with a towel. "I told you. Only one here is me and has been since the place opened."

Shock covers Dahlia's face. "Since it opened? Void, man, this place is older than dirt. Everyone knows that."

Setting the glass down and flipping the towel over one shoulder, the bartender who is not Wart stares her down. "I'll say it one more time, lady, so listen close. There is no Wart Langley. This establishment has been here for coming up on ten years. I am the owner and anything else you fancy. Now, I suggest you and your friends leave before I have you tossed out for causing trouble."

Eyes narrowed, Dahlia rises. The suspicion and confusion in her expression are impossible to miss. "Very well. Let's go." She hops down from the stool and navigates back toward the door, knocking over a chair as she walks by. The man at the bar watches us go. No one breathes until we're through the croaking door and standing beneath the sign we missed before.

I bring it to Dahlia's attention.

She stares up at it, her normally wide eyes now two slits. "Something ain't right, y'all."

Yeah, no kidding. It started with the absence of someone Dahlia seemed to be sure would be here, and now this?

"What an absurd name for a pub. Green Glasses? It's not even original." She huffs. "Well, I'm afraid I'm at a loss for what to do next. Without Odessa—"

"Did you say Odessa?"

At once we all turn to the man half my size who's leaning against the wall on the other side of the door. A newsboy cap sits low over his eyes. His pants go to just below his knees where his socks meet the hems. He's wearing a diamond-patterned vest and a cigar hangs from his mouth.

So we have traveled back in time then. Fine. But we still don't know if it's the right time or place.

"What's it to you?" Dahlia asks the man.

"Not much. I just like to be a helpful citizen. Doing my duty to the community and all."

"Sure." Typical Wren can't keep her mouth shut.

"I'll handle this." Dahlia scoots past her and stands before the man, looking down at him with both hands resting on the shelf of her hips. "What do you want?"

"I want in." He looks up. His face is like the human version of a bulldog. He drops his cigar and puts it out with the toe of his shoe. "I tell you where the Matron of Munchkins is and you smuggle me in with you. She owes me a sizable sum, and I'll be green if she doesn't pay me every last penny. Hard to get to her on my own, but with you lot I might just stand a chance."

"You got a deal." And just like that, Dahlia shakes his hand.

No interrogation, no making sure we can give weight to anything he says. Being around as long as she has, Dahlia can probably tell a lot about someone sooner than most. I trust her. Let's hope she's not wrong.

The small man, who I can only assume is also a Munchkin, pushes off from the wall. "We have to make a stop first. Otherwise we'll never get in."

"Get in where?" Wren again. Always talking and never listening.

The bulldog man glares at her. "I'll tell you something, girl. If we stand a chance at slipping past the guards, you're gonna have to learn to keep your trap shut."

She growls with lips pursed but doesn't say anything else.

I underestimated this man. Maybe he's not as untrustworthy as he seems.

He nods at her. "Better. Now as I said, follow me. We can't go into a masquerade looking like a bunch of filth off the streets."

The four of us exchange another glance before trailing behind him down the street. A masquerade, huh? Not what I expected but something I can deal with just the same.

Good thing for us I'm an excellent dancer.

TWENTY-NINE

Because I Love You

The Verity is mine.

If Isabeau thinks she's going to be the vessel again, she's mental. I won't sleep, won't eat. I won't rest until I've tried every mirror in whatever place we're headed. I will find my way out. Better watch it, Lion Lady. The only place the Verity is going is to destroy the Void. Get ready for a heart attack. The kind that makes it so darkness never was.

Rain pound, pound, pounds. I blink, wipe the hard drops away. No use, of course. The relentless pour won't cease. Lightning and thunder explode the sky, splitting the clouds with every clap and rumble.

Odessa waves me forward. Is she shouting something? Can't hear over the downpour. Don't need to, really. From my short time spent with the woman, I can guess it's something such as "Hurry up." Or "This way." Or "Keep close." Does the Matron of Munchkins ever stop telling people what to do or where to go?

A glimpse over my shoulder reveals my grandfather behind me. He tips his hat, rain spilling from the brim. He's unreadable. Is genuine coldness a thing? Because if so, he pulls it off. What's the forties phrase I'm searching for?

A real humdinger.

When I face forward once more, I watch my footsteps. My sneakers slosh in the inches of water flooding the streets. An Ozident bumps me, not bothering to apologize, and she sprints across the road and into the nearest doorway. My shoulders are heavy. My mind. My heart. This always happens when it rains. As if darkness looms and the only way to go is the wrong one. When the clouds free their tears, I can't help but get sick to my stomach.

The farther we walk, the more the shadows fold over me. I lift my head to find a palace at the end of the sopping road. The street seems to narrow the closer we get, the buildings forming an arrow herding us to the palace doors. Unlike the domed governmental building, this one's all sharp edges and angles. The spires spear the clouds, disappearing within their mist. But this, by far, is not the most noteworthy detail. Rather, the entire structure is stained glass. And the best part? The rain washes away the grime, shines and polishes. Like a first snow in Manhattan.

I can't help but stop and admire the sudden beauty of it all. Odessa climbs the winding narrow steps to the doors. Yet I am glued in place.

Jasyn stands beside me. "What is it? What do you see?"

The anger-fueled girl bursting to be let out again screams to be heard. She can't take this moment from me, though. The Verity swirls in rhythm with my heart.

Thump, beat, pitter.

Patter, thrum, pulse.

I sigh and swallow. Close my eyes. I'm the girl in the snow, imagining the white washing my mirrormark away. Only now, the scene has altered. As the rain makes everything new, the sinking sensation I had minutes ago drains too. And all that's left is this single stirring deep inside, where even my worst self can't get to.

"What is it?" the teen boy asks again.

I open my eyes and take my first step. My answer isn't for anyone but myself.

Hope. I see hope.

⋘⋙

"You look ravishing, darling. Simply stunning." Odessa busies herself tucking me into this unbreathable dress.

I'd expected it to be green like my coronation gown and every-thing else around here. But, oddly enough, it's not. Instead, this dress is a soft gold, forties-style gown, with puffed sleeves and a V neckline. The fabric is a stiff brocade with sage vines embroidered throughout. It's far less extravagant than what I wore in the past—future—but also exceedingly less comfortable. No mistaking the thing wasn't designed for me. Too long. Too tight. Size zero is really more of an Ebony thing. But hey, who's counting?

As if addressing my unspoken dilemma, Odessa snatches a corner of the gown's skirt and shoves it in my open hand. "You'll just have to hold this away from the floor. We've no time to make alterations."

How am I supposed to cover my chest *and* keep myself from tripping? Where's Rodgers and Hammerstein's fairy godmother when I need her? She'd argue, but the task is simply "Impossible." If I bend over, I'll fall out of this thing. I don't fill out the chestal area, which is part of the issue. There's just this huge gap between fabric and bra. Tiny waist and big, well, you know. Whoever this dress belongs to is a supermodel. The airbrushed kind. And that's when it hits me.

The dress belongs to Isabeau.

"Come, come, we must do something with that hair."

I sit on a low cushy stool before an old-fashioned vanity while Odessa stands on an even lower stool and does my makeup. She powders my nose with something sneeze worthy, then she curls my lashes and paints my lips. The pampering is relaxing and nerve-racking at once. In an unexpected instant, the dress feels tighter. But it isn't the gown that's giving me heart pangs.

I miss my sister.

If Ebony were here, she'd ease my fears about what's to come. She'd flip her hand in the air, roll her eyes, and tell me what a big deal this is so not. We have our differences, more than our simi-larities, for sure. But our opposites help the other grow. I was just getting to know her. Will I ever see her again?

Will I see anyone again after tonight?

Drip, drop, drip. The rain creates a rhythm. *Drop, drip, drop.* My head sways along to the tune.

"Hold still." Odessa tugs on my greasy locks, powdering them with the forties version of dry shampoo. "How do you expect me to fix you up if you keep squirming like a child?" She teases and combs, twists and pins.

The style is elegant and classic, and I like it better than I expected. I turn my head this way and that, admiring the Munchkin woman's work. I've never seen myself this way, face clear of blemishes, right side matching my left with makeup and hair done up like a calendar girl. Is this how Joshua sees me all the time? Perfect?

I don't like it.

Pitter, patter, drip, drip, drop . . .

It's too much, too . . . fake. I want to stand out in the rain, let it wash the paint away. Draw my mirrormark. Then at least I'd be me.

Odessa grabs my hand and drags me toward the door. She really needs to stop treating me like a dog on a leash.

"What about my shoes?" I pick up my dress and point to my sneakered toe.

She waves a dismissive hand. "No one will be looking at your feet, dear."

Her very *Ever After* line reminds me evil never triumphs. It didn't with Drew Barrymore and it sure as Cinderella won't overcome me.

A half smile tugs at my painted lips.

Then we're out the door.

There's no prelude. No waiting in the hall to be presented. No butterfly nerves fluttering until my name is called. We're simply there, in a great hall, surrounded by what must be every resident of the Emerald City and then some.

Like the Second Reflectioners, these Ozidents clean up nicely. All prim and proper and matching the decor. Which is, hello, green.

Similar to my Fairy tale coronation with a woodland color scheme, yet oh so far removed. Because one thing is lacking here. Light. This place is dull and *dingified*, not to be confused with dignified. Unwelcoming. No friends or family greet me with joyous smiles or Kuna-friendly waves. Still, an anticipation buzzes through the air that sets my heart pounding.

"Stay here. I will return for you shortly."

"Whatever you say, ma'am."

I'm unacknowledged and abandoned at the punch table while Odessa disappears into the crowd. Isabeau and Jasyn have yet to appear. I'm sure they'll make some sort of grand entrance. Anything less would make me question their identities. Joshua told me how the Troll showed up after the coronation. She took on her most hideous form and issued threat after threat. The woman is insufferable. No matter where I turn, she's there. Waiting in the wings. Ready to strike. Asking Haman for Mom's baby or crashing a party and killing my friends.

"You can't break me," I say. "I'll unbreak you first." I squeeze my drink cup until punch spills over the sides and splashes the copper floor. The hem of my gown takes a hit, stained permanently pink. Good. I don't bother picking up the dress. Let it drag. I hope the gown gets ruined. I'm sure Isabeau owns a hundred more like it.

Despite Odessa's order to stay put, I wander, taking in the eccentric group of attendees. It's bad enough they all wear masks and I'm the only one with a barren face, but then there are no two alike— some animal, some human, and some a bit of both. A man with an ax for an arm. A woman with hair made of actual feathers. As is fitting, her costume is reminiscent of a peacock, complete with a yellow-beaked eye mask and a gown fashioned from blue and green quills. Another woman is dressed as a mirror, her dress and mask reflecting anyone who passes by. Still another man wears a kilt and green-shaded spectacles, his mask resembling the Phantom of the Opera, which suits his dark, slicked-back hair.

I feel like the girl from Kansas, sticking out like a sore thumb. Why didn't Odessa give *me* a mask? This *is* a masquerade. Isn't it?

As if on cue she returns, shoves something into my hand before briskly disappearing once more.

I turn the mask over in my hand, tracing its frame with the tips of my fingers. Of all the masks, what would lead her to choose this one? Of all the masks, how would she know this is the perfect one for me?

The music changes, transitions into a Renaissance-happy dance. Fitting the piece into place, I tie the ribbon at the back of my head. The guise hides my right eye while curving up and over my left. Intricate, ruby-colored filigree cambers and coils over my right cheek, stopping at the corner of my mouth. Beading completes the accessory in just the right places, like little roses blooming among thorny vines.

A flashback ensues. I'm aboard a boat in the middle of the Second Reflection sea. My first brush with the *Mirror Theory*—the *me* theory—collides with my heart. But it's not even so much the theory as it is the prelude. The poem I feel I'm living now, in this moment of clarity. The words in my soul drown out the music. I can't stand it. I have to see. To witness the piece of me that's been missing for such a short time but also far too long. I compose them into a song, dancing and moving as I search the room.

"Once upon a time is ne'er what it seems . . ."

The bodies jump this way and that, the dancers clapping and skipping.

". . . and happily ever after oft a mere device of
     dreams . . ."

A woman bumps me. I keep singing.

". . . What wicked snares are vines, and thorns cause
     many throes . . ."

Many throes indeed. This place is a madhouse. Still, I keep going.

> "... but peer beyond the surface; you may there find a
> rose."

I twist left, right, rise on my toes. Yes. There, at the center of the room, stands a column. The green marble is draped in chiffon, the fabric adorned with gems.

Mirrorglass gems.

Another shove, two squeezes, and an *oof!* "Sorry!" gets me where I need to be. The biggest stone is the size of a CD, just what I require. I peer at my reflection, relief and realization erasing the world.

There I am.

And I love it.

Me as I was. Me as I've been since Joshua kissed my baby cheek. The rose beyond the thorns. Only a Kiss of Infinity from the Verity's vessel can create a Mirror. Why didn't I think of it before? *I* am the Verity's vessel. Could I love this girl enough to create a Mirror in myself once more?

Placing my palm over the mirrorglass, I cast it all away. Every jab. Every kind word. Each and every definition given to me by another, negative or positive. I asked myself once how I could possibly fulfill my purpose as a Mirror without first loving the girl within. So much has taken place since the day I first smiled at my own reflection atop the castle hill. I once desired to change everything about Eliyana Olivia Ember.

And now? Now I wouldn't change a thing.

The transformation that takes place is internal, the Kiss of Infinity unseen. It's a kiss from my heart to my soul. An acceptance of the person I am. A binding promise, making me complete and whole. Because for the first time in my life, I don't want to hide.

I want to sing.

And I feel it. Feel the mirrormark returning as my lips part. I breathe deep as I prepare for my song to flow.

> *"I've lost my way, nothing left to give,*
> *Yet I cannot break, my soul does live.*
> *Past or present, future or beyond,*
> *I'll find my song until my voice is gone.*
> *This song is mine. It's been here all along."*

The lyrics are scarce, the ballad short, but it's original. My very own mirrorsong.

Someone taps me on the shoulder.

Unashamed, I turn to face the curious listener.

I step away.

Then I move closer.

He's here.

ACT IV

In my life . . .
a heart full
of love

joshua

No, he will not steal this moment. Josh will not be the first to hold her after too much time apart.

"You're such a baby," he says in my head. *"It's only been a few days."*

A few days, an eternity, what is the difference?

The trek toward the light is less daunting than the last. I know my way this time. I have gained enough rest, and the time has come to resurface once more. Taking over my own body is easier now. I have no qualms. Soon I will be in permanent control.

Move over, Shadowalker. Eliyana is mine.

THIRTY

KY

I see her before he does.

The triangular ballroom has a tilted feel. Probably due to all the stained glass pieced together at odd angles to create the vaulted ceiling. Or perhaps it seems askew due to the way I stagger when she comes into view. I dart my gaze to Josh. To her. He's not even looking up. His mouth moves, his eyes trained on the floor.

Ah. David is on the way. I don't know if that makes it better for me or much, much worse.

We descend a spiral staircase, following the Munchkin man we've learned is Pierre, as if we belong. When we reach the end he scampers off, leaving us to fend for ourselves. I watch Josh. If I make a sudden move, he'll notice. Do I make a scene? Or play it cool?

Decisions, decisions.

"Odessa'll be here somewhere," Dahlia says from behind her golden mask. Shoulders slumped, she coughs several times, her breaths coming in huffs. "I'll get on with findin'—"

I lean toward her. A stale scent surrounds her. Like dead leaves. She really is ill. All this traveling has gotten to the old Ever woman. "We don't need her," I say as low as I can manage.

"Where are you runnin' off to in such a hurry?"

I follow her line of vision.

My brother is gone.

Crowe, why'd she have to go and ruin it?

"Run for her." Kyaphus is all talk, but he's not the one who suffers the consequences of my actions. Not really. *"Don't let him get there before you. Take what's yours. Be a man."*

A man, huh? A man who does what he wants. Takes what he wants. What kind of man is that?

Sounds more like a coward, if you ask me.

I clear my throat and begin my controlled, out-of-character walk. This is not the time to fight over her. She's made her choice, and she chose me. I have to trust that's enough.

The Void makes me weaker with every step, though no one seems to notice the charcoal veins covering every inch of my arms. One guy even comments on my "costume," asking where in Oz did I get my work done. At least I blend in.

Didn't need much of a disguise. Pierre suited our group up within an hour, ready with forged invitations, cheap masks, hats, and other odds and ends.

A green boa for Wren that's more snake than feathers.

Dahlia squealed, delighted at her wide-brimmed hat and dress made from a set of drapes. Really?

David was pleased his only addition was a simple eye mask in such dark green, it almost appears black.

And me? The mask I wear is much lighter, almost white, covering my face from hairline to upper lip. The Munchkin man thought it would be of good contrast with my "strange tattoos."

I chuckle. Em loves musicals. Will she see me as the Phantom of the Opera? I could always break out in song, render my own version of "All I Ask of You." Too soon? Maybe, but I'll try anything at this point.

David has a twenty-foot lead, surfing with ease through the throng. A peek over one shoulder informs me Dahlia has gone off to who knows where, probably looking for Odessa, even though an informant has become unnecessary. I haven't kept track of Wren, but I'm sure she's watching everything unfold from some shadowed corner. Sulking and defeated. I feel the slightest iota of pity. It's truly awful to love someone who doesn't love you back.

That's my reality as well. "But not for long." The assurance is for myself alone.

I'm reminded of the first time I encountered the girl at the center of the room. Different but also the same. Her hair is pulled off her face now, shoulders back and squared with confidence. The sight makes me fall in love with her more than ever, and a sudden burst of strength plus a shot of resolve quickens my strides. Not too fast, but not sluggish either.

The Verity inside her soul is tethered to the Void inside mine. I need her. I choose her. The light in my darkness.

When David reaches her, I don't stop. Watch her expression for some sign she wants nothing to do with him. Disgust, repulsion, disinterest? I'll take any and all. We've been apart three days, but it feels like a lifetime. If I can just touch her, everything will be all right. We'll be the way we were and everything will be—

Over. Done.

Because he kisses her. Full on the mouth. Hands in her hair. Thumb on her face. But this isn't what rips me.

It's the way she doesn't push him away. The way her arms wrap around his neck. The way she rises on her toes to be closer to him.

My world falls apart.

"*See what patience has cost you? This is why you need me.*"

"No." My vision blurs. "The only person I need is kissing my brother."

Then everything clears and I'm tearing my shirt over my head, charging for them. If I was a Mask, I'd be a lion.

"*Paralyze him. Use your Shield and take what's yours.*"

"Shut *up.*" The command reaches deep, a resounding boom telling him to back the Void off.

Kyaphus trembles.

I promised myself I wouldn't use my Calling for anything other than self-defense again. Granted, I could justify this as defense of some sort. He thinks he can trick her into loving him again? She's smarter than that.

And so am I.

"Em."

Either they don't hear me or they don't care. My brother backs her against the mirrorglass-decked column just behind. His entire person takes her over. I could ask him to please remove himself from the love of my life. Or I could do this my way.

He releases a soft moan and she echoes the sound.

My way it is.

I tear him off of her. I'm so close to punching him, but I growl instead, releasing my hold on his bicep. No doubt I look like the monster many believe I am. But this isn't the Void acting, it's me. Just wait for it. I know exactly what I'm doing, and it's not what they think.

She screams and . . . here it comes. Just as I knew she would—because I do know her better—she shoves me. How else was I going to gain her touch? If I'd approached with a calm, timid demeanor, she would've backed away. And David? No chance he'd let me get close after that. Nah, this is the only solution. Thank you, element of surprise.

When her palms meet my bare chest, skin on skin, her expression transforms, just as it did before the Threshold swallowed her. She keeps contact as her gaze passes between me and my brother. Confusion, disbelief, anger, rage, sorrow. All are present, shredding my heart as it connects with hers. I told him our connection was stronger, but he wouldn't buy it. Does he see it now? Does he feel the slightest bit of remorse for what he's done?

"Ky?" Her voice shakes. "Ky . . ." She blinks. It's like watching someone wake from a nightmare. *"Ky."* My name on her lips lifts the pain of the Void. I hardly even notice it now.

She starts to fall backward, but I take hold of her hand before she can break contact. Then I draw her in. I'm about to kiss her when a guard bangs his staff on the floor three times.

Tap, tap, tap.

"And now a special dance will commence in honor of Her Grace, Her Royal Excellency, the Lioness of Oz!"

A wave of excited titters passes through the crowd. Then

they begin to call out in caws and hoots. Barks and meows and whinnies.

Apparently this isn't a party at all.

It's a zoo.

ebony

Why did I wander off? Following a smell? A river embedded with ebony wood? Seriously, whose story is this? Because it sure as Prada isn't mine.

"Unreal."

I know I spoke, but where's my voice? Left behind in the Fifth? Existing between Reflections inside a Fairy Fountain is weird. More than weird. Insert word here that describes something other and strange but also amazing and magical. I'm not a Scrib, people. Synonyms aren't my forte, capiche?

"Testing, testing, one, two, three."

Nothing. Not a sound.

El and I watched a movie once, on one of our many movie nights back when I pretended to be her friend before I realized I actually liked her and *wanted* to be her friend. It was one of those comedies where the main dude dies, but he's like between lives or something? Anyway, everything was white and some woman with a clipboard took down names and told people where to go. This is like that. Except my woman with a clipboard is a Fairy named Huntra whose voice gets higher pitched with every breath.

"This way, Princess." She drags me into light so blinding I have to squint to keep from tripping over myself. And Ebony Archer does not trip over her own two feet.

"Where are we going?"

"Where you belong."

Belong, huh? And where is that? Truth is, I've never felt more at home than in recent days. I'd like to turn back, to find Tide and say I'm sorry for chickening out when we started to get close. To make sure Khloe's okay and not totally stunned by my Dennielle transformation. She's seen me shift plenty, so what gives? Why, now of all times, did she act petrified at my shape-shift? I'd also thank Stormy. I may be more than slightly jealous of her, let's be real. But it's a good jealous. An I-can-love-my-sisters-better-than-you-can jealous. A please-don't-replace-me-because-I-really-am-trying-to-do-better jealous.

Double sigh on a stick. Enough wishing. I can't turn around. Where would I go? There are no paths between Fairy Fountains. Look left and oh, there's some light. Look right and what's that? Yeah. Light. Not a beam or ray jogs my memory, though. Which makes me think I may have played near a Fountain as a child, but I've never actually traveled through one.

"Hurry, hurry," Huntra says. Who knew a person no taller than my pinkie could be so flipping strong?

"Excuse me? No one tells me what to do." Call it a character flaw. I'll refer to it as independence.

The light grows brighter the farther we walk. Float? Swim? Fly? No way of knowing what's really happening here. I can't feel my body, can't even really tell if I'm alive. It's an unusual sensation. Dreamesque. Like when you're falling and your whole body jerks awake.

Wake me up anytime now. This is getting creepy. 'Kay thanks.

When the light is so bright my eyes might corrode in their sockets, the cool and welcoming relief of darkness blankets me. "Ahhh." Much better. For a minute there I thought I was dying.

Humid air stunts my breathing. I blink several times before I orient myself. "Huntra?" Where has that Fairy flitted off to? Did she really abandon me in this . . . am I inside a *tree*?

I stand, wring out the hem of my blouse. The ends of my hair. Swimming then? I was swimming through the Fountain but breathing as if on land? Didn't notice I was sopping until like just now. Is this what it's like for Tide when he dolphinizes himself?

Or Khloe when she adapts? Nice. Though I'd rather come out perfectly dry if it's not too much to ask.

Bark on every side winds and twists around and above. I wouldn't call this a hollow tree. More like several individual, rather slender trees all twisted together to form a single mass. Water pools around my ankles and all that's left to do is climb.

I'm not the outdoor type, but circumstances have forced such atrocities upon me. If I had the option, which I don't, I'd stay inside all day. Venture outdoors only when totally necessary. And no, I wouldn't read. I'm not that kind of introvert. Libraries don't call to me, and I don't sniff books as if they're candles. My interests are much more of the cuisine persuasion. Shocker, I know. I like to cook. So sue me. There's just something so invigorating but also relaxing about dicing fish and veggies, rolling them into sushi rice and seaweed. Perfection.

But I'm getting off topic. Climbing. Right. "Let's get this over with."

The way up is easy with plenty of niches to grab or to place my foot. A few boosts and heaves and I'm inside the main branches, a landing of sorts spreading out from the holey center. I couldn't call this a trome, per se. Not enough room for so much as a footstool. But it's the same idea, just on a smaller scale. Except you can't get out through a door and you have to go up to get down.

I scoot to the edge, letting my feet dangle outside the tree, which grows at the heart of a much larger pool. Like the cavern beyond the waterfall, these stone walls contain blue writings too. How can anyone make sense of it? Nonsense, that's what it is.

"Ebony?"

I narrow my eyes. At first I don't see her, sitting below just off the pool's shore, perched on a seat made of stone. Overgrown ivy frames her figure, the vines snaking and slithering, embellishing her serpentine-like persona. Lavender flowers with soft but pointed petals grow between the leaves. "Are those Oden Lilies?"

"Main ingredient in Illusoden?" She shrugs. "Why, yes, I believe they are."

That's when everything comes into focus.

"I've been here." The memory is hazy, but some things you just know in your core. "The tree. The scents. Those flowers."

"Well, of course you have." Cool much? One might think a mother-daughter reunion would be more joyous.

"What Reflection is this?" I turn and climb down, using my feet to judge when it's safe to let go. The pool splashes when I land. I move to the shore but don't get too close. Not yet. I don't trust her and won't anytime soon.

"The Third." Her voice comes off unamused.

What else is new? No "Hello, Daughter, lovely to see you." Or "Ebony, what a surprise! I've been looking everywhere for you." Did I expect more? Kisses and hugs and sappy tears?

That's not us. This is.

"Where in the Third?"

I try to listen for sound above the low ceiling. A pop or shout or siren to indicate we're back in NYC. Yes, I do realize the Third is bigger than an island, but for the smallest fraction of a second, I wish I could forget it all and be back in Manhattan. No more Tide or Khloe or Stormy or El. Yes, I'm selfish, but give me this. This moment in which a shopping trip on Fifth Avenue would be nice. Not a care in the world. Just me and Jasyn Crowe's Third Reflection credit card. The way it used to be.

"Does it matter where in the Third?" my mother asks. Tiny details in her features begin to stand out. Her sunken eyes and cheeks. Bony frame. Even her breathing is labored. Someone needs a spa day.

"No. Not really."

She rises slowly. The radiance has vanished from her being. No color perks her skin. She looks awful. "You came looking for *me*, not the other way around, darling."

Darling? Spare me. Her sickly sweet endearment never meant anything then and it doesn't now. "I need to know what I am. Am I a Shield same as my father? Or am I . . . like you?" I'm afraid I already know the answer.

"You are both. A breed of mortal and immortal."

"Can immortals bear children?"

She half coughs, half laughs. "Can Evers feel pain? Immunity to death does not inhumanity make."

Oh really? Could've fooled me. "And my Calling?"

"Tell me, Daughter." Her fingers run along the throne's arms, nails scraping the stone. "Do you recall tasting Threshold water? Do you bear a Seal as other Called?"

A Seal? "Yes." I'm not stupid. The rose and thorns adorn my shoulder blade as much as the next Shield. "I remember when it appeared. Saw it with my own eyes."

"Did you, now?" The sinister sneer I'm oh so familiar with appears on her pale lips. "Look again."

I hate to give her the satisfaction of proving me wrong. Then again, I'd relish a chance to do the same to her, so why not? I unzip the pocket of my jacket and remove the antique silver compact.

Her almost-invisible brows lift a hair. "You still have that old thing, do you?"

What's it to her? "So?"

"Never pictured you as the sentimental type, precious." There she goes with her pet names again. "It is not even real silver. Simply a shoddy, timeworn trinket your unfaithful father proffered. As with all his promises, the gift is garbage. In fact, I distinctly recall throwing it out when he left us." Her glare is not lost on me. I know where she's going with this. "I do not appreciate defiance, Ebony. Is that why you saved it? Simply to disregard my authority?"

"Why do you care?" I clutch the compact so tightly the edges cut into my skin. "You didn't want it. It's mine now." Okay, so she's right. I keep the stupid thing partly because she didn't want it. But also, no one has ever given me a gift. Not a real one. This may not have been handed directly to me, sure. Still, it was *a* gift and now it's mine.

"Did you miss him when he left, dear?" She yawns. "Did you think he loved you and might one day return?"

I will not cry in her presence. I came for answers and I'm

getting them, for myself and for our cause. I won't let her affect me. I promised myself a long time ago those days were over.

"*Come with me. Join us at the Haven.*" Dennielle's words haunt me now. She could've been a mother to me, at the very least a friend. Why did I run?

Because you were afraid, that's why. Afraid of being rejected again. Afraid of getting your hopes up only to be let down.

Going into business for Jasyn seemed the better option at the time. I didn't have to care about the man. The job didn't require me liking him either. I just had to do my thing, and I'd be taken care of, left alone for the most part. Granted, I had to bolt my door every time I entered my room, but still.

There are worse things.

Mouth turned down, my mother stares at me. She's waiting for an answer, is she? Sorry, too bad. This isn't your lucky day, Mom. I refuse. Yet, I have to know . . .

I remove my jacket and set it on the ground at my feet. Pull down my blouse collar over my right shoulder. Flip the mirror open and angle it so I can see—

Gasp! My hands become noodles. I drop the compact and it shatters. The one possession of my very own I managed to keep all these years is broken. Just like that. It's gone. I want to get on my knees and pick up every last shard. To surrender my final shred of dignity and beg my mother to fix it. I know she must have the power—

One breath, then another. My lower lip wants to quiver. Sorry, but no, not today. I don't allow my gaze to fall to the ground. *Don't react. You can't. It would please her too much.*

My mother laughs. The sound echoes throughout the claustrophobic cavern. "There, there. As I said, the mirror was a piece of junk."

Don't look at the mirror. Don't pick it up. "What happened to my Seal?"

"The one you recall was a counterfeit. A transient mark that eventually faded. You were young, and I have a talent for convincing people to believe what is not true. Your mind was shapeable. You ate up whatever I said. Until you started to rebel, that is. I had hoped you would follow in my footsteps, but as with every other human I have had the displeasure of encountering, you were an utter disappointment."

I can't breathe. So it's true. I'm not a Shield. I'm part human, part immortal. What does this mean? I don't voice my question. Too much pride.

She answers anyway. "Your power is beyond what you comprehend. The fact you can alter personas, as I can, shows you are far more than a Shield. More than Tiernan. More than his wretched, adopted son Kyaphus."

My jaw laxes just enough.

"Oh yes, love. I know about Kyaphus." A sinister leer that could rival the Grinch's spreads across her close-to-transparent skin. "As I was saying, you may not be able to modify your wardrobe, but the detail is trivial compared to what else you might be capable of, if only you would join me." She offers a skeletal hand.

I snatch my jacket and the broken compact, leaving the dislocated pieces in the dirt. "Be real. I may be less than pleasant company most of the time, but I'm not like you. I'm not a monster. You killed Nitegrans. And Tide's mother? She died because you had to have your stupid Rose." Hot tears leak and I don't care. I'm so angry I could throw this shattered mirror at her conceited face. "I won't kill or steal. I won't choose darkness. I will follow the Verity."

I gaze down at my reflection in the water. The scrap of fabric woven through my braid stands out more than ever. "I can't help it if my power doesn't come from being Called. But I can still choose how and when I use it. And I'll do nothing to help you."

"Oh, I wouldn't be so sure about that, my sweet."

My hands find their favorite nooks on my hips. She's got nothing. Where's that Fairy? I'd like to go back now. I'll get Tide and Khloe and Stormy. Huntra referred to me as Princess. Maybe she's loyal enough to take me through the Fountain to the Sixth. They connect to each Reflection, right? If I'm my mother's daughter, a

Fairy princess, maybe I can travel through the Fountains on my own. With El and her mirror walking and me and Fairy travel, we'll be okay even without the Thresholds. Even if every last one drains.

"Huntra should be back any moment." Must she read my mind? Do I have no secrets when it comes to her? "Ah, and here she is." My mother checks her nails.

Gotta stop making a habit of that one. I whirl.

Splash. Huntra has returned, but she's not alone. "As you requested, Your Majesty."

"Thank you, Huntra."

I swallow hard. She has the upper hand now. Fine. "What do you want? I'll do it, but let my friends go." If El were here, she'd use her Amulet voice all up in this place.

"Eb, it's okay." Tide speaks for them all.

Khloe holds fast to Stormy. I can see in her wide eyes she's warring between cowering and acting like the girl outside Nitegra Compound.

Her inner Supergirl wins. Sort of. "Don't listen to her." Khloe's spitfire plea contradicts her arms wrapped tight around Stormy's tinier-than-mine waist. "She's just a sad old woman who needs someone to love her."

Oh, the wisdom of my youngest sister. If I were a writer, which I'm not, I could pen a novel full of all the sage advice she's given.

My mother approaches, tilts my chin up with her finger. Her nail slices my skin. "I thought you might agree. How very disappointing. You are just as weakhearted as I remember."

When she turns, I follow her down a hall and into her chambers. Weak? I do a mock curtsy behind her back.

We'll just see about that, *Your Majesty.*

THIRTY-TWO

my life seems to stop

Insanity. Clearly this is not Oz. It's Wonderland. Because I've gone mad. In fact, we're all a little mad here. Crazy mad. Angry mad. Take your pick. There's plenty to go around.

One minute I'm reunited with Joshua. He's kissing me and I'm kissing him. It's no Kiss of Infinity, but the passion, the connection, the chemistry between us is undeniable. He's my best friend playing guitar. His embrace is a cup of hot cider. His kiss ignites a fire and everything is where it belongs.

"Cheer up, sleepy Jean." His tenor pierces my ears and my heart. He sways me to his own melody. The song never changes. We are us. Forever the same.

Leave it to Kyaphus to ruin everything.

A split second before he tore us apart, I sensed him. Maybe it was the Verity recognizing the way-too-close proximity of the Void, or perhaps I became aware my reunion was about to be spoiled. He does that. Weasels his way in, gets in my head. My heart.

When I touched him, my insides passed through the shredder.

And now, here we are. Just as when we collided in Wichgreen Village, embracing for the first time, everything has changed.

His heartbeat against my skin brings it all back, drowning me in emotion, pouring out the truth behind my twisted, turned-around memories. Behind my blind hatred.

Ky saved me from Gage.

Ky played a song composed for me alone.

Ky kissed me on the beach of the Fourth.

Ky. Ky. *Ky.*

I want to hit him and fall into his arms in the same instant. How dare he let this happen. How dare he let me believe Joshua was—is—the one.

"Em," he says, lazy half grin and all.

Oh, ouch. My heart. I can't take it. Can't take knowing what I knew since we connected before I fell through the Threshold. Whatever Joshua gave me is strong. But not strong enough. Touching Ky is key, and I won't lose him again. I can't.

"I said always and I meant it." He tucks my hair away from my face and behind my ear. The first time he did this I hid. Now I lean into his touch.

Ky smells of spring and earth and all things green. He's the Emerald City as it's intended to be. With the rain pouring down, washing everything anew. Alive and thriving and bright. Colors seem to enhance, and the world shifts into focus.

"I found you." Be still, my soul—his breath smells like a first kiss. "You said bound souls find one another. You were right, Em. You were so right." His eyes close.

"Yes. She was." Joshua takes hold of his bicep.

I have a mind to slap him. He can't do this to me. Not again. "Joshua," I plead. "Don't."

I search his eyes. There's a light in his cerulean gaze, but a darkness swirls beyond them too. He's sorry but determined. Forever trying to make my choices for me.

A new dance ensues in honor of the Lioness, who has yet to rear her hairy head. It's a wild ruckus of a song. A few glasses of punch and these people turn this ball into a party. They jump and clash and bash their heads. The music isn't quite so much Metallica as it is Hot Chelle Rae, and all I hear is *"la, la, la"* and *"oh well"* and *"whatever."*

Except not whatever. Because this music is so wrong for the seriousness of the situation. Like standing at the precipice of a rave, watching everyone go crazy but you can't bring yourself to join in. The DJ has it all backward. This song doesn't fit and please play something else. Anything else. Taylor Swift or Christina Perri or Jamie Scott or Snow Patrol. Music that *means* something. I don't want to get lost in the beat. I need to be found in it.

"Joshua." I face him fully, keeping a hand on Ky at all times. "Listen." The music drowns my voice. I raise it. "Don't take him from me again. I beg of you."

He shakes his head. His jaw works. In all the time I've known him, I don't believe I've ever seen him this drenched in emotion. His eyes glisten enough for tears. But none fall. "I . . ." He reaches for me, then draws back. Shifts his glance between Ky and me. "I cannot live without you. I . . . need you."

The admission appears almost unbearable for him. As if saying these words removes some part of his manhood. Yet somehow these mean more than any of his "I love yous" ever did.

I sniff. Blink. The truth stings my throat as I force myself to admit, "I . . . need Ky."

Joshua's nod and pursed lips bring relief and heartbreak. He's going to relent. At last he'll let me go.

I give Ky my full attention once more. The invisible thread between us is mending. Will a physical link recharge our connection? If we stay attached long enough, will the spell break?

Our minds reel. He hears every memory restored, removing Joshua and returning to the place he's always belonged. I see every moment of his from start to finish since we've been apart. His decision to go it alone. A conversation with Mom causing him to change his mind.

It was you? I think. I lift my hand to my cheek and he covers it with his. *All this time. You* gave me the mirrormark? *My mom said . . . soul love? Really? That's . . . amazing.*

He shrugs.

But then how did the wounds Haman inflicted heal? Joshua's Ever blood—

"—was connected to me." He finishes my thought. Hands that have become so familiar wrap my waist.

But Joshua can't see my mark—

"A side effect of his Ever blood. Living outside time."

I assumed the Verity lived outside of time, but Evers? Whoa.

From the corner of my eye, I notice Joshua staring, watching the scene unfold. Why does he torture himself? I don't want to hurt him, but I can't lie either. He'll never fully leave my heart. But it no longer belongs to him. Maybe I gave it to Ky years before I knew him.

Joshua said we were connected. Our foreheads touch and I'm home. He sensed me his entire life.

"The Verity joined us at birth. His blood still healed you. But only by way of the love you and I were meant to share from the beginning."

The triangle. Our battle with Jasyn. I thought I was the link, uniting us all. But the common thread was never me.

It was Ky.

"Kiss me." His soul breathes the words into my heart.

You read my mind, my soul breathes in return.

I see Joshua move before I can register a reflex. I hold tight to Ky, but my first love is too strong. He pulls his brother away. The Void in Ky has made him too weak to win this one.

Focus. Don't blink. Keep eye contact. Don't . . . lose . . . him.

Sing.

My lips part. I still know Ky. We're not touching, but he remains. I can overcome this. I can—

Enter the cowardly lioness. The woman who wants it all but has nothing. An immortal who only takes and never gives.

"Loyal subjects." The Lioness enters the room, in feline form once again.

The crowd parts. Masks lower. Music ceases.

No. Don't let it distract you. Stay with—

Joshua pulls Ky away.

"Stop!" I don't care who's watching. I follow, push past, through, and around. Why won't they get out of my way? Don't they see this is a matter of life or death? And by death I mean a life, not without Ky, but in which I hate him. Which is almost worse.

If I forget him entirely, he might have a chance at charming me again. I fell for him before, right? Yes, I hated him once, or thought I did. This is different. The anger and spite I harbored were enough to turn me into a Shadowalker.

"I welcome you to the most splendid of evenings." Voice booming, Her Grace is the female version of Jasyn. "For I have found the answer to our Shadowalker infestation."

Not me, no, ma'am. How did we get here? This is a revival of my eighteenth birthday, complete with a new cast. Ky, not Joshua, is the one snatched away. The Lioness, not Jasyn, plays the lead. And me? I'm still fighting the Void, but instead of planning to take it on and become its vessel, I'll do whatever is in my power to destroy it. Then we can all finally be free.

The Lioness roars. French doors fly open on cue, like two wings flapping, beating the walls, making way for the circus to come. Instead of Soulless—those mindless, lifeless drones forced to obey the Void against their will—these are people who have chosen this fate. A death march featuring those trapped by the darkness they've allowed to reside inside them.

And they're all in cages.

Cage after cage is carried forth, some formed from bent branches, others fashioned from iron. All sit atop guard-supported poles. As if on display, each one is placed on a different platform throughout the room. Spotlights rotate toward them, shining bright gold and green filtered lights onto the accused. The lights cause a prism effect, bouncing off the glass walls and ceiling, like something from a dream.

But what's inside is truly nightmarish.

Not because the Shadowalkers are particularly frightening. Aidan's outlook makes so much more sense now that I see them for who they truly are—now that the Verity sees who they are. I see them through eyes of light, much in the same way I saw myself in the mirror minutes ago. These citizens aren't dangers to society. They're merely human, each and every one of them experiencing an indescribable pain that eats away until all that remains is darkness.

A middle-aged woman cries, fingers spread over her flat belly. Did she lose a child? I can't imagine.

A balding man clutches his head, rocking back and forth as if tortured. Who did he lose? A wife? A mother? A friend?

The worst sight of all, however, is not a person entrapped. Not in a physical cage, at least. No, the sight that grips me, that has me bracing myself against a nearby column, trying to find my voice so I can do something, is the change in Joshua's eyes. Not in color. It's deeper than that. The eyes are the windows to the soul? The saying speaks truth. I'm witnessing it right now.

"Behold, your peers, men and women who have bowed to the Void." Her Lioness prowls to and fro, looking as if she seeks to devour the Shadowwalkers one by one. "It would be something if we gave them another chance. I am not called 'Grace' without cause." Cheers of agreement and praise erupt from the attendees. "Yet I am afraid they have wasted all opportunities for redemption. Would you not agree?"

The people jeer. Shout. Call. At first their cries are inaudible, a jumble of yells and screams. But then I begin to translate what they're actually saying, separating the words, picking them out. One. By. One.

My core trembles.

"Destroy them!" a Munchkin man demands.

"Throw them into the Deadly Desert," the beak-masked woman yells.

"Bury them alive," a couple shouts in unison.

I look to Ky. To Joshua, who continues to hold him back. Their expressions are polar opposites.

Ky's brows draw together, shadowed veins covering his face. But he's looking at me. Gaze never turning from the light.

Joshua's eyes, however, look down on his brother. Anger fills them. The rage I felt for Ky plagues him too.

And, slowly, I sense my heart slipping away from the boy who can't take his eyes off me, falling onto the one who can't seem to let me go.

"Curse them!"

"I say we have a hanging!"

"Make it so they never come near us again!"

The more Her Grace's subjects call for justice, the brighter her fierce teeth gleam. Her approval eggs them on, manipulating them into making the choice for her. Then her eyes lock onto the quarreling brothers. She licks her lion lips and rolls her ferocious head.

"No."

I don't have to read her mind to know what she's thinking. The Shadowalker in Joshua is clear, the Void in Ky obvious. Both will become victims of her mass murder. Both will be destroyed.

Whatever her intentions for me, I can't allow them to suffer the same fate.

I hitch my skirt and climb onto the nearest platform. One hand finds the bar of a cage. I curl my fingers around it. The distraught woman inside grabs my wrist.

"Please," she implores, much in the way I pleaded with Joshua not to take Ky. "Help me."

Swallow. Nod. This is what I was meant for all along. Because it's here, Reflections away from my throne, where I may finally act as queen.

"Listen!" My outcry draws the attention of the people.

A tangible shift takes place as all eyes whip toward me. Some frown. Others show surprise, curiosity, interest.

But the Lioness? She's the kicker. No longer the center of the Reflections, she wears a scowl that could bring an army of Soulless to its knees.

Been there, done that.

"You would do well to step down, Elizabeth."

I turn my head to discover my someday-grandfather standing just below.

He reaches for me. "Come. Her Grace's wrath is inevitable. You cannot save them."

I narrow my eyes. "Why are you doing this?" I'm on the verge of tears, but who gives a crowe? Where is the compassion? The grace the Lioness claims to be? "I thought you wanted to be rid of the Void, yet you only aid in strengthening the darkness."

His mouth turns down. "She understands me in a way Aidan does not. She accepts my darkness instead of pretending it is not there. Surely you can understand." He glances from me to the Lioness and back again. "With Aidan, my shadow is something to remain hidden. But with Her Grace? I am free to be who I truly am." His façade shimmers, and for a fraction of a second I see his Void-blackened veins. But then he seems to think better of it, conceals his flaws once more.

"The Void is not *you*," I say to him alone. "And as long as you let the darkness define you, true freedom you will never know."

I look away from him, speaking loud enough for all to hear. "Can't you see what these Shadowalkers need is love, not punishment? Is their crime not one we all are guilty of?" My lip trembles. I steady it, momentum coursing through me, empowering me, mirrorglass in my veins.

The people exchange glances, murmur in hushed tones.

I gulp a dose of courage, then another. They've been misled to believe a lie. What is the Verity for if not to expose the truth? "Which one of *you*"—I point to a trio of women who laugh behind their hands, pointing at their childless peer beside me—"has never made a mistake due to grief?"

They shut off their chatter. Not a single one makes eye contact with me. But the roses in their cheeks play witness to their shame.

"And *you*." I pick out a guard poking his staff through a cage at the tortured balding man. "Have you never lied? Cheated? Stolen? Have you never heard the voice of darkness at your door and it's everything you can do to turn the bolts and shut out the din?"

The guard ceases his fun, withdraws his staff, and lowers his head.

Time for the clincher.

I lower myself from the platform, refusing Jasyn's help as I do. Then I walk directly toward the Lioness, Isabeau, Troll, original vessel of the Verity herself. I stand before her. I do not cower. I do not bow.

"And you, Your *Grace*." My emphasis on the word *grace* is impossible to miss. Good. "Have you forgotten where you've come from? You created the Void." Her eyes widen. Do I see a hint of a tear, there in the corner of her right eye? "How can you now condemn those who live caught in its snares? How can you accuse, when you yourself felt so much agony at Dimitri's rejection, your shattered heart caused the very thing that afflicts theirs?" My chest is an earthquake, my heart beating so fast it rumbles my core. But I am rooted in light.

And I will not be moved.

The Lioness, speechless for a moment, stares.

Have I come through loud and clear? Will my voice make a difference when it's needed most?

"Eliyana Olivia Ember." Joshua stands feet away. The way he looks at me, says my name? It's all the explanation I require. He's fighting something too. We all are.

I convey a silent plea as the last bit of my Ky melts into Kyaphus. I hold on to my love for him as long as possible until he's—

The Void's vessel. What's *he* doing here?

"*He's here to take everything from you,*" Miss Shadow in my soul says. "*Just as Jasyn Crowe tried to destroy your life, so Kyaphus—*"

A hand on my shoulder. I whirl. My teenage grandfather stands there, liquid brimming in his eyes and hat to his heart. "You *are* the one. The girl with the light. Her Grace has spoken of you as a long-lost treasure. I scarcely believed you existed."

I scrunch my forehead.

"When I became the Void's vessel, I believed it less daunting to use its power than to fight it. But perhaps there is another way? If I ever have a daughter, I hope she is like you."

Innocence, pure and simple. Jasyn is the orphaned boy looking up to Aidan, trying to figure out where he belongs.

I consider Kyaphus again, but with the same eyes that loved the Shadowalkers. Rather than hatred building, compassion rises, squashing every stone I wished to throw his way.

"No!" The darkness within me wars against my head. My heart. Her voice is stronger than ever, clawing out with screeches and cries.

This is the moment that counts. Give up? Give in?

"I will never stop fighting. Someday I will be free. Try to deny it, but you will choose me. And when you do . . ."

She goes on and on, so loud and long and never taking a breath. I physically cover her ears. Why, when I finally sense a breakthrough, does the moment of truth arrive?

The Lioness becomes Isabeau in a seamless swirl. Approaching me, she leers, the almost-change I saw before vanished with her fur. "Ah," she says. "It appears the boys will not be the only new additions to the Shadowalker execution." Her chin lifts left, then right. "Guards, lock them up." With her widest smile yet, she adds, "Let the games begin."

THIRTY-THREE

joshua

I growl.

"Troll."

Isabeau. Fairy Queen. Lioness. She is the same no matter which form she assumes. The immortal can smell darkness. She, after all, is to blame for its creation.

"Yes. Isn't she beautiful?" Josh's voice is faint, but it's there.

The Shadowalker I believed I at last managed to lock away lingers, a mark not quite removed. He will always exist, anticipating a chance to escape. But I will never cease fighting him. From here on out, I vow to choose the light.

I release my hold on my brother.

He grunts and stumbles, catching his breath in heaves. When I offer him a hand up, I utter the words I never thought I'd say. Not to him. But now they must be spoken. Now they are my truth.

"I'm sorry. For everything."

The unblinking eye contact between us sets me on edge. I almost think he might not accept my offer.

But, as I've learned, this is Ky—not Kyaphus. Not Josh. This is my brother. A better man than me.

He takes my hand.

I pat him on the back and he nods. "Thanks," he says.

"Sure thing."

But the moment doesn't last. In unison, we turn to find the one we came for.

"Get off me." El kicks, but she has no need. The guards obey her Amulet command without protest. The dilemma she faces is in her eyes. She's fighting something no one can see, a battle I am all too familiar with.

"You can do this, El." I go for her but three men close in. Not even guards. They simply want to impress their queen. I'm restrained without a word. My crime? Being human.

"Silence her." The man with the bowler hat returns it to his head. Next he withdraws a handkerchief, does a quick swipe beneath both eyes, then stuffs it in his blazer pocket. Whatever moment he and El shared has end—

Wait. I do a double take. Is that . . . ? It cannot be Jasyn Crowe. At first I didn't make the connection, but . . . "Impossible." I scratch the back of my head, then take three steps toward him. "Jasyn?"

He stands before me, looks me up and down, though he's shorter, scrawnier. Nothing has changed, not when he's fifteen or fifty. An air of superiority remains. "How do you know my name?"

"You're . . ." Did we really travel to the past? "You . . . know my father."

"Who is your father?"

"Aidan Henry."

The lines on his forehead tighten. "You must be mistaken. Aidan does not even have a wife to claim, let alone children."

"I said don't touch me!"

My attention shifts. Two guards back El into a corner. One is a shorter, thinner version of Preacher, all scruff and scowl. The other is much broader, a double Kuna if such a thing exists.

Managing to escape his sole jailer, Ky says, "You heard her." He attacks the whiskered guard, grabbing him in a chokehold while he bucks my brother this way and that.

The burlier guard attempts to aid his comrade, prying Ky's arms off, though my brother regains his hold each time.

"Didn't your mother teach you to fight fair?" He pokes the guard in both eyes with his free thumb and forefinger. "No? Well, I guess all moves are fair game then."

The smaller guard yelps. Forgetting El, Ky puts his energy into getting the leech off his back.

Nice. I knew my brother was a good knife fighter, but this? He doesn't need his weapon to make a dent in his enemies.

"Elizabeth, really," Jasyn chimes in. You would never know he almost shed a tear moments before. "It is best for you to relent and allow the inevitable to take place."

Elizabeth? I blink. Realization weighs heavy. El knows this is her grandfather, the future vessel of the Void, if he isn't already. She's given him another name. "What year is it?"

The Jasyn Crowe look-alike who cannot possibly be who I think he is replies, "What an odd question to proffer during such a time as this."

Struggling against my captors, I say, "Answer me."

"It's 1945."

The wormhole transported El to 1945? Then the Rose dew brought us here as well? How do we return?

"I said leave me the Void alone!"

We'll have to figure that out later. For now, all my efforts must be poured into this, the here and now. Or then, it seems.

El's voice grows weaker with each demand.

The guards act less confused, overcoming the small bit of Amulet left in her words. She's not even singing, just shouting until the sound fades to a dull hum.

"She's losing it again," Ky calls. "Her voice. This has happened before. We have to *do* something." He relays all this while continuing to ride his guard like a bronco.

The anger shrouding the girl I know is like nothing I have ever witnessed. Oh yes, I have seen her angry, but not like this. This is different. This has Shadowalker blueprinted all over it.

The people look on, raising their masks or adjusting their spectacles as if watching staged combat. They're worse than Soulless. Crowe's army was held against their will by his Void injections, but these men and women? They are choosing to stand back and do nothing.

"Is it fear of your queen that keeps you in place? Are you all so twisted you will not help innocents?" I'm able to free one arm from the man on my right. He yanks it back, causing pain to rip through me. I bite my tongue, refusing to let him in on my weakness. "I saw it in each of your eyes. You must know your queen is not for you. Any ruler who chooses suffering over saving is no ruler at all."

The only response I receive to my reprimand comes in stares, ogles, and select guilty frowns.

I draw a deep breath, search the room for my cohorts. They've waited in the wings until now. Perhaps they still see me as king, loyal to the end. I grow an inch at the notion. If these brainwashed citizens will not help us, so be it. Dahlia's nowhere in sight, but no matter. When I lock eyes with the Preacher, his gaze transfers. I follow it to Wren, who stands fifty feet to his right. She catches his stare, then touches two fingers to her brow and tucks her hair behind one ear.

Anyone else might witness the natural ticks and assume she's just being a girl. But I know better. This is the Silent Code of the Guardians.

These men aren't going to know what hit them. The countdown commences, and I cease my struggle. *Ten, nine, eight . . .*

Wren walks backward through the throng, pivots, and runs.

Preacher sidesteps, left, left, left. He's almost to the stairs we descended not twenty minutes ago.

Both are in position now. Our numbers are few, but together we're strong. I clear my throat and shout, "To the crown until death!"

"To the crown until death!" Preacher and Wren cry in unison.

With more skill than I've ever seen him use, Preacher chucks his battle-ax straight toward the glass roof. The execution is flawless. Time to duck.

I'm released a second after the roof shatters. It doesn't take much to charge past the burly guard, snatch El, and lug her beneath an archway. "Stay here."

I leave her, then go for my brother. The glass storm has sent everyone to their knees, hands and arms covering their heads.

Those in cages have more protection than the rest. But the fight between Ky and Isabeau's guard of the year goes on.

I launch myself over a man curled into a kneeling ball. Then I grab the staff the burly one dropped and use a sweeping motion to bring the final guard to his knees.

My brother is relieved.

"Thanks," he says.

"You're welcome."

But the fight isn't over.

With the roof in pieces across the vast room, it's time for Wren to make her move. She's disappeared from view, but I don't have to see her to know what's coming.

"Watch." My brother receives an elbow to his rib cage. I jerk my chin toward the dark clouds swirling above the open ceiling. "Five, four, three, two . . ."

A screech-like roar that could rival the Lioness version of Isabeau sounds.

"One."

Wren in griffin form swoops down through the roof's opening. She soars low over the people.

They scream, bowing as close to the floor as is physically possible.

Cawing and clawing, Wren uses all her best moves. When she lands on top of a cage, her front talons clacking against iron, the people of Oz lie officially spooked. No one rises. In fact, we're the only ones still standing.

Aside from Isabeau.

"Joshua!" My name on El's lips doesn't sound like her at all. She runs for me.

But that's when guard after guard closes in, some piling in through the double doors where Isabeau entered and others marching down the stairs. They create a barrier between us and the Verity's vessel.

There's no way out on this one. We are completely trapped.

"Did you believe it would be easy to defeat me with a few stunts and circus tricks?" The immortal who seems to be the source of all our troubles glides to where we stand. She steps on the broken glass as if it's ice. She acts as if we didn't just crash her party and destroy the place. "This day was set in stone long before you were born, gentlemen."

"What day?" Ky clenches and unclenches his fists, then rubs the back of his neck. The pain the Void causes is obvious. With each moment that El forgets her love for him, the greater the Void's hold on his soul becomes. If we wait much longer, it will consume him as it did Jasyn.

Guilt and remorse devour me, blacking out my vision for a breath. When my sight returns, I resolve to make the switch. She can't fight without her Mirror, and she can't spark her Mirror without him.

It will kill me to do so, but my brother and El must be reconnected. And I am the only one who can do it.

⌀∞⌀

"Mirrorglass reverses, my boy."

Rafaj's words return to me, guiding me along the path I swore I'd never choose. Along that path that will mend her heart.

"Is there a way to undo this?" I asked.

"Oh"—he rubbed his hands together—"is there not always a way?"

"Tell me." The break was meant to be permanent. I couldn't take any chances Kyaphus might discover a loophole.

"What else?" Rafaj said. "Mirrorglass. It reverses. The severing of two souls is not immediate. The break will not be complete in the same moment the tear touches her tongue."

"How long?" I worked my jaw. My grandfather was a cryptic one. I didn't know the details behind his imprisonment, but I could wager his irritating personality had something to do with his chains.

"Depends on the strength of their bond, my boy. A few days, a year."

"Could you be more specific?"

"Until her hatred for him subsides. There is a fine line between love and hate. When she no longer feels anything toward him, anger included, that is when the Elixir will have done its deed. That is when she will at last be able to let him go."

"And before then? You said mirrorglass reverses. Would you care to elaborate?"

"Certainly." He twiddled his fingers. "The only way to reverse the curse you will place is to take on the curse yourself."

Rafaj, at last, went into detail. Sharing what I must do if and when I ever regretted my decision to sever my brother's tie to El.

"But remember, it must be done before she lets him go. If she releases him from her wrath, nothing can be changed."

My head lifts and I am back in the present.

"What day?" Ky asks again.

Now I see it. The difference between them together and apart. Restoring their link will make her stronger and able to fight. The Elixir I concocted had nothing to do with her memories. The change ran far deeper. Unless her heart is restored to its original state, much like Isabeau's heart must be mended to destroy the Void, El will never regain full use of her Mirror Calling.

"Why"—Isabeau brandishes her arms and the sentinel wall splits, forming a clear path between us and Eliyana—"the day the prophecy is fulfilled."

"Prophecy?" El speaks, her voice hoarse, not her. "What prophecy?"

El's deadened eyes, the way her shoulders slump. She's letting go just as Rafaj said she would. Her hate for my brother subsides. She no longer looks on him with disdain.

She no longer looks on him at all.

I feel the mirrorglass bottle inside my pocket. Never thought I'd need it again. But here we are.

Ky sacrificed himself for the sake of the Verity once. It is my turn to pay the price.

Isabeau creeps toward El. "You foolish girl. Did you truly believe you could somehow turn my people against me? I am queen. I have been around for many years. I have seen it all. I have witnessed vessels come and go. I have watched betrayal after betrayal. I have seen those unworthy to take on the light waste it as you mortals waste everything." The disgust twisting her expression brings out the Troll within. She does not need to transform to be a true monster.

"I have waited years for the girl with the light the Scrib Dimitri spoke of in the Garden," she continues. "Before darkness overtook him, he cried out, screaming at me it was not over. Warning me one day I would meet my match in a girl truly worthy of the light I lost." Isabeau squares her shoulders. "Now here she is in the flesh. Now I want what is mine. Jasyn." Her words confirm this man is indeed the one we will battle years from now.

He approaches. "Your Grace."

"You brought the crown?"

"Yes, Your Grace." He removes his bowler hat once more, but this time takes out the lining. There, hidden within, is none other than the Verity's mirrorglass crown. He hands it to Isabeau.

"That belongs to my father." I shouldn't know this, yet I do. Was this Jasyn's first betrayal of many when it came to Aidan?

Isabeau caresses the crown. "That is where you are wrong. This was stolen from me years ago. With it in my possession once more, I will at last be free."

I am unsure what she means by free, but I'd hate to stick around and find out. "El." Why does she stare off into space as if she's not here?

"Em." Ky joins me in trying to bring her back. I'm so thankful for the aid, his nickname doesn't even bother me. "Use your Mask, your Magnet, your Shield. Come on, Princess. I know you have it in you. This stuff's cake for a Mirror."

She's physically here, but nobody's home.

Crowe, what now?

I look to Preacher, tackled to the ground by five men. Useless.

Wren thrashes, fixed in place by whips around her four legs. One man muzzles her beak while another wrenches her tail. The most devastating sound I've ever heard, whether from human or beast, emerges from her throat.

"Stop this." I fight harder than ever to be free of my captors. "El, please. Come back."

Each second I watch her do nothing. The queen I saw on the platform is no more. She slips away, letting the Shadowalker take over. My brother's suspicion was partly correct. Another Kiss of Infinity is the remedy. But they will never share one again unless I make this choice, here and now.

I hang my head. The power I felt as Josh gratified me in a way I cannot describe. No control, just freedom. But the cost that came after has been too great. The price of realizing my wrong and knowing I may never be able to go back and correct it. Countess Ambrose cannot be brought back to life. But this? This I can correct.

"Please." Pathetic. "Give us a moment, Your Grace." The words are the most bitter I've spoken. "Allow us a chance to say good-bye before you execute your punishment." Using my body weight, I force the guards to kneel with me. I bow my head. This is disgusting, but it may work yet. "Let us say farewell. A final request before our execution."

I glance up at Isabeau beneath my eyelids. My entire body waits on full alert. Is there a sliver of hope she'll grant my request?

Her glare suggests not. But then she returns the crown to Jasyn's hat. "Very well. I am nothing if not gracious." The leer she offers says the opposite. "Release him." She waves a commanding hand.

I fall face forward to the floor, but I'm quick, catching myself with my hands before a nose break follows. Quick as a fastball, I'm on my feet. I cross to Wren first. When I reach her I bury my face in her feathered shoulder, using her mass to hide what I'm about to do.

I withdraw the palm-sized bottle from my pocket, hold it up to my left eye. All it takes is the thought of El in my brother's arms for a tear of true heartbreak to fall.

Wren moans and nuzzles my head.

"You are a true friend," I tell her. "And I will never forget it until the day I die."

She lowers her muzzled head, blinks a single tear that slips down her facial feathers.

I touch the lone blue feather toward her neck, bright as ever. Wren has remained loyal to the Verity despite all that's happened. Life has hardened her, but never so much she's turned to darkness.

All my strength goes into turning from her and toward Eliyana. This is it. The rest of my life draws near. My precise gait is slower than usual. Each step is a decision, one I will not turn back from.

When I walk past my brother he stares at me, eyes wide.

"I really am sorry." I stop before him and hold eye contact, letting the words sink in.

The guard loosens his hold long enough for Ky to shake my hand. "It's forgotten."

I nod my thanks, then take my next step. I go to her for the last time.

ASIDE

KY

What's he—?

Son of a Shadowalker. "David—Joshua, wait."

My brother moves toward Em. He's fluid, purposeful, and ignoring me completely. I don't like this. The tiny bottle in his hand. Maybe no one else noticed it, but I sure did.

The remedy. Must be. I ought to be thrilled he's come to his senses, elated Em's about to remember me in the way she should. Instead, feelings of dread and doomsday rush me.

Why do I sense my new beginning is about to become my brother's end?

THIRTY-FOUR

Ebony

I'd go for a coffee, but let's be real. I'm so over the whole Starbucks thing.

"Hey! Watch it, lady!"

I continue my trek from this curb to that one, dismiss the cabbie with his head out the car window. Can't he see I'm walking here? Places to be and things to retrieve. His royal taxiness can wait. People use Uber now anyway. Or is it Lyft? Hard to keep up when you don't live here anymore.

Dodging a puddle of melted snow and street grime, I hop up onto the final curb. Just a hundred more yards and . . . Well, it hasn't changed, but what did I expect, for the thing to grow wings?

This is the part where I'd generally reach into my purse and reapply my lip gloss, pluck a stray eyebrow hair or two. But I travel lighter than a Fairy these days. Oh wow, did I just think a bad joke? I shake my head and approach the bottom step. *You really must be tired, Ebony. You're starting to sound corny.*

Tide loves corny.

Sigh. I know.

I take the stone steps to the abandoned home in style. Never thought I'd find myself here again, standing before El's brownstone on Eighty-First, seeking a way in. Not into her home, but into her life. Back then I believed I had it all figured out. I could sum up every goal into hurting her. But the blame game is so last year. Time to take on a new hobby. No longer out for *revenge*, I'm ready to *a*venge. Give me knee-high boots and a pair of black leather jeggings, because this girl's ready to become a true Shield.

Out of habit I take the knocker and rap it three times. Listen. Nada. Good. First rule of breaking and entering? Appear as if you know what you're doing. Look like you belong and no one will think otherwise.

The key's in the same place she left it when we were here last—behind the loose knocker. My eyes roll because, hello, it may not be as cliché as a key beneath the mat, but this hiding place is so obvious.

When the door opens inward, the most freezing draft ever seems to explode in my face. Sheesh, it's colder in here than it is out there. Kinda sad, really. I only lived in this city a few months, but El's home was a source of warmth despite how much I despised her. Elizabeth would offer me tea and ask me where I was from. I'd make it up as I went along, of course, adding lie upon lie. As I creep through the lower level, our past conversations flood me, remorse weighing heavy with each one.

"Eliyana said your mother works in fashion, Ebony. I would love to meet her sometime." Elizabeth sipped her Earl Grey, the tea tag fluttering with each tiny move.

I couldn't bring myself to look her in the eyes. Instead, I busied myself pretending to take interest in a Pottery Barn catalog on the kitchen counter. "Yeah. She likes to change styles a lot. What can I say?" It wasn't really a lie. Tell me which part of that sentence isn't actually true.

"Perhaps she and I can set up a coffee date. I might as well get to know—"

I flipped a catalog page, receiving a lovely little paper cut in the process. "She's out of town quite often." I didn't hate interrupting. I was used to it. And again, which part of what I said was a lie? No part, exactly.

"Oh. Well, perhaps sometime when she *is* in town." She stared me down over her teacup, tapping the ceramic with a fingernail and arching an eyebrow as if to say, "I'll be watching you."

It was no secret El's mom didn't like me. I didn't use proper grammar in texts, and I never said *please* or *thank you*. If I ever see her again, I've already decided the first thing I'll say.

"Thank you for showing me what a real mom looks like."

I think of my most recent conversation with my own mother as I exit the kitchen and make my way down the hall. She didn't offer me tea, or coffee, or so much as a glass of tap water. Her words run through my head with each step up the creaking stairs.

"You have become close with Tiernan's illegitimate child, have you not?" my mother asked with a sneer.

I didn't need to answer. I mean, given she can see right through me and all. Hate it, can't help it.

I don't have to go far when I reach the second floor. The first door on the right calls to me, inviting me to a place I've been many times but never truly appreciated.

The door with the crystal knob? El's room. Been her room since before she could walk. A dose of outdated jealousy pours down my throat. I swallow, forcing it gone. Me, jealous of a seven-by-ten box? Yep, guess so. This was hers. She didn't have to move. Never needed to run until Jasyn found her.

"Answer me, Ebony. Or will you insist on being difficult?"

She wanted an answer? Fine by me. "*I* am Tiernan's illegitimate child too, Mother. Come on. Enough pretending. He didn't love you any more than he loved Elizabeth."

My response stung more than I wanted. I ignore the ache in my stomach, turn the crystal knob, and enter El's space.

Must and the scent of unwashed clothes cloud the air. It's like a time capsule in here, a museum of my sister as she was. A complete and utter hot mess. Not that I turned out much better. My room on the Upper East Side was anything but tidy. At least I had some organization to my clutter, though.

"This is just gross," I mumble to myself, glad no one's here to witness my snobbery. Which, by the way, I *am* trying to suppress. Give a girl a break. Sometimes you just have to say what's on your mind, am I right?

Where to begin? "You don't have all day, Ebony. Time to put that conniving but brilliant brain of yours to good use." I start in on the closet. Shirts and sweaters slide off hangers, land in a heap on the wood floor. "Doesn't she know sweaters should be folded?"

Swift but efficient, I rifle through more of her things. Dirty clothes lie scattered, but that's about it. I check under her bed, inside her open backpack. With each drawer I open, Isabeau's words sink deeper. Mallets to my already-butchered heart.

"He loved me," she said, voice quavering though she tried to conceal it. "What we had was a love unrivaled." The cool calm I've come to know returned to her words. Verity forbid she show a little emotion, lose a little control.

"He didn't love you." I clutched the broken compact inside my pocket. If anything, the discarded mirror was only more proof of my father's indifference. "And he didn't love me." My heart raced. Was I really going to say what came next? "But I could've loved you, Mother." And there it is. The little-girl plea I've been denying. "But you never let anyone in."

Like me with El. And Tide. Anyone and everyone. Even Dennielle, who offered a warm bed and a good meal, couldn't thaw my frost.

I rub my hands together, blowing hot air into them. Then I sit on El's unmade bed, trying to envision the last time I saw her with what I've been sent to retrieve. But instead of focusing on my task, I allow the chill in the air to take me back to my mother's chambers. Cold and bleak, they were perfect for the ice queen of the millennium.

When she offered me a stool beside her vanity, I tilted my head and narrowed my eyes. "I'll stand, thanks."

"Very well." She sat on a chair directly before her mirror then. The scene became a flash forward of my future. She powdered her nose the same. Turned her face this way and that. Her high cheek-bones belonged to me too. Was this my destiny?

"You and Elizabeth?" I continued. "You're the same. Except not so much really. She actually loves her daughter."

My mother glared at that and swiveled in her seat, tapping her long fingernails together. "You know nothing of love. You are a child."

My skin crawls. I dig my nails into the rumpled bedsheets. Move things around on El's dresser, lean over and peer behind it. A book gets knocked off and falls to the floor. Nothing.

"I am tired," the Fairy Queen said. "Tired of things being stolen that once were mine. The Rose was never meant to remain in the Fourth. It was taken from me years ago by Ambrose's grandfather. When I at last discovered its whereabouts, I ventured to reclaim it. But the countess placed an alternative. She was aware of my identity, though she would not divulge the source of her information."

Once Upon a Reflection. Tide's mother kept the book in her archives for who knows how long. I'll bet my favorite pair of Gucci shoes, if I ever see them again, the book was Ambrose's source.

"The Siren held my identity over my head as blackmail. We shared a Kiss of Accord. She swore not to breathe a word of my nature, and I promised never to come for the Rose."

I eyed her. Clever woman. Ambrose didn't actually tell us Isabeau is the Fairy Queen and original Verity's vessel. She only aided us in coming to the conclusion on our own. And my mother? She sent Joshua to capture the flower. Both broke their promises while technically never breaking them at all.

"Why do you care so much about who knows what you are?" Even as I asked the question, the answer was clear.

"The same reason you do not wish for your friends to know what *you* are. Other, special, more powerful than their mortal minds can comprehend. I once made the mistake of allowing others to see my true self. And it cost me more than the control over them was worth." She messed with her thinning hair, pulling some forward to make it appear fuller. "You are going to make me a promise too, dear."

She had to be dreaming. My lips weren't going anywhere near her hand.

"Oh yes, you will. Because, though you are the spawn of a wretched man, I also know, deep down, you desire to do good. You will fail, of course, but you do try."

Try, my derriere. Failing is not a category in this scenario. I'll save Tide and Khloe and Stormy. I'll find her wretched trinket and use what I've learned to help end the Void. Boo and yah. How's that for trying?

I jump up and rip El's sheets off her bed. "Ugh!" A pillow goes flying. Not here either. Where did she put it?

"I am aware of far more than you realize." Rising from her chair, my mother crossed to her boudoir. "You know about the Garden. Jonathan is a good little spy, you see. Told me all about how the Countess gave you a book from her library. *Once Upon a Reflection*, was it?"

She thinks she knows everything, but she doesn't. She doesn't know we're going to stop her from becoming the monster she is today. If the Void never was, neither was she. There will only be the Verity in the end. I may not exist, but the others will survive. They'll go on. All that matters, far as I'm concerned.

"You needn't speak," she said. "But I know. I know you and your friends are aware of what I am. Of who I am. But what you don't know is our goal is one and the same. I do not relish the Void's existence any more than you do."

I kneel beside the bed. Rest my head against the mattress edge. How could El sleep on a twin? This thing is tiny. I twist and open each dresser drawer, moving clothes aside and—*there*. Yes. Here it is, tossed aside like a generic something or other. I stuff it in the satchel my mother provided, tromp out of the room and back down the stairs. I lock the door, hide the key. As I head in the direction of Central Park, my mother's words continue to berate me.

"I want the Void done for as much as anyone else." Her eyebrows became the focus. She tweezed and brushed, forcing each hair into perfect, proper place. "We are all on the same team. My methods are a bit unconventional, I will admit. Which is why I need my mirrorglass crown returned. And I expect you know just where to find it." She caught my eye in her reflection, but then her gaze returned to herself, always the main attraction in any case.

I hug the satchel to my side. The naked trees seem to taunt me. Their branches are talons and I'm about to be ensnared. I don't know the backstory behind how the crown ended up with the Second's ruler, and I don't really care. Tide, Khloe, and Stormy? They're what matters. Not some diadem. It's a thing. A charm. Let the Fairy Queen have her prize. I don't believe a word she says. She wants the Void extinguished? Not buying it.

The way back to what I'll refer to as her lair is a slice of pie. Now that I know a hidden cavern lies beneath Bethesda Fountain, Central Park will never be the same. It's not too busy, which is nice for me. What's not nice, however, is the frigid air numbing my bones to icicles.

A salted sidewalk clears my path, snowdrifts plowed off to one side. I make a beeline for the terrace. I know the way well enough. El had a sort of fascination with the Park. To me it was just another outdoor venue, complete with dirt and leaves and animal droppings people so conveniently forgot to pick up. I'd much rather spend a day at the museum or culinary institute, but whatever. Our time spent here did me some good. For starters, I'm not lost. And I don't even have my GPS. *Score one, Ebony.*

I cross the intersection into the Park without waiting for the Walk signal. Horns are like "what the bleep?" as cars and taxis slow. So sorry to inconvenience you, but this is an emergency. Excuse me if I don't stand by for Mr. Walk Light.

The path past the Lake is the quickest route. I dodge weirdos sporting every fashion and beauty trend you can think of. From wavy eyebrows to glitter beards, New York has it all and then some. Call me old-fashioned, but I think I'll keep my natural brows. And Tide had better not grow a beard and sprinkle it with glitter. For that matter, if he starts pulling his hair back into a man bun, we're going to have problems. Thank the Fairies the other Reflections don't seem to go too crazy with jumping on the trend wagon.

When at last I reach Bethesda Fountain and the terrace, I

pause. The angel statue seems to look down on me, though I can't tell if she's meant to guard or condemn. Her hollow eyes almost look angry. I feel like her outstretched hand is pointing at me, telling me to stop, wait, don't give Isabeau the crown.

I have to give her the crown.

Just across from the fountain, a terrace waits. The passage beneath leads tourists through arches and into a colorful, tiled tunnel. Night falls, marking the end of day three since my sister's vanishing act, and the lights in the tunnel bounce off the ceiling. If I look up I can almost see my reflection there. But I don't look up. *No time for sightseeing, Eb.* This isn't one of my missions for Jasyn, though stalling helps me think. I know my mother won't harm them as long as I possess what she desires. But the second I hand it over, that's when all bets are off.

The façade within one of the tiled arches is easy to find for those who know where to look. I pass through it with ease, keeping the mirrorglass crown close. When I'm through and exiting the mirror into my mother's chambers, she rises from her perch on the bed.

"Well done. It appears you are more competent than I realized."

I toss her the satchel, wishing the crown would break but knowing it won't. "Why did you need me? Or Joshua for that matter? If you're so powerful, why can't you retrieve your junk on your own?"

She removes the crown from the satchel. Her ice-blue eyes widen as she examines it. "There are some tasks even I cannot achieve without aid. My reach has been limited for many years. I have remained confined to the Fountains, to the shadows, cursed to walk the Reflections as the opposite of my true self if I venture too far. Light reveals my flaws. Only in the darkness have I been allowed to be myself."

I cross to the door. I want to be done with this, to take my friends and go. But I have to stay, don't I? I didn't come here for myself alone. I came to learn as much as I could about the original Verity's vessel. I'm close to discovering a missing piece, something none of us expected. I feel it.

Then again, I could just have indigestion.

Moving to her vanity once more, my mother takes a regal stance, sets the mirrorglass crown on the vanity. "I am cursed, Ebony. I may remain close to the shadows and, in so doing, keep my youth and beauty." Fingertips to her crow's feet, she lifts the skin around her eyes. "The Broken Bridge in the Second was as far as I could venture without being forced to transform. Any other place I went, if I was away from the shadows too long, my curse would take over. I was forced to take on my Troll or some other form aside from my true self. Here I was alone, but myself. Out there I was every form but my own." Releasing her lids, she sits before her mirror again.

How much time does she spend here? Remind me never to take more than an hour doing my makeup again. Now I know why they call it a vanity. Is this what others thought of me? As vain and selfish and Ebony-absorbed? Ewww. I wouldn't want to be friends with me either.

"But now." She smiles at herself. A wicked, self-satisfied smile. "With your help, I can finally be free of this cage. With this crown I will be myself once more, and one step closer to my goal. I came close once before. Unfortunately, my plans were foiled."

There's a story I'd like to hear. My mother didn't get her way? Pass the popcorn and turn down the lights. I'd pay to see that show.

"Tiernan used to come to me in my prison, tired and in need of unadulterated affection from someone who could please him in all the ways his wife could not. Do you remember our home in the Second, my darling? The cottage near Pireem Mountain?"

I clench my fists. Oh, I remember it all right. All too well. It was from said home I fled. If I never see the place again, it will be too soon.

"But I am getting away from myself. What was I saying?" Her airy voice gives me the creeps. Everything she says is backhanded.

Ick. Didn't I do the same to El? To pretty much anyone? How did I fail to realize the person I most wanted to stay away from is the person I've become?

I grew to be my mother's daughter. Worst career ever.

"Oh yes," she continues, no reminder needed because the question was rhetorical. Does she speak just to hear her own voice? "My curse." Hands on the crown, she lifts it above her head. "No more shadows, no more hiding. I was running out of time, growing old. Destined to be immortal but unable to hold on to my youth. Now that will all change, for now I will be able to return to the place I have always belonged."

My mother places the crown upon her head. Her form takes new shape after new shape. She shifts from Isabeau to Troll to . . . Whoa, a Lioness?

"Mirrorglass reverses." She confirms my greatest fear. "While before I was limited, now I will be in control. I may go anywhere, be anything. But, most importantly, I may return to my Garden, no longer held within boundaries by an invisible chain." She cackles with each new transformation, becoming whomever and whatever she wants. An old woman, a swan, a sunflower. A unicorn, a blue jay, a Fairy. The shifts are quick and seamless. When she pauses on one form in particular and turns to face me, I stumble backward, grope for the handle on the door.

"Why, hello, darlin'," she says.

I find my voice and spit her name. "Regina?"

ASIDE

joshua

Some good-byes are short-lived.

Others last forever.

If this is my final moment with El, what else can I do but end where we began?

"Hold this." I press the mirrorglass into her palm. Then I find my way to the stage. Everyone watches. Heads turn and bodies shift. Forget a private farewell. Our ending is a spectacle, but this makes no difference. Not to me. When I'm with her I feel as if I am the lone man in the room.

The band has abandoned their post since the party unofficially ended, probably off boozing somewhere. Not a problem. I do not need the guitarist, only the guitar.

Several to choose from, I decide on the simple acoustic. The wood the craftsman used is much darker than the pine my own is made from. Still, lifting it off its stand feels similar to shaking hands with an old friend. I strum and find the instrument already in tune. Then I turn, ignore those who consider these final moments as entertainment, and begin.

Every song I always desired to sing to her, all the lyrics I restrained when I pretended I felt nothing. Now I pour it all out, holding nothing back.

"One, two, three, four . . ." Ed Sheeran opens the serenade. ". . . fallin' for your eyes . . ."

"Joshua. What are you doing?" El's tone is deadpan. She

stares at me. Through me? Her love for me is present, but no life resides behind it.

Because I am not the one she needs.

I move on to Secondhand Serenade, combining lyrics and reworking melodies to create a new piece just for her. "... *fall for you ... break the silence ... impossible to find ... my heartbeat ...*"

She's feet away now. I've commanded the room's attention. From the corner of my vision I see my brother war between stopping what's about to take place and letting it happen.

His foot slides forward.

I face him but continue to play. *This is my choice,* I mouth.

His foot slides back.

My gaze meets El's again. Each song I touch becomes mine— ours. From the works of A Great Big World to The Fray, the refrain flows as if it's never been sung before.

"... *unspoken ... the stars had aligned ... you found me ... I'll look after you ...*"

No tears form in her eyes that have always reminded me of rich chocolate—sweet and irresistible.

When I'm so close I can smell her indescribable scent, I set the guitar on the floor. With a deep breath I take her hands in mine and finish the lyric I've been saving for last. "... *daydream believer ... daydream.*"

All of me wants to kiss her then. I lean in, ready to steal what I know she will freely give.

Her eyes close, and she waits for me to make the first move.

But I don't. Instead, I take her hand, which now holds the bottle, and guide it to her lips. Her eyes open and search mine.

"Everything will be okay." *Keep it together. Almost there.* "Drink this and you will understand."

She nods and her lips part. This trust will vanish soon. She'll no longer be mine. A thought occurs, and I ponder it as the tear slides slowly to the bottle's lip.

Was she ever really mine?

Our short time together plays on a reel before my mind's eye. I take a snapshot of each moment, holding on as long as possible.

When my tear touches her tongue, I wait, watch for the change in her eyes.

I know when it happens. Because when her gaze leaves mine, I know it's been undone. I've lost her.

"I am so sorry," I say for the second time today.

She says nothing, instead abandoning me for my brother.

I want to run, but the denial would not last. Why delay the inevitable? I turn and take in the scene as it plays in slow motion.

Their reunion is bittersweet. She's crying and he's taking her face in his hands. He hugs her and mouths a *thank you* to me over her shoulder.

I nod and wait. This is not over until . . .

Their kiss is the final blow. The last cut, severing our link. The heartbreak that follows is physical and emotional. I can almost hear the crack down the center of my sternum.

I grab my chest with one hand and the wall with the other.

What is it Romeo said?

"Thus, with a kiss, I die."

as if something is over

There's nothing quite as invigorating as finding something you've lost.

I draw back from Ky's kiss. Just look at him. His hair, honeyed cowlicks curling away from his ears. I twist a lock around one finger. He tugs on my hair in response and we both laugh.

Three full days. How fitting. When I believed Joshua drowned, three days passed before he came to life before my eyes in the Forest of Night. Now Ky lives and breathes as himself in my memories again. My Ky. Mine.

"I remember." The words squeeze through choked, happy tears. "I didn't even have to touch you. I remember."

Ky traces the lines of my face. The bridge of my nose. The arch of my brows. "But you *want* to touch me, right? I mean, come on, who wouldn't?" He shrugs. Half grin and all.

This is the part where I punch him playfully and we go for a walk. Fingers and souls intertwined. Because, yes, that was a Kiss of Infinity just now. Rare as they may be, infinity seems to come natural to us.

"I missed you," I say.

His two-tone eyes say everything his lips can't. *"I missed you more,"* he thinks, for my heart alone.

The Reflection seems to have faded around us, leaving Ky and me in our own private bubble. Everyone else is a blur. No Joshua. No Lioness or Matron of Munchkins.

Only. Us.

"Em—"

Not yet, I think. *Stay. Just a bit longer.* The knowledge of who Ky is and, more importantly, who he is to *me* sparks something deep inside, piercing the darkness in my soul with spears of light.

"Won't you stay with me?" My heart croons the Sam Smith lyrics. *". . . you're all I need."* Except it's clear to see this *is* love and this *will* work. With Ky everything works.

"Em—"

I hear the ache in his heart. The urgency behind his thoughts. But I'm not ready for this moment to be ripped away like everything else. Yes, I know this isn't a scene from *Once Upon a Time.* There's no screenwriter to guarantee a happy ending. No loophole every other episode, giving us a way out. As Joshua once told me, *"This is real life."*

It appears my broken heart's mended. I lean into him, inhaling his green scent. *Shall we mend the Fairy Queen's as well?*

Ky swallows and his Adam's apple bobs. He tucks my hair behind my ear. "Em." My name is an out-loud plea. "Look." His gaze passes over me then. Our bubble pops.

The room becomes clear once more, the Ozidents ogling us through the eyeholes of their masks. Cages filled with Shadowalkers surround us. A griffin I'd know anywhere as Wren thrashes and sways. Her agony strengthens her as she rips from her restraints and takes flight. She soars over us and lands ten feet away.

To my right stands Isabeau. Watching. Waiting. Expecting. What? She's yet to place the mirrorglass crown upon her head. Did Jasyn steal it from Aidan? How did it end up back in his possession?

"Will you just stand there?" Isabeau rests her chin on her cupped hand. "Will you not attempt to save him?"

My head whips toward Ky. He's fine. No one is stabbing him or harming him.

"No, not him, dear." She gestures toward the griffin.

I look over to find the Mask kneeling beside—

That's when I see it. A body so still it could be dead. No, not it. He.

And I'm frozen.

I clench my gut. The warmth. The Verity isn't rejoicing. It's crying.

Colors flash before my eyes and fade to gray. The world around me tilts. "Joshua." His name rasps from my throat. I scramble to him. Trip. Someone laughs. A few scoot closer. If they had smartphones, I've no doubt they'd post this on every live feed across social media. They're Shadowalkers, all of them. I don't fear those in cages. I'm more afraid of those who taunt and tease, standing by while others suffer.

"Wren." I touch her feather-and-fur shoulder.

The griffin rounds on me, snaps her beak, and assumes a protective stance over him.

I reach out a hesitant hand, lowering myself before her.

"What are you doing? How can you kneel before her? You are a queen. She should be your servant!" The worst version of myself rages in her internal cage.

I glance over my shoulder at Isabeau. *No,* I think, returning my attention to the griffin and her charge. *A good queen must first learn to be the least before she can become the greatest.*

Ky interrupts my silent conversation. *"Well thought, Em."* Pride fills the words unspoken.

"Wren," I say again. "Let me see him."

She stares through me. With a shake of her shoulders, she transforms. Naked, she falls to her knees. Uncontrollable sobs rack her body. She hides her face in her hands as jeers and taunts sound from a crowd enjoying their show.

My heart wants to wrap her, to comfort her in a way only Joshua could.

I rise slowly, using my frame to block the exposed girl on her knees before me. Then I remove my dress and drape the garment over her like a blanket. I'm in nothing but a thin slip, bra, and underwear now. In my time this might be considered modest compared to what some Walmart goers wear, but here I feel more naked than Wren. Exposed.

But I am not ashamed.

I sense Ky's presence a few paces back. When I glance at him he's frowning. But he's also not surprised. Did he know this would happen to Joshua?

"Yes," he says in my head. *"He caused you to drink my tear from the mirrorglass bottle, which made you forget you loved me. Now it's his tear you took. The remedy, I believe."*

My hands cover my mouth. With anyone else, this might not be so bad. My bond with Joshua broken and my link to Ky restored. All would be as it should be. But this?

I love you, I tell Ky's mind before I shut him out. I don't hear his response, but I don't need it. He traveled through time and Reflection to find me. If I ever doubted his affection, it wouldn't be now.

I skirt a sobbing Wren and approach Joshua. When I'm behind his head, I draw him into my lap. He's heavy. I can manage. Because we've been here before.

But we won't come back again. Not this time.

My lip quivers.

Joshua blinks.

When he looks up at me, my breath is twice removed from my body. His eyes shine, the cerulean more brilliant than I've ever seen. He doesn't bleed. No bruises cover his skin.

"Joshua." I choke on my own tears. "Why?"

Wren wails. She places a hand on his boot, then rests her forehead there.

He smiles all the way to his eyes. "Because." One small word. All his energy. "It was the right thing. The good thing. I—*inhale*—spent—*exhale*—my life . . ." Inhale. One swallow. Two. Throat cleared, he starts over. "I spent my life believing I was meant to save. It was time to fulfill my purpose. To be the man my father knew I'd become."

I trace his brow, feel every single hair roughing up his cheek.

"A tear spilled from true heartbreak plus the reverse effect of the mirrorglass makes an Unbinding Elixir," he says. "Ky's tear made you forget. Mine made you remember."

Right hand over his heart, I feel his pulse slow. Left hand

clutching my treble clef–heart necklace, I feel mine race. We don't
have much time.

My mind screams in a place no one hears. Resolve takes over.
This won't be like Kuna. I slip my hand beneath his shirt, touching
skin to skin.

> *"Here we are again,*
> *At the edge of good-bye.*
> *Please don't leave me now,*
> *Let this death be a lie . . ."*

I sing the words over and over. A tear slips and splashes onto
Joshua's face. Nothing changes.

"El." Joshua covers my hand on his chest with his. "It's okay.
I'm ready."

"I'm not." I sniff, remembering Ky's words.

"No matter what . . . if someone is already meant to die, if it's their
time, nothing can change that. Not a touch from a Physic or a drop of Ever
blood. Death is a Calling all its own."

No. I'm not going down without a fight. We've lost too much.
My touch can heal his heart. It *has* to. I just need to try harder, to
believe with all my heart it's possible. My lips near his ear. Then
my song releases, stronger this time. One for him alone.

> *"Take my heart,*
> *Listen to my mirrorsong,*
> *Let my voice give you*
> *Everything you need . . ."*

Joshua uses every effort to lift his hand to my face. His thumb
traces my lip. His touch is so light I almost don't feel it. When his
right hand finds my left one, my curled fingers open.

Holding the charm he gave me, he asks, "You . . . still have this?"

Is it working? "Of course I do. I always will." I have to keep
singing.

"Take my hands,
Feel my healing touch,
Let my touch give you
The life that you need . . ."

His eyelids flutter. He's fading. His broken heart is too much for him to bear. This solidifies the truth. Joshua is dying. And there's nothing I can do about it. Because the only thing that can mend his heart is me. But I love Ky. This is where it ends.

"It's okay," Joshua whispers. "I'm ready." He's so far gone he's repeating himself.

"You idiot." I swipe my stupid tears. "Why would you do this? There had to be another way to undo—"

"No," he says. "When I sought out the man who told me about the Elixir, I made certain the only one who could reverse its effects was me. It was a risk I was willing to take. A side effect I never thought I'd have to endure."

My forehead meets his. I've come all the way to the past, only to destroy my future? A future without Ky or a future without Joshua? If he had given me the choice, which one would I have chosen?

I can't make that choice. But I don't have to. Joshua did it for me. He made the choice he knew I'd never be able to.

"El," he says. "The mirrorglass crown. It reverses."

I furrow my brows. "I know." I swipe at my nose, my eyes.

"El. Mirrorglass reverses." Then he winks, and I get a small glimpse of the boy and his guitar once more.

Mirrorglass. It reverses.

I peer at Isabeau. She has yet to wear the crown. Jasyn never wore it. The reversal effect too much for his Void-infested soul. Because the mirrorglass would have counteracted his darkness. What was it Nathaniel told me?

"The crown would have put a cap on Crowe's darkness like a Confine on an underage soul."

I kiss Joshua's forehead. He's a genius.

If Isabeau wears the crown, she believes it will reverse the darkness in her enough to take back the light—the Verity. "She's going to try and kill me," I breathe into Joshua's ear. "She's going to try to release the Verity and take it back by way of the crown at the same time."

"Let her," Joshua says. "The Verity cannot be fooled. Taking on the light by way of force will be catastrophic." He wheezes. "But it needs to be done now. Ky will save you." He finds the rose-button charm now. A slight smile lifts one corner of his mouth. "I'm a full supply of Ever blood as long as my body's still warm." He laughs.

I shudder.

Joshua reaches out, but Wren is too far. "Song."

She looks up. Will she tell him she loves him?

"To the crown until death," he says.

She fists her heart. "To the crown until death." Then she transforms once more, taking flight and disappearing past the gaping hole in the ceiling.

"Your turn." He looks at me. "Time for you to go too."

I kiss his knuckles, bating my sobs as I force myself to rise.

I am the Verity's vessel. Queen of the Second. I have experienced more than one Kiss of Infinity. I've fought against the Void and felt the sorrow of a Shadowalker. Now it has to end. Here. For good.

The entire room is still frozen in silence. I know none of them. I want to go home.

So I do the only thing left to do. I stand before the immortal Fairy Queen, waiting for her. She said this is a game? I say game over. How does she plan to kill me? By sword? Knife? Hanging?

Ah, much more clever, and most unoriginal. She's going to do this the old-fashioned way.

Isabeau becomes the Lioness. And I'm the prey in her den.

Behind me the best Ever I know takes his last breath. The small connection remaining between us vanishes.

When she pounces I don't fight her. This is no game of cat and mouse. She wanted a struggle? Too bad. It only takes her teeth to my arm and her weight to my head to make me drop like a sack of nothing. I'm shaking and heaving. This isn't like the time I died in Jasyn's façade. This death is more painful. I have no out-of-body experience. There is no Ever linked to Ky to immediately restore me. The Verity leaves my body, but I don't see it. I am dying a slow and painful death.

Correction.

I am already dead.

joshua

What is this place?
　　Death is a Calling.
　　And it is beautiful.

ebony

"Where are the others? Ky and Joshua. Preacher. Wren."

Regina looks so much different now I know the plot behind her gaze. Funny how a person changes when they, I don't know, turn out to be your ruthless mother?

"I left 'em back in the Fifth. There's a Fairy Fountain beneath the palace in Oz where I used to live. I got tired of it o' course, back then I mean. So many people bowing and groveling. It's exhaustin' for anyone."

Oh, she really is a classic, isn't she?

"What was the point?" My mind reels. She's been with us the entire time? At the castle in the Second? Helping hide Elizabeth in the Fifth? Journeying to find my sister? "Why go off with Ky and Joshua? Why attack Nitegra Compound? You could have had your revenge on Elizabeth more than once. You flippin' raised her, didn't you?" Everything we thought we knew? Lies. Assumptions. Big fat Fs.

My mother leers. It's the smile she gives when she's about to transform. Except this time she becomes someone altogether new. Another persona. Another lie. Who is the real Isabeau? Does such a thing exist?

Regina thins, her skin fading into a shade neither dark nor light. I don't even know how to describe it. The hue is other, does that help? My brain can't register the color. I'd almost go so far as to say it doesn't exist. Then again, here I am, looking right at her.

It's as if this color is being created here and now. A completely new shade made for Isabeau alone.

Her eyes are swirls of rainbow light, the irises shifting with every blink. Sapphire. Burnt orange. Lilac. Cinnamon. And don't get me started on her hair. It appears as if it's alive, locks curling on their own, securing themselves on top of her head. Wings grow from her back, bright crimson, making her appear as if on fire.

I back up. Ouch. Wall.

"The point, *Ebony*"—she comes toward me—"is this." Her altered voice sets me on edge. Neither musical nor monotone, the sound is unsettling and soothing at once. "Revenge is a side note. Sure, it adds flavor, but as sweet as it may be, revenge is not the main course."

Oh brother, she's using food metaphors. Kill me now and never mind about cooking. I'll find a different passion to pursue when this is over. Anything but what my mother spent doing as Regina Reeves for the past whatever years.

"If being immortal teaches you anything, it is patience."

Riiiight. Because you were so patient with me when I was younger.

"As much as I weakened when away from my Fountains, never able to show my true self when apart from my shadows, I needed to learn all I could of the woman I believed would bear the answer to my prayers." She comes so close I feel her breath on my face.

"El." I look down, then back up at her, realization kicking me in the behind. "This was about El?" Again, I can't help it, but I'm jealous. Everything is always and forever about my sister. Her mark. Her Kiss of Infinity with this guy or that. Saving her mom. Saving her. The queen of the Second. Vessel of the Verity. For once, I mean, just for like twenty-four hours, could anything be about me?

Sigh and I'm over it. Wow, that was fast. What was it, like, two seconds and I'm fine? Moving on? Not bad if I do say so myself.

"Eliyana is an anomaly. A Mirror like Aidan's precious Ember. Vessel of the Verity with traces of the Void *and* Shadowalker. The

Verity is meant to enter the purest soul, yet Elizabeth's child seems to be like any other human. Which led me to ask myself, why? Why would the Verity choose her?"

Oh. My. Word. I know this one. For once, the answer lies at my fingertips. So simple. What El has is the answer to the Fervor Dragon's riddle from the story Ky read. "She loves." My downcast gaze lifts. Is it really this easy? "She loves like no one else." I laugh out loud at that. "Her heart. The Verity chose her because of her heart."

"Ah, the heart. Yes, what a tricky organ indeed. Needed for life, yet connected to the soul in a deeper way than any mortal could imagine." She taps the mirrorglass crown. "Let me ask you, Daughter. Do you know where mirrorglass comes from?"

Ha. I know this one too. Thank you, Tide. "It was discovered in the Fourth." I think of the thousands of glittering pebbles on the shore of Tide's home Reflection. As rare as mirrorglass is, it seems to be everywhere. Maybe it's not the substance that's scarce but the wielding of it?

"Silly girl. Discovery of something does not an origin make." She paces the room. Her hair continues to change styles. Her eyes mix new colors, ever altering as she always has. Her wings glow hotter, twitching as if ready to take flight. "You mentioned the Verity chose your half sister because of her heart." She glares over one shoulder. "But do you know what the Verity did to mine? Or rather, what Dimitri did?"

The story of *The Scrib's Fate* was tragic. The purest light giving up everything for a man who did not love her. "He broke your heart," I say. Is this what compassion feels like? I want to reach out to her. To let her cry on my shoulder and help her heal.

"And do you know what became of my heart, Daughter? Do you?"

My brain hurts. All these questions. Is there a test later? Can I get an exemption because I am so not prepared? She waits. Watches. My eyes dart as I search for the answer I'm sure is right in front of my nose. I think of *Once Upon a Reflection* and the childlike *Heartsong* rhyme written in blue ink—a.k.a. sap—from Fairy Fountain–watered trees.

". . . for as mere glass will shatter, her heart remains strong."

My hands cup my mouth. I wish El could hear this. She'd flip. "Mirrorglass is . . ." I squint and really look at her for the first time since returning with the crown. "Mirrorglass comes from your— the Verity's—broken heart."

She claps a sarcastic, nonpraising clap. "Well done. You are brighter than I believed. You are, in fact, correct." She adjusts the crown on her head. "This piece in particular was taken by none other than Dimitri himself. The first shard of my heart among thousands of pieces that shattered across the Reflections. At one time I ventured in search of them. Trying to collect them all, hoping if I could put my heart back together, I would be returned to my former glory."

Her head turns this way and that. She brings some hair forward over one shoulder. "But in the end the task proved impossible. I would have to find another way to change the past." She brandishes the Rose. "Which is where this little beauty comes in."

The Rose. The Fountain. Take your pick.

"I come from the Garden. The Rose was my final parting gift. I plucked it upon my banishment, stored its life-changing dew. I had three small vials. That was all. Evers live outside of time, and as immortal as I am, I could not know what would become of me in the end. The Midnight Rose has taunted. For as much as a drop of dew allows the drinker to save a life, the only thing it did for me was take me on a recurring loop. Ever blood upon the petals mimics the dew, its life-giving properties similar to that of the Garden's. Yet every attempt was futile. One sip and I ended up where I began. My deepest desire never matches up with anyone else's need."

So much to take in. I need to sit down. I slide down the wall. "None of this was about Elizabeth?"

"Oh, nonsense, dear, were you not listening?" Isabeau leaves me to sit on the stone-cold ground. "I raised her. Her safety has always been of the utmost importance. When I asked Haman for her new child, it was only to startle Eliyana and drive her to reach her mother that much faster. She had to be the one to save her mother. She needed to become the strong girl you have come to know today. Every step was to get her to where she is now—the Verity's vessel. I planned all of this down to the very last detail. All to get her exactly where I want her. She had to come to me in the Sixth. I had to fail that day in order to succeed now. So *her* deepest desire lines up with *my* greatest need."

"You don't hate Elizabeth?" Just making sure I get all the facts in order.

"What do I care for her?"

Hello, isn't it obvious? "She and Dad—Tiernan . . ." Do I really need to elaborate?

"Tiernan? I promise you that man was not worth a single tear, let alone years' worth."

Okay, um. Now I'm lost. "I thought you—"

"Love is a fool's dream. I dared to believe in that dream once." Her eyes hold a fierceness behind them. "I was never so foolish again. I used men, yes. I used your father to get you. I wanted a daughter and oh, I got one." She looks me up and down. "I thought perhaps you would become my shining star. That you would grow to be the remedy I required."

My hands find their comfort zone on my hips. "Oh yeah, and what remedy is that?"

"You will see." Then she vanishes.

As quickly as she arrived, my mother is gone.

⚬✖⚬

"I can't get over how bright it is." Tide holds tight to my right hand. "I mean blinding, right?"

I squeeze his hand and laugh. Weird. Still can't hear my own voice between Reflections, but theirs come through loud and clear. Is it the same for them? Are we even speaking or merely thinking to each other? Whatever the case, my heart wants to burst because Tide and Khloe and Stormy are just fine. I have no idea where my mother went or what she's up to. But we are all going to be okay.

"Where do you think the light comes from?" Khloe holds tight to my other hand. She's linked to Stormy on her left. My sister still hasn't shared what freaked her out when I Masked into the Physic Dennielle. I hate to push her, but I have to know.

"Hey, Khlo?"

"Yeah?"

I squeeze her hand three times. She squeezes back the same amount. I'm not sure when we started doing the silent "I love you" squeezes. She's never had an issue expressing herself, but words are difficult for me when they're real. Snark-free, as the case may be. She's understood this since the moment we met.

"You want to know why I had a meltdown?" She reads my mind as always.

Another squeeze to her hand. "Basically, kind of, totally, yeah." I release a soundless laugh, though I know she hears me.

She huffs. "You can't just turn into someone's mom like that and expect them not to be a little weirded out."

Shock radiates through me and I stumble forward, out of the Fairy Fountain light and into the day. I'm drenched from head to toe, on my hands and knees in soft sand.

Khloe joins me rather than helping me rise. She looks down at the tan grains, draws circles in them with her fingers. "When my mom died it was like, not real, you know? I never got to tell her good-bye. She was just gone, and my dad took me, and that was . . . it."

Oh, ouch. *Crud, don't cry. Don't do it.* "Khlo . . . I don't know what to say."

She bites her lower lip, so much like our other sister. "Can I ask a favor?"

I place a hand on her shoulder. Tug on one of her still-tight braids. "Anything."

"Could you . . . ?" She peers at me beneath her long, dark lashes, which, unlike mine, will *never* need mascara. "I just want a hug. Even if it's not really her. Even if I'm just pretending."

The other two have joined us. They stand back and to the side of the waterfall we passed through. The stones around the fall's pool bear the same blue writing, which I now see are years' worth of laments from my mother herself. The Fountains were her world, the elements her pages.

Tide and Stormy look on. Tide gives a little nod of encouragement as if to say, "Go ahead. It's okay." Stormy seems to smile in agreement.

I take a deep breath. Close my eyes. And find my way back to Dennielle's form. My hands the Physic's once more, I draw her daughter in.

Khloe inhales and snuggles against my shoulder. "Mama," she whispers.

And I can't take it. I begin to sob.

She joins me and our forms quake as one. When she lifts her head, her eyes glisten. I wipe her tears with her mother's fingertips. Then I kiss her forehead in the way I imagine a mother should.

"Where does the light come from?" she asks again.

"Where else?" Dennielle says. "The Verity." The answer comes easily, as if I've known it all along. What else could allow travel between any and every Reflection?

Khloe smiles at last, her sadness melting into joy. She looks more childlike than ever, a five-year-old waiting for her mother's story. "I'm all right now. You can go." One more hug and then she's up, the original Khloe once more.

I rise as well, becoming myself again as I do. Dusting the sand off my clothes, I take in our new surroundings. We need to find El. I have no idea if this is the right Reflection, but I feel it is. I trust the Verity brought us to the Sixth where Ky and the others wait. The Fairy Queen has been after El all along, waiting for what she would become. Still don't know what she meant by that. But I have a sinking feeling we're going to find out too soon.

Fairy Fountain Falls, as I've dubbed it, hides in a hidden cove off the shore of a private beach. I've never visited the Sixth, but this certainly isn't anywhere in the other Reflections I've visited. The bay around us is shaped like a crescent moon. The water greener than any ocean I've seen. Definitely not the Fourth Reflection ocean. The ground is different as well. In the Fourth the sand is glittering with mirrorglass pebbles. Here the sand is barren, not a shell or shard of seaglass to be found. No wonder it's so soft.

"Where to?" Tide comes up beside me and shakes the water out of his hair like a dog. He leans in, speaks for my ears alone. "I'm proud of you, by the way. That was something, what you did for Khloe. Really something."

That's it. I'm not going one step farther until I take care of this. I turn toward him, my face closer to his than it's ever been. Ever.

Tide's scared, I'm-innocent expression makes him all the more adorable. "I didn't do it." He puts his hands up.

"No. But I'm going to." I grab him. And kiss him. It's fast and not at all the romantic first kiss I would have liked. But it's there. Here. And now I can't deny how I feel. Not even if I tried.

And I won't. Not anymore. Never again.

Stormy whistles.

"Whoa." Tide slicks back his black hair only for it to fall in his eyes again. "That was—"

Khloe giggles. "It's about time."

Tide looks at her, and they exchange some kind of glance that says I'm out of the loop. Stormy slings an arm around my sister, and *they* share a look too. Am I really the odd girl out?

"What?" I place my hands on my hips.

"Oh, nothing," Tide says. "It's just that—"

"Just that what?" Spit it out, someone, please.

"That was horrible." He strokes his chin. A hair couldn't grow there if he tried. "I mean, really, truly awful."

My cheeks catch fire. "I take it back, then. The kissing train has passed." Ugh, lame.

He closes the space between us. Takes my hand in his and kisses it. Stormy shields Khloe's eyes with her hand, and my little sis shoves it down.

I don't care that they're watching. His lips are so soft. "Care to try again?" His eyebrows wag.

Khloe and Stormy turn away. "We won't watch this time," Stormy says. "Guardian's honor." Back turned toward us, she salutes no one.

Oh brother. Or is it sister? Whatever. "Think you can do better?" I tease Tide back, squeezing his hand as I do.

"You bet I do."

And three, two, one . . . what is it they say? Blastoff.

He kisses me like there's no yesterday or tomorrow. There is only us and now and him and me. I've been kissed before. By Guardians too old for me in the shadowy alcoves of the castle. By Third Reflection guys like Blake Trevor who've had way too much to drink, leaving the taste of alcohol on my lips for days after brushing.

But this? I've never been kissed like this.

Tide's lips move against mine with a sort of sweet timidity. There's no push, no expecting this to go too far. He's simply kissing me for the kiss itself. He keeps one hand tangled with mine, his body just close enough but not too close. When he draws away, his soft smile breaks into a full grin.

I mirror his expression, but I don't look away. Don't push away, though it's my go-to reaction when things get too close. "What?"

"Oh, nothing." He winks. "It's just . . . I told you I could do better."

No quips or words of defense come to mind. All I can think to say is, "Yes. Yes, you did." Then I let him kiss me again.

THIRTY-SEVEN

KY

The Lioness is laughing. She's gone completely mad. I don't care. I only care about the girl tossed aside by the feline's jaws.

"Give me the knife, Crowe. I know you always carry one on you." I take a fistful of young Jasyn's shirt. I have a window. Very little time to save her. Can she be saved? Please, let her live through this. She has to live through this. I've already lost my brother today. I can't lose Em too.

The stricken look on Crowe's face doesn't make my hold on him any less firm. "Calm down." He withdraws the old-fashioned pocketknife I knew he'd be packing. "Here."

Coward. Scum. Pansy. A slew of names I could call him but don't spins through my mind. He might've won Em's compassion, but his final decision to side with our enemy seals the deal. Once our adversary, always our adversary. Some things can't be fixed.

I snatch the weapon that will never compare to my mirrorglass blade and fall to my knees beside my brother. My lifeless, will-never-breathe-again brother. His open palm is the most accessible. I make a small, clean incision the way my Physic mother taught me, scrape the blood off with the dull edge of the knife. "Looks like you came in handy after all, David."

The joke is one he'd laugh at if he were here. In the end he became much more than blood supply. If he had stuck around a bit longer, we may have even become friends.

"You saved her," I say to him, though he can't hear me. "Now it's my turn."

I go to her. For both of us.

The Lioness's laughter continues. Would she shut up already?

Keeping Em as covered as possible, I lift her slip and survey the gaping wound in her side. I've been around blood enough, the scent doesn't faze me. No, it's the stillness that grips my heart. Her nonrising chest. The way her hands lay limp. She's my mother, Dennielle, lifeless at the bottom of the stairs.

Focus blurs. Shifts. Then zooms in again. *Get it together. You're on your own now. Do it for David. For Em. For Verity's sake, do it for yourself.*

The wound is the worst I've seen. Even a Physic's hands couldn't heal this. Without David's blood, Em would be gone for sure. The Ever in her Calling gives her a fighting chance, along with David's blood already in her veins from the last time he saved her. Still, a little more can't hurt.

I lower Crowe's knife over the wound and let David's blood *drip, drip, drip.* Then I take off my shirt and do my best to clot the bleeding. Pressure. So much blood. I lean over and kiss her like I've done before. The way she kissed me after Jasyn's Void injection. A miracle worker, right? My lips move against her cold ones. I shake her shoulders. Push her hair away.

Please come to, please. There is no loophole for my brother, but Em? She's the heroine. She can't— Oh Verity, she *can't* die. This is not that ending. I refuse to—

She gasps. Coughs.

The rigidity in my body I didn't realize I possessed relaxes. I knew it. No sweat. No problem at all.

That's when I heave, clutch my stomach, and vomit to the side.

My head swims. Okay, maybe for the tiniest second I thought she really might be dead. I wipe my mouth and gain my bearings. Never smiled bigger in my life.

"Has it happened?" She attempts to look around, then winces.

I knit my brows. I search her thoughts as she reopens her mind to mine.

Ah, so that's what the hag was up to. Steal the Verity? Doesn't the immortal know anything? Has history told us nothing about the forces of light and darkness? I glare at Crowe. He did everything in his power to harness the Void. Created an army of Soulless, hoping to spread his power across the Second. Has what he's witnessed here influenced his bad decisions in the future? He thought he could hold on to the Void and use it for his own gain. In the end, it destroyed him. I watch the Lioness now, cackling as if she's won.

Joke's on you, Your Majesty.

I help Em sit. We watch the Lioness revel in her victory.

"She has the Verity now," Em says in my head. *"But she won't for long."*

I hear my brother's words replay in her mind. *"The Verity cannot be fooled."*

A sudden flash of light. The Lioness screams. Roars. Then the crown falls to the ground, unbreakable due to its nature. "No," she cries, hind legs shaking. "What have you done?"

A delicious grin spreads across Em's lips despite her injury. Man, have I mentioned I love this girl?

"You cannot fool the Verity, Isabeau," she says. "The light knows the difference between a good heart and one made of stone."

The original vessel of the Verity passes through her myriad transformations. Lioness. Troll. Isabeau. And . . . Dahlia? Whoa. Didn't see that one coming. Explains where she's been, at least. Guess it was never about helping us at all. She had her own agenda, though we've yet to discover exactly what it is. No wonder her story kept changing. The Rose did this, it didn't do that. What a bunch of crud. Should've smelled bad from a mile away.

"She wanted me," Em's thoughts relay. *"All this time, it wasn't about Mom. She wanted the Verity. I thought she cared. I thought she was my friend."*

She was, I think back. *As long as the role suited her.*

We watch as the woman keeps shifting until, at last, a burst of darkness billows, as if the Void itself has—

A cooling sensation runs through me, replaced by warmth I haven't known in too long.

I gaze down at my arms, at the darkness fading, melting away. My torso belongs to me once more, only burns and scrapes and bruises to show for past battles, but nothing close to the charred color of Void-infused flesh. The blackened veins? The Void? Gone. But where—?

A whimper followed by a bloodcurdling scream gives me my answer.

The moment Isabeau takes on the Void is unmistakable. The show she invited all to witness has become her production alone. "Don't look at me!" She claws at her hair, pulling it over her face. Locks fall to the floor in clumps. "Close your eyes and bow! Bow to your queen!"

But no one moves. Not a single subject obeys her screeched commands.

I rise and help Em do the same, becoming the strength she has yet to regain. Arms around each other, we take in the unfolding scene.

Isabeau backs away, bumps into a Guard who doesn't bother to get out of her way. "You are wretches, all of you!" Another stumble, she ends up on her rear. Gets back up with a fumble and zero help from anyone. "Just wait! I will have my day. This is not the final chapter. I will rise again."

I sense Em's heart sink and hold her firm against my side. "Empathy won't help her," I say in her ear.

"But what will? What can we do?"

"I don't know." My lips curve down. Here we thought we were heroes, ready to unbreak a heart that's been in pieces for years on end. Naive is what we were. A bunch of kids playing a game. At this point we're back at square one. Where do we go from here?

When at last Isabeau departs, the room is left in frozen awe. I'm about to take Em away too. She needs rest, clothes. I nudge her.

"Wait." Her gaze passes mine.

I follow it.

"Look," she says.

And I do. The Shadowalkers. Are they . . . ?

Some remain in their cages, as before. But the others . . .

My jaw goes slack. "Well, I'll be—"

"They've turned into Fairies." Em lifts a finger, extends her arm toward the nearest cage.

A transformed Shadowalker flits from his prison, dark wings flapping. The tiniest cry emits from his miniature mouth. He flies fast, follows the direction of his queen. One by one, those altered follow suit, until only a handful remain caged.

"They've chosen the darkness." Em leans her head against my shoulder. "The Fairy Queen holds the Void they worship. Their choice to continue as her servants has cursed them to do just that."

"And the others? What of them?"

She smiles softly. "What else? They've chosen to be set free."

In the aftermath of it all, there's one thing Em keeps thinking over and over.

"Talk to me," I tell her.

Sadness radiates from her wide eyes. "We didn't change anything." She releases the final no-longer Shadowalker from her cage. The woman who lost her child. "Isabeau was always going to take on the Void. The Shadowalkers who preferred darkness were always going to become Fairies, doomed to serve the infamous Fairy Queen. And . . ." She swallows. Her eyes brim with tears. "Joshua was always going to die. We changed nothing."

I take her hands. "But we did what we were supposed to. And now we understand what we're up against. Now we know she's carried a portion of the Void all these years. The Void is bigger than Crowe or me or my brother. One vessel tries to contain it, but it's like an infection, spreading and doubling throughout the decades. It's why Crowe could inject it into his victims. Why darkness shrouded the Second for so long."

She presses her hands into her side. Cringes. "Don't you see, Ky? We can't stop the Void from being created. We can't change the choices people make. Where has the Verity gone? It didn't return to me. What now? We have less than when we began."

"Not quite." I turn her toward the nearest reflective surface. "The Verity left its mark on you. Unless the new Verity's vessel gives a Kiss of Infinity to another, you'll stay the only Mirror in existence." I rub her back to reassure her. "According to my birth mother's theory anyway." I wink, then add, "I don't know what happens after this or where we go from here, but I do know we can't go on without doing one thing first."

Reading each other's minds is easy. Like breathing. I nod and glance at my brother's body. She does the same.

A grand exit deserves an even grander send-off. And I know just the thing to make his ending epic.

THIRTY-EIGHT

NO ONE LIKE HIM ANYWHERE

J asyn Crowe is gone.

He will probably become the same man I met. Nothing I did changed him, though I understand him better. And now I know where Mom's name originated. At the very least, perhaps I touched him in some small way. And . . . I guess I wouldn't try to change him—only he can do that for himself. But I would live out my own moments differently. Treat him a bit more kindly. With more empathy and compassion. It's such a different perspective, knowing where one's been.

The mirrorglass crown vanished too. Focused on freeing those who chose not to follow the Fairy Queen, we didn't even notice when my teenage grandfather slipped away, crown returned to his possession. We know Aidan ends up with it in the future. Did Jasyn return the crown, or do we only assume Aidan wore it? If mirrorglass reverses, I can't imagine the crown would do the Verity's vessel any good. The thing ought to be tossed into the sea.

"I smell it," Ky says. "A sailor always knows his way to the ocean. Just a bit farther."

He and Preacher carry Joshua on a stretcher. Wren follows in griffin form close behind. I walk along with one hand on Joshua, two fingers wrapped around his thumb. He could be sleeping. I wish he were.

The farther we tread, the more the houses thin out. When the briny aroma of saltwater hits me, I know we must be near. The feeling is good and bad. We've made it, but am I ready to say good-bye?

His crooked smile flashes in my memory. I'll never forget the first time I heard his voice. The song in my heart come to fruition.

"Please don't stop," he'd said. *"That was . . . you have the most beautiful voice."*

He was a prince in every meaning of the word. Joshua saved me from myself. He saved us all, if I really think about it.

"With a voice like that you could do anything."

I squeeze his thumb. Imagine he still smells of my favorite autumn holiday. I want to tell him I have and I will. That, like Ky, he helped me find my true voice in a way no one else could. Joshua is, and always will be, the white knight on his steed from my favorite Monkees song. Now I feel the cold sting of the razor in the lyrics. Not much longer now. Soon our tune will end for good, only a memory. A daydream.

When the Sixth's ocean comes into view, we head down to the beach. I abate the inevitable sobs and bite the inside of my cheek. Hold fast to his thumb before at last letting go.

Ky and Preacher set Joshua on the shore and begin gathering large pieces of driftwood. They attach it to the stretcher with rope from Preacher's supply pack.

I'm not much help. Instead, I sit in the sand beside the boy who gave everything for me. I don't touch him again, knowing if I do it will be too hard to let go. I mull over lines of lyrics before finding some worthy of him. Remembering his life, honoring his death.

> *"I've been thinking of all you've done,*
> *How you changed me and shaped me and taught me*
>   *to run.*
> *Your place in my heart will always remain.*
> *Because of you I am changed.*
> *Because of you I will never be the same."*

"Are you ready?" I look up to find Ky offering his hand.

I nod, dust the sand off the clothes Wren loaned me. She hasn't changed into a human again since Joshua died. This is how she copes.

By hiding behind her Calling. Not a bad idea. I long for my butterfly form. To flutter away and grieve apart from it all. But this must be done first. Here, at the water's edge, is where we say good-bye.

The men lift Joshua and carry him down to where the sea and shore meet. I open my mouth to speak when I hear it.

Someone is shouting my name.

I shade my eyes, twist, squint. When I see Ebony and she sees me, we break into a run. I'm dirty and dingy and smell awful. But I don't care. My sisters are here. And Stormy! This is what Joshua would've wanted. All of us together.

The three of us collide with each other. Laughing. Hugging. Making sure the other is real. Ebony tells us of Isabeau and the Rose and the crown formed from a broken heart.

"Reggie is the Fairy Queen," she pants.

I nod. "We saw the shift. I still can't believe it. All this time. She could've hurt me or Mom. All this time she had part of the Void."

We fill her in on what's happened to us. She shares how the Fairies were Shadowalkers, and we bring the story to life. When everyone knows everything, Ebony takes my hand.

"I'm sorry about Joshua," she says.

I smile. "Don't you mean Josiah?" I tease her, remembering the days when she called my best friend anything but his name.

She shakes her head. "Not anymore." Her eyes sparkle and—

"Eb." I cover my mouth. The girl with the light. She's— "The Verity. It's you."

Her brows pinch. "What? Impossible. You're—"

I shake my head. "The Verity enters one pure of heart. When the Verity left me, it found you. Brought you right to us."

"Pure of heart?" Her stunned expression relays more than her words. "*Me?* You've got to be joking." My sister's shock quickly contorts to worry. "It doesn't make any sense. My mother . . . hates me."

I shake my head. Shrug. "Apparently not. You are the one the Void's vessel cares for most."

Disbelief widens her eyes and parts her lips. She doesn't take her eyes off me. I hold her gaze until she blinks.

And now I think we've found our way. We may never be able to destroy the Void. Darkness will always exist. But a broken heart can be mended. We may come out of this the way we'd hoped after all.

We all join hands and stand in a line, our toes and shoes kissing sea foam as we say our farewells.

"He fought fair. Never cheated in a duel." Preacher breaks the chain and holds his knit cap to his heart. "A true Guardian and mate."

"He was . . ." Ebony pauses, as if searching for the right words. "He was never not kind to me. Even when I was a—" She clears her throat. Starts again. "Even when I was sort of rude to him."

"I didn't know him much." Tide's voice quivers.

I almost think he won't go on. I wouldn't blame him either. But then . . .

"He was humble enough to seek forgiveness when many run from such encounters. For that he gained my respect."

Khloe's next. Something tells me her words will be the wisest of all. "He was my brother's brother. Which makes him my brother too. And if he was my brother, then I loved him. No questions asked."

It comes down to Ky and me now. He goes first.

"My brother may have battled darkness, may have even been subject to the Void in the worst ways." His glance shifts to Tide. Joshua killed his mother, but even *he* shared a kind word about the best Ever I've known. "But in the end, David chose light."

I don't have to look at Ky to know he's tearing up. His slightly off voice gives him away. A quick squeeze to his hand tells him to keep going. The gesture is all he needs.

"Joshua died for what we all must live for. His last breath was spent doing what was right. I can only hope to live worthy of that legacy." He turns his head toward me.

My breath catches. How can I follow him? What else can I say? There's nothing to say. There is only what remains of his song.

As Joshua drifts out onto the water, I follow him with my voice.

"No, we will never be the same.
Your body has passed, but we will carry on your name.
And when someone asks for a tale of noble, right, and
      good,
We will tell them how you lived.
We will tell them how you fell.
We will tell them how you stood.
We will tell them of your good . . ."

My voice trails, no melody left on my lips.

When he's vanished from view . . . when we can't see him anymore, it's Ebony who asks, "The Seventh?"

Blink. Gulp. Breathe. "The Seventh."

Back to where it all began.

Passing through a Fairy Fountain is similar to passing through
a regular Threshold. Except it's brighter. Rainbow light like the
Verity. Colors I can't even begin to describe. Ky is the only one I've
shared the Verity's true form with. Maybe now he can see what I
witnessed the night I took on the light.

"No, Em. That's all you," he says in my head. *"All I can see is
white."*

My heart leaps. Emotion stirs. *But . . . the Verity left me.*

*"Yes, but you're still a Mirror. And after all you've accomplished, all
the good choices you've made, I suspect this is a little gift of its own. The
Thresholds drain, the passages between Reflections crumble, but these
paths remain and you, of all people, can see the truth of the light."*

But even the light can't help what we find when we reach the
Seventh. Death. Nothing. Void. Now I know where the name of
the Darkness stems from. This wasteland isn't a Garden.

It's a nightmare.

"Are we in the right place?"

Ky shrugs. "Beats me."

"She's here." Ebony takes the lead. "I can smell her."

No Dragon guards the Garden's gate when we approach. Barren hedges form a maze of thorns and twigs, woody claws reaching out, snagging our hair and clothes. The place is so abandoned, there aren't even leaves left to crunch beneath our soles. Nothing has grown here for a long time.

"Do you hear that?" Khloe grabs Ky's arm. "Is that a baby?"

I listen for the sound she describes. No, not a baby. A woman is crying. Déjà vu moves me forward, has me racing past my sisters. I'd know her voice anywhere. *Mom*. Were we wrong? Did Isabeau decide to carry out revenge after all?

But the figure I see at the heart of the Garden's weeds is not my mother.

I fall to my knees and look on Isabeau with new eyes. I feel like Wendy from *Peter Pan*. Watching a boy cry over his shadow. Except I need not ask why the heartbroken woman before me sheds her tears. The Rose has been planted at the center of what used to be *her* Garden and the crown sits atop her head once more. And . . . she's singing. And I know this is the true lament of the Fairy Queen.

> "I have only longed for love; I have waited all these years
> To return to the only love I have ever known, to return to
>   my garden home.
> But it has died with everything else, withered away
>   while I was gone,
> And now not even my song can bring what I have been
>   missing all along."

The words break my heart. Shred it in two. When she looks up, her face is streaked in tears. But this is not what stills my soul. No, it's the face beneath the mirrorglass crown that fills me with new understanding. Void-blackened veins cover her skin. The Void's vessel cannot hide them now. The darkness has returned to where it began, taking over despite her many efforts to control it.

She sought to take back the light, only to end up in shadows. And Dimitri's story comes full circle.

"*She bestowed on him the most perfect of kisses, a Kiss of Infinity . . .*"
But the love was never returned.

It all makes sense. The story is the key. My Scrib memory recalls the tale in detail now. Piecing the final fragments together.

"And this was the Scrib's fate, cursed to walk the earth consumed with darkness crafted by the woman he did not love. Eventually he grew old and the darkness left him for another, latching onto one who loved the soul infused with light. The switch had to occur, for the light's purpose was to be loved."

And now I know what must be done. We were never meant to reverse what happened with Dimitri.

Ky's words float to the surface of my mind. "*You can't be forced to love someone, Em. A Kiss of Infinity comes from the deepest part of you.*"

Love can't be forced any more than the Verity could be compelled to choose Isabeau.

"The Rose is the Fountain," Ky thinks. "*Need and desire go hand in hand.*"

Now Ebony breaks off from the group. Tucks her hair behind her ears. Folds her arms over her chest. Something flashes in her brown eyes that reminds me of the old Ebony—Quinn as I knew her then.

But then . . .

The light—the love Isabeau sought all along—kneels beside the Void.

THIRTY-NINE

Ebony

I've waited for this day. Imagined it. What I would do if I ever had the chance to make my mother feel the way she made *me* feel for so many years.

Trash. Garbage. Unwanted. Nothing.

"Mom." I touch her shoulder.

She wrenches away. "Just go." She claws at her hair, pulling it down over her face. "Don't look at me. Just *go*."

Her Void-infested arms bear scrapes and bruises. Did she try to rid herself of the Void with her bare hands?

"I said leave!" Rocking back and forth, my mother hugs her stomach.

Her wailing. Weeping. I . . . It's too much.

"Get out! Go! Leave!" Sob after racking sob. "Just . . . leave." Her voice falters on the last word. Not a command. A plea.

I draw back. My hands don't know what to do with themselves. It feels too condescending to plant them on my hips. I let them fall to the sides of my bent knees. Feels kind of nice to let them relax for a change.

Still . . .

I *should* go. I ought to leave her here to rot in this wasteland. Garden of Epoch? More like Field of Death. There is nothing—and I mean *nothing*—gardenish here. I'm talking more than weeds. This is the equivalent of a foliage apocalypse. Besides, we can make it back on our own. The Fairy Fountains make the way a cinch. With our resident Mirror, we don't even need them. El can take a few, and I'll lead the rest. We'll be in the Second again by midnight. Poof! Glass slipper totally not necessary.

What else is left? We thought we could destroy the Void. Were we wrong? Will darkness forever remain something we must battle? I look at each of my friends in turn. I thought El would be the one in the end, the girl at the center of it all. But here I kneel, all eyes trained on me, myself, and I. And the woman who wanted nothing to do with me? She's my accessory. Except I've no flippin' clue where to go from here.

I make eye contact with Tide. Khloe. El. Ky. Stormy. Preacher and Wren stayed behind at the Garden's entrance, opting to keep watch, though I have a feeling they had other reasons for staying behind. Now it's just those who've grown close standing here. They're tired, starving, smelling of all things gross. But they're *mine*. They've all fought. All won and lost in different ways. Maybe, in the end, winning isn't about ending the darkness. Perhaps the victory lies in overcoming the battles we face each day. In a sense, we each destroy the Void every time we choose the light.

I consider my mother, so opposite the woman I know. Hair falling out and skin sunken. She has a choice too. Fight or give in. Clearly, she's chosen the latter. There's nothing else we can do for her. I straighten. Square my shoulders. Take a deep breath and prepare to rise.

"I thought . . ."

Her soft-spoken words stop me where I kneel.

". . . if I could just get back to the Garden." The word *Garden* sounds sacred on her tongue. "If I could get *her*"—outstretched arm shaking, she points at El—"to drink the Rose's dew once she was here, in *my* Garden, perhaps my fate could be altered." My mother lifts her head, just enough so I can see her eyes. No longer blue, they're a shade of rotting apple green.

"When I killed you all those years ago in the Sixth"—she addresses Eliyana—"I thought the Verity would choose me. I truly believed the crown would complete me, that the piece of my heart Dimitri kept for himself would make me whole again."

El stares at her, wide eyed.

Did my mother just admit she was wrong about something? Go figure.

"But all I did was curse myself yet again. I followed that boy"— she points to Ky—"and his dead brother into the past in hopes I'd gain perspective on what happened in the palace that day. But all I found was nothing. The more I try, the farther I fall, it seems."

The laugh she looses bears a sad kind of creepiness. The giggle of someone deranged. "The Void entered me, forcing me to hide in the shadows. I thought, with the crown back, the Void would be suppressed. I could go anywhere and be anything again. I wouldn't try to fool the Verity. Instead, I would use it to my advantage. All I wanted was to come home."

Her head raises another inch. Chin quivering, she surveys the destruction around her. "But home is gone!" She sobs into her hands. "Just leave. I am finished trying to change anything. There is no hope for the hopeless."

Every awful thing she's flung my way rushes back. This is my sweet revenge, this broken woman on her knees, begging us to let her be.

But instead of relishing the karma, I'm . . . I lift my fingertips to my eyes . . . weeping? Her broken heart is my own. Because it is not the Void alone who cares for the Verity. The combo takes two.

I care for the Void as well. Like my sister and the brothers. Like every Verity's vessel, I suspect.

"You aren't hopeless." Tears swiped and shoulders back, I do something I never, in this Reflection or the next, thought I would do. I scoot closer to my mother. And hold her.

She loses it then and we weep together.

For all *she* lost.

For all *we* lost.

For all *I* lost.

She doesn't apologize. Still. But this hatred I've harbored, I can't take it anymore. I bow my head next to hers. Wipe away her

sorrow as if she is the child and I'm the parent. Despite all she's
done, I can't help but mourn for her shattered heart.

"It's okay. Shhh. Everything is going to be fine. You'll see." My
tears fall, drop to the hard, cracked ground. "I love you, Mama." I
use Khloe's term for Dennielle, finding I like the way it sounds on
my lips. "I know I'm not Dimitri, but if you'll let me, I'll love you."

More tears spill and I can hardly see now. Flippin' emotions.
I haven't cried like this since I was told to shut up for doing so at
the age of eight. Now everything I've held in for years pours out.
I'm a dam.

And the Garden begins to bloom.

Shut the front door. Is this real?

Colors burst to life. As if the Seventh is a black-and-white photo,
retouched stroke by stroke. The blank spaces fill with warmth and
light. Scents like you wouldn't believe expand in the air. Honeysuckle
and cherries and rose blossoms and pine. Maple. Cinnamon. Cilantro.
Cranberries. This isn't Epoch—it's epic. Literally.

My own warmth surrounds my mother until she's too hot to
touch. My hold on her loosens, and I back away. Shielding my eyes,
I rise and join my friends. Tide takes my free hand and kisses it. I
don't even deny this is my guy and I'm his girl. And I'm totally in
love with him, by the way. We watch in silent wonder as the cold,
deserted Garden warms, the light now radiating off Isabeau touching everything around it.

Mom transforms right before me. But not into a Troll or a
Lioness. She's just a girl. Not plastic like the woman she tried to
be. She's about my age with hair and eyes like mine. The Void has
melted away to leave soft but far-from-perfect skin, curvy hips and
thighs, and a face shaped like a heart. Is this how she appeared to
Dimitri? She's lovely. How could he reject her?

When she stands, she examines her hands. Her hair. Then her
eyes find mine. "Ebony," she says.

Though I can't recall her ever appearing to me this way, I know
her. This is my mother in her truest form. "Mom?"

She opens her arms and I run into them. She smells of the Fairy Fountains and I know I'm home.

"I was lost," she says into my ear. "I'd forgotten who I was. You . . . helped me remember the girl in the Garden all those years ago." She kisses the top of my head. "We must go. The Garden is meant to guard the light. It is no place for us mortals."

"Mortal? You're . . . ?"

She nods. Tears of joy ensue. "Let's go home."

"Sounds good to me."

"What of the Fairies?" El speaks up, stepping forward. "The Shadowalkers?"

My mother wraps one arm around me and smiles. "They will be keepers of the Garden now. Given a second chance. They will guard the light instead of darkness."

We walk hand in hand to the entrance where Preacher and Wren wait. When we're standing outside the Garden gates, vines and thorns and roses and ivy grow over the opening. Unless one knew where to look, they'd never know the Garden was here.

"What of the Void?" Ky asks.

My mother frowns. "The Void will always have a chance to grow where it is welcomed. We may never defeat it entirely. But if we remain aware, we will always have a fighting chance."

"How do we get home?" Khloe tugs on my jacket.

"The Fairy Fountains are not for us anymore. But now that the Verity is restored, we will still have the Thresholds." My mother looks at El. "But there is always mirror walking."

My sister touches her cheek.

"You are the last Mirror," my mother says. "Use your Calling wisely."

"I will," my sister promises.

And I know she'll keep her promise well.

I look over my shoulder once more, hoping I'll at least catch a final glimpse of the Garden's beauty. Instead, I find something else. I eye my sister. Did she see it too? I tap her shoulder. "El. Look."

She follows the direction of my gaze. "What?"

I blink and shake my head. "Nothing. Thought I saw something."

She shrugs, but I continue to watch the spot where he vanished.

He's alive. But we buried him.

And it's in this moment I realize the truth.

The First Reflection—the place where those passed are not really gone—was in the Seventh all along.

joshua

I hover in the shadows of a rosebush as I watch her part. My throat grows tight, but my heart is not heavy. For once I have chosen what is best and right for her. For once I have finally acted as the king my father wanted me to be.

"You will not say good-bye, dear one?" The Verity speaks. I have a feeling the sound is not for human ears but for the ears of her Guardians alone. "After today you will be able to neither see nor hear her if she returns."

"This *is* my good-bye. I am letting her go. This is the best way I can love her. This is my purpose."

I walk deeper into the Garden. I will never forget the sound of her voice or the way she made me feel. But my brother is the best one for her. He loved her enough to risk losing her. To risk her forgetting all about him just so she could live.

And . . . that is why . . . I live.

CODA

ELIYANA

one year later

Go on, I'll be right here when you get back." Ky kisses me on the forehead and gives a little shove. He slides down the tree trunk behind him, lazes at its base. Closes his eyes. But he's not sleeping. He doesn't have to watch me to hear everything in my mind.

"Nice try," I say.

His lids flash open. "Hey, we're connected. Don't hate on a guy who wants to spend every waking moment in your head, love." He shrugs.

"I'll be back." Then I shut him out, collecting my thoughts for myself alone.

I didn't tell Ky why I desired to return here. When Ebony came to me and said she saw *him*, I had to find out for myself.

Unaccompanied, I follow the rest of the path to the familiar hedges that form the labyrinth that is the Garden wall. I navigate the maze easily, finding the Fervor Dragon at the Garden's gate in no time.

She rises from her relaxed state, rolls her head in a full circle. "Your Majesty." The Dragon bows, though . . . should *I* be bowing to *her*? Something Ky said following our last venture to the Seventh returns. A conversation we shared before journeying home to the Second.

"I have a theory." He elbowed me as we walked. It was the first time I'd felt at ease in what seemed like ages.

I shook my head. Watched our feet stride in sync. "You and your theories." I laughed. The sound was so light and free, it made me never want to stop. "Go on then. Tell me."

He peered over one shoulder, toward the Garden gate quickly vanishing from our view. "The Dragon in Dimitri's story? The one with the riddles who guards the entrance?"

I followed his gaze. No Dragon waited there now. Would she return? "Uh-huh."

With a signature smirk, he leaned in. "I'll bet my mirrorglass blade, if it ever comes into my possession again, the Verity *is* the Dragon. Her first encounter with Dimitri was when she allowed him into the Garden. His correct answer regarding love intrigued her. That's when she started to fall."

He winked and left it at that. I never thought too much about his crazy idea.

Until now.

I nod to the far-from-mythical creature before me now. Not only am I starting to believe Ky's theory is true, but I realize the Fountain in the Second's castle courtyard was inspired by this. The Dragon statue with the rose between its teeth? Yeah, that's the Fervor Dragon, the guardian of Epoch herself.

"At a loss for words, Queen Eliyana?"

I blink and meet her piercing gaze. I may no longer be the Verity's vessel, but the people of the Second chose to keep me as their queen. For whatever reason the Dragon recognizes this. Has it truly been a year since we stood inside the Garden's dead walls? Last spring seems like a lifetime ago. "I'd like to enter." I glance past her toward the high hedges, now vibrant with the green of life.

Eyeing me down her scaly snout, the Dragon replies, "You know very well what the rules are here. Only the purest of souls may enter." She turns in a circle, her dark skin shimmering with each move. "Even if you make your way in, the keepers of the Garden cannot see you. Cannot hear you. They exist in another Reflection entirely, and I—the Verity—will not allow you to disrupt the way of things."

My heart sinks, but Ky's theory is confirmed. I am speaking
to a form of the Verity. Reverence and awe strike my core, and I
tremble. The Dragon is a sort of vessel, a protection in and of herself. "I understand." I lower my head. "Ask what you will."

A long pause ensues. At last the Dragon offers her riddle.
"What is stronger than a hundred men but breaks with a word?"
She huffs and heaves, passion igniting her words. "What is kept
in a cage but never locked?" Voice booming, she sends birds into
flight. "What is small as a fist but as ferocious as a lion? What races
against anger and stops with a breath?"

I let her finish, but I knew the answer at "breaks with a word."

"The heart." I palm my chest. Feel my pulse *thump, thump,
thump*.

The Dragon's nostrils flare, though she shows no other signs
of annoyance. "Indeed. Only one who has known what it is like to
be truly broken would hold the key to such certitude." She moves
more swiftly than a jungle cat and as slithery as a snake. "You may
enter, but be careful you do not speak to those who reside here.
New protections have been put into place. Unlike Dimitri, if you
make contact with any inside the Garden, you'll ne'er be allowed
to leave."

One gulp is all I need. I muster the courage to continue. Almost
allow Ky into my thoughts again but refrain. I wanted to do this
alone, and I will.

The path between the hedges is narrow. A small opening I
have to sidestep through.

Rustle, thud, stomp.

I whirl to find the gate guarded once more. Sigh. My lips form
a flat line. I swallow any and all words I know I'll want to say.
Silence is my ticket out. But only when I'm ready. For now, I turn
toward the Garden. Take a step closer to my goal.

"I saw him by the roses," Ebony shared before Ky and I left. "I
know it was him."

I search the perimeter for any flower that might resemble
a rose. Morning glory, orchids, daffodils. Some sort of bud that

appears to be a breed between a lilac bloom and a water lily. Pretty much every blossom but the one I seek. Moving deeper into the foliage, I find a paved path that winds into an orchard. One deep breath and I'm following it.

Still no roses.

But I didn't doubt Ebony then and I don't now. My closest friend and confidante, she's become the Second's sweetheart. Public relations? Piece of cake for my older sister. Everything my introvert can't handle, her extrovert takes on. We're so in sync these days, it's difficult to contemplate we were once enemies. And even more of a task to remind myself Isabeau is no longer Isabeau. Ebony's young mother looks our age but speaks as someone years beyond us. She keeps to herself mostly, cautious to build relations with anyone aside from her daughter. There's a gentle calm about her as she kneads dough down in the kitchens, a position Ebony insisted her mother continue. It's strange not to hear Reggie's joyful humming. And yet, Isabeau's silence is almost a song of its own. After years spent living in resounding bitterness, her lack of noise makes her seem . . . happy. Content. Maybe one day she'll even sing a new Heartsong.

My thoughts turn to my own full heart as I think of all I've gained amid so much loss. I always wanted a best friend I could trust, and now I can claim a handful. Stormy and Robyn and Khloe and Eb. And Mom, of course, who is pregnant *again*, a baby sister on the way this time. Discovering her lifelong friend and caregiver, Regina, was also our greatest enemy came as nothing short of a shock. She took the news as if mourning a death, but didn't stay heartbroken too long. How could anyone remain downcast around Evan? My brother is all giggles, closer to taking his first steps each day. Makai can't keep up with his crawling, carrying my brother on his shoulders constantly just to keep him out of mischief.

"My hair will be nothing but gray by the time your sister arrives." The only father I've known turned Evan upside down, only to initiate another fit of squeals. "This boy's Shield Calling will be a disappearing act, you watch."

I smiled. "Like father like son." Arms folded, I leaned against

the cobblestone wall of their Second Reflection cottage. So similar
to the one in the Fifth, but surrounded by lush flora and fauna
rather than dry desert. Dewesti Province is home now. Can't
remember the last time I longed for New York.

Birds chirp a tune reminiscent of my first mirrorsong, pulling
me forward. Overgrown grass tickles my exposed ankles, and every
sort of fruit imaginable decks the orchard tree branches. When we
departed the Seventh twelve months ago, I caught a small glimpse of
the beauty Dimitri described in his journal. The dead space exploded
into life, but we only remained long enough for a taste. Now my
sensory palate takes it all in. Every new color and scent.

Something moves behind me.

I freeze. Inhale through my nose. Look back but nothing's there.
A memory surfaces easily, as they all do now, my Scrib ability fully
restored. My first encounter with Wren, she hid inside a trome in
Lynbrook Province, her blue lock of hair catching my eye. I thought
I'd imagined it, but it was her, waiting for me. Same as she was a few
months ago when I found her in the castle stables.

Joshua's horse, Champion, hadn't been the same in his owner's
absence. Not even apples cheered him. At a loss for how to help, I
still made it a point to visit the horse every day. Wren beat me to it
as last autumn came to a close.

Dressed all in black, she brushed Champion's white mane. Their
contrast was stark. A colorless photo come to life.

"I can feel you standing there. You might as well stop staring
and just come over."

She didn't make eye contact as I approached. I watched as
Champion leaned into her touch.

"How'd you get him to do that? Anytime I've neared him, he's
thrashed and bucked. Like he's spooked."

Wren rolled her eyes.

I couldn't help but grin. An eye roll meant she was still Wren.
Meant she'd be okay.

"He likes potatoes." A pat to his side. A stroke of his nose.
"Give him potatoes and he'll be your friend forever."

"Thanks." Ready to walk, I paused. Tossed the idea back and forth before deciding. Part of me didn't want to let go, but the other half knew it was the right thing. "You should take him. It's what Joshua would want."

I expected a smart remark. Something like, "How would *you* know what Joshua would want?"

Instead, she shrugged and replied, "Fine."

I haven't seen her, but Robyn says Wren rides Champion every day. Though the elder Song sister hasn't been seen in griffin form since Joshua passed, something tells me she's soaring high on the back of Joshua's steed.

A breeze shudders the leaves as I think of all we've lost. But what's more is everything we've gained. I no longer fear the future, but welcome it. As long as we keep our eyes on the light, the darkness poses no real threat at all.

The trees thin and the path widens until it disappears into a meadow. Again, I want to let Ky in, share with him everything I see and feel. But then my breath is stolen and I'm glued in place and, for now, I don't mind being just me.

Ky's brother is here.

He looks . . . different. The changes are hard to describe. Hair a shade lighter, almost as if grayed but not quite. When he throws his head back and laughs, the sound comes to me as a whisper. Like the voice of a ghost.

And yet . . .

He's still him. Still Joshua. He walks like a Guardian, a king. He's the man Nathaniel and Makai raised him to be. This is what he was meant for. Though I miss him, though he can't see or hear me, this is all I need.

Joshua walks along the riverbank fifty feet ahead. Hands in his pockets, he overlooks the shore on the far side of the rushing water.

Ebony was right.

"The First is the Seventh Reflection. The Seventh is the First," she said. "The Verity guards the souls we've lost. The Garden is their new home. Their new Calling."

Tears well. The best kind. The kind that leave my heart so full, I can't imagine ever feeling more joy than I do in this moment.

I can't tell him how much he's missed. How he's changed my life for good, and I live every day thankful I knew him. I hold my contrasting charms against my heart, the silver treble clef sharing one chain with the copper rose button now. Different, but equally treasured. Never forgotten. I drink him all in before I turn and ease my way back to the entrance.

I've done what I came for.

I've seen the heart of the Verity.

What could be more beautiful?

The End

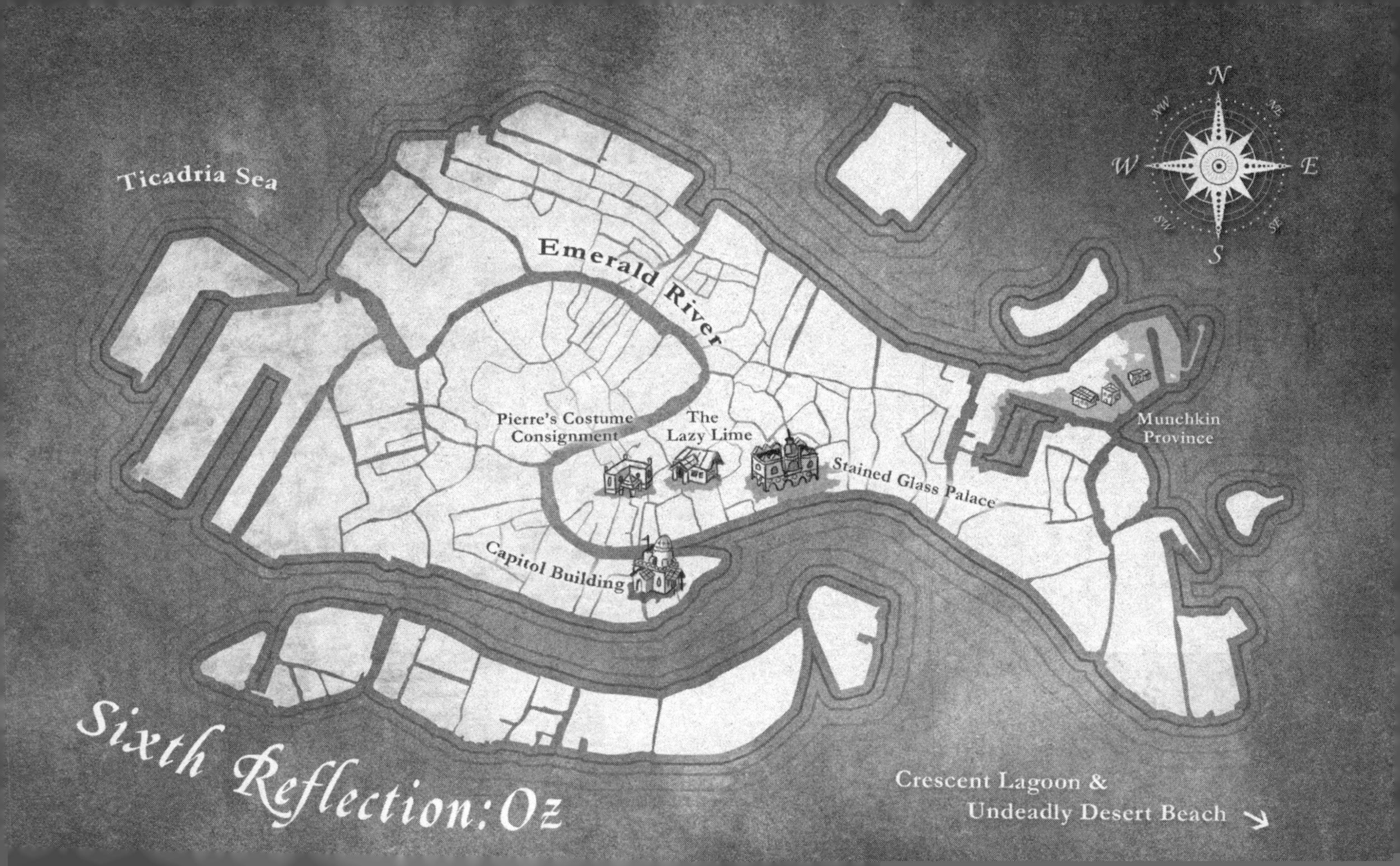

Munchkin Province

Stained Glass Palace

The Lazy Lime

Emerald River

Pierre's Costume Consignment

Capitol Building

Ticadria Sea

Crescent Lagoon & Undeadly Desert Beach →

Sixth Reflection: Oz

Garden of Epoch

Seventh Reflection

First Reflection

Garden Gate & the Fervor Dragon

Midnight Rose Garden

The Living Tree

Oden Lily Field

Orchard of Epoch

labyrinth of hedges

Epoch River

family tree

Nathaniel Archer
Physic

Bianca Moretti
Shield

Makai Archer
Shield

Tiernan Archer
Shield

Dennielle Rhyen, wife
Physic

Aidan Henry
Ever

Ember Archer
Mirror

Khloe Rhyen
Shield

Joshua David
Ever

Kyaphus Rhyen
Shield

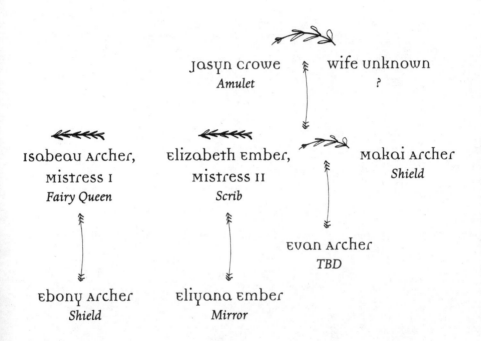

Jasyn Crowe
Amulet

wife unknown
?

Isabeau Archer,
Mistress I
Fairy Queen

Elizabeth Ember,
Mistress II
Scrib

Makai Archer
Shield

Evan Archer
TBD

Ebony Archer
Shield

Eliyana Ember
Mirror

Notes:

- ❀ Tiernan married Dennielle—but had affairs with Isabeau and Elizabeth.
- ❀ Khloe, Ebony, and Eliyana are all half sisters.
- ❀ Ember Archer was treated as a daughter by Nathaniel's parents, and eventually took their name as her own. They are not related by blood.
- ❀ Ky was raised by Tiernan. Joshua was raised by Nathaniel and Makai. They are the fraternal twin sons of Aidan and Ember.

Not shown:

- ❀ Rafaj Niddala (Ever) is the father of Aidan Henry.
- ❀ Countess Ambrose (Mask) is the mother of Tide Toshiro (Mask).
- ❀ Song Family: Wade (Physic) and Lark (Mask) are the parents of Robyn (Mask) and Wren (Mask).

author note

Twenty-Third Day, Tenth Month, Final Year of the Queen
Eliyana's reign . . .

It is with a full, while also heavy, heart I pen this final
journal entry in what we will call the closing volume of
The Reflection Chronicles. Though the series name didn't
make it onto the cover, the *Unblemished* trilogy will always
and forever be *The Reflection Chronicles* to me. These
characters have been with me for so long, I'm not quite
sure how to let them go. Eliyana has grown *with* me. Ky
and Ebony have grown *on* me. And Joshua? He and I have
grown apart and closer together than ever. Each character
ended up exactly where I always knew they would, but also
where I never imagined at the same time. I hope you have
loved with them and mourned with them, as I have. I hope
their stories will live on in your hearts far after this novel
hits the shelves.

    If you have struggled with feeling ugly or less than or
never enough, I hope you see now just how valued you are.
You are more than enough. Your flaws make you who you
are. Embrace them. Recognize what you and you alone can
offer the world. Whatever your Calling may be, go for it.
Never let anyone discourage you from becoming the best
version of yourself. Others don't define you. There are so

many quotes I could use here, but I think one taken from the deck of *The Seven Seas* is most fitting. Dear precious reader, "Dive deep if you ever hope to rise."

Sincerely yours,
Sara Ella

discussion questions

SPOILER ALERT! Don't read until you've read ALL of *Unbreakable*!

1. This story explores the idea that we all have the potential for light and darkness. Do you agree with this philosophy? To which character's struggle do you most relate?

2. *Unbreakable* introduces Ebony's point of view to the series. Discuss this character's journey from *Unblemished* to the end of *Unbreakable*. In what ways has she changed? In what ways has she remained the same? Do you feel differently about her at the end of this journey than you felt when you first met her as Quinn?

3. Eliyana endures changes in her memory throughout the novel. Is there something in your life you wish you could forget? Or do you believe that all memories, good and bad, shape who you are today?

4. No matter the hope El held for him, Jasyn Crowe's fate remained the same in the end. If time travel were possible, is there a moment in your life you would like to alter? How would the alteration affect your life today?

5. Throughout the series, we witness firsthand how anger and bitterness can grow like the Void and turn a person dark. Isabeau did and said some horrific things over the

course of her life. Do you believe she deserved to be forgiven for all she had done? Does forgiveness heal the person offering it as much as it helps the person who is forgiven? Consider Tide's forgiveness of the murder of his mother. Is forgiveness an action, a feeling, or a bit of both?

6. Now that you've visited each Reflection, which is your favorite and why?

7. Khloe certainly shows she's tough for her age, but when Ebony shifts into her mother, Khloe falls apart. Discuss a situation in which you allowed yourself to be vulnerable to another person. Describe how that vulnerability helped make you stronger, and maybe even helped you heal from past hurt.

8. Ky fights hard to suppress the Void, even without Eliyana around. In the end, he proves love is stronger than any Elixir. Ky has faced many hardships and much pain, but rather than falling prisoner to the darkness, he chooses to do what is right. Compare and contrast him with Joshua. In what ways have each succeeded or failed in reaching his ultimate goals?

9. Joshua has certainly undergone quite the transformation throughout the series. How do you feel about his final sacrifice? Do you believe this proves, in the end, he truly did love Eliyana more?

10. Eliyana comes to the realization that she had the power all along to create a Mirror within herself. Is there a difference between self-love/acceptance and arrogance/pride? Discuss the differences and what they look like. Name three things you love about yourself, and three things you wish you could change. How would it transform your perspective and behavior if you accepted your flaws rather than criticized them?

acknowledgments

The Reflections weren't built in a day, just as a novel takes far longer than a few months to write. This story is my heart. I'll move on to new worlds, but nothing can ever take the place of this debut series. So many souls have earned far more than a "Thanks" from me. It is here I'll leave their names, hoping in some small way this will show them how very much they mean to me.

First, my King. You gave up your life so I might live. To You be the Honor and Glory. Any and all talent I have comes from You.

My husband. You met me when I was in the worst of places. Stayed with me through it and continue to show your love each day. You are my fairy tale. As you wish, my love.

My girls. Oh, my girls. You are my favorites. Thank you for showing me unconditional love and for always being patient. I couldn't ask for better mini-me's.

My parents. Mom, who is no longer with us, but forever lives in my heart. Daddy and Mama Jodi, who go above and beyond for me every day. My Aunt Terri, who has been a mother to me in so many ways, and continues to love me like her own. Without you all I might go crazy. I love you with all of my heart.

My new family, Jen Mom, Paul Dad, and Madisyn. Tosh, Erika, Hannah, and Asher. I love being a part of your big beautiful family! Thank you for accepting me and for cheering me on. Love you guys.

Jim Hart. My agent. I forgot to thank you in *Unraveling*, so you bet your favorite novel I'm going to give you a double, triple "thank-you" here! You stay behind the scenes, always watching out for me and answering my questions. There's no one I'd rather have on my team. You're stuck with me, sir. I'm so proud to say your name every time someone asks who represents me.

My partners in crime, Mary Weber and Nadine Brandes. You are two of the most amazing women I have ever met. I love you both dearly and am blessed to call you friends and publishing sisters. Thank you for taking time to listen to my Voxer rants, surprise me by flying across the country, and talk me down from my constant ledges. Without you girls my world would be gray. Thank you for making everything colorful.

My editor, Becky Monds. You make everything okay, even when it's not. I love you. Thanks for putting up with my constant extensions.

Jodi Hughes, answerer of all questions, etc. . . . You bring light and encouragement to my days. I love you.

Amanda Bostic. You make me cry with your loving kindness and encouragement. I love you.

The team at HCCP. As always, you amaze me with your astounding awesomeness. Paul Fisher and Allison Carter, you both work so hard to make my books seen. Kristen Golden, you make sure my stories get into the hands of Fiction Guilders. Kristen Ingebretson and the design team, my covers never fail to make jaws drop thanks to you. Matt Bray, your social media graphics are fantastic. Matthew Covington, my readers drool over your maps. Kayleigh Hines, you never fail to help me with the business side of things. Julee Schwarzburg, you catch everything and I am continually amazed by your attention to detail. Jolene Barto and my audiobook team, and my narrator, Hayley Cresswell, you bring my stories to life. Cat Zappa, I know you are working hard to make my stories even more visual. To all of you and those I have failed to name, thank you for your countless hours of work on these novels. I am truly astounded I can call Thomas Nelson my publishing family. There is no place I would rather be.

To the folks at ECPA for being so warm and welcoming. It is an honor to even be considered for your prestigious awards.

Kayla Kunkel. I couldn't have finished this book without you. Thank you for being my friend and for making my work days better.

My friends for life. Elizabeth VanTassel, bringer of joy. Christen Krumm, forever my first reader and helper of social media things. Neysa Walker, your voice never ceases to make me smile. Becky Dean, critiquer and encourager in one. Shannon Dittemore, most inspiring mom-slash-writer EVER. Carolyn Schanta, soul sister no matter the miles between us. Brooke Larson, my most gracious sister and friend and (now) fellow reader and coffee drinker. Janalyn Owens, you are a light in the darkness. Karine Krastel, my sister and introducer of leggings (you were right). Lauren Brandenburg, getting to know you more this year has truly made a difference in my life. Each and every one of you ladies have touched me. You will never know just how deeply you have blessed my heart.

My first editor, Deirdre Lockhart. Did you ever think I'd make it this far? Thanks for helping shape me in my early author days.

My fangirls (and boys) and dear friends. Too many of you to name, but I'll sure try. Deena Peterson, Gabrial Jones, Valeria Hyer, Laura Pol, Damian Last, Steven Mannasse, Betsy Haddox, Emilie Hendryx, Hannah White, Ingrid Corbin, Nancy Kimball, Ari'El Soukkaseum, Kristy Neufeld, Trina Ruck, Hope Ortego, Abby Woodhouse, Mandi Alva, Sophia Springer, Ann Springer, Sarah Springer, Alexis Goring, Stephanie Warner, Austin Ryan, Sage Marie, Elizabeth Newsom, Ashley Schaller, Emileigh Latham, Savanna Kaiser, Galaxy Adventurer, The Bookish Menagerie, Rissi JC, Bookish Babblings, Carrie from Reading is My Superpower, Bookworm Mama, Moriah Reads, and the countless other authors, BookTubers, bloggers, and bookstagrammers I am failing to mention. Each and every one of you have taken time to encourage me and build me up, writing reviews that make me cry happy tears and shooting the most lovely photos of my books I have ever seen. From the bottom of my book-loving heart, thank you. I see you. I appreciate you. This is me hugging you and throwing a random dance party in your honor.

And to you, the person I have forgotten (because I KNOW I must have forgotten someone as I always do). Thank you for your heart and humility. Whatever you did, it didn't go unappreciated. If I didn't mention you it just means that you perform quietly and graciously behind the scenes. You are amazing! For whatever you have poured into this book or me, thank you from the bottom of my heart.

about the author

Photo by Emilie Hendryx

Once upon a time, Sara Ella dreamed she would marry a prince and live in a Disney-style castle. Today, she is winner of the ECPA Christian Book of the Year Award for her debut novel *Unblemished*, which released to magical applause: "a stunning journey into a fascinating new world of reflections" (*RT Book Reviews*). Sara spends her days throwing living room dance parties for her two princesses and conquering realms of her own imaginings. She believes "Happily Ever After Is Never Far Away."

Visit Sara online at saraella.com
Facebook: writinghistruth
Twitter: @SaraEllaWrites
Instagram: saraellawrites
Pinterest: Sara Ella
YouTube: Sara Ella